MOONSHINE AND MERCURY

By Harriet Smart

The Butchered Man: Northminster Mystery 1
The Dead Songbird: Northminster Mystery 2
The Shadowcutter: Northminster Mystery 3
The Hanging Cage: Northminster Mystery 4
The Ghosts of Ardenthwaite: Northminster Mystery 5
The Echo at Rooke Court: Northminster Mystery 6
The Fatal Engine: Northminster Mystery 7
The Witches of Pitfeldry: Northminster Mystery 8
Moonshine and Mercury: Northminster Mystery 9
Tarleton's Coffer: Northminster Mystery 10
The Wounded Oak: Northminster Mystery 11
Mummer's Night: A Northminster Novella
Carswell's First Case: A Northminster Novella
Emma Vernon's Northminster Ghost Stories
The Dolls at Heron's Reach
The True Value of Pearls
The Daughters of Blane
Green Grow the Rushes
The Wild Garden
The Lark Ascending
Reckless Griselda
A Tempting Proposal

MOONSHINE AND MERCURY

by

Harriet Smart

Published by Anthemion

First Edition

ISBN 978-1-907873-61-4

Made with Jutoh

Chapter One

September, 1842

Felix came back from dressing to find that Eleanor had brought Miss King into their bedroom, and had installed her in their bed. She was sitting next to her, stroking her forehead.

"She had another wretched night," Eleanor said. Miss King managed a wan, apologetic smile. "Her tooth."

"We should send for Morris," Felix said.

"No, no, no!" said Eleanor, and there was the same alarm in Miss King's expression. Eleanor pulled her a little closer and kissed her forehead. "No, we shall not do that. I have a much better idea. Felix will write to his friend Hamilton, and we will go to Stanegate and see him. Yes?"

"I don't think –" he began, but Eleanor had abandoned Miss King and was now ushering him from the room. She carefully closed the door behind them.

"I will not have that man mauling Jenny," she said. "He is unbearable. That time he came and drew Jacob's tooth –" She gave a shudder. "It will make it worse. She is already exhausted and terrified."

"And trailing over to Stanegate will help her? An hour and a quarter on the train –"

"We will simply stay there a few days," said Eleanor. "We can go to the opera. Bartelozzi's company are in Stanegate. Canon Fforde said that they heard them in London and Mrs Fforde said –"

"Yes, I remember," said Felix. The topic had come up at a recent dinner at the Treasurer's House. "Are you sure you want to go somewhere so public as the theatre?"

"I'm not horribly fat yet," said Eleanor, caressing her swollen stomach. "And if you took a box, who would notice?"

"It would be much better for Miss King, if we sent for Mr Morris now," said Felix.

"If this man of yours is as good as you said he was –"

"He is not my man," Felix said. "I only know him slightly."

"But you were impressed by his article."

"An article doesn't mean anything."

"Said by the man who never manages to finish one," said Eleanor.

Felix let this pass, though with a slight struggle.

"I really think Morris should look at her, and as soon as possible," he said. "He may be brutal, but that's the nature of his business, and one can't fault his knowledge. Even Mr Harper submits to him, and he has had a wretched time with his teeth."

"Probably because he insists on patronising that ghoul Morris," said Eleanor. "Now will you write to Mr Hamilton, or shall I? It will look strange if I do, of course."

"Oh, very well, I will write!" said Felix. He had no great wish to go to Stanegate, but he could not be insensible to Miss King's suffering. "But if she seems any worse today, you will send for Morris, do you promise?"

"Yes, of course," said Eleanor. "The idea of going to Stanegate will be a tonic for her, especially the opera. She is frightened of Morris. Another, kinder fellow – that is what she needs."

She had a point; Morris was competent, but he did represent an old-fashioned remedy to a common misery. There was certainly a need for better and gentler treatments. Miss King had endured a great deal of excruciating pain in silence out of a mixture of fear and stoicism. When she had finally confessed to it and allowed him to examine her, she had been rigid with terror, and the mention of the dentist and an extraction had filled her with horror. She had asked him if he would think of attempting it, but he had hesitated. It was not his speciality.

"She will say anything to please you," said Felix. "That's the truth of it. She would walk across hot coals. Now, make sure she has a warm poultice to hand at all times, and not too much laudanum."

"Of course, of course," said Eleanor. "Now you had better go, or you will be late. Did you not say the Major wanted you early this morning?"

"Yes," said Felix. "But Miss King's inflamed bicuspid will excuse me. Now, remember what I said: if there is any deterioration, even any slight sign of fever, you will send for Morris and for me, for that matter."

"Is that because you do not entirely trust him?"

"I do, but if she is afraid, then perhaps –"

"Then we must arrange things so she is not afraid! Your friend sounds like the remedy to that. Now, you had better go." She kissed him and turned him towards the front door.

He went out, where a servant was waiting with his horse. He mounted up and reflected on how typical of Eleanor it was to spring such a scheme on him just as he was about to go to work. She now followed him out of the house, and waved him goodbye. In her pale silk wrapper, her hair still down, she looked delightfully plump and rosy. Pregnancy suited her and she was not the slightest bit indisposed by her condition. He had experienced the intense pleasure of listening to the tiny heartbeat and wondering nervously about the character and destiny of the small individual awaiting its introduction to the world. It made him think of all the times he had reassured anxious parents, without understanding at all what they might be feeling. It was an instructive process.

It was easier to go by horseback than by carriage into Northminster at this time of day. The roads were liable to congestion as trade increased in the city. Felix had found that taking a field path from Hawksby and then following the canal saved him a good ten minutes.

Despite the brightness of the morning, the towpath was cast into heavy shade by the massive new manufactories that had recently been completed on either side of the canal, and the noise of the machinery was clearly audible within. As he passed through this canyon of progress and modernity, he considered James Hamilton. He had been a brilliant, diligent student, but shy. He had not cared to go drinking with the rest of them. Tall and stooping, he had a gentleness that would no doubt put the most fearful at their ease. Felix had been surprised to learn he had turned to dentistry: it was a lowering step for a medical man, and yet, when one saw the suffering caused by teeth, it was perhaps shrewd for a man who had an inclination towards it and needed to make his own fortune. Setting up in a watering place such as Stanegate was equally sensible. The paper in The Lancet had been on the use of ether in extraction, with which he had been successful. That Hamilton had dared to do this was intriguing. It would certainly be of great interest to talk to him about it.

However, a jaunt to Stanegate was not appealing. He had experiments in hand that he had no wish to leave, and Mr Harper was in great need of him at the Infirmary.

As he negotiated the traffic-crammed streets of the city he resigned himself to the visit, experiments notwithstanding. Eleanor's will would prevail, as it usually did. The only comfort was that Stanegate was liable to be as busy as Northminster, and it was unlikely that he would run across a certain person whom he had heard was now living there.

When he arrived at the Northern Office, he hurried straight up to the Major's room, rather than going down to his laboratory as usual.

"Good morning. Excuse me, I meant to be earlier, but Miss King has toothache."

"Poor woman," said Major Vernon, with a grimace. "I hope you were able to help her. And you are not late."

"So, what did you want to speak to me about?"

"We are to have a visitor. Captain Lazenby will bring him over shortly."

"Not Prince Albert?" said Felix. It had been a private joke between them that they would receive a royal inspection one day.

"Not this time, thankfully," he said, with a smile. "But from the way the Captain broached the subject I thought that it was. No, this is a gentleman from the Home Office: Mr Edward Fitznorton, private secretary to the assistant secretary. Winchester, Cambridge, Lincoln's Inn – he was called to the bar earlier this year, but has determined on a career in government service –"

"Until he gets a safe seat somewhere?" said Felix.

"He does read as that type, yes," said Major Vernon.

"I wonder if Lord Rothborough has anything to do with this," said Felix.

"I don't think so. It was apparently all Fitznorton's idea. He has been studying policing in Europe, and now he wishes to study us. Well, the Northern Office in particular."

"For how long?"

"A month."

"A month? What are we to do with him for a month? At least Prince Albert would be gone by lunchtime. Did Lazenby even ask you whether you wanted him?"

"No," said Major Vernon.

"That is because he wishes to scrutinize us," said Felix.

"That may be an added benefit for him," said Major Vernon. "And he is perfectly entitled to scrutinize us – it is part of his job. On the whole, I don't think Lazenby is as zealous as he might be. I would be watching us like hawks, in his shoes. But I don't suppose he had much choice about this. If the Home Secretary considers it a good idea, then none of us have much choice, do we?"

"I liked it better when we only had to convince Alderman Todmartin and the Watch Committee to give us so many guineas. They never insisted on looking over our shoulders for a month!"

"I shall have to find him something useful to do," said Major Vernon.

There was a knock at the door.

"The gentleman is here now, sir," said the head clerk.

They went downstairs and found him studying the large map of the city that hung in the hall.

"Mr Fitznorton?" said Major Vernon.

"Major Vernon?" he said, turning from the map. Tall and flaxen-haired, he had the bearing and physique of a guardsman combined with the showy good-looks of a fashion plate. "Captain Lazenby sends his apologies – he was called away, and I thought it might be best to try and get here on my own account. Edward Fitznorton at your service."

"How do you do?" said Major Vernon, shaking his hand. "This is my colleague, Mr Felix Carswell."

"The Northminster labyrinth did not defeat you, then?" said Felix as they shook hands. "When I first came here, I was constantly getting lost."

"No, seemingly it did not," said Fitznorton, considering the point and then turning back to the map. "It must be the difference between the structure of a medieval city such as Edinburgh, and that of Cambridge, for example. There are more points in common between Cambridge and Northminster, despite the colleges which, of course, might be considered anomalous, as they occupy so much of the town."

"And Winchester, where you were at school," said Major Vernon, turning now to the map himself. "The pattern there must be similar to Northminster, I should think."

"Yes, quite," said Fitznorton, "although Winchester is by no means as developed as Northminster. The scale of manufactories is striking."

"And the smell," said Felix. "Particularly delightful this morning."

"This time of year is always pungent," said Major Vernon. "It usually clears by the end of September. It's best to get lodgings as close to the Precincts as possible, though. Did Captain Lazenby suggest anything?"

"I'm putting up at Pratt's Family Hotel," said Fitznorton.

"You'd be better off at The Black Bull," said Felix. Pratt's was a large temperance hotel that had recently opened in the Market Place. Built in yellow brick, it had an austere, uncomfortable look about it. "Wilkes keeps a good cellar."

"It's certainly a convenient spot," said Major Vernon, pointing out The Black Bull on the map. "You might consider it. But now, shall we get to business? A quick tour of the premises, in the first instance?"

"Certainly," said Fitznorton.

"I'll be downstairs," said Felix.

"We could start there," said Major Vernon.

"Get the worst over first," said Felix. "Speaking of smells, I apologise in advance – it is not exactly pleasant down there. I've been working on decomposition rates. Let me go and open the windows."

So he hurried down and opened the windows, which made precious little difference as the day was already still and warm. The smell of rotting flesh was sickening. He noted the temperature of the room on his chart and the presence of flies on the window, and then turned to the various legs of mutton that he had placed in large glass jars, filled with different substances.

The Major and Fitznorton came in soon after.

"I was thinking," Felix said, noting their expressions, "that I ought to try this in the attic. I want to observe mummification."

"When I am next on leave," said Major Vernon, reaching

for his handkerchief. "Mr Carswell is relentless in the pursuit of scientific truth."

"The great question we are faced with is time of death," said Carswell. "And after twenty-four hours it becomes increasingly difficult to be accurate. How long has a body been on the ground or in the water? – or as, happened last month, a manure pit."

"Was that a homicide?" said Fitznorton.

"No, accidental death," said Major Vernon. "A wretched case. The pit had been left uncovered, and the poor fellow was in his cups and stumbled in at night. He was buried the next morning when a cart load of night soil was thrown in, and he died before anyone noticed he was there. He was not reported missing for some time."

"The results were extremely confusing," Felix said. "It was hard to say when he had gone in, the state of decomposition was so advanced. So I thought I would try and simulate the effects of various natural environments – soil, brackish water, gravel and so forth. It is of course, not a perfect experiment, but no experiment is, to tell you the truth. One can never reproduce what happens in reality, but if I can establish some helpful markers then it will be worth it. The progress of maggots for example."

"I see," said Fitznorton, gazing at one specimen that was crawling with them. "And one would presume that each species of insect has its own timetable?"

"Correct," said Felix. "Those grey ones will be common house flies, and those ones, like pearls, are bluebottles, which are slower to develop. But I'm not only observing the insects. There is the matter of the texture, the colour, and of course the smell. Yes, at first it seems indiscriminately foul, but my theory is one might learn to distinguish between different stages of decomposition, just as one can distinguish between a Burgundy and a claret. Or rather between a good claret and a bad one, or a bottle that has been open too long. In fact, it was spoilt wine that got me thinking about that. Canon Fforde taught me how to spot it. I was thinking of asking him to come and smell these samples for me. He has such a precise way of talking about wine."

"Canon Fforde is the Treasurer at the Minister here," said Major Vernon, "and my brother-in-law. Yes, Mr Carswell, he would be the man to do that, though I can't imagine it would be a pleasure for him."

"He says that smelling wine is like listening to music," Felix said. "And there may be something in that. The nose is as discriminating an organ as the ear, though it has to be said, we still know very little about the processes involved in either smell or hearing."

"I suppose you will publish this," Fitznorton said. "The Lancet?"

"I don't know," said Felix. "I ought to try –" He saw Major Vernon smiling in sympathy. He was aware of Felix's frustration on this point. "We are often pressed for time," he finished.

"I should be interested to read it," said Fitznorton.

There was a knock at the door and a constable came in with a message for Major Vernon.

"From Inspector Harris at Stanegate," Major Vernon said, having read the letter. "Our assistance is requested. They have a body and it looks like murder. You'd better come with us, Mr Fitznorton." He turned to the door. "I'll go and look up a train."

Chapter Two

"When is your train?" Emma asked.

"Midday," Giles said. "I hope I shan't be away long." He fastened the buckle on his travelling bag.

"You will be away as long as is necessary," she said, kissing him. "And I can always send more linen with Sally."

"Sally?"

"They are going on Thursday, for the opera, and then to take Celia to school, don't you remember?"

"Ah yes," said Giles. "I didn't realise that was so soon. I had it fixed later in the month."

"There is some particular company that Lamb was anxious to hear. They are there for a full week. At The White Hart, I think."

"That's some comfort, then, if things become prolonged," said Giles. "You should come with them, just for a night or two, perhaps? That would be even better and we could all go to the opera."

"And leave the children?" she said.

"Greene can manage them for a few nights, surely? And since we have Miss Frey coming in most days, it ought to be possible. And Holt will keep Hamish in line."

"Will you not want Holt with you in Stanegate?" said Emma.

"No, it would be too much of an inconvenience for you, were I to take him. He's better left here. I can always get Mr Fitznorton to brush my coat."

Emma laughed at that and said, "How is Mr Fitznorton?"

"Inoffensive, at least so far. He took Carswell's vats of rotting mutton in his stride."

"Poor man. I hope he has the right waistcoats for Stanegate. It's quite fashionable now, I hear."

"He has a good London polish about him. Carswell and I will look shabby in comparison."

"Is he handsome?"

"Yes, very. Are the children in the garden?"

"Yes." She wrapped her arms around him. "Oh, it is such a nuisance you have to go! I was hoping to take you with me to call on Mrs Madderly."

"Who is she?"

"The mother of a little girl in Sophy's sampler class. She is throwing a children's entertainment, and apparently I must call if Sophy is to be invited. It is rather high and mighty of her, but Sophy will be heartbroken if I do not. She so wants to belong."

"Is that the class Mrs Lazenby prevailed on you to put her in?"

"She did not prevail, Giles – I thought it a good idea that Sophy should find some friends here. Especially now Celia is going away to school."

"Who is this woman to demand you call on her?" said Giles. "She should be calling on you."

"She does sound quite a specimen, so I thought it would amuse you to go. Catherine Lazenby is terrified of her. Her husband owns the Penkirk Mills."

"Oh, I've met him. He's reasonable enough. Where do they live?"

"Banfield Lodge."

"Really?" Giles said. This large house, set in a garden that might almost be described a park, was constantly under siege by builders and painters. "Yes, that would have been interesting. You can give me a full report, down to the last curtain tassel."

"Oh, I shall. If I am not eaten alive."

"She will be glad to know you," said Giles.

"I doubt it. I don't think I'm serious enough for that set."

"A children's entertainment doesn't sound too serious."

"It's to raise money for something or other. I suspect it will be edifying rather than entertaining."

"And Sophy still wants to go?"

"She wants to belong, as I said. It's hard for her. She wants to go to school with Celia, but they don't take such little girls."

"And that place is ruinously expensive, except for the daughters of clergy," said Giles. "How much was the sampler class, for that matter?"

"Two guineas a term," said Emma.

"Patton would have done just as well," said Giles.

"I entirely agree," said Emma, "but I thought the social aspect would be useful. And we do have the money, Giles. I would not overspend, you know that."

"Yes, of course, that's not what I meant. You are never careless with money. I only wonder if it is wise to throw her into circles that we know so little about."

"It can't do too much harm," said Emma. "She is not so impressionable, and I am being prejudiced against poor Mrs Madderly. She may be charming, and I may have got entirely the wrong end of the stick."

They went out into the garden where Hamish and Sophy were enjoying the last few minutes of their morning break kicking a ball about, while Miss Frey was drinking her tea in the bower. She was a calm, experienced teacher, employed by Lambert and Sally for some years, and she had got the measure of Hamish and Sophy. They had already had long debates about whether they should embark on some more formal schooling for them and had decided that for the present, the daily governess three times a week, with Emma making up the rest, would suffice. But as he joined the impromptu football game, he began to wonder if Hamish would not benefit from being with companions of his own age as much as Sophy.

Mark Hurrell's nephews had been sent to board with a sensible young clergyman and his wife, who kept a small school, and were thriving there. It would have been an excellent solution for Hamish, but Giles was not ready to send Hamish away, for his own selfish reasons as much as anything.

Miss Frey called the children back to work, and he made his own farewells, fending off a long, enthusiastic embrace from Sophy, intended no doubt to delay her return to her copybook. He agreed with her. Though Miss Frey was not a savage taskmaster, it was not a day for work. He would happily have stayed in the garden and played with the children for the rest of the day.

Emma saw him to the gate.

"I really don't want to go," he said after a lingering kiss.

"I suppose Mr Carswell might be reluctant as well," she said. "Is not Mrs Connolly there now?"

"Lord, yes," said Giles.

"I can't remember what her new husband's name is," Emma said. "But I did hear he is the doctor in charge of that new place, where they pack you in wet sheets and all that horrible nonsense. Does Mr Carswell know about that part?"

"Kennedy?" Giles said, having searched for the name in his recollection.

"Kennedy! Yes, that's it. It's just the sort of thing Mr Carswell is so caustic about."

"With luck, their paths will not cross." It would be awkward for the former lovers to meet.

Fitznorton was waiting for him at the station coffee room, as arranged. He was reading a blue book – the recently published second volume on the mining commission. This struck Giles as ostentatious, for the size of the volume was hardly suitable for travelling.

"What's your thinking on it, Major Vernon?" he said. "It is an appalling business. Boys made to sit twelve hours underground in a degraded state."

"I've only seen the extracts in the newspapers and it's clear something must change. There is no excuse for child labour of that sort."

"Quite," said Fitznorton. "It is barbaric. There must be substantive reform."

"But the industry must feel it is reforming itself rather than having reform imposed upon it – that usually gets a better result, at least in my small experience of these things," Giles said. "Make the mine owners feel virtuous about what they are doing to change things. Certainly don't hector them about what they have done in the past."

"You don't think there should be reparations?"

"You cannot punish people for something that up until recently no one thought very wrong. No one thought it particularly immoral to send a child of eight into the fields to help his parents put bread on the table until recently, after all."

"That does not make it acceptable," said Fitznorton.

"Of course not, but now, because trade has demanded it, little boys sit twelve hours a day underground operating gates, which is shocking, yes – I entirely agree. But the important thing is that it should not continue, surely? It is easy to cry and lament and point fingers. But to find a solution to it that does not make things worse for everyone, especially for the boys themselves? Not so easy. If they are forbidden to work in mines, their parents will send them into some even worse situation out of sheer desperation. You should talk to Lord Rothborough about this – I am only parroting him."

"I hope I might have the honour of meeting him while I am here," Fitznorton said.

"I'm surprised you don't know him already," said Giles. "He must know your chief. I'll gladly introduce you."

"And he is – forgive me, I must ask – connected to Mr Carswell?" Mr Fitznorton said. Giles nodded. At this moment Carswell himself came into the refreshment room, carrying his bags.

"Well, it is done!" Carswell said, throwing himself down in the spare chair at their table.

"What is?" Giles said.

"I have made my last set of observations, and asked Fenton to dispose of the experiment."

"I hope you gave him a tip," said Giles. "That is well beyond his usual duties."

"I did," said Carswell, pushing his hands through his hair. "It really is irritating to have to abandon it now!"

"It is better abandoned," said Giles. "You cannot say how long you will be away."

"If only there was someone I could have trusted to make the observations! I tried to get Sam Tolley to do it, but Mr Harper would not spare him. He was not pleased to let me go, to tell you the truth. He never likes it when the dead take precedent over the living."

"Mr Harper is surgeon-in-chief at the Infirmary here," said Giles. "We have a half-share in Mr Carswell's services."

"It's an approximate arrangement," said Carswell. "We are short-handed. You don't happen to know any young medics looking for work, do you, Mr Fitznorton? The stipend is not attractive, nor the hours, but Mr Harper is a genius. I have learnt more from him in the last few years than I ever did in Edinburgh. It is a pleasure to watch him operate."

"The rest of us would struggle to find any pleasure in that," Giles said. "But he does seem to perform miracles."

"Have I time for coffee?" said Carswell.

"Yes, such as it is here," said Giles, draining his own cup.

"Then I will have tea," said Carswell, summoning the waiter. He ordered tea and bread and butter. "Who knows how long it will be before we get dinner," he went on. "Can I see Harris' letter?"

Giles took it from his pocket and handed it to him. He scanned it. "Not much to go on there."

"He wouldn't want to anticipate your observations."

Tea and coffee taken, they went to the train. It was busy and they were obliged to share their carriage with three well-dressed women – a widow and her middle-aged daughters – who looked as though they were going for the cure.

They were met at Stanegate station by Sergeant Dale, who Giles remembered as one of his first recruits in Northminster, now promoted to plain-clothes duty.

"So where are we going, Sergeant Dale?" asked Giles. "The Inspector did not give me any details."

"The menagerie, sir," said Sergeant Dale.

~

It was soon clear why Inspector Harris had chosen to be laconic. There really were no words to describe the sight that met them. When Carswell lifted the sheet covering the remains he grimaced, while Fitznorton at once turned away, his hand covering his mouth. Giles, for his part, murmured: "Dear God, what was he doing in here?"

"That is one of a hundred questions," said Carswell, reaching for his hand lens and crouching down.

"Did the animals kill him?" Giles said.

"Impossible to say at this stage," said Carswell.

"When was he found, precisely?" Giles said.

"This morning, sir, at about nine," said Harris.

"I suspect he's been here a couple of days," said Carswell, "as far as I can judge from what is left, and given the amount of depredation. There are two of them?"

"Yes, sir," said Harris. "Leopards – Moonshine and Mercury."

"How much meat does a leopard need a day, I wonder?" said Carswell.

"That was the thing that brought it to light, sir," said

Harris. "The keeper only went in because the beasts rejected their usual food."

"Because they had feasted on this and lost their appetites," said Carswell.

"I suppose the keeper might not have noticed he was here at once," said Giles, looking around him, "given the size of the cage."

It was set into the hillside, and had the look of a rockery combined with an aviary. There was a great deal of shrubbery. A stone wall, formed of decorative Moorish arches filled with iron bars, provided visitors with their view of the exotic beasts. More bars made a roof that extended to the hillside, leaving no space for the animals to escape. It was hard not to be impressed by the ingenuity of it, allowing the animals to have some freedom of movement and some privacy. It had also allowed a body to lie concealed for some days, if Carswell had it right.

"I don't suppose you can see this spot from the path down there," he went on. "Perhaps you could go and check, Mr Fitznorton?"

Fitznorton looked relieved to be sent away on this trivial errand.

Steeling himself, Giles crouched down beside Carswell.

"Poor fellow," he said. "First your legs of mutton, and now this." He scanned the corpse for any details that might help with identification.

"Be careful what you wish for," said Carswell, reaching into his bag for his sketchbook. "But he could have come to Northminster and there would have been nothing, whereas this is –"

"Something to tell his grandchildren about. Leopards, of all things!"

"Where are they, by the way? I presume they shot them. I'd like a look at their teeth."

"No, I don't think they did," said Giles. "And what is that

over there?"

He got up and went to investigate. A large white blanket had become tangled up in a thorn bush. It was a struggle to extricate it and when he did, he found it was marked with dirty brown patches. "Bloodstains, perhaps?" he said, holding it up for Carswell.

Carswell glanced up from his sketch.

"Possibly."

"And it's a Hudson Bay blanket."

"A what?"

"It's a trading blanket, made for the export market. We had them on our bed in Ontario. Strange to find one here. The coloured stripes were particularly desired by the natives. They made them into coats and so forth. And these embroidered lines here – these show the number of beaver skins it's worth. Three and a half, in this case."

Carswell now stopped his sketch and gave the blanket some consideration.

"That might be blood," he said. "The pattern is interesting." He glanced back at the mangled remains. "If he was already wounded when he got here, then the animals would be attracted to feed on him. That might explain it."

"Wounded?"

"I can't really say at this point, but some of these wounds look like stab marks. If he was lying, for example, face down on that blanket, that type of staining might occur. All highly speculative at this point, but –"

Giles nodded, and began to fold up the blanket.

"So where are the leopards now?" Carswell asked.

"I shall go and find out. We had better get him out of here as soon as possible. It looks like rain. Inspector Harris said that the Incurables Hospital will have a suitable room for you."

Carswell nodded and returned to his sketch, while Giles made his way out of the enclosure.

He found Fitznorton looking slightly more composed.

"I'm sorry," Giles said. "That was shocking, even by our standards."

"I cannot begin to imagine what manner of person might feed one's fellow man to wild beasts, dead or alive."

"And that, Mr Fitznorton, is the whole business in a nutshell. We have to start to imagine, difficult though that may be. For a start, is this the only way in?" He went in, going back to the gate through which he had just emerged. There was a chain and an open padlock dangling from it. "I wonder who has a key for this," he said.

"But if you knew there was a pair of leopards in there," said Fitznorton, "why would you go in, in the first place? It would be madness."

"The keeper must go in to feed them," said Giles, "and presumably he has some means of controlling them that would lessen the risk. We must talk to him and the owner." He swung the door shut. "I suppose you could open the gate, shove someone in and lock the door behind him. If our victim was drunk, for example, or in some other way incapacitated. But that doesn't explain the Hudson Bay blanket."

"The blanket, Major Vernon?"

"Stuck in a bush near the corpse. You didn't notice it?"

"No," said Fitznorton. "Forgive me, but all I could see was his face, or rather the lack of it." He looked pained and then turned away again, and began to retch. "Excuse me, sir –" Giles felt some sympathy for him. Cambridge and the quiet corridors of the Home Office were no preparation for this.

"Mr Carswell usually has some brandy on him," he said. "I'll get some for you."

"No, thank you, sir," said Fitznorton. "I don't drink. This will pass, I'm sure."

"Let's go and find the keeper," said Giles.

Seeing them approach, Fitznorton still with his handkerchief pressed to his mouth, Sergeant Dale said,

"There's a spring over yonder, sir, if the gentleman needs a drink."

"One of the famous Stanegate springs?" Giles said. "I'm not sure that would help. It's foul stuff." With some pain, he remembered Laura at the Bowerswell, valiantly taking a second cup.

"Nay, sir, that's only if you're not used to it," said Sergeant Dale. "I've drunk it all my life. Cures all ills," he added.

"Don't let Mr Carswell hear you say that," said Giles. "At your peril, Mr Fitznorton. It tastes of rotten eggs as far as I'm concerned."

They had reached the spring, which was contained in a picturesque garden building. A large sign indicated that the pale pink mugs were a ha'penny to hire and a shilling to buy. They bore the legend 'Askham's Famous Stanegate Menagerie and Pleasure Ground' and on the other side, a crude transfer image of two leopards.

Taking the role of spring attendant, Sergeant Dale filled two mugs from the pipe that was gushing into a marble basin. One he handed to Mr Fitznorton, and the other to Giles. "You really should try it again, sir. It comes out warm here. As refreshing as a cup of tea, and much better for you."

Giles took a sip. It was surprisingly warm, and salty to the taste. "That's almost bearable. Better than the Bowerswell, certainly."

"Quite peculiar," said Fitznorton, "and quite refreshing. Thank you, Sergeant."

"I had to have some myself after I first saw that poor fellow," said Dale.

"Where's the leopard keeper?" Giles said, setting down his mug. A sip had been enough.

"With his beasts," Sergeant Dale said. "His name is Bobby Farr."

Farr, a small, weather-beaten man, was sitting on the steps

to a large circus van. The van was painted in crimson and yellow, and decorated with large letters that announced 'The Celebrated Moonshine and Mercury! Leopards Extraordinaire!'

Seeing them, Farr came over, his pipe stuck in his mouth.

"You have the animals in there, then, Mr Farr?" Giles asked.

"They're not themselves," Farr said. "Rattled, they are. When can they go back? They don't like that van."

Giles had no immediate answer to that question.

"Tell me what happened this morning," he said instead.

"I went in at seven as usual, to give them their meat. Usually they come to me, a bit wary like, but they come. They know I won't hurt them and they won't hurt me, so they come. But this morning there was no sign of them, and yesterday it had been the same. They didn't touch the meat I left. So I went in, careful like, of course, and found 'em fast asleep. And I couldn't think why, unless... and then I went along a bit, and there it was."

"So yesterday morning when they didn't take their meat you didn't think to go in?"

"It happens some days, but not twice in a row. We've had the odd fox in there, you see."

"And that gate is the only way a man can get in, would you say?"

"Aye, pretty much."

"Only pretty much?"

"There's a bit at the top that needs fixing, but..."

"Show me, would you?"

They went back to the leopard cage. As they arrived, the victim's remains were being carried out on a covered hurdle. Carswell was behind them, carrying the Hudson Bay blanket.

"You were right about the rain," he said, as the first drops began to fall.

"I need your opinion, Mr Carswell," said Giles. "Sergeant Dale, will you look after that blanket for me?"

Bobby Farr had begun to climb up what passed for a path in the rocky outcrops to the side of the cage. Giles followed, with Carswell behind him.

"Someone's been messing with this," Farr said, stopping. He was standing on a ledge that overlooked the cage. Giles joined him and saw that two sections of the cage roof had been tied to each other to hold them fast. "I had it different," Farr said. "I noticed it were loose a week or so ago, so I fixed it with that bit of rope, and I told the master to get a man to fix it proper."

"So there was a gap when you did that?"

"Aye, a foot or so. Enough for the cats to get out, so I fastened it pretty swift. Moonshine, when it takes her, can leap as high as you like. She'd have been out of there."

"And you say that rope has been retied?"

"Certain of it."

Giles glanced back at Carswell who had edged along behind him.

"Large enough to insert a wrapped body?" he said.

"Yes. But it's still no small undertaking to get a dead or unconscious man up here and insert him through that hole, is it?" said Carswell.

"No. You'd better go with the body. I want to talk to Mr Askham, and then I must find the coroner."

Chapter Three

Giles was directed to find Mr Askham, the proprietor of Stanegate's famous menagerie, in an office reached through what was grandly described by one of the employees as 'The Museum'. This was a warehouse of dusty taxidermy: stuffed birds and animals of every sort, thrust together in an incoherent jumble, so that a roaring wolf was attended by parrots and a walrus lay down with fancy chickens. The effect was not helped by the ridiculously inept stuffing of the specimens. It was a veritable house of horrors, full of gazing glass eyes and bared teeth – both disturbing and hilarious.

"Whoever did this has no regard for the basic taxonomies of natural history," said Fitznorton, who clearly found the disorderliness offensive. "What is the point of this?"

"Spectacle?" said Giles. "A child would adore it – if they weren't scared witless."

Mentally he placed Hamish in the first category and Sophy in the second.

"They would learn nothing in either case. It would be a waste of time and money."

"You don't have children, I take it, Mr Fitznorton?"

"No," said Mr Fitznorton.

"Wasting time becomes an object for a parent, and once you do have children, money slips away without you even having to think about it. So in those terms, I would rate this as a horrible but useful excursion. I would have had to drag my nephew out of here. Only a promise of iced cakes would do it. I would have been the same at his age, I dare say."

"Major Vernon?"

A man's voice addressed him as his attention lingered on

a knock-kneed gazelle. Giles turned and saw a white-haired gentleman in his shirtsleeves. He wore a broad-striped waistcoat and a spotted kerchief at his neck, while gold hoops decorated his ears.

"Mr Askham?"

"The inspector said you wanted a word, sir."

"Yes, thank you. This is my colleague, Mr Fitznorton."

"I see you are admiring Gertrude," Mr Askham said, reaching out and stroking the gazelle's head. "She was always popular on the circuit, in particular with the ladies. That was a sad day, when she left us."

"So, some of these specimens are from your travelling days?" Giles said.

"Yes."

"Then I probably saw some of them in their prime," said Giles. "I remember Askham's coming to Alnwick Fair when I was boy. There was a tiger – Tiberius, is that right?"

"Tiberius, yes! He was a magnificent fellow. I have him in my office here, if you'd like to come in?"

"Certainly," said Giles.

"Alnwick – that was always a good pitch for us," said Mr Askham, showing them into a tiny room that opened off the hall. Here, Tiberius in all his magnificence stood next to his master's desk, a red velvet coat draped over his back. There was hardly room for the three of them, so Fitznorton was obliged to stand in the doorway. "All round the northern counties and into Scotland too we used to go, and sometimes we would go to Edinburgh. Thirty years ago now, sir."

"It must be," said Giles. "How do you come to be here, Mr Askham? I thought you would prefer to be on the road still."

"I do love that life, but you get too old for it. Well, my missus did, God rest her soul, and we got the lease here at a good price, and it made sense to make a go of it. And when the railway opened – well, that changed everything. People come to us, instead of us going to them! But for how much longer, I don't know."

"Why is that?"

"My landlord. The property has changed hands – it was the nephew who got it from his uncle, who was as good a fellow that lived, and loved coming to see the animals, especially the camels – but the nephew, who inherited the place from him, he's not from round here. He wants to sell up, and he wants me out."

"Has he served notice on you?"

"Not yet, but it's been talked of. I've offered to pay more rent. That's where it stands for now, but I'm not hopeful. He wants to sell, and with the price of land round here these days, I can hardly blame him. I wish I could buy him out, but there's no way I could lay hands on that much money." He sighed.

"Can you give me his name and address?"

"Yes, as you wish," said Askham. "I have it hereabouts somewhere." He began to search his desk. "And now this business! I suppose I shan't be able to open for a day or two?"

"No, I think not, Mr Askham," said Giles. "I would also like a list of everyone who works for you here, and when they usually come and go."

"Yes, I'll see to it," said Askham, handing him a letter. "Here you are – that's the solicitor dealing for him."

The letterhead indicated a firm in London. Giles scanned it.

"The owner's name is Henderson?"

"Aye, it were John Henderson I first dealt with. That's the nephew's name as well, though I've never heard from him directly."

"May I borrow this?"

"As you like, sir."

"Do you live on the premises?"

"No, I live with my daughter and her husband in Broad Street."

"What time do you usually come into work?"

"About half eight. Not as early as I used, I have to admit. We don't open to the public until ten."

"And you haven't seen or heard anything suspicions over the last few days?" Askham shook his head. "Bobby Farr said he asked you to have the leopards' cage mended. That it needed a farrier to fix it."

"Aye, that was last week. He had it patched up with a rope. It looked safe enough, but I had sent for someone. It's just that the town is so busy you can't get a good tradesman in a hurry."

"Safe enough for the animals not to escape, you mean?"

"Of course. I wasn't thinking of anyone getting in that way. Why would anyone be so daft?"

"They may have had no choice about it," said Giles.

~

Dr Greville of the Incurables Hospital was waiting outside to meet Felix and the cart containing the corpse. They shook hands.

"I shall be glad of some assistance," said Felix.

"I must explain, I'm not a medical man, Mr Carswell," said Dr Greville. "My doctorate is in divinity. We are not so much a hospital as an almshouse. But we have a room suitable for your purposes, especially if an inquest is called. And we are a sanctuary of sorts, so it is my sad duty to bring this poor soul to a decent rest after such violence. This way, if you please."

They went through a pair of gates into a most picturesque and serene courtyard resembling an Oxford quadrangle, with beds of wallflowers and pinks filling the air with their sweet scents. In the middle, an ancient fountain burbled, while on the lawn several of the patients were sitting in bath chairs, enjoying the sunshine.

They turned into a cool, stone-flagged passageway, and then went through an ancient, iron-studded door to a pillared and vaulted room, lit with lancet windows. As far as Felix was concerned, it was perfect for the purpose.

"It was formerly a dispensary," said Dr Greville. He indicated a stone basin set in the wall. "Our own warm spring feeds this basin, by means of ancient plumbing."

"That will be useful," Felix said.

"There is a theory, advanced by some antiquarians in the district," said Dr Greville, "that this building, which was once a friary, is on the site of the original Roman bath house which in turn was built on the sacred spring of the ancient Celtic goddess Brigantia. I like the theory, for in pre-reformation days there was a devotion to St Bridget here – surely the two must be related?"

"I'm sorry, I don't know," said Felix. "Might it be possible to have a key to the door?" The constables had laid the hurdle containing the body on the floor, for the room was empty. "And perhaps a couple of trestle tables?"

"I'll get it seen to, sir," said Sergeant Dale, placing the blanket down on the floor beside the hurdle.

"Inspector Harris said that he met with an accident in one of the animal cages," said Dr Greville.

"It was probably more than an accident," said Felix.

"That menagerie is a curious place," said Dr Greville. "It has become very popular over the last few years. I suppose it is commensurate with the increase in trade here. Working people come from Northminster on cheap excursions in great numbers just to visit it. Sometimes we can hear the beasts roaring, if the wind is in the right direction. And then there is the smell. My wife does not like the smell of the camels. She notices it particularly when she is upstairs in our quarters, which are at the back here. But apparently it is to be closed. It will have to be, I suppose, after this." He gestured towards the hurdle. "How terrible."

"If it was doing well, why are they closing it?" Felix asked.

"It was doing too well," said Greville, "with the wrong sort of people. Some of the landlords in Stanegate have been alarmed at the recent growth of the place. It is a question of tone. This has always been a genteel resort, and perhaps the menagerie is not the right sort of entertainment. It was tolerated until the railway introduced those cheap tickets from Northminster. Captain Carrington of the Hydropathic Institute has been exercised about it."

"Is that what used to be The Queen's Hotel?"

"Yes, but you would not recognise it. It's been transformed. They found a hot spring in the grounds and have built a bath house. Quite a sight. It is like Rome restored! Extraordinary. Now, I had better leave you to your work. Here is the key to this door, and another to the main gate."

"Thank you," said Felix, and saw him to the door, locking it behind him.

Left alone, he got down on his knees and took the sacking from the body. In the clear light of the dispensary, the damage was much easier to see, and far more disturbing. He had read accounts of bodies mangled by wild beasts, but had never seen it for himself. Thankfully, it was a rare occurrence.

Just before he had come away from the menagerie, he had climbed the steps and looked into the van containing Moonshine and Mercury. The leopards had been lying in semi-darkness, wrapped up in each other like a pair of lovers. They were magnificent, supple beasts, full of power and hostility even in repose. One had closed eyes, the other gave him a cautious stare. What struck him was how like domestic cats they were. He had seen Byron, the tabby cat who had the run of Hawksby, lie in the same languid pose, a massive paw outstretched, perhaps to remind the onlooker to be wary. Byron, if petted correctly, would melt like butter in his arms, but even then, he would sometimes turn and scratch.

He looked down at the torn flesh, and remembered something he had read about wild beasts only feasting on corpses with flesh wounds. A corpse without blood might not have attracted them, given that they were well fed.

He sloughed off his coat and searched out a scalpel and tweezers from his bag. Rolling up his shirtsleeves, he delicately began to fold back the ripped layers of linen and flesh from the victim's abdomen, searching for any sign of wounds that were not a result of the beasts' depredations. He did not like to presume that there might be any, but it seemed unlikely that any man, other than the keeper, would have entered the leopard cage willingly.

He was interrupted by the arrival of the trestle tables, and the business of transferring the body onto one of them. Soon after, Major Vernon, Fitznorton and the coroner Mr Boothroyd came in, and the necessary preliminaries were discussed. Mr Boothroyd decided that he would defer the inquest until they had established more facts, signed the chit for the post-mortem, and then happily excused himself, having only glanced at the body.

"So," Major Vernon said, having seen him to the door, "identification has to be our first priority. Who is he? The more we know about him, the better. If we know who he is, we can then ask: why is he dead in this particular and peculiar location?"

"Nothing in his pockets," Felix said.

"But that is a reasonable quality cloth, I would say. And his shirt – the linen is very fine," said Major Vernon. "Braces, nice quality too. Can you remove them, Mr Carswell?"

Felix disentangled them from the mauled rib cage and laid them on the other table.

"Embroidered," said Major Vernon. "Not cheap and not exactly commonplace. So he's well turned out. Well nourished? What is the girth of his trousers?"

Felix measured it. "Forty and three quarters. So he had

some flesh on him – once."

"Sir..." murmured Fitznorton in reproach.

"Have a care, Mr Carswell," said Major Vernon, for Fitznorton had gone pale and looked on the verge of collapse.

"You should sit down," Felix said. Fitznorton went and perched on the stone bench that abutted the wall, and Felix made him put his head between his legs before he passed out.

"Do you want a drink?" Felix asked when Fitznorton had straightened up again.

"I won't, thank you."

"Are you sure? I have reasonable French brandy or illegal usequebah."

"No, thank you."

"Then hold on to this," Felix said, handing him a flask of smelling salts. "It may recur. It's nothing to be ashamed of," he added. "You should see the students at Edinburgh dropping like flies at far less than this. We all do it at one time or other. Practically a rite of passage."

Fitznorton nodded, and then stood up and walked deliberately over to the corpse and looked down at it for a long moment, as if trying to harden himself to it.

"Do you know shorthand, Mr Fitznorton?" said Major Vernon.

"Yes," he said.

"Perhaps you would take notes?"

"Certainly," Fitznorton said, taking a notebook from his pocket.

Felix continued his inspection of the corpse.

"Height: five nine," he said. "Hair: fair, with a touch of white, would you say?"

"Late middle age?" Major Vernon said.

"I would say so. Looks like a bit of birthmark on his forehead, but I can't say for sure. Good teeth for his age, and all his own. Eyes: blue grey."

"What can you say about his physique?"

"As I said, he had some flesh on him, and he's well set up. Broad shouldered, wouldn't you say?"

"Yes," said Major Vernon, who was now examining the man's boots. "Everything suggests prosperity and position. Perhaps a wealthy visitor to Stanegate for the season? We shall have to scour the hotels to see if anyone has gone missing – unless... may I?" he added indicating the boot.

"Yes."

Major Vernon removed the man's boot.

"Patent leather and a dressy article. Worn on the heel." He glanced inside. "Excellent, a bootmaker's label: Smithsons, the Parade, Stanegate. So perhaps not a visitor?"

"Not a great deal to go on," said Felix.

"There's enough," said Major Vernon. "Come, Mr Fitznorton – let's go and see if Dr Greville will give us a cup of coffee and some local gossip."

"Oh yes, he will be good for that," said Felix. "He was telling me about the Hydropathic Institute and how they have built a Roman bath house and how Mrs Greville does not like the smell of the camels from the menagerie."

"These are the scraps by which we live!" said Major Vernon.

~

Dr Greville was clearly inclined to be hospitable and took them straight up to his wife's drawing room.

"Your colleague, Mr Carswell, will be joining us?" he said.

"I'm afraid not."

"I shall have something sent in for him," said Dr Greville. "Such an interesting young man. He reminds me of someone, but I cannot think who – ah, Matilda, you are here after all. I thought you might be in the garden. I have Major Vernon and

Mr Fitznorton for you!"

Giles had the feeling he was being served up as the main course, as the introductions were made. Mrs Greville was not alone – she had a lady with her, a Mrs Stuart.

"Stuart with a 'u', mind, Major Vernon," said Dr Greville. "I always wonder at the two spellings, but for my part I find the 'u' version has a more distinguished look to it."

The Mrs Stuart in question smiled at that. Distinguished was a good word to describe her: Giles guessed that she was in her mid-twenties, with smoothly arranged chestnut braids framing a well-constructed face. Her clothes suggested wealth and style, but without any touch of show about them, and her carriage and manners were graceful.

"My husband's family no doubt changed it for that very reason," she said.

"You must be Mrs Fforde's brother, Major Vernon," said Mrs Greville, offering him a cup of coffee.

"I am," said Giles.

"It's unfortunate to have to meet you in such circumstances," she said. "But I suppose that's the nature of your work. I'm only happy we can be of help to you."

"Do you have any idea who he might be?" said Dr Greville.

"Only that he got his boots at Smithsons in the Parade," said Giles.

"Now, that is an expensive shop," said Mrs Greville. "Very nice, but expensive."

"One might say that of all the shops here," said Mrs Stuart.

"Yes, it is scandalous how dear everything is here," said Mrs Greville.

"The whole town is a temptation," said Mrs Stuart. "I have to keep myself in check."

"Nonsense," said Dr Greville. "You are not at all that kind of woman. I cannot tell you how rare it is that a visitor to

Stanegate strays over our threshold, let alone comes and offers to help. Mrs Stuart has been visiting all the old women here."

"It is no chore. They are lovely old creatures, and I confess I adore places like this. It is like sitting under an ancient oak tree. So much time has passed here!"

"Are you here for all the season, Mrs Stuart?" said Giles.

"Yes, we came in May. My husband is taking a course of baths at the Hydropathic Institution."

"And has it done him good?"

"A little."

"Are you staying there? I understand it used to be The Queen's Hotel."

"Oh no, we have taken one of the cottages on the hill. Just a few minutes' walk from here."

"Up a great many steps," Mrs Greville said. "Oh, to be as young and fit as you, Mrs Stuart. I walked up there the other day and I was utterly out of breath. But the views are worth it. All the houses have verandahs. It is delightful."

"Have these been built in the last year or so? I have been here before and I do not remember them."

"Oh yes, it is all part of Captain Carrington's developments," said Dr Greville.

Giles felt badly in need of a map.

"Where are these cottages in relation to the menagerie?" he said.

"They overlook it," he said. "You are troubled by the smell of the camels as well, I think, Mrs Stuart?"

"We are. It is not pleasant."

"Dr Greville, you don't happen to know anything about the Mr Henderson who owns the land on which the menagerie is situated?" Giles said.

"I'm afraid not," he said. "You should ask at the Rothborough Estate office. Mr Tait will be able to help you."

"I shall, thank you," said Giles. He finished his coffee and got up. "Thank you, ma'am. We must get on, I'm afraid, though I would much rather stay and talk."

"Rothborough, of course!" said Dr Greville as they went downstairs. "That is who Mr Carswell reminds me of. Is he –? Though perhaps I should not enquire. Mrs Greville would consider it vulgar."

Chapter Four

"I need a map," said Giles to Fitznorton. They turned into the first booksellers they came to in the Parade, an establishment that had opened since his last visit. It was as glossy as it was spacious, with a large subscription library section, full of smartly dressed ladies. Some of these favoured Giles and Fitznorton with the searching, interested gaze of those who wanted to know exactly who they were and how much they were worth.

"Do you get the feeling that Stanegate is a marriage mart?" Giles said to Fitznorton, when the shopman had gone away to fetch the maps.

"Or worse," said Fitznorton. "I would not care to find my sisters idling in such a public place. I suppose that in towns like this, where strangers are thrown all together, those girls fancy themselves invisible."

"I suspect they would hate to be invisible," Giles said. "They wish to be noticed: that is the whole point, surely?"

"To act with such bold carelessness suggests to me that they do not think they will be observed," Fitznorton said, "let alone judged."

Giles glanced back at the library section. A woman of his own age, in mourning – her bonnet crowned with a halo of expensive black lace – smiled at him.

"No," said Giles, "they expect to be judged, just as they are judging us. The cut of your coat, the polish of your hat – it is all being assessed. These are women who make excellent witnesses. They never forget a detail, however trivial."

"It would be better, surely, that they stay at home and make themselves useful?"

"How do you know they are not useful at home? A woman who takes trouble with her appearance usually takes care of her household with great diligence. At least that has been my experience. Take Mrs Greville, for example."

The bookseller now came back to the counter.

"If it is a plan of the town you are after, sir," he said, "might I recommend the one in Captain Carrington's pamphlet? It folds out, you see, and it is very clear." He opened the book on the counter, and unfolded the map. "All the principal attractions clearly marked. The new opera house, the Hydropathic Institute, of course –"

"But not the menagerie?" said Giles. "That's a curious omission."

"It's not a place that is of much interest to most visitors, and I understand it will be closing soon. I suppose the Captain had it left off for that reason. Will this suffice, sir? There is also a good map of the district – less detail of the town, but it is useful for planning excursions by carriage and so forth. May I suggest the drive to Holbroke, for example? That is a house worth seeing. The gardens are particularly fine this time of year."

"No, the pamphlet will suffice."

"Yes, of course, sir. That will be a shilling. I cannot interest you in a library or newspaper ticket? Most families coming to town find our selections very much to their taste. We have all the latest novels, of course, and plenty of them. Ladies like nothing less than waiting for the next volume of a favourite author, and it always pays to keep the ladies happy when travelling, sir."

"A good maxim," Giles said. "No, just the book at present."

"Yes, of course, sir," said the shopman. "Shall I wrap that, sir?"

Giles shook his head and handed over his money.

"Would you write a receipt for that, please?" said

Fitznorton. The shopman went away to attend to it, and Fitznorton went on: "Would you like me to keep a tally of your expenses, Major Vernon?"

Giles did not answer at once as he was flicking through the pamphlet that contained the map.

"Yes, if you would, that would be helpful," he said. He had paused at a full-page engraving that showed a large, impressive building. The illustration was entitled 'The Hydropathic Institute at Stanegate. Proprietor: Capt. C. Carrington. Physician in charge: Dr P. M. L. Kennedy, MD Dublin.' "We will have to go and talk to Captain Carrington in the near future. But first, I want to talk to Mr Tait."

~

"Major Vernon, a great honour to know you, sir," said Mr Tait. "His Lordship has spoken of you, and of course we all read The Bugle! How can I help you?"

"Can you tell me anything about Mr Henderson, the man who owns the land the menagerie is situated on?" Giles asked.

"That's an interesting question, sir. It's a strange parcel of land all in all. His Lordship, you see, has had his eye on it, and we have made an offer on the land – a fair and generous offer. But for some reason, Mr Henderson is reluctant to make up his mind, one way or the other."

"So if the Rothborough Estate acquired it, Mr Askham would be evicted?"

"Yes, certainly. That place has had its day. His Lordship is opposed to it on humane grounds. But we are not the only ones interested. I suppose that accounts for Mr Henderson's failure to answer us. He is biding his time."

"I had heard Captain Carrington would like to acquire the land."

"Yes, we think that may be the case."

"That name is on everyone's lips here," said Giles.

"He has transformed the place," said Tait.

"Have you met him?"

"Once or twice."

"And what do you make of him?"

"He is ambitious and he seems to have a genuine flair for promotion. He has raised the profile of the place wonderfully. This summer has been extremely busy and land values in the town are increasing as a result. His business has been good for our business, I have to say."

"So do you think he might outbid you?"

"I don't know. As I said, it was a fair and generous offer, perhaps more than would be usual. Lord Rothborough would very much like the land. He is of the opinion that that part of town needs to be properly landscaped and turned into an area for public recreation. When those houses were thrown up on Carr's Crag –"

"Are those the cottages above the menagerie?" Giles said, reaching for the map. "Could you show me where, exactly?"

"Here," said Tait, pointing to the spot. "His Lordship was most annoyed about that, as he had also attempted to buy the Crag. It's too splendid a place to be built on, but unfortunately those fancy cottages have gone up now."

"Is that Carrington's doing?" asked Giles.

"I'm not sure. He has some stake in it, but I have struggled to find out exactly what. We have enquiries in hand on that, as it may still be possible to purchase the area back, but it would be very expensive now, even for a man of Lord Rothborough's means. I will set one of my clerks on this, and I'll send you a more thorough report. There may be something of use to you. I imagine some serious business has brought you here?"

"Yes, that is the case."

"Where will you be staying, sir, if I may ask?"

"I'm not sure."

"Let me send my boy to The White Hart and tell them you are here. I'm sure that is what Lord Rothborough would want. He keeps a set of rooms there. I take it Mr Carswell is with you?"

"Yes, he is. Thank you."

"It's under new management – a Frenchwoman has it in hand. A lady from France, I should say, because she certainly is one – and she is just what the place needed. The food there now – I've never tasted anything like it, and I've had the honour of dining at Holbroke."

"Stanegate is full of surprises these days," Giles said.

"Oh, it certainly is, that's true."

"About Captain Carrington," Giles said. "Could you describe him for me? His appearance, I mean?"

"I'd say he was between forty and fifty. He has his hair still, but it's on the thin side, like mine is. You can see he has a birthmark about here," Tait said, touching the crown of his head. "He's solid looking, and looks well looked after, if you know what I mean. Very smartly turned out, with a swagger about him. Handsome enough, and of moderate height."

When they were in the street again, Fitznorton said, "Why did you ask for his description?"

"He appears to be a man playing for high stakes. That can attract enemies."

"And you think he might be the victim?"

"I shall not rule him out until I have laid eyes on him. Tait's description was too close for comfort, don't you think? It's time we went to the Hydropathic Institute."

~

Giles was pleased to see that the Hydropathic Institute,

formerly The Queen's Hotel, had not sacrificed its beautiful gardens. The enticing bowers and rose walks were all flourishing, and the guests, who did not look remotely like invalids, were enjoying the late-afternoon, end of summer sun. It was curious to see it all again, and more curious still to realise, as they approached the entrance, that the woman in white muslin walking with a baby in her arms on the broad terrace, was none other than Sukey Connolly. He corrected himself: Mrs Kennedy.

"Excuse me," he said to Fitznorton, and went over to her.

"I thought that was you!" she said, smiling. "I thought I was seeing things for a minute, but it is!"

"It has been too long," he said.

"Yes, yes, certainly it has. I would shake your hand but my hands are full, as you can see, Major."

She had one finger in the child's mouth.

Without thinking much about it, he bent and kissed her, and she returned the favour.

"We are old friends, after all," he said.

"Oh, it is good to see you!" she said. At this moment the baby crumpled its face and began to cry. "Oh dear."

"May I?" said Giles, gesturing to take the child from her.

"Are you sure?"

"Quite." She eased the baby into his arms.

"Be good now, Lorenzo," she said, "or Major Vernon will not like you."

"Of course I shall like him," said Giles, jiggling the child gently in his arms. He felt strong, sturdy and delightfully wilful. "Lorenzo?"

"I call him that. He is properly Laurence, after Dr Kennedy's father."

"Lorenzo suits him."

"Goodness, what did you do?" said Sukey, as the baby fell quiet. "He has been fractious all afternoon. Ah, but you could subdue the oceans, if you cared to, that is it!"

"I don't think so. How old is he?"

"Three months," said Sukey.

"I'm surprised that Mrs O'Brien did not mention his arrival," said Giles.

"That is because –" She broke off with a sigh. "That can all wait for another time. You should go back to your friend, Major – he looks awfully forlorn."

"He's an acquaintance at most," said Giles. "He has been sent from the Home Office."

"So you are here on business?" Sukey said.

"Yes, the usual," said Giles.

"Does that mean that Mr Carswell is here?" she said.

"Yes."

"What has happened?"

"A body has been found in the menagerie – in the leopard cage."

"What? Moonshine and Mercury killed someone?" said Sukey. "Surely not? My stepchildren love those leopards. I do, for that matter. They are so beautiful!"

"No, we think he was most likely dead when he went in. At least, Mr Carswell is attempting to establish that that is the case."

"Oh, goodness! Major Vernon, I do think you should rescue your Home Office gentleman."

"Yes, of course," said Giles, and went over to him, Lorenzo still in his arms. "I have found an old friend who may be able to help us, Mr Fitznorton."

Fitznorton obediently came with him and Giles presented him to Sukey, and then added, "Mrs Kennedy, I take it you know Captain Carrington?"

"I do," said Sukey.

"I wish to see him. Where is the best place to find him?"

"You won't find him at all today," said Sukey. "He's away on business."

"Do you know when he left?"

"On Friday morning. I remember because my husband was pleased about it. Oh dear, I should not have mentioned that, should I?" she said, and reached out to take the baby from him.

"They are in dispute?" said Giles, relinquishing the child to her.

"No, I don't think so," said Sukey. "It is just that when two men are in partnership there is bound to be friction from time to time. It is like marriage."

"What does the Captain look like?" he said.

"Oh, why are you asking me that, Major?" she said.

"Perhaps you can guess?"

She nodded and said, "He is a little under six foot, with pale, thin hair. He is stout but in a vigorous way. And he dresses beautifully – he always wears patent leather boots, I have noticed that. Oh, and he has a port-wine stain on his forehead, but he combs his hair over it."

"I need you to look at a body," Giles said.

Chapter Five

"He was dead before he went in there," Felix said, opening the door to Major Vernon. "Come and look at this –"

"Not just now," said the Major, shutting the door behind him. "I have someone here who may be able to identify him. What state is the body in?"

"I haven't begun to dissect," said Felix.

"Good. Can you make him vaguely presentable?"

"Yes, but I do wonder that anyone will be able to recognise him."

"That is a risk. But this is a reliable witness."

"Who?" said Felix. There was something about the Major's manner that merited the question.

"Mrs Kennedy."

"What?" said Felix.

"I have a feeling this may be her husband's business partner, Captain Carrington."

"Then cannot her husband come and look at him?" said Felix. "I really would rather not –"

"Of course. I entirely appreciate that, but needs must. She is a far more suitable person to do it than her husband, who we do not know from Adam. This is Sukey, Mr Carswell – she understands what we are about. And it will be only a few minutes' work. She has to get back to her child."

"She has a child?"

"It's to be expected."

"How old?"

"Three months. She is nursing him, so she cannot be away long."

"Three months? She's not to be relied on, then. She is still postpartum."

"That's a little unfair," said Major Vernon.

"Not at all. There was a judgement only last month –"

"Yes, I know the one you mean, but the circumstances are hardly the same. That woman had a predisposition to mania, did she not? Five minutes, that is all. If it were anyone else I would agree with you, and I know this will not be pleasant for you. It will not be pleasant for her, for Heaven's sake, but she has agreed to it, like the sensible woman she is."

"Oh, very well," said Felix. "Let me tidy him up first, though."

"Thank you," said Major Vernon, going to the door.

"I'll come out and get you," he said.

He closed the door and leant on it, wondering at himself. Why did the thought of seeing her disturb him so, when time and their respective circumstances had surely healed all the wounds they had inflicted upon each other?

Turning back to the cadaver, he reflected that the Major was right to have brought her there. There was no disputing that. She had the strength of character to face such a task, and make an honest assessment of what she saw. Yet he wished it were anyone but her, for all the expediency of it.

He did what he could to make the cadaver decent, covering it entirely, and hoping that only showing his ravaged face would be enough to make the identification. He really did not want to inflict the full horror of it on her. Then he went to the warm spring basin and washed his face and hands, before going out to the courtyard.

She was standing by a bed of pinks and gillyflowers talking to Mrs Greville. She was dressed in white, with a blue shawl wrapped about her, and because of the conversation she did not notice him at once. He had the chance to study her at his leisure, a painful exercise in some respects, but he did not desist from it. He thought of how Fitznorton had forced himself to look at the corpse earlier. It seemed analogous – to look at her was to force himself to look at the rotting cadaver that had been their affair. He remembered the quarrels, of which there had been many, the awkward apologies and the hot and tender kisses that had followed as an inevitable prelude to the ultimate intimacies. However, that last part, when they had shared a bed, was curiously distant now. He had purged it thoroughly from his memory, like a housemaid scrubbing away a stain.

"Mrs Kennedy, this way, if you please?" he said.

She turned and nodded, and came towards him. Major Vernon followed them into the dispensary and shut the door behind him.

"Now, if you give a positive identification," the Major said, "I shall ask Dr Greville to see who he thinks it may be. We have not mentioned our suspicions to him, yet."

"A good plan," said Felix. "I'll just show you his face. That should suffice." She came over to the trestle and he folded back the sheet. He saw her swallow and grimace, and take a deep breath to steady herself.

"Oh, that's him all right," she said after a silence. "Yes. Captain Carrington."

"Is there anything that particularly makes you say so?" Felix asked.

"The port-wine stain. Or rather what's left of it." She pointed to it. "Did the leopards really do this to him?"

"The superficial damage, yes, but he was stabbed before that," Felix said.

The Major covered him over again.

"How well did you know him?"

"Only slightly," she said. "I can't say I liked him."

"Presumably he knows your husband well?" Major Vernon said.

"You will have to talk to him," said Sukey. "I don't really know much about their business arrangements. I have been too busy with the children. And I really should get back."

"Yes, of course," said Major Vernon. "But if I could just ask you to wait until Dr Greville has seen him?"

She nodded, and Felix was left alone feeling the raw unpleasantness of the situation. It was obvious she knew a great deal more about Carrington than she said. She had been evasive, but that was to be expected. She had new loyalties and he hoped to God it was done willingly. Was she happy? Could he determine that from such a brief encounter?

There was no time for reflection. Major Vernon brought Dr Greville in shortly afterwards.

"Do you know this man, by any chance?"

Greville scanned the ravaged features.

"I cannot think why it should be – but it looks to me like Captain Carrington. That mark..." He waved his hand towards the port-wine stain, and then turned away, his hand over his mouth.

"Thank you, sir," said Major Vernon, and hurried him out.

Felix covered the corpse and followed them, locking the door behind him.

As Dr Greville staggered across the lawn, Felix said to Fitznorton, who was standing some six foot away, "Do you still have those smelling scents on you?"

Fitznorton dug in his pocket and tossed them to him. Felix was so surprised at this that he almost failed to catch them. He hurried to Dr Greville, who was on the verge of fainting, and thrust them under his nose.

"You're a cricketer," Major Vernon said.

"Now and again," said Fitznorton.

"He's a Cambridge Blue!" Dr Greville managed to say, coughing and spluttering as the salts did their work.

"You should sit down, sir," said Felix, guiding him to a bench.

"Thank you, I will," said Dr Greville. His wife came and sat beside him.

"I will take Mrs Kennedy home now," said Major Vernon. "We are putting up at The White Hart, Mr Carswell. Shall we rendezvous there?"

"Certainly," said Felix.

"You will forgive me if I don't get up and say goodbye, Mrs Kennedy," said Dr Greville. "I hope you will not have bad dreams. I am sure I will. But I will be right as rain to do my duty on Sunday, you may be sure of it! And of course, if you wish to speak to me at any time, I am at your disposal."

"Thank you, Dr Greville. Mrs Greville," said Sukey. "I'm sure it will all go splendidly. We are looking forward to it."

"I do so love a baptism," said Mrs Greville. "It is my favourite sacrament."

~

Giles handed Sukey into the carriage and sat down before he asked, "So Dr Greville is to baptise your son?"

"Yes, he is."

"That's rather unexpected. Is there not a priest here?"

"Yes, but we have left the Roman Church since we came here," she said.

"I see. Is that why you have quarrelled with your sister? And why I have heard nothing about Lorenzo?"

"Yes, it is. Nothing in her eyes could be worse. She thinks my husband is the Devil incarnate for making me do it."

"And is he making you do it?" said Giles. "Excuse me, but I must ask."

"No, I'd never do such a thing if I didn't want to. Dr Greville has explained it all to me, and I find I like it. It's more comfort to me than anything I had before, which is just as well given all the trouble it's caused."

It was only a short drive back to the Hydropathic

Institute, and the driver, who belonged to the place, dropped them in a courtyard behind the main entrance.

A man came marching out to meet the carriage. In the doorway behind him, a woman servant could be seen holding the screaming Lorenzo.

"What is going on?" he said, seeing Giles handing Sukey out of the carriage. "Who are you, sir?"

"This is Major Vernon, Paul," said Sukey. He was a commanding figure: long, dark sideburns outlined a well-sculpted, yet rugged face that would not have disgraced a warrior king. However, his manner at once put Giles on his guard.

"Dr Kennedy?" said Giles, offering his hand. Kennedy did not take it.

"You need to get inside," he said to Sukey in an imperious tone that Giles could not like. "Your child –"

"Yes, yes, I know!" she exclaimed. "As if I'd forget!" she said, running past him and into the house.

"The fault is mine, sir," said Giles. "I kept her longer than we anticipated. But it was in a good cause. I'm afraid something serious has occurred. Perhaps I might talk to you in private?"

"You're with the police, aren't you?" said Kennedy.

"Chief Superintendent of the Northern Criminal Investigation Office, yes," said Giles.

"So?" said Kennedy.

"About Captain Carrington," Giles said. "I understand he is away on business at present."

"He is," said Kennedy. "What is going on?"

"Can you tell me when he left?"

"Last Friday. He took the connecting train for London."

"And do you know when he is expected back?"

"Friday, he said. What has this to do with you taking my wife off like this, sir?"

"It was necessary, I assure you," said Giles. "You see, a

body was discovered this morning at the menagerie. I asked your wife to identify him. I apologise if it has caused any domestic inconvenience."

"You took my wife to identify a corpse?" said Kennedy.

"Yes. She gave me a description of Captain Carrington that tallied closely with my dead man. It was expedient to ask her to see whether he was in fact the Captain. Which he was."

"Are you saying Captain Carrington is dead?"

"Yes. His remains were discovered this morning in the leopard cage at the menagerie."

"His remains? Are you saying that he was mauled by them?"

"Yes, there was serious depredation by the beasts – that is the word my medical colleague used. And I apologise again for submitting Mrs Kennedy to such an ordeal. There are very few women in the world I would allow into such a situation. But she was, of course, equal to it."

"Did the beasts kill him?" said Kennedy.

"That is not yet certain."

"Mother of God," said Kennedy. "What was he doing in there?"

"I was hoping you might help me with that. After all, he is your business partner, I understand?"

"We have an arrangement that amounts to that."

"But no formal articles of partnership?"

"No. I have only been here since the spring. We thought it best not to commit to anything until after the season, in case we were not temperamentally suited. So we had an informal arrangement, but we were to sign an agreement at the beginning of October. He had asked his solicitor to draw it up. Is it really him? Are you absolutely sure?"

"Dr Greville also identified him."

"In the leopard cage?" Kennedy said. Giles nodded. "Well, that will be the end of the place now, thank goodness! That is something. Askham is a rogue of the first order. I trust you have talked to him?"

"I have, yes," said Giles.

"That place is a blistering sore. It attracts the wrong sort of people, and the guests here do not like it. One of my patients has been reduced to hysteria by the noises of the animals, particularly the braying of those camels."

"You can hear them from here?" said Giles.

"Her room was in the new wing, on the top floor. It overlooks the menagerie. It's unfortunate."

"I understand that the Captain wished to buy the land?"

"Yes."

"You don't happen to know who the landowner is? Askham was only a tenant."

"No, he didn't mention it. But I know that he was in negotiations. I suppose that would explain the threats."

"Threats?"

"Askham sent some nasty letters."

"Did you see them?"

"No, the Captain mentioned them in passing. He was not the type to be bothered by such things. I think he burnt them."

"Did Captain Carrington live here on the premises?"

"Yes, he has rooms in the old building. Had rooms, I should say."

"Thank you, Dr Kennedy – I will leave it there for this evening. You will want to get back to your family. I'm sorry to be the bearer of bad news. It's a difficult thing to lose a colleague, especially in such circumstances. My regards to Mrs Kennedy."

Giles walked back to the main entrance and went in. The interior was much as he recalled it, although it had been redecorated and at the foot of the staircase was a white marble statue of a Greek goddess. Far larger than life, she was beautifully sculpted and she gazed down with a mixture of benevolence and power, a large snake twisting elegantly about her. Sitting nearby were Inspector Harris and Sergeant Dale who he had asked to meet him there.

"Apparently that is Hygeia, sir," said Inspector Harris, getting up to greet him. "The goddess of health. She's quite the lady, isn't she? Mr Fisher, the general manager here, said she's made from a solid block of Italian marble and cost over five hundred guineas."

"They certainly haven't stinted here, have they?" said Giles looking about him.

"Wait until you see the bath house, sir," said Harris.

"So what did Mr Fisher have to say?" Giles asked.

"He was surprised, certainly, and I can't say it wasn't genuine. He said everything has been going smoothly and that they are turning people away. Dr Kennedy is popular, especially with female patients."

"Did you secure the Captain's rooms?"

"Yes, sir, all ready for you."

"We will leave that tonight. I want to get a full report from Mr Carswell before we proceed and I'd like him here to help the search. We are looking at murder. He was dead before the beasts got him."

"Speaking of the leopards," said Harris. "What do you want done about them? They will have to be destroyed, I would think. They're a public danger."

"I suppose it will have to come to that. It seems dreadful to condemn them for only being true to their nature."

"The town is going to be jumpy enough after this. Captain Carrington was very well known. It will calm nerves to know they have been dealt with."

"You are right," said Giles. "But let me sleep on it. I will let you know tomorrow."

"Of course, sir."

"I'm putting up at The White Hart," Giles went on. "I suggest we all take our rest and start again tomorrow. At least we know who he is. That's a good day's work."

"Of all the people," said Harris, shaking his head. "As I said, sir, Captain Carrington was quite the celebrity here."

Chapter Six

Felix sincerely hoped that he would not be left alone to dine with Fitznorton, and was anxious for the Major's return. For this reason, when the waiter enquired where they would eat, in their rooms or downstairs, he chose the latter, although he would have preferred to dine in shirtsleeves in privacy.

"This is as good a place as any to judge the lay of the land," said Major Vernon, finding them installed in the lavishly decorated public dining room of The White Hart. "Have you ordered for me?"

"I settled on the 'propositions de jour,'" said Felix, "and a bottle of the '29 Burgundy."

"That sounds excellent. I'm surprised we could get a table. It's busy in here. Who are all these people? Not health-seekers, surely?"

"Gourmands, I should say," said Felix, "given the menu."

"I recognise some of that party of gentlemen in the corner," said Giles. "They are from Northminster. Is that not Miller the attorney?"

"You are right," said Felix. "Where is Mrs Miller, then?"

"Perhaps she is at the Hydropathic Institute drinking gruel and worshipping Hygeia," said Major Vernon. "It is a shame there are no ladies here. The room needs them. All the gilding and looking glasses – it's more like a drawing room."

"Surely you cannot be in favour of respectable women dining in public?" said Fitznorton.

"I can't see the harm in it," Giles said. "Not in a place like this. And what right have we to deny them our pleasures? I caught a glimpse of our hostess as I came in, and she looks as if she could be an archdeacon's wife."

"A handsome archdeacon's wife," said Felix, who had also seen this elegant person when they had arrived. "And French."

"It is extraordinary how this place has changed in two years," said Major Vernon. "It was torpid previously."

"All thanks to the late Captain Carrington," said Felix, "and his parcel of nonsense. That pamphlet – I read it in my bath, which did not, incidentally, miraculously cure me of anything – is all specious quack nonsense of the worst sort."

"But profitable, apparently," said Major Vernon. "And that makes for enemies."

"He certainly must have had those," said Felix.

The wine had arrived and it fell to Felix to taste it. It was excellent, and he was glad for his informal lessons from Canon Fforde. Otherwise, he would have remained ignorant and liable to order expensive vinegar. "I really cannot tempt you to a glass, Mr Fitznorton?" he said, seeing him turn his wine glass upside down. "For the sake of hospitality and in the name of fellowship? After such a day –"

"No, thank you."

"Do you even drink beer?" he said.

"No, not even that," said Fitznorton. "I'm aware this makes me awkward, but I cannot condone it. The evil it does: you gentlemen must be more aware of that than others. You must see it daily in your work, what degradation it causes. I feel that our class should set an example."

"To be frank, I'm not sure your self-denial would change any poor drunkard's opinion," said Felix. "And they will only poison themselves with something else if it is forbidden. Beer is wholesome and nourishing, by the way. A working man can get a good meal from a glass of well-brewed stout, and if that helps him with his work, then so be it."

"And if he drinks to excess and beats his wife as a result?"

"Then he's a wicked fool. I have drunk to excess on occasion and it has done me no good, and I try not to do so now," Felix said. Even as he said this, he had drained his first glass and knew he would have liked to indulge heavily. He felt primed to such stupidity by the wretched business of the day, and even more inclined to it by Fitznorton's sanctimonious attitude. "But it is my choice what I do," he said, and refilled his glass. "And it is the same for the drunkards."

"Society makes it too easy for them. For you, for that matter."

"You would regulate?"

"Of course. A civilised society would enact a complete ban."

"Would you ban wine from Holy Communion?" said Major Vernon.

"Good point," said Felix. "Our Lord asked us to drink wine, and I imagine he meant us to enjoy it. Take the wedding at Cana!"

"In the case of the Eucharist it would be necessary to find some acceptable substitute," Fitznorton said.

The soup arrived, and Felix knew he ought to endeavour to be less abrasive, no matter how vexing Fitznorton might be. He drank his soup and let Major Vernon make enquiries about Fitznorton's cricketing career, which made him unbend a touch. Felix, who knew little about cricket and cared less, found himself thinking of Sukey. How had she managed to marry a quack? For that was what Kennedy must be, if that pamphlet of Carrington's was anything to go by.

The soup was removed, and a dish of bream in a sauce fragrant with wine was placed in front of them. Felix was tempted to renew his arguments as he watched Fitznorton eating it without objection, but decided the food was too good to spoil with quarrelling.

He did not have long to enjoy it. The head waiter approached them, and bending over, whispered to Felix: "Mr Carswell, Madame Jacquot begs a favour. There has been an accident in the kitchen."

"Yes, of course," said Felix, getting up.

He followed the waiter out of the dining room, through a swinging door and down a narrow staircase into a large but low-ceilinged basement kitchen which was best described as an inferno. The heat punched him as he entered. The room was packed with men in white tunics, all diligently involved in some culinary process or other, all apparently under the orders of a stout gentleman in a white toque who was shouting at them in French. The waiter hurried him through these ranks into a warren of smaller rooms beyond, and finally into an office-cum-storeroom. Here he found Madame Jacquot sitting on the floor with a man writhing in her arms. He showed all the signs of having just slit his wrists.

Felix threw himself down beside them and began to give what assistance he could. Madame Jacquot had shown considerable resourcefulness and fashioned some tourniquets out of napkins, but they, and the pressure she was valiantly applying in addition, were not equal to the case. The artery on the right wrist had been severed and Felix began to doubt if the damage done could be repaired. Whatever the case, the man was at the brink of death.

"Get my medical bag and Major Vernon," he said to the waiter, and attempted to tighten the tourniquet on the right arm, but at the same time was acutely aware of the man's fading pulse as the blood continued to flow. The man gave a shudder, gasped and fell back against Madame Jacquot.

"Victor," she said. "Victor, non..." She began to mutter to him in French as if to encourage him back to consciousness, but Felix, reaching forward and feeling the vein of his neck, was forced to meet her gaze with a shake of his head.

"He's dead, madame," he said. "I'm sorry."

She continued to gaze at him, as if she could not understand him. So he repeated the words in French. His concern must now be for her, he realised, for she would be in a state of shock after such an ordeal. She was sitting with a dead man in her arms, in a pool of blood that was seeping into her petticoats. There was also blood on her broad lace collar and on her long white frilled cuffs as well as on her face and hands.

"I shall move him so you can get up," he continued in French. "If you are ready," he added, wondering who this man might be to her.

"Yes, of course," she replied. "Thank you, sir."

He gently detached her hands which were still pressed to her improvised tourniquets, and slid his hand under the man's head before taking him into his own arms. Fortunately, Major Vernon had now arrived, and was able to assist him in completing the task. They laid him flat on the tiled floor.

In the meantime, Madame Jacquot was now awakening into realisation of what had happened. She attempted to get to her feet, but was struggling. Felix went to assist her, and together they staggered from the room into the dismal passageway. The Major fetched a chair and they helped her into it. She sat and stared at her bloody hands, and then leant back, gazing up at the ceiling.

"Thank you, sir," she said.

"Would you like some cognac?"

She shook her head and got up from the chair. Felix went to offer his assistance, but she waved him away.

"I must get changed," she said in English. "Please excuse me." She moved past him and went to the door of the room they had just left, and looked down at the dead man, crossing herself as she did.

"I will be in my rooms," she said, turning back to them. "You will want to talk to me, I'm sure."

She left, and they turned their attention to the dead man.

"Suicide?" said Major Vernon, when she had gone.

"Yes," said Felix.

"He's dressed like a chef," Major Vernon said.

"She called him Victor and spoke to him in French,"

Felix said.

"This looks like the culprit," said Major Vernon, crouching down and retrieving a knife that was lying under a table. "Poor woman – what a thing to discover."

"She tried to staunch the bleeding," said Felix, pointing out the tourniquets. "Quite a feat. Though he must have been on the verge of passing out for her to attempt it. She could not have saved him, though. He did too thorough a job. Look at the depth of that cut." He exhaled, feeling suddenly exhausted. "Dear God, what a wretched end to a wretched day! I see you did not bring Fitznorton with you. That's just as well. I think he's had too much blood for one day. As have I, to be frank!"

"We will have him moved in the morning," said Major Vernon, taking a tablecloth from one of the piles of linen and covering the corpse. "Fortunately there is a good lock on this door."

~

They left Fitznorton in their rooms, scribbling away at something, and went to speak to Madame Jacquot.

"A damning report, no doubt," said Felix.

"If you will down two glasses of brandy in front of an abstainer, then..." Major Vernon said.

A maid showed them into a pretty chintz-papered sitting room where Madame Jacquot was sitting at a tea table, dressed in a spotless white wrapper. Only her red-rimmed eyes suggested that anything strange had occurred.

"I have lived in England long enough to understand the value of a good cup of tea in times of distress," she said in her charmingly accented English. "Will you join me?"

"Is that teacake you have there?" said Felix.

"You missed your dinner, of course," she said. "I can

send for something more substantial, if you like?"

"Teacake will be excellent," said Felix.

"There is new butter there, too," she said.

She made the tea and dispensed it with a calm formality that he had to admire. The ritual was extremely soothing in the circumstances, and had a better effect than the brandy.

"So, can you tell us what happened, madame?" said Major Vernon, taking out his notebook. "A brief statement of the facts is all we need at this stage."

"Yes, of course. What I cannot get over is that it was by chance I found him. I was not looking for him," she said, "although I knew he was not in the kitchen where he should have been. Monsieur Lanier had already told me so. He had given me an earful about it – is that the right word?"

"Yes," said Major Vernon.

"You see, Victor was my responsibility. I had insisted we employ him, although Monsieur Lanier was dubious. He did not like him at all. But we were short-handed, and Victor was experienced and talented. But he was also unreliable, and that is why Monsieur Lanier complained to me. He told me I must dismiss him or he would leave himself, and of course, I cannot, cannot lose him. So I said I would deal with him, when he showed himself again, and went to get a fresh tablecloth. And there was Victor, and the knife was on the floor and he was standing there and..." She stopped and looked down at her hands. "It was like a fountain. A red fountain. And then he collapsed and so I tried to help him."

"You did more than many people would have done in such circumstances. It was a heroic act," said Felix.

"But futile," she said. "Yes? Absolutely futile!" She threw up her hands, shaking her head. "If I had been there earlier, just a minute or two, I might have been able to stop him, to talk him out of it. I knew he was – how do you say – il a un humeur un peu inegale, un peu fantasque –"

"Mercurial?" suggested Felix.

"That!" she said. "And you take such people with care, of course, and you try to even them out, yes?"

"Yes, I see," said Major Vernon.

"I wish I could have spoken to him," she said. "Just for a while. I might have stopped him."

"How long had he been working for you?" asked Major Vernon.

"Just a few weeks," said Madame Jacquot. "Before he was at the Hydropathic, but he was let go."

"Do you know why?"

"Pilfering," said Madame Jacquot. "And of course you must ask why I took him on. Why I risked such a person in my well-run kitchen, and risked Monsieur Lanier being very cross and threatening to leave. Yes, it does seem stupid now, I have to say. I took pity on him – and he was very good. Exceptionnel, and now –" She frowned and looked away. "Le pauvre."

"He was definitely working at the Hydropathic Institute?" said Major Vernon.

"Yes, and Captain Carrington himself dismissed him. Victor said that he did nothing, but they didn't believe him."

"That's interesting," said Major Vernon, glancing at Felix. "Do you think he was likely to be a thief?"

"No," said Madame Jacquot. "That is one of the reasons I took the chance on him, but who can say?"

"No indeed," said Major Vernon. "Did he have any family here?"

"Not here," she said. "He is from near Dijon. I am Dijonnaise. Another reason I let my heart rule over my head. Is that right?" Felix nodded.

"Did he have a sweetheart or any particular friends?"

"Not to my knowledge. His full name is Victor Morgueillon."

~

It was a relief to find that Fitznorton had retired when they returned to their rooms. They had given him Lord Rothborough's bedroom while they had taken the other, less commanding room. But it was still nicely appointed, although they were obliged to share a bed.

Feeling a mixture of extreme fatigue and mild feverishness from the brandy, Felix went to the window and opened it. It had a pleasant outlook and the cool breeze was most welcome.

"It must cost Madame something not to let these rooms when it is so busy," said Felix. "It is just as well."

"Yes, at least we will be comfortable," said Major Vernon, getting into bed. "So what do you think about Morgueillon being involved with Carrington's death? He had a grudge and a volatile character."

"And a guilty conscience, yes," said Felix.

"We shall find out what happened tomorrow at the Institute," said the Major.

"What was Kennedy like?" Felix asked.

"Hard to say. A gentleman, certainly. Perhaps a little irritable –"

"Irritable?" said Felix, turning back to him.

"He was concerned abou: her returning late, that was all. The child was roaring. That's apt to set a father on edge."

"God forbid that he should be involved with this," said Felix, coming and sitting down on the end of the bed. "For her sake. That is what I fear."

Major Vernon nodded and said, "We cannot yet rule him out. But with luck we shall. That is all that can be said for now."

"This is all utterly preposterous, you know," Felix said, getting up again and pacing the room. "I feel I am having an insane dream and I shall wake up any moment in my own bed. Only this morning, Eleanor told me she wanted to come here to take Miss King to the dentist and the opera, and now what is to be done about that?"

"Does she need the dentist urgently?"

"Yes," said Felix. "So I had better send for them. Though of course, now Eleanor knows I'm here, she will probably arrive tomorrow anyway. Do you think Madame has any rooms to spare?"

"Fitznorton and I will look for other quarters in that case," said Major Vernon. He lay back on his pillows. "And then there is the question of Moonshine and Mercury and what should be done with them. What do you think? Should they be destroyed? There was a time, you know, not so long ago, when animals were tried for crimes. Perhaps that is what I should suggest."

"Yes, this is an absurd dream. You will be suggesting a jury of their peers next," said Felix, climbing into bed and blowing out the candle. "It is all beyond ridiculous!"

Chapter Seven

James Hamilton had set up his dentist's practice in an elegant house overlooking the extensive public parkland known as the Stray. It was a part of town that Felix was familiar with, for it was here that Major Vernon had rented a similar house two summers ago.

Hamilton could not see him at once. He had a patient in hand, and Felix was politely asked by the servant to wait with a throng in a front parlour until a smartly dressed young woman came in and addressed him.

"Mr Carswell? I saw your card – won't you come this way?" She led him from the room and into what was obviously Hamilton's private study. "I recognised your name. My brother will be pleased to see you! But I am afraid he will only be able to give you five minutes at most, this morning. It is not something urgent, is it? On Wednesday morning he always sees those with Infirmary tickets, and as you can see, there are a lot of them today."

"To tell you the truth, Miss Hamilton, I don't have much longer myself," Felix said. "I was going to write, but business called me here, so I thought I would come in person."

"Business?" she said. "Is that connected with the police? We read The Bugle sometimes, you see, Mr Carswell. Has there been a –? Oh dear. Is that what you wanted to see James about?"

At this moment James Hamilton came through the door. He was dressed in a dazzling white smock.

"I apologise for my wretched timing," said Felix, as they shook hands.

"No, don't. It's so good to see you. I've been meaning to

write," said Hamilton.

"As have I," said Felix. "But correspondence seems to be the last thing I have time left for. It must be the same with you. Your article in The Lancet – I have so many questions. You will come and dine with us? You as well, Miss Hamilton, of course – my wife will be joining me here."

"Your wife?" Hamilton said. "Congratulations. When did that happen?"

"A year ago, this past midsummer," said Felix.

"That's another thing I've had no time for," said Hamilton. "But I have the sweetest housekeeper and companion in Lucy here," he said, indicating his sister. "I'm worried she is going to beat me to the altar, and then where will I be?"

"Oh, don't be silly," said Miss Hamilton. "Now, I shall leave you to your five minutes, but no longer than that, Jamie. Mrs Hobbes' boy is sitting there in agony." She left them.

"Then perhaps I should go?" Felix said.

"You might want to stay and observe it," said Hamilton. "It's an interesting case. I shall etherise him."

"Do you do that very often?"

"More and more," said Hamilton. "I'm attempting to build up a body of cases."

"It's remarkable," said Felix. "I should love to see it. But I cannot this morning, unfortunately. And I must tell you why I came – I wonder if you would see a friend of my wife's? She has an inflamed bicuspid, back right, and as far as I can ascertain, it is almost hollowed out. I have suggested she see our local man in Northminster, but my wife will not have it. She maintains he is a brute, which is perhaps true, but an efficient brute."

"That would be Mr Morris?" said Hamilton.

"Yes. And Miss King – that is the lady – is now mortally afraid, so Eleanor thought that you might look at her. Which is a good notion."

"I will certainly do what I can. How old is she?"

"She is almost thirty and in good health," Felix said. "She has been living with us since February and this is the first time she has been indisposed."

"When did you say your wife was arriving?"

"They will be here tomorrow, certainly, perhaps this afternoon. We will be at The White Hart."

"I could see her tomorrow morning," said Hamilton, consulting his diary. "At nine?"

"Thank you. I'm glad to see you have so much work in hand," said Felix.

"It was a good idea to come here, yes," said Hamilton. "And this season has been better than the last. Thanks to the puffer Carrington, that is."

"The puffer Carrington?" said Felix.

"That is what Lucy and I call him," said Hamilton. "We ought to be more respectful, I suppose, given what he is doing for the place, but there is something ridiculous about him. The Roman bath house – have you seen that yet?"

"No. I have read his pamphlet, though. Puffer is about right." Felix noticed a plaster cast of a set of teeth lying on Hamilton's desk and thought of Carrington's well preserved teeth. He picked it up and examined it.

"Was that taken post-mortem?" he asked.

"No. That's a new fad of mine. I have the patient bite into a softened block of beeswax, and then Lucy, who is clever with her hands, makes a cast of it. It is most convenient when one is attempting to make repairs and construct prosthetics and so forth."

"And you have a few sets of these?"

"Oh yes."

"And all unique to the patient?"

"Yes, of course."

"Do you think this will catch on?"

"I hope so!" said Hamilton. "Why do you ask?"

"It strikes me that it would be useful in my line of work if it were more universally adopted. Sometimes it's a struggle to put a name to a victim. If a man had a sensible dentist, with a cast of his teeth, we could identify him more easily."

"You're here on a murder case, I take it?" said Hamilton. Felix nodded. "And you don't know who he is?"

"No, no, we know exactly who he is," Felix said, putting down the plaster cast. "I'm only speculating. No, it is the puffer Carrington, as you so elegantly put it."

"You're not in earnest?" said Hamilton. "He's been murdered?"

"Yes."

"How astonishing," said Hamilton.

The door opened and Lucy Hamilton came in. "Jamie, you have to come now. That boy is on the verge of running away. I cannot say anything to calm him!"

Felix made his farewells and left them to their crisis, which was soon resolved with a few well-chosen words from Hamilton. He displayed the same mesmeric authority over patients that Felix had often observed in Mr Harper. It was perhaps the defining quality of a truly great medical man, and he wondered how he might cultivate it better.

He wondered whether it was that same authority that the quacks used, as he made his way to the coroner's office where he had arranged to meet Major Vernon. He was already there, along with the inevitable Fitznorton.

"My duties are usually so light as to be imperceptible," Boothroyd said, when Felix joined them. "And yet we must meet again so soon, gentlemen. It will disturb the business elements of Stanegate when the news of both these unhappy deaths gets about. Captain Carrington –"

"Ah, yes, I must anticipate you there, Mr Boothroyd," Major Vernon said. "We have now identified the body at the menagerie. It is the Captain himself."

"Heavens," said Boothroyd. "That is distressing."

"You knew him, I take it, sir?" said Major Vernon.

"Yes, I did some business for him last year, but he was not the easiest client. I was glad when he took his custom elsewhere, although it would have been lucrative. Now, I must say I am very glad!"

"What kind of business was it?"

"Leases, in relation to the houses up on Carr's Crag, the Rustic Cottages as they are known. He wanted some short pro forma leases drawn up for seasonal visitors. He drove a hard bargain on the price for the work, and the terms he put in – although understandable – struck me as rapacious. Of course, one does not get successful by being sentimental, but I was glad to see him go. And also" – he leant across his desk to a basket of correspondence – "there is this. The Italian Marble and Stone Company Limited of Hull wishes me to pursue Captain Carrington for various unpaid accounts." He offered the letter to Major Vernon. "His solicitor, Mr Webb in Northminster, says that the contractors Messrs Breckonbridge and Sons are responsible for it. I'm not so sure. I spoke to Joe Breckonbridge myself about it, and he maintains that the customer – that is, the Captain – was to supply the stone and marble. According to Joe, the Captain boasted about getting a better price for it than Joe ever could, which put old Joe out, and he's not the sort of man you want to put out. Not that he would murder anyone, Major Vernon," Boothroyd said with a nervous laugh. "I did not mean it like that. Joe would not hurt a fly. It's simply that Carrington's way of going about business was frankly abrasive. Joe will back me up on that, I'm sure. He will have some tales for you."

"May I keep this?" said Major Vernon.

"Yes, of course. You may have all the correspondence. It will now be evidence, after all. Now, turning to this man at The White Hart, Morgueillon – do I have it correctly?"

"Yes – it is bit of a mouthful," said Felix.

"Will a post-mortem be necessary?"

"I should prefer it to be done," said Felix, "if only to establish he was acting of his own free will. There have been cases when suicide has been induced by ingestion of toxic substances."

"As you like," said Boothroyd, scribbling out the authority. "I wish you good luck and a speedy result, gentlemen! I have to say, I am pleased to see you here, Mr Fitznorton, for purely selfish reasons. We have a modest cricket club here, formed mostly of Oxbridge men, of which I have the honour of being the secretary. We play each Saturday at the east end of the Stray. We have a match against the Amberleigh men this Saturday and would be honoured if you came and joined us. We are short of men and they are a formidable crew, I regret to tell you. But you might enjoy that! Major Vernon and Mr Carswell, you are also most welcome, of course, though I am afraid I'm entirely ignorant as to your sporting predilections. Mr Fitznorton's reputation, of course, precedes him in this area."

"We will spare you our dubious assistance, shall we, Mr Carswell?"

"Yes, certainly," said Felix. "I don't even understand the rules. Edinburgh men do not generally play cricket."

~

"So, to review," said Major Vernon, as they walked away from Boothroyd's office. "We have an employee with a grudge against a former employer and a marble supplier suing for settlement of an account, which our dead man claimed was the responsibility of the builder."

"Is an unpaid account sufficient cause for murder?" Felix said. "That seems too commonplace."

"No, not of itself, but it may hint at other wrangles."

"It was an extremely large amount," said Fitznorton. "Where was the marble from? If we are talking about the southern part of Italy, then business can be conducted in a lawless manner."

"That is an interesting thought," said Major Vernon. "I have read about these secret Italian brotherhoods. Connected with the lemon trade, yes?"

"I was in Sicily last winter," said Fitznorton, "and heard some accounts of it for myself from the British consul. It is ruthless and organised, and unfortunately seems to be flourishing wherever there is a high profit to be made. It strikes me that the import of marbles and so forth might be an area of interest to them."

"Then perhaps you would work on that line of enquiry, Mr Fitznorton, and see if there is anything in it?" said Major Vernon, taking the letter from his pocket and giving it to him. "They are based in Hull."

At this point their ways parted. Felix had to go to the Incurables Hospital where he had arranged for the Frenchman's body to be delivered, while the Major and Fitznorton continued to the Hydropathic. He was relieved that his duties called him away, grateful to have been spared a chance encounter with Sukey or her husband.

Sergeant Gale and his cortège had not yet arrived, so Felix went first to find Dr Greville and ask his permission to receive another cadaver, which he granted readily enough, though with some distress and surprise. Felix was then left alone to his work.

~

Inspector Harris was waiting for them at the Hydropathic, and they went to Carrington's rooms. These were not at all impressive for the proprietor of such an establishment, being on the ground floor, with an outlook onto an internal court. He shared his austere bedroom with a wall safe.

"Do we know who had access to that?" Giles said to Harris.

"I'll go and find out. He has a servant too. I'll find him as well."

"This feels like a butler's parlour," said Giles, glancing into the adjoining sitting room, "only less comfortable. How strange he should choose to live like this. Perhaps he didn't spend a great deal of time here." He opened the wardrobe and saw a row of boots. He took one out and examined it. "Same maker. Mr Fitznorton, if you will start on his desk?"

"What am I looking for?"

"Diary, letters, account books. We shall have to go through it all. I want to know who his family is, who are his friends? Who does he do business with? Does he have a mistress? A wife and children?" He looked about him again. "These rooms are so impersonal. I wonder when he last slept here."

"The drawers are all empty, Major Vernon," said Fitznorton from the other room. Giles had found nothing but clean clothes in the drawers in the bedroom. He examined the fastening of the safe and decided it was far beyond his lock-picking capabilities.

Harris came in.

"I have Captain Carrington's servant waiting, sir," he said. "A Mr Pember. But no one seems to have the key to that safe."

"Thank you, Harris. I will be with you in a moment."

"There are some books in here," said Fitznorton, who was investigating a satinwood chiffonier.

"What have we got?" said Giles, joining him to examine the titles. "Volume Two of Mrs Bramhall's 'Devotion' and it's a library copy. From the establishment we visited yesterday –

that might be worth pursuing. 'Waverley', the Bible, Loundon's 'Cottage and Villa Architecture'." This volume was bristling with bookmarks. He opened it at one and saw an engraving of a rose-embowered house entitled, 'Cottage Orné in the Ancient English Style'. "I wonder if this inspired the Rustic Cottages that everyone was complaining about," he said. "And what is that?"

"It's a box, pretending to be a book," said Fitznorton. "Curious."

"Ah, I have seen one of these before! Yes, they are ingenious," said Giles, reaching into his pocket for his lock-picking tools. He carried it over to the window to get what light he could, and set to work on the well-concealed lock. The lid sprang open to reveal a cloth bag.

He spread the contents out on the table: there was a bunch of keys and a bundle of documents.

"Have a look through those for me, would you, Mr Fitznorton?" said Giles. "I need to go and speak to Mr Pember."

He left Fitznorton settling himself at Carrington's desk and went to speak to Carrington's manservant.

"When did you last see Captain Carrington, Mr Pember?"

"It was on Friday morning," said Pember. "Just before he went away."

"And did he tell you where he was going?"

"London, sir, but I don't believe that was where he was going."

"Why?"

"It's just that what the Captain said and what he did – it was hard to tally up sometimes."

"That's interesting. You mean he was not straight with you?"

"No, sir. I suppose he'd no reason to be straight since I'm just here to do his boots and keep his coats brushed, but other masters, they let you know their comings and goings pretty much."

"And you would run errands for them, and so forth?"

"Yes, sir. I always did in my last place, that was true enough. But Mr Wilson was a married man with a family, and it was different. The Captain, well –" Mr Pember hesitated. "I don't like to speak ill of the dead, but when he said he was going away, there was a woman in the picture."

"And what makes you think this?"

"His linen, sir," said Mr Pember. "He'd come back with handkerchiefs and so forth, with embroidery on them that he didn't have before. And his shirts nicely mended. Not what you'd think if he'd been going to London and a hotel there. Mr Fisher, the manager here, he thinks the same as I do."

"Do you and Mr Fisher have any idea who this woman might be?"

"No, sir. He wasn't one for talking to the likes of me."

"You never saw him arguing with anyone?"

Pember hesitated.

"He could have a temper on him. Some of the kitchen staff will tell you that."

"Do you know Victor Morgueillon?"

"Yes – he was a troublemaker. The Captain was not happy with him. He was dismissed a couple of weeks ago. Do you think he has something to do with the Captain's death?"

"Why do you ask?"

"Because it wouldn't surprise me. He was always causing trouble. Called himself a syndicalist or something, and was always talking about revolution and all that nonsense."

"Would you say he was prone to violence?" Giles asked.

"I think he likes a fight. Some of the younger lads will tell you about it, I dare say. Talk to them."

Giles went with Harris to the kitchens, which replicated on a larger scale the same regimented frenzy he had observed the night before at The White Hart. Here, though, the chef was an elderly Italian called Luchetti and his English was not good. Fortunately, his son was on hand to interpret. He spoke English with the local accent and had an air of authority about him. As they spoke, he was deftly trussing and then stuffing some small game birds that Giles thought were partridges.

"Are you in charge here, Mr Luchetti?" Giles said.

"My father is happy to let me run things now. He gets tired," said Luchetti. "So what is this about?"

"Victor Morgueillon."

"What about him?"

"He committed suicide last night," Giles said.

"And that's a police matter? A lunatic like that?"

"You would say he was predisposed to it?"

"Aye, and I'm surprised it didn't happen earlier. He was always strange in the head. A good saucier though, but he had to go."

"I heard that there was some accusation of pilfering," said Giles. "That was why the Captain dismissed him?"

"That would be right," said Luchetti. "But the main reason was that he was insubordinate. Politics, always politics! Typical bloody Frenchman. A kitchen only works if everyone keeps to their place. But talking to the kitchen maids and the porters about bettering their lot by forming a union – no, sir, we can't be having that."

"I see."

"And of course those daft girls will listen to a handsome foreigner. I didn't want women in my kitchen at all, to tell you it plain, sir, but the Captain said we had to make do. It's a business getting staff in this town at the moment, and of course the girls come cheaper, so that suited the Captain, as does the fact that most of them are as pretty as they are daft." At this point they were interrupted by a young man with a sauce for the chef to taste. He did so and then considered briefly. "More thyme."

"Aye, chef," the young man said and went away again.

"For these," said Luchetti, indicating the birds he was

working on. "Are you staying for lunch, sir? You should. These partridges are at their best just now."

"Perhaps," said Giles. "Do you mean that Captain Carrington likes young women?"

"Young woman, old women, anything in a skirt. I try to keep an eye on those girls, sir, but he is the boss, and he will do what he will, and I'm not able to do much about it. I was speaking to Mrs Kennedy about it – she's a sensible lady, and she suggested we find a sitting room for them, and an older woman to look out for them properly. She's been bothered about the chambermaids as well. A very good lady, Mrs Kennedy. She said she'd talk to Dr Kennedy about it."

"So the Captain has been preying on the female staff?" said Giles.

"Not if I can help it, sir. But some of them won't be told, will they?"

"Do you know if he has any more permanent arrangements with women? A mistress, perhaps?"

Luchetti eyed him warily.

"What is all this about, sir?" he said. "These questions? What has the Captain to do with Morgueillon killing himself?"

"Captain Carrington has been murdered," said Giles.

Luchetti stared at him and mouthed an obscenity. "He never has," he said, laying down his knife. "But what will happen with this place now?"

"That I can't say," said Giles, glancing in the direction of the sculleries and the young women hard at work on endless piles of pots.

Chapter Eight

Giles returned to Fitznorton, who was diligently making a list of the contents of the bag.

"So, what have you found?"

"A marriage certificate: George Edwin Carrington to Birgitta Halverson. A Swede, judging by the names, and the marriage taking place in the Swedish Church in Wapping."

"What's the date?"

"July, 1819."

"I wonder where she is. Has she gone back to Sweden?" said Giles, taking the document from him. "Or is she dead?" He laid it down on the table. "What else have you found?"

"I scarcely know how to categorize them: letters of various sorts. These three in the same hand, a woman's hand. I cannot make out the signature but the contents suggest a woman. Unfortunately," he added, and pushed the letters across the table to Giles.

"Why unfortunately?"

"They are... indecent."

"Ah, I see," said Giles, trying hard not be amused by Fitznorton's discomfiture. He took up one of the three letters: it was two pages and cross-written, in a tiny hand. The paper was of good quality but there was no embossed heading. "*My only darling* – I wonder who she is addressing. Not helpful of you, ma'am, not to give us your lover's name." He frowned. "And your handwriting could be better."

"I could make a transcription," Fitznorton said. "Omitting the objectionable parts."

"That would be pointless," Giles said. "The objectionable parts are the important parts."

"Surely it is enough to say that they express warm feelings of this unknown person to another?"

"No, Mr Fitznorton, that is not enough, I'm afraid."

"This person must surely be a gentlewoman," Fitznorton said, "by birth, if perhaps not in behaviour. Is it appropriate for us to read her personal correspondence? What if your wife were to write such a letter and it were to be read by strangers, Major Vernon?" Then he began to redden. "Forgive me, I did not mean to imply that your wife would ever write such a letter."

"Of course," he said. "I appreciate your delicacy on the point, but it is the nature of this business to deal with the less fragrant aspects of human behaviour, I'm afraid. These letters may explain why Carrington ended up in that leopard cage. We cannot omit the details because they offend our ideas of how women ought to be. I know it is not gallant, but there it is. What does she say?" he said, handing the letter back to Fitznorton.

He began to read.

> My only darling, I have thought of nothing but you since we last met. Do you realise that as I write this it has been two days and five hours and twelve minutes? The old clock on the mantel, such an old friend in former times, I now hate to distraction, for every tick-tock reminds me of how long I must wait until I am again in your loving arms. Know now, my dearest, dearest love, I shall never forget a minute of that sweet afternoon, and how I constantly remember each and every detail. When I was putting my stockings on this morning and fixing my garters, I remembered your sweet fingers struggling with the clasp and then how you slid them down my legs with a hundred gentle kisses –

Giles realised that this was a worse torture for him than looking at Carrington's ravaged remains, and put up his hand to stop him.

"Very well, a transcription will suffice, but with nothing

omitted."

"As you wish, Major Vernon."

"There was no envelope with them?"

"No, sir, not that I found."

"And no indication of the recipient in the contents? A nickname, anything?"

"She does call him 'my lord', but that may just be rhetorical."

"Interesting. So we have several possibilities: one is that they were addressed to Carrington and he has kept them as keepsakes."

"Keepsakes?"

"To get a woman to write a letter like this to you is a triumph, and if you are that kind of man, which perhaps Carrington was, then it would be worth keeping. Of course, there may have been genuine feelings involved here. We cannot know, and just because he has a reputation for goosing kitchen maids, does not mean he was never in love. Maybe this poor lady is dead. Might she be the Swedish wife? What is the signature?"

"Only her initials. She had some idea of discretion there, at least," said Fitznorton. "They are formed into a monogram. I think there is an 'A' and an 'S'. This one is slightly clearer," he said, showing Giles another letter. "And the contents are even more unconstrained."

"Any mention of husbands?"

"There is talk of another man. She compares his actions to those of the lover. Intimate actions, that is."

"And I don't suppose the comparison is favourable?" said Giles.

"No," said Fitznorton.

"Of course, the other reason for Carrington having such compromising letters is that he has acquired them for the purposes of blackmail," said Giles. "This makes me wonder what may be in the safe. Did you try the key?"

Fitznorton shook his head and Giles wondered at his lack of curiosity. He went into the bedroom and tried it in the lock of the wall safe. It turned, and revealed a stack of ledgers and paperwork.

"This looks promising," said Giles. There was a knock at the door. "Answer that, would you, Mr Fitznorton?" Hearing himself asked for, he went to the doorway.

"Major Vernon?" the waiter said. "Chef says your partridge is ready, with his compliments."

"I hope you are hungry, Mr Fitznorton," Giles said, locking the safe and handing the key to him. "You can have a look through those this afternoon, if you don't mind."

The waiter showed them to a private dining room, where they were served an excellent meal, if rich for that time of day. As if to offset any pleasure in it, Mr Fitznorton took to asking him some searching questions about prison management, which Giles was not able to answer satisfactorily. His earnestness was, in truth, tiring – it was born of being in a strange situation, Giles supposed, but at the same time he wished for a more congenial companion. It was a relief when the younger chef Luchetti came in to ask how they had enjoyed their lunch.

"It was excellent," said Giles. "I shall need to go for a brisk walk now, or perhaps to the baths to sweat it off. That's the usual regime here, I understand?"

"Yes, and a good one," said Mr Luchetti. "That was a great innovation of the Captain's, and it's brought us a lot of trade here. We were at The Queen's Hotel before, but perhaps you know that, sir?" Giles nodded. "My father came here in '23 and built the kitchens up from nothing. People came here for the food and they still do. And the baths are a nice addition for them. But of course, Dr Kennedy keeps telling everyone that they should be eating nothing but gruel and boiled vegetables, and they will listen to him, so it's nice to serve a couple of appreciative gentlemen. Now, will you take anything else? A cup of coffee?"

Fitznorton declined and excused himself shortly afterwards. Feeling in need of artificial stimulation, Giles asked for coffee and was rewarded by a surprisingly intense and envigorating brew. On asking the waiter about it, he was told it was made by Mr Luchetti himself with his new contraption.

"A steam fountain, it's called, sir," said the waiter. "Chef himself drinks a dozen cups a day of the stuff. I stick to tea and beer myself, sir."

"What's your name?" Giles asked, reaching for a coin to tip him.

"Jackson, sir," said the waiter.

"I suppose you know why I am here? You've heard about what happened to Captain Carrington?" Jackson nodded. "What did you make of him as an employer?"

"I never spoke to him more than once," said Jackson.

"But he was generally liked?"

"Not really, sir. He was always rushing about, here and there, changing things, telling us everything had to be done in such and such a way, and if not, then he'd turn folk out without warning. Mr Luchetti had a few run-ins with him."

"As did Victor Morgueillon, I understand?"

"God rest him, yes," said Jackson. "Is it true, what I heard, sir, that he killed himself?"

"Yes."

"Wild as they come," said Jackson. "He had lots of bad habits. He liked to gamble. You know the sort, sir, I dare say, that will bet on raindrops running down a window pane."

Giles let him go back to his work, and gathered his thoughts before leaving the room. It was as well he did, for in the passageway he encountered Dr Kennedy.

"Do you have a moment, sir?" Giles asked.

"I'm afraid I don't, Major Vernon. I have patients to see."

"Perhaps you might tell me when we might talk?"

"About what?"

"When a man dies in troubling circumstances, as Captain Carrington has done, it's useful to form a picture of his habits and so forth."

"I'm not sure how I can help you," said Dr Kennedy. "Given you seem to have spoken to everyone else here, what can I add?"

"A great deal. As his business partner –"

"I really don't know what information you are hoping I will supply you with, Major Vernon, but I assure you I don't know anything that could assist with this."

"You've heard about Victor Morgueillon's suicide?"

"No," said Kennedy. "Should I? Who is that?"

"One of the chefs. He worked here until recently. The Captain dismissed him."

"I don't much concern myself with domestic matters here. If you will excuse me, sir, I must get on."

"Yes, of course. Perhaps Mrs Kennedy might help me, then?"

"In what way? I would say she has done enough for you already."

"That was regrettable, yes, but it has moved things forward. I don't think she would object to helping further – with your permission, Dr Kennedy, of course. I know she has concerned herself with domestic affairs here, in respect of the women staff, some of whom Carrington seems to have been preyed upon. I dare say you discussed it?" The moment he said this, he could tell from Kennedy's expression that it had not been discussed. He went on: "That he had such unpleasant habits is relevant to our enquiry. Did you know he was a libertine?"

"As I said, I don't much concern myself with domestic matters. I'm not aware there has been a difficulty. I didn't see anything in Captain Carrington's conduct that would give rise to such an allegation. I suspect my wife has been misled by her natural sympathy for her sex. Some girl or other has gone complaining to her for some perceived slight and she has taken up their cause. But as to the truth of such cases –"

"You know as well as I that they are common enough," Giles said. "And Mr Luchetti is also concerned about it. He told me he discussed it with Mrs Kennedy. Are you sure you can't tell me anything useful about the Captain's habits? His valet implied there was a mistress or two. You can't work with a man and not notice such things."

"No. I'm sorry, Major Vernon, I have nothing defamatory for you. You will excuse me now, I have a great many things to do." He went on his way a few paces and then stopped and turned. "And I would prefer that you did not speak to my wife. She does not like to be reminded of that period in her life."

Giles went back to Fitznorton, disturbed by Kennedy's manner. His protestations of ignorance were far too convenient, and Giles did not at all like his way of speaking of Sukey.

Fitznorton had been joined by Inspector Harris, and the table in the centre of the room now bore an impressive number of documents, all lined up as if for a game of patience.

"Just logging the evidence, sir," said Inspector Harris. "Mr Fitznorton has a nifty system, I must say."

"That is all of interest, then?" said Giles.

"Blackmail, sir," said Harris, "is looking likely, as you suggested to Mr Fitznorton. But there is a lot to get through."

"I thought it best to secure it and remove it before we examined it further," said Fitznorton.

"Excellent," said Giles. "I shall meet you back at the station house at about five. We should have a report from Mr Carswell by then. But before that, I have to take back a library book," he added, taking up the second volume of Mrs Bramhall's 'Devotion'.

~

"Would you like Volume Three? We have a copy to hand, although that's a popular title at the moment," said the clerk at the circulating library. "Do you have your ticket?"

"No, I'm not a subscriber," said Giles. "I found this book and I wondered if you could give me the name of the lady who borrowed it."

"I'm not sure I should, sir," said the clerk. "That's confidential information."

"Usually I would agree with you," said Giles, taking his badge from his pocket. "But in this case, it is a police matter."

"Is this to do with Captain Carrington?" said the clerk.

"Why do you say that?" said Giles.

"Everyone's saying he's been murdered and the leopards ate him," he said. "Someone shoved him in the cage and they ate him."

"I wouldn't listen to the rumours, if I were you," said Giles.

"But he is dead, sir?"

"He is. Now, if you want to help, can you give me this subscriber's name and address?"

"Oh, certainly, sir." He returned with a card. "Mrs Thorne. Laburnum Cottage."

"Where is that?" Giles said.

"That's one of those new houses up on Carr's Crag. The Rustic Cottages, they are called. We have a few subscribers there. This lady, Mrs Thorne, also subscribes to our delivery service. That book should just have been sent back with the others. I suppose she lent it to someone. As I say, it's a popular title just now. Mrs Bramhall seems to know exactly what the ladies want in a novel."

Giles retraced his steps to the menagerie, and took the lane which ran alongside its boundary wall. It was a warm afternoon and the smell of the animals caught the breeze, but the wall itself was high and gave no glimpses of what lay on the other side. It was also hard to imagine anyone climbing over it, especially with a body. Further on, the lane diverged from the boundary and became steep, with large gorse bushes growing over the side. Only when he reached the summit and what appeared to be the rear garden wall of one of the Rustic Cottages, was he able to get a glimpse of the menagerie itself. He realised to his annoyance that he had an imperfect knowledge of the orientation of the menagerie, and resolved he would go back and rectify this after he had seen Mrs Thorne. He also wanted to determine if there was any truth in Dr Kennedy's allegation that Askham had sent Carrington threatening letters.

He continued up the hill, noting how there were three properties backing onto the rocky terraced hinterland that was terminated by the walls of the menagerie, and how the wall itself at this point turned from a brick affair into the more traditional dry stone style common to the area. It was also lower and perhaps more accessible, although it would still be no easy procedure to haul a body over it. He wondered why he was hypothesising that Carrington may have been murdered outside the walls of the menagerie. It was surely more likely that he was killed within the walls and then thrown into the leopard cage.

Ruminating on this, he set out to find Laburnum Cottage. The Rustic Cottages were laid out in a circle, some seven of them, with a curious rock formation in the centre, presumably an immovable geological object that had been turned into a picturesque rockery and planted with ferns. Perhaps the spot had lost its raw grandeur – Giles felt sure Mrs Felix Carswell would protest at such a violation – but there was no doubting the attractive seclusion of the cottages themselves, all set in generous gardens and decidedly private.

Laburnum Cottage was at the far edge of the circle, in the

most secluded setting of all. There was a picturesque, almost artificial air about the place. The roof edge was trimmed with fancy patterned barge-boards, and the windows were glazed with diamond lattices. It was a fine stage set for a mistress, and Giles could not helping wondering at the irony of Carrington's apparent indiscretion in this regard. A blackmailer ought not to lay himself so open to the very thing he inflicted on others. It was a sign of the confidence of the man, though, which was interesting in itself. This was Captain "Puffer" Carrington, after all, as Mr Carswell's friend had called him.

A pretty, elegantly dressed maid showed him into an attractive though cluttered sitting room. Here, Mrs Thorne was doing some fancy beadwork, with many small dishes of different colours laid out in front of her. She was deftly picking up the tiny beads on a needle, and looked up in enquiry as he came in.

"Major Vernon, ma'am," said the maid.

She looked puzzled and laid down her needle. Seeing her, in her frills and lace and ribbons, he sensed her vulnerability. She was a delicate-looking creature, with a roses and cream complexion. He was about to tell her some wretched news, after all.

"I'm sorry, sir, do I know you?" she said.

"No, you don't, ma'am. I have some bad news for you. May I sit down?"

"Yes, of course."

"I'll get some tea, ma'am," said the maid, and hurried out of the room.

"Am I right that you are a friend of Captain Carrington?" he asked.

She nodded and burst out, "What has happened to him? Is he all right?"

"I'm afraid not, ma'am. I regret to have to tell you that he's dead."

"Oh," she said, and looked away. "Oh, that is very –" She

broke down in tears, as the maid returned and laid down her tray. "The Captain's dead, Mary."

"Oh, dear Lord, ma'am," said the maid and sat down beside her, taking her into her arms. "What happened, sir? Was he sick with something? He's been away from here so long, we've been wondering, and not hearing anything from him..."

"When did you last see him?" Giles asked.

"At least a fortnight ago," said Mary. "That's right, isn't it, ma'am?"

"Fifteen days," said Mrs Thorne, "and not a word. I would have gone to him. I would have nursed him. Why did you not send for me?"

"I'm afraid it isn't a case of that, ma'am," said Giles. "Captain Carrington did not die from illness. He was murdered. About three days ago, we think. His body was only discovered yesterday."

"Murdered?" said Mrs Thorne, staring at him. Her maid, however, wore an expression that suggested that she was less than surprised that he should meet with such a fate. "But who would want to do that to him?"

"I was hoping you might help me with that, Mrs Thorne," said Giles.

"Who are you, sir?" said Mary.

"I'm from the County Constabulary. I've been charged to investigate Captain Carrington's death." At this, Mrs Thorne collapsed into sobs again and clung to Mary.

"Let me get you some tea, ma'am," said Mary, detaching herself. She went and poured tea, putting plenty of sugar in it. When Mrs Thorne was calmer, she said, "Perhaps I should talk to the gent, first, ma'am? Let you get yourself more composed?"

"A good idea," said Giles, getting up. Mrs Thorne was unwilling to be left at once as Mary moved towards the door. "I will not keep her long, ma'am."

"It will be best to let her cry it all out on her own," said

Mary, closing the sitting room door behind her. "It's a shock for her."

"You don't seem similarly astonished, if I may say so, Miss –?"

"Carter," she said. "I always thought he was a fast one, and they are the sort that come to sorry ends."

"You didn't care for him?"

"No," she said.

"He didn't expect you to act as his mistress as well?" Giles said. She was a handsome woman, after all.

"You're sharp, sir," she said. "Yes, he would have liked that, but I didn't let him. I don't let my heart rule my head," she added, gesturing towards the sitting room, "unlike some. She is going to be..." She shook her head. "Lucky I have put some of the money by. I made sure of that. It only seemed like good sense."

"Speaking of money," said Giles. "Are you aware of where the Captain got his money?"

"I have some ideas," she said. "He was a fast one, as I said, and I don't imagine any of the ways he got it were straight."

"What makes you say that?"

"Come and see for yourself," she said, and took him into the dining room. She opened the sideboard and revealed shelves stuffed, not with china and linen, but documents. "He was forever cramming stuff in there, and he didn't like it when I saw him do it. He told me not to meddle with them."

"So you did?" Giles said.

"I've had a bit of a look, yes, sir. Perhaps I shouldn't have, but I have to think of her – she's a helpless soul and that's the truth. I don't know what it all means, but there was just something about the way he was shoving it away in there, I didn't like. I mean, if it was just his business papers, why would he keep them here? He didn't come here to do business. I think he put them there so that no one should find them, sir."

"You may be right," said Giles, liking her acuteness. "Thank you, Miss Carter. I shall send someone up to collect them."

"What will happen about him being buried?" she asked. "She will want to know. She will be putting on widow's weeds, I dare say," she added with sigh.

"That's a good question. I can't say just yet, but I will let you know. Do you know if he had any relatives? Was he married?"

"He was," she said, "although he never said so. I saw him once, when I went down into the town, with a woman about his age. A great tall woman she was, with blond hair. I've never seen such fair hair, great big ringlets of it coming out of her bonnet." She gestured to indicate the style and size of them. "They were up a side lane – it was off the Parade; there is a lane that goes up to the Church, and I looked up it and saw them. I stopped because they were having words – that was clear enough – and then he stomped off one way and she another."

"When was this?"

"About three weeks ago."

"Why did you think she might be his wife?"

"I can't say. It just had that look about it. Oh, and she walked right past me, and into the Parade. Her expression was something to see. She had the most beautiful printed muslin dress on as well. That's what made me remember it, because Mrs Thorne had been eyeing up one just like it for herself and was going to ask the Captain for it."

Having exchanged a few more words with Mrs Thorne, who was still not in a state to talk about anything, Giles set off down the hill again, and this time abandoned the path to follow the dry stone wall. The terrain was as inhospitable as he had suspected, better suited for sheep than men. Parts were so rocky and steep that they were better described as scree. He was about to abandon his efforts when he noticed that there was a stile of sorts, apparently leading into the menagerie. He climbed over it, but with some difficulty for it was in a wretched condition with many fallen stones. He stumbled, and then descended what remained of the path at some speed before emerging into a clearing, at the centre of which was a large aviary. He turned and looked back up the path, wondering again if it made any sense for anyone to bring a body down it. In that moment, as the parakeets squawked at him, it seemed absurd.

He walked from the aviary to the picket-fenced enclosure which was the residence of the camels. This was a sorry sight, and extremely unpleasant to smell. The beasts themselves had a truculent look about them – they resented being there as much as the locals resented them, and one of them bellowed at him as he passed.

Ahead of him lay the crimson and gold van containing the leopards, and as he approached, their keeper Bobby Farr came running up to speak to him. He was clearly agitated.

"You ain't going to kill my beasts, sir!" he said. "You'll have to kill me first!"

"Has someone told you they are to be destroyed, Mr Farr?" said Giles.

"That sergeant fellow said it was being talked of."

"Nothing has been decided, yet," said Giles.

"Then I beg you to spare them, sir, if you can," said Farr. "It's only Christian. They did nothing wrong."

"True enough," said Giles, gazing into the depths of their wagon. It was a wretched space for two such creatures. The male cat, Mercury, was pacing, evidently both frustrated and miserable. The other, Moonshine, lay on the ground apparently asleep, but the petulant drumming of her tail indicated otherwise. "They are beautiful creatures."

"I'm glad to hear you say that, sir," said Farr.

Mercury now stopped a moment to regard Giles, with a

disconcertingly frank gaze. He knew a great deal about what had happened that night, Giles reflected. How vexing it was that animals could not speak when he had so many excellent witnesses to hand.

Chapter Nine

By four o'clock, Felix had done as much on Carrington's remains as he could, and was at that moment unwilling to begin on the late Morgueillon. That, he decided, could wait until the following morning. He finished his notes, or rather the inelegant, pencilled aide-mémoire that formed the basis of his proper notes, and then stripped off his shirt and took full benefit of the warm spring and the basin. Mrs Greville had kindly sent in some rough towels, and feeling sufficiently refreshed and stimulated, he put his shirt back on and wandered out into the court to get some sunshine. He sat down on a bench and lit a cheroot; trying to empty his mind of his work, he closed his eyes and turned his face up to the sun.

"Excuse me, is it Mr Carswell?" Felix started at the sound of a woman's voice. "Oh, excuse me, sir!"

"No, that's all right," said Felix, staggering to his feet and throwing down his cheroot. "Ma'am?"

He took stock of her: a young woman, beautiful and elegant in manner. She was wearing a plain apron over a fancy muslin dress.

"I'm sorry to disturb you," she said. "There's an old woman who needs a doctor. Would you come and look at her?"

"Of course, ma'am."

"My name is Mrs Stuart," she said. "I have been helping Mrs Greville with her work here."

This explained a great deal.

"Forgive my appearance," he said, suddenly conscious of his shirtsleeves.

She made a dismissive gesture and indicated the door

through which she had come.

"She is wheezing most horribly," she said. "I'm really afraid for her."

Felix followed her.

The old woman was sitting hunched in her bed in a pleasant ground floor room, with the windows thrown open onto the court. She was in the midst of a most uncomfortable coughing spasm.

"I have a found a doctor for you, Mrs Watts," Mrs Stuart said.

Felix did what he could for her, and then as the spasm subsided, helped her to rest back on her pillows. He returned to the dispensary and fetched his bag so he could examine her, leaving Mrs Stuart sitting beside her, holding her hands and speaking in soothing tones.

"You have done more than I could have," he said, on seeing this. She yielded her place to him with a graceful smile. "You are lucky in your nurse, Mrs Watts."

Mrs Watts nodded and smiled at that, and he proceeded to examine her, sounding her chest with particular care.

"I do not think it is anything serious," he said. "I suggest a syrup of rosehip diluted with boiling water, and a little laudanum at bedtime to help you sleep. I will come and see you tomorrow morning, if I may?"

"So long as you don't charge me!" Mrs Watts managed to say. "Although I shall be a rich woman soon enough, shan't I, ma'am?" she said, with a glance at Mrs Stuart. "Then you may charge me as much as you like, sir!" The thought of this amused her and she started to laugh.

"Hush now, Mrs Watts," said Mrs Stuart. "You should not talk, let alone laugh. You really should rest."

Mrs Watts checked herself before any damage was done and they left her to rest.

"Is she coming into money?" Felix said as they walked into the garden.

"I don't imagine so," said Mrs Stuart. "She likes to imagine it may happen. It is a pleasant fancy for her to think that one day she will drive away from here in a horse and carriage, when the truth is she will never leave, at least in life."

"Compared with some places I have seen," Felix said, "she is lucky to be here. I presume that the women who are admitted are destitute?"

"I believe so. They are lovely old creatures, and Dr and Mrs Greville do their best for them. If I were in such an unhappy state, I should think it paradise to be admitted here. And now, alas, I must find my bonnet and go home."

"Do you live near here?"

"Just up on the hill. Goodbye, Mr Carswell, and thank you!" She turned back and went into the building without another word.

Felix went back to his cadavers, and finished tidying the dispensary for the next day's work. He was just putting on his coat when Major Vernon arrived.

"Any progress?" Major Vernon said.

"Some," said Felix. "The animals definitely did not kill him. That I've established beyond doubt. There are three, if not four, deep knife wounds to the thorax which would certainly have killed him."

"So there must have been a struggle?"

"Not at that point. He was restrained and then stabbed. If you look at his left wrist..." Felix flipped back the sheet covering the late Captain Carrington's remains. "It's not easy to see at first, but that bruising is consistent with a restraint – most likely a rope. The same on the right – although it's scarcely visible because of the teeth marks. But he may have had his hands tied behind his back."

"So, he was overwhelmed in some fashion, then restrained and stabbed?"

"Yes."

"More than one person at work, perhaps?" said Major

Vernon.

"That did cross my mind, given the location of the body. Two men can move a body much more easily than one."

"I've just been at the menagerie," said Major Vernon. "There is a stile where you might get a body over, if you were determined about it and there were two of you, but then it would still have be dragged up and down some fairly steep slopes. Why take such a risk just to hide a body in a leopard cage?"

"Because it was important he was not recognised, given Carrington was so well known?" said Felix. "Or perhaps they imagined he would never be found because the leopards would destroy him entirely. It must have been convenient in the moment, given that the objective was to conceal the death."

"Might he have been sitting when he was restrained?" Major Vernon said.

"That's possible, yes."

"Easier to overwhelm a man if he is taking his ease with you," said Major Vernon. "Imagine you are sitting at a table with people you take to be friends, or at least not outright enemies. It's a warm night. You have taken your coat off, as have your companions. You have had a few glasses of wine and a hand or two of cards. Then one of them gets up, walks behind you and grabs your arms, and before you know it you are trapped in your chair."

"Interesting," said Felix. "And plausible."

"Perhaps he sat down with people he ought not to have trusted and they have got the better of him?"

"Or they executed him," said Felix. "The depth of the stab wounds would attest to that."

"A great deal of anger and resentment, then," said Major Vernon. "We are going to have our work cut out. It seems that the Captain was a prolific blackmailer. A good way to make enemies."

~

They went back to The White Hart. Here, just as Felix had predicted, Eleanor had arrived, accompanied by a grey-faced and miserable Miss King. It was a good thing that Hamilton would be able to see her the next day. The journey had not agreed with her and she was already sequestered in her bedroom. Fortunately, Felix had told Madame Jacquot that it was possible that they might appear unannounced, and she had done everything to make them comfortable, including making up a serviceable poultice for Miss King and finding two more rooms for Major Vernon and Fitznorton.

"I'm afraid they are not our best rooms," said Madame Jacquot.

"So long as there's a bed, I'm happy," said Major Vernon.

"The gentlemen will dine with us, of course," Eleanor said to Madame Jacquot.

The Major and Madame Jacquot left, leaving Felix alone with Eleanor.

"It is so strange that you should have to come here," she said, "just when we were discussing it."

"It's a wretched coincidence," said Felix, pulling off his boots and stretching out on the sofa. "If Miss King's toothache had not been so serious, I would have told you to stay at home. Last night one of the chefs here slashed his wrists."

"No!" said Eleanor. "Why?"

"We don't know. It may be connected with the first murder, it may not. Whatever, this all looks set to be a miserable tangle and I shall be busy. Once Miss King has seen Hamilton, you should go home again."

"But what about the opera?" said Eleanor. "And the Ffordes – they will be here tomorrow, you know."

"I don't think Miss King will want to go to the opera,"

said Felix.

"Perhaps not, but she will not mind if we do. She told me so. And no doubt when she has seen your friend she will feel better." She handed him a playbill. "Look! They are giving La Sonnambula tomorrow, Maria Stuarda on Friday, and on Saturday, Norma!"

"Norma – is that the one with the Celtic priestess and the Roman soldier?"

"Yes, and it has some wonderful music," said Eleanor, perching on what was left of the sofa, and then insinuating herself into his arms. "Oh, don't make us go home, Felix, please. I want to see the animals."

"The animals?" he said, stroking her hair.

"The menagerie. Jacob was telling me about it. He and his brother took the train to see them. There are two beautiful leopards –"

"Moonshine and Mercury," said Felix.

"Yes!" said Eleanor. "What does that great sigh mean?"

"The menagerie is closed," said Felix. "That's where the body was found – in the leopard cage."

"No, surely not? They did not kill him, did they? What a fool he must have been to go in the cage. No doubt he angered them."

"No, no, they did not kill him. He was dead when he was put there. They merely ate him. But that will probably mean they will have to be destroyed."

"What? They cannot do that. That would be utterly barbaric! That cannot happen, Felix, you must make sure it does not."

At this moment the door opened and Mr Fitznorton came in.

"Oh, excuse me!" he said, seeing them entangled on the sofa. "I did not realise you had company."

He said it as if Felix were entertaining some loose piece he had discovered in the back alleys.

"Eleanor, this is Mr Fitznorton," said Felix, releasing her and sitting up properly. "Mr Fitznorton, my wife."

"Mr Fitznorton, how do you do?" said Eleanor, putting out her hand. "I'm afraid we have turned you out of your bed, or rather Lord Rothborough's bed. I hope you don't mind. Madame Jacquot has found you another. You will have dinner with us, though?"

Fitznorton took her hand and said, "Yes, of course, ma'am, thank you. My luggage," he added, "has it been moved?"

"Oh yes, Jacob saw to that," said Eleanor. "And he was careful with it, you may be sure, Mr Fitznorton."

"Who is Jacob?" said Fitznorton.

"My servant," said Felix. "He is extremely reliable."

"We were just talking about the leopards, Mr Fitznorton," Eleanor said. "It would be a scandal if they were to be destroyed. It cannot happen, surely?"

"I don't know ma'am," said Fitznorton. "It's a matter of public confidence. If it is not indelicate to say, they may have got a taste for human flesh."

"They must not be killed," said Eleanor, jumping up. "Something must be done!"

Felix burst out laughing.

"What?" she said.

"It's that expression," Felix said. "Lord Rothborough is always complaining about people shouting at him: 'Something must be done! Something must be done!'"

"He will agree with me on this!" said Eleanor. "You may be sure of it. I will tell him about it. He will be at Holbroke on Saturday, by the way. Another reason for me to stay here. There was a letter from Charlotte this morning."

"He's changed his plans?" said Felix.

"May he not?"

"Yes, of course, I'm just surprised," said Felix.

"Perhaps Charlotte would like to hear Norma," said

Eleanor. "Do you like the opera, Mr Fitznorton? There is a first-rate company here this week. You will join us, I hope? My husband is going to take a box."

"Oh, is he?" said Felix, smiling.

"Of course he is," said Eleanor. "Now I am going to see to my poor Jenny. We dine at seven, Mr Fitznorton."

~

"Ah, Mr Fitznorton, I see you've found your new quarters," said Giles, meeting him in the passageway. "I hope they are comfortable."

"Perfectly, sir," said Fitznorton.

"And did Inspector Harris tell you about the additional papers at Laburnum Cottage?"

"Yes, he and Sergeant Gale went to secure them. In fact, I am now going back to the station to have a preliminary look at them. It may take me some time. For it strikes me we need to have a proper system in place in order to extract the full value of them as evidence –"

"What we need to know is if any of the names we turn up are in the neighbourhood," said Giles. "That's task enough for now, I should say."

"Yes, but a much broader picture of Carrington's activities needs to be determined surely? I will send my excuses to Mrs Carswell for dinner. There is too much to be done."

"We do not need such detail at this point. Go and look at them now, if you like, and consider how you will attack them tomorrow. But I really think you ought to come back and dine with us." Fitznorton looked offended at this so Giles went on: "Believe me, in this business of ours, you will soon begin to realise that it is sensible to close the door on your labours and enjoy a good dinner. These are not dry statistics you are dealing with."

"I'm sure, sir, that I'm equal to anything this business throws up," said Fitznorton. "However, on reflection, it would not do to offend Mrs Carswell. She was a Miss Blanchfort before her marriage, I understand?"

"Yes," said Giles.

"I believe there is a distant connection between that family and my mother's," Fitznorton went on. "I remember the marriage being spoken of by my mother and aunt in lively terms." He glanced away as he said it. Giles repressed a smile, imagining what those 'lively terms' might be, and how perhaps Mr Fitznorton was not supposed to have heard the conversation.

"Ah, then, you will have to come," said Giles. "What else will you write in your letter home from here? You cannot go into details of the case. Better to describe the beauty of your distant cousin."

"No, no, nothing so close as that," said Fitznorton. "I can't remember what the connection was."

"Perhaps Mrs Carswell will know. You will have to ask her."

"She also asked me to the opera," said Mr Fitznorton.

"That you should definitely accept. Indeed, we should all go and make a show of ourselves. After all, it is the height of the season here and everyone of significance will be in the audience. Someone there may well know what has happened to Carrington. An opera house audience is likely to contain a blackmailer's clientèle – people with money and nasty secrets that they would like to protect."

Chapter Ten

Felix ate his breakfast the next morning in the company of Miss King. She was evidently anxious about their forthcoming visit to Mr Hamilton, so Felix said, "Shall I go and wake Mrs Carswell?" He had left her sleeping soundly.

"Surely it is better she rests this morning?" Miss King said.

"She would want to help you," said Felix, getting up. "She will be cross if I don't."

"That's true. But let her sleep and then scold me," Miss King said.

Jacob came in carrying their boots and Felix's freshly brushed coat.

"I saw to the Major and the gent from the Home Office, like you asked me, sir," he said, helping Felix into his coat. "And the carriage is waiting at the door."

"Thank you, Jacob," said Felix.

"Shall I help you with your boots there, Miss, or shall I get Miss Stevens?"

"If you do not mind being a lady's maid, that would be helpful," said Miss King.

"Not at all, ma'am," he said, kneeling down to help her. "But there is one thing, sir, if I might mention it now, since we are here, in this establishment."

"Of course," said Felix.

"It's just I was thinking, sir, last night, that I'd been with you and the family nigh on two years now, all that time acting as a proper gentleman's servant, up to the standards of Mr Bodley, who taught me all I know –"

"Where is this going, Jacob?" said Felix.

"There, sir, that's exactly where I am going. Jacob. My name."

"And the difficulty with that is?" Felix said.

"Perhaps, sir, you don't understand how it is with gentlemen's servants. They reflect their master's position, you see, and plain Jacob, though it's the name my mother gave me, it's a lads name. Not my proper name. I only ask for the respect that someone in my position in the house should be shown. You understand me, I think, ma'am?" he said, looking up Miss King like a baleful spaniel as he finished buttoning her boots.

"Yes," said Miss King. "You would like us to call you Moore, henceforth?"

"Thank you, ma'am."

"Oh, I see," said Felix, trying hard not to laugh. "As you wish, Moore."

"Thank you, sir," said Jacob. "Will that be all for now, sir?"

"Yes, that will be all," said Felix.

When the door had shut behind him, Felix could not long contain his amusement.

"Mr Carswell, you ought not to mock him," Miss King said. "He is well within his rights and he is an excellent servant."

"I know, I know, but... oh dear! And you are smiling too, and I've not seen you smile for days."

"Very true," she said.

"How will I ever remember not to call him Jacob? He is so entirely Jacob that Moore will not do at all."

"You will have to, or he will give you notice."

"He would not dare. I will bring the wrath of the great Mr Bodley down on him if he attempts to do such a thing. I cannot manage without him, and that's the truth of it. Now, shall we go?"

They drove to Mr Hamilton's, where both brother and

sister met them at the door, and showed Miss King the greatest solicitude. Felix found himself admiring Hamilton's consulting room at the back of the house. It had been painted a brilliant white, even the floor, and its large windows were screened with white opaque blinds that admitted a clear but diffuse light. He had a special examination chair, designed in conjunction with a cabinet-making cousin in Glasgow, which tilted the patient back into the most comfortable position possible and allowed the surgeon an excellent view of the patient's mouth. In addition he wore a white smock and a tight white cap, like a night cap, which suited him well and gave him a look of authority. Likewise, Miss Hamilton, who acted as his nurse on such occasions, was swathed in white, almost like a nun. The overall effect was of exceptional orderliness and cleanliness, and Felix could see that Miss King was greatly reassured by it.

Hamilton examined her with great care and said, "I advise an immediate extraction. Are you willing to allow me to etherise you?"

"What does that mean?" she asked.

"I shall ask you to inhale a gas called nitrous oxide, that will sedate you. You will remain conscious but feel no pain as I remove your tooth. It is a novel process and there is an element of risk. But you are young and healthy – in short, a good candidate."

"Is that what they call laughing gas?" she asked.

"Yes, but the aim will not be to make you dance around the room as in the demonstrations you may have read about. Did you eat breakfast this morning, by the way?"

"No. I cannot eat at the moment. I had a scrap of supper at about nine last night."

"That is excellent. It is better to fast before such a procedure. I have ample time this morning, if you are willing. Perhaps you would like to think about it and discuss it with Mr Carswell?"

"No, let's try it!" said Miss King. "I cannot bear this pain any longer. I want to go to the opera."

"I'd better get that box, then," said Felix.

"You had better go fast. The stalls were all sold out," said Miss Hamilton. "We were hoping to go to Maria Stuarda. I love anything to do with Mary Queen of Scots."

"Then you will join us, if I am lucky?" said Felix.

"Oh yes, and I hope you are," said Miss Hamilton.

"Now I'm going to prepare the nitrous oxide, Miss King," said Hamilton. "I shall not be long. Perhaps, Carswell, you'd like to see the process?"

Felix followed him into an adjoining room, his curiosity now thoroughly piqued. Hamilton's laboratory arrangements struck him as perfect and he was consumed with ideas about how he might improve his own. The process of creating the gas, by heating iron filings with nitric acid, had been rendered almost idiot-proof by means of a special double flask, set on a spirit lamp.

"A vast improvement on Davy's system," said Felix, examining it.

"Again, I have my cabinet-maker cousin in Glasgow to thank. He has the mind of an engineer. He looks at such things and is always able to suggest an improvement. We are thinking of taking a patent for that. Now, it looks about ready, and you simply open the spigot here, and fill the oiled silk bag thus..."

The gas inflated the bag in a few seconds.

"All ready for the lady," Hamilton said, tapping the bag.

The operation then proceeded without any difficulty. Felix watched, with astonishment, as Hamilton gently coached Miss King on inhaling the gas, and how, as a result, she went into a state on the margins of sleep, without any agitation or distress. Then, with the strength and skill of a truly accomplished surgeon, he adeptly removed the infected tooth, while all the time Miss King lay as if in a trance, her eyes half-closed, holding Miss Hamilton's hand, which she had been told to squeeze if she felt any pain. But there was no pain, no screams of terror, no limbs rigid with agony. The tooth was removed into a bowl, covered with a white napkin and carried out of the room before Miss King was even aware what had happened.

Felix stood in silent awe, as Hamilton gently packed a lint swab into the bleeding gap where the tooth had been.

"There, ma'am," said Hamilton, "that should be sufficient for now. You must not move for a while, as you may find yourself weak and dizzy. But the offending item has been removed." He looked across at Felix at that moment. "Why are you shaking your head, Carswell?"

"Out of sheer wonder," said Felix. "I have glimpsed the future. You must come to Northminster, Hamilton. Mr Harper must see this." He gestured about the room. "Every medical man in the country should see it! It is extraordinary what you are doing."

When Miss King had recovered a little and the bleeding was checked, Felix took her back to The White Hart to find that Eleanor was barely out of bed and deliberating with Stevens about what to wear.

"You shouldn't have let me sleep," she said. "But I was so tired – oh, Jenny, you look so much better! What happened?"

"Mr Hamilton took out the bad tooth, and I felt nothing."

"Nothing at all? Goodness."

"I will let you explain it all, Miss King. I must go," said Felix, taking up his hat. "And mind you eat a good breakfast and don't let Eleanor drag you about the place if you are tired. Your body has had a shock, even if it does not feel it. A quiet day is in order," he added, kissing Eleanor.

"Of course, of course," said Eleanor. "I will look after her very carefully. And you will get the opera tickets?"

Felix walked to the theatre and discovered he was in the

happy position of being able to take the last remaining box for the three nights desired by Eleanor. That it had remained unsold was unsurprising, for the price was exorbitant. He then made his way to the Incurables Hospital, to begin his second post-mortem in two days.

As he settled himself into the work, he remembered the perfection of Hamilton's arrangements and the ease and swiftness with which everything had been accomplished. It hardly seemed possible, and yet he had seen it with his own eyes. That was the future of medicine, for certain. He turned to wondering what his part in that might be, if any. He was twenty-six and still had not published. He had won a gold medal at Edinburgh, but since then he felt he had achieved nothing substantial. Yes, he had served the cause of justice in some small ways, but that was not what he had intended in his career. He felt hungry for a different kind of glory.

Scalpel in hand, he stared down at the late Victor Morgueillon. He suspected that the post-mortem would reveal little. Dissection could not see into a man's mind, and in the case of self-murder, that was what was required. That was more in Major Vernon's line, to make those acute speculations that seemed always to lead to the truth.

He pushed aside his dissatisfaction with himself, and pressed on with the work. The conclusion he formed, soon enough, was that there was no sign of anything untoward in his stomach contents. Morgueillon had not been drugged, neither did he seem to have been inebriated. Whatever had driven the man to suicide was purely mental. He examined the shape of the man's head, which was not difficult as Morgueillon had worn his hair close-cropped. Had he been inclined to phrenology, he might have run his fingers over it, feeling for the bumps that were supposed to indicate melancholic or criminal tendencies. That was utter quackery, of course. There could be no relation between a man's characteristics, in all their infinite complexity, and the shape of his skull. But as he looked, he wondered if there was in the nonsensical nature of that theory some attempt at grasping a truth as yet undiscovered by science. Were there perhaps structures in the vast complexity of the organ of the brain itself that had some hand in making men's characters, or if not that, in driving their behaviours? It struck him that there had not been much work done on the physiology of the brain, and as the tools to hand for the anatomist improved daily, especially in the field of magnification, there were possibilities that might be pursued. It would mean, of course, a systematic course of study, leaving little time for other pursuits.

He was deep in his notes when there was a knock at the door. It was Major Vernon.

"Anything I should know about?" he asked, indicating Morgueillon's body.

"Nothing to indicate that he was not in perfect physical health. Nor had he been drugged. He acted of his own free will."

"He has been described as wild, and a trouble-maker, with a liking for gambling," said Major Vernon. "I wonder if he had debts."

"That has made plenty of men kill themselves," said Felix.

"Quite. We need to talk to the staff at the Hydropathic."

"Do you still think he may be connected to Carrington's murder?"

"I can't rule it out yet. Do you fancy trying the Roman Baths there?"

"I'm sorry?" said Felix.

"I know you like to take a hot bath after performing a post-mortem."

"True enough," said Felix. The idea was highly appealing.

"I need to understand Carrington's empire – or perhaps we should call it his folly? That seems a good place to start. And there is something else, though it will not please you. I tried to talking to Dr Kennedy and he was distinctly unhelpful,

I'm sorry to say. It made me uneasy."

Felix nodded, not trusting himself to speak with any moderation on the subject. He went and put on his coat.

"Yes, why not?" he said. "What have you done with Fitznorton?"

"He is still deep in Carrington's paperwork. I suspect we will have a most thorough analysis."

"It should bring out a lead or two," said Felix.

"My worry is that there will be too many," said Major Vernon. "From what I have seen so far, the blackmail seems to have been a flourishing business. And perhaps that is not where the answer will lie after all. I have set Inspector Harris trying to find the Swedish wife. She may be in Stanegate. Now, shall we go?"

"I have to go and check on one of the old women here first," said Felix.

They crossed the courtyard, and on entering Mrs Watt's room, Felix found her entertaining three other women. She was sitting up in bed and apparently in fine fettle. The other women were seemingly visitors from the town, on their way back from that morning's market, judging by their bonnets and groaning baskets. One even had a chicken in a cage. They all looked wary as he came in, and the woman with the chicken immediately gathered it up and left without another word.

At the same time, he noticed Mrs Watts pushing something beneath the blanket that she did not wish him to see. Given that this was obviously a most inopportune time and she was in no medical need, he made his excuses and retreated.

Major Vernon was in the courtyard with a chicken under his arm. In her precipitate haste, the woman had allowed her precious cargo to escape.

"A fine bird," he was saying.

"God willing, a good layer, sir, yes," she said, opening the basket. Major Vernon inserted the chicken, and she hastily fastened the catch and walked away, with some briskness.

"What is going on there?" he said.

"I can't imagine," said Felix. "If they were not all respectable bodies I would think it suspicious. She hid something from me just then, under the coverlet. It was curious – when I saw her yesterday, she was insisting she was about to come into a great fortune. Mrs Stuart considered it all fancy, and she was probably right."

"But an interesting thing for her to say all the same," said Major Vernon. "So you have met Mrs Stuart with a 'u', then?"

"Yes, although I wasn't aware of the 'u'," said Felix.

"Dr Greville was careful to point it out," said Major Vernon. "Perhaps he can tell us what is going on with Mrs Watts and her court."

"Later, perhaps?" said Felix. "You have tempted me with visions of hot water now."

"Of course," said Major Vernon.

They walked down to the Hydropathic Institute where Mr Fisher was happy to sell them two tickets for the Roman Baths for the sum of five shillings each.

"That makes the opera box seem reasonable," said Felix. "I wonder if Fitznorton will let us put this on expenses?"

"I doubt it. Do you still think that is why he is here?" said Major Vernon. "To spy on us?"

"Who knows? Do you have a better theory?"

"I imagine that his godfather, or perhaps his parents, or someone influential in his life, has asked his chief if he cannot send him about and make him more worldly. Though whether this is what they had in mind, I don't know."

They had now arrived at the entrance to the Roman Baths, which was reached from the main building by way of a colonnaded terrace that gave a commanding view of the gardens and the town beyond. One side of the colonnade opened onto a large hall that served as a pump room and which was full of people sipping the water, gossiping and strolling about, enjoying the views. Beyond the terrace, Stanegate glittered in that peculiar rich sunlight that sometimes came on in late summer, a distillation of all the good weather that had preceded it.

"A northern Bath," said Major Vernon. "You have to admit that Carrington had some vision to create all this."

It was easy to agree with this as they entered the bath house, which called to mind the baths of ancient civilisation. A circular entrance hall with jasper columns and a domed ceiling led to the various bathing departments. An attendant examined their tickets and showed them into a luxuriously appointed changing room. The etiquette, it appeared, was to strip and then wrap a Turkish towel about one's waist and proceed from there.

They passed into the steam room, an octagon in form with glittering mosaics on the walls and towel-covered couches placed in arched recesses about the room. In the centre, completing the magnificent effect, was a gilded, steaming fountain, supported by mermaids.

"How is this all done, I wonder?" said Felix. "The temperature is perfect."

"It must have cost a fortune," said Major Vernon. "I've yet to see the account books."

"Another job for Fitznorton, perhaps?" said Felix, stretching out on one of the couches. "I prefer this. It is outrageously pleasant. Why cannot we have this in Northminster?"

"Is all this resting on a fragile foundation of blackmail? Who are the other investors, I wonder?"

"You should lie down," said Felix, "to get the full benefit."

Major Vernon did so, and they lay in silence for a while. Felix closed his eyes, and encouraged by the delicious steamy temperature, allowed his mind to picture various voluptuous scenes suitable for such a decadent setting: beautiful women, scarcely clad, rubbing each other with scented oils.

He was startled from his fancies by a hand on his shoulder.

"Perhaps we should sample the cold bath?" said Major Vernon.

They went through to the next room, which if anything was more impressive. Here, a large, blue-tiled pool stretched out in front of them, with a vaulted ceiling above, painted to imitate a bright Italianate sky. To one side, an arcade formed of arches made in coloured brick opened onto a gymnasium area, where several men were engaged in stretching and lifting according to the latest fashionable notions. One, with the shoulders of a ploughman and a broad chest thick with dark curled hair, was hauling at some contraption mounted on the wall that made him look like a horse between the shafts of a wagon.

Major Vernon addressed him. "Dr Kennedy!"

Felix had not realised until that moment how little he wished to know Sukey's husband, who now left off his self-imposed torture. Wiping the sweat from his well-formed features, he stood for a moment, surveying them. Sensing a critical eye, Felix straightened, realising that in this state of undress, he had none of the subtle advantages given him by his tailor.

"Major Vernon," said Kennedy. "Is this part of your investigation?"

"After a fashion. I'm glad to have caught you. You are not scurrying off after patients today, I hope," he said, indicating Kennedy's state of undress. "Dr Kennedy, may I present Mr Carswell, my colleague. He has been conducting the post-mortems of Captain Carrington and Victor Morgueillon."

"But I thought he committed suicide?" said Kennedy. "Why was that necessary?"

"One can never be too careful," said Major Vernon.

Kennedy nodded. "I'm glad you appear to have time to experience some of the benefits of the facilities here."

"It is certainly a wonder!" said Major Vernon. "Is it not, Mr Carswell? This bath house is a luxury that those of us from Northminster can only dream of."

"It has certainly drawn many people here," said Kennedy. "But it is not the heart of our work, although it has a great deal of therapeutic value. It is our cold water treatments in the German manner that are the real wonders of this establishment. Priessnitz's system, as I'm sure you are aware," said Kennedy.

"Yes, I have read Carrington's pamphlet," Felix said. "And some of the cures outlined there – you must have quibbles yourself over such hyperbole, sir? Patients must come here with inflated expectations. It must be awkward, when they have been promised so much."

"No. They are rarely disappointed," said Kennedy. "We have many testimonials to the efficacy of these methods, and I would not persist with something in which I had no confidence."

"Of course not," said Felix. "But there was one case mentioned of a complete removal of the symptoms of phthisis after a course of cold water wraps or some such. You will have to excuse me, but I find that hard to credit. Was that one of your cases?"

"I see a great many people," said Kennedy. "I don't recall that one in particular. But as I say, there are many testimonials, which you are welcome to consult."

This was evasive at best, and struck Felix as insincere. Surely no man with any medical education could be comfortable making such claims. He had to struggle not to respond bluntly, and was relieved when Major Vernon stepped in and said, "You told me the other day that you were about to formalise your partnership with Captain Carrington." Kennedy nodded. "How did your association come about, may I ask?"

"We met in County Down," he said, "where I was in practice at the time. In Ballycoghlan."

"What was the Captain doing there?"

"He was on business of some kind," Kennedy said. "We met – do you know, I can't remember the circumstances, but whatever it was, we found we had interests in common. He told me about what he was doing here, and how he was looking for a medical man to partner with. The German physician with whom he had developed the plan had decided he preferred to return to his home country – family commitments, I believe."

"So you saw this as an opportunity to be pursued?"

"A man can easily stagnate in this profession," said Kennedy.

"And I presume you made some financial commitment to the project?" said Major Vernon.

"Yes, I have put some capital in."

"What return were you promised?"

"A sensible one. Why do you wish to know this? How is it relevant?"

"I'm attempting to form a picture of the Captain's financial circumstances," said the Major. "Although we have found a certain proportion of his papers, it is difficult as yet to form a view as to whether he was solvent or not. There was a dispute about a bill for the marble here, for example. I was hoping you might be able to fill in some of the details. I take it you were privy to such things?"

"No," said Kennedy. "I'm not really a man for figures. The Captain understood that and did not trouble me with them."

"Perhaps because he thought you might be troubled by them?" said Major Vernon.

"Because I trusted him. He was a person who invited one's trust. If you had met him in life, sir, you would have understood that. And I cannot see how his financial dealings have any relevance to this appalling business. It's my understanding that murder is usually a brutal, impulsive affair, committed by ruffians."

"There is something in that, Dr Kennedy, but even the worst ruffian usually has a reason for his actions, beyond a lust for bloodshed. I must find those reasons if I am to find Carrington's assassin. If anything does occur to you that may help us, I would be grateful if you would tell me. Now, I think it is time for us to sample the cold bath, Mr Carswell, don't you?"

Felix was grateful for the suggestion. The abrupt plunge into the chaste, cooling embrace of the blue-tiled pool was exactly what his temper required. He and the Major swam several lengths and then paused at the far end.

"I do not trust him," Felix said. "I certainly cannot like him. It would not surprise me –"

Major Vernon raised his hand to silence him. "Let us not rush to conclusions, no matter how tempting. Shall we have a race? Five lengths?"

Chapter Eleven

Carswell beat him easily, which was to be expected given the difference in their ages. Giles' pride was not hurt. He had only suggested it to allow Carswell to deal with his irritation in a harmless way, and for that matter, to allow some necessary blunting of his own temper. Carswell's feelings on the subject of Dr Kennedy were all too easy to imagine. Giles had witnessed first-hand the intensity of the affair between Carswell and Mrs Kennedy, and he had been the confidant of both parties. She had been his friend as well as his employee. Her welfare was of no small concern to him, and as he had ploughed up and down the pool in pursuit of Carswell, he was forced to conclude, even on such slight acquaintance, that Kennedy was exactly the type of man he would have advised her not to marry.

As they dried and dressed themselves, he turned that question over in his mind. How had she come to marry him? Yes, he was handsome with a powerful physique. He was established in his profession and presumably her family thoroughly approved of him at the time. He was also a fellow countryman and of the same religion. He surely could be charming if he chose to be. Yet even on the slightest acquaintance, Giles could not begin to comprehend how Sukey, so fierce and discerning, had fallen for such a man.

Carswell was giving his hair a final vigorous towelling, the result of which made him look particularly wild. Giles pointed to the looking glass. Carswell studied his reflection, smoothed his hair and said, "I need Sukey to cut it. She is the only person who could ever tame it adequately. The only person who could ever tame me, for that matter." Giles was about to respond, but Carswell went on, "Yes, yes, I know. I shouldn't indulge myself!"

"It's quite understandable," said Giles.

"I can imagine him killing Carrington," Carswell said. "He has the physical strength, that was clear enough. Can you not just arrest him and go at him until he admits it? If anyone could do it, it would be you. Yes, I know, that is utterly ridiculous, but I cannot rid myself of the most unpleasant suspicions about him."

"What would he gain?" said Giles. "That is the question, and it all comes back to the books –"

"About which he was so vague. 'I'm not a man for figures.'" Carswell repeated the phrase in a feeble mockery of an Irish accent. "Any medical man who consents to sit on top of a confection of quackery such as this must be a man for figures. This is all about profit, is it not?"

"That is the unavoidable conclusion."

"And who's to say Carrington wasn't blackmailing him as well?" Carswell said, putting on his coat. "Perhaps he has some nasty secret, and that's why he consented to make a mockery of his qualifications here, because Carrington had him on a leash of some sort. He was wonderfully vague about how they met, don't you think? We should go and see what Fitznorton has turned up."

"Yes, certainly. But first, I want to speak to the kitchen maids."

~

Signor Luchetti greeted Giles like a long-lost friend.

"I hear you enjoyed your coffee," he said.

"I did. I should like to know the secret of it."

"Let me show you!" he said, and took Giles and Carswell

into his office. "My father and I were about to have a cup." The elderly Signor Luchetti, sitting at a table with some paperwork, nodded and smiled at them. "I was talking to Papa about Captain Carrington's death," Luchetti said. "He remembered seeing the Captain on Sunday afternoon."

"When he was supposed to be in London," said Giles.

"Si, si!" exclaimed Luchetti senior.

"So where did you see him, sir?"

"Near the menagerie," said Luchetti the younger. "He likes to go for a stroll about four o'clock."

"I like to look at the animales," Luchetti senior interrupted, "and have a cup of the water... yes? Very good for the digestion," he added, patting his stomach. Giles nodded. "I saw him when I come out. He was with a man. A giovanotto – and he was arrabbiato – how you say it, Giancarlo?"

"Angry," said his son.

"Si, angry. He was shouting!"

"The man with Carrington was angry?" said Giles. The old chef nodded. "And the Captain? How did he seem?"

"Angry. You said they were nearly at blows, Papa."

"Yes, yes," said Signor Luchetti. "That's true."

"Where were they exactly?" Giles said.

"On the corner by the lane, yes, Papa?" The old man nodded.

"By the bottom of the hill," he added.

"And can you describe this man, sir?"

"He was a young man, and tall. Gold hair – he didn't have his hat – and red, red here," The old man touched his cheeks. "Big shoulders – ben construito."

"A strapping lad," said Giancarlo Luchetti.

"Thank you, sir, that's interesting to hear," said Giles.

"And now, caffe?" said the old man.

"Si, Papa! The kettle has boiled so we are all ready. Here is our wonderful machine!"

"Is it Italian?" enquired Carswell, examining it.

"I wish I could say so, but no – Birmingham," said Luchetti, pouring boiling water into the bottom of the machine. "Now as you see, there is a spirit lamp here, which heats the already boiling water."

"And forces it up the tube in the middle?" Carswell said.

"Yes, exactly, sir, and through the grounds, which are in here, and then it flows out, like a fountain. And the glass dome keeps it hot and preserves the aroma. And there is a filter, so there are no grounds."

At this moment the coffee began to spurt out and collect at the bottom of the machine in an impressive fashion.

"Most ingenious," said Carswell. "It is a little like a distillation."

Luchetti placed a coffee can under the tap at the bottom and drew out a cupful, which he handed with great ceremony to Giles.

"It is truly excellent coffee," Giles said.

"That is a great compliment," said Carswell, sipping his own cup, "given how much of a slave to coffee the Major is."

Having drained his cup, Giles said, "I want to talk to the girls in the scullery, if I may. Were any of them particularly involved with Morgueillon, do you know?"

"La bella Polly," said Luchetti senior, and then he added something in Italian which made his son grimace.

"What did he say, if I may ask?" Giles said.

"That she's probably pregnant. Stupid lass. Well, not stupid, that's the trouble with Polly Roberts. Are you sure, Papa?"

"She told me 'erself," said the old man. He got up from the table, and went to his son, laid his hand on his shoulders and again spoke to him in Italian, in a sharp tone. Luchetti bridled at this and responded in the same tongue, but the old man persisted, apparently scolding him, given the gestures involved. In the end Luchetti junior seemed to concede the point, but with some exasperation.

"He wants me to marry her!" he exclaimed.

"You need a wife!" said Luchetti senior. "Thirty-five, he is, Dottores, thirty-five! And Polly is a good girl."

Luchetti the younger sighed and shook his head.

"Ignore him. Let's go and find her," he said.

Polly Roberts was 'bella', just as the old man had said. Built like an Amazon, she was standing at a stone sink scouring copper pans, with strong bare arms. While the three other girls who were working alongside her looked fearful at the sight of Chef Luchetti, she threw him a disdainful glance that only enhanced her impressive features.

"What is it now?" she said.

"These gents want to talk to you about Morgueillon, Polly," said Luchetti.

"What have you said about him, Giancarlo?" she said.

"The truth. But I didn't tell about him getting you in the family way. Why didn't you tell me?"

"I told your old man."

"Of course you did! And you're certain?"

She shrugged. "Not certain whose it is," she said.

Luchetti muttered an oath and turned away.

"Perhaps, Miss Roberts, we might talk elsewhere?" Giles said. "Thank you, Mr Luchetti, that will be all for now."

Luchetti looked glad to retreat, for the other girls were now staring and giggling.

"Get back to your work, all of you!" he shouted as he left.

"Shall we go outside?" Giles said to Polly.

They went from the scullery into a dank courtyard.

"Who are you anyway?" she asked, and Giles explained. "Is this about the Captain being murdered?"

"Yes, and Morgueillon's suicide. Were you sweethearts?"

"Aye, but there was nothing sweet about it. It was – well, he was as mad as they come and I jumped right in the fire, and if I got burnt I've only myself to blame for it. But I don't think Giancarlo will see it that way. I don't suppose he'll forgive me in a hurry."

"So you and Mr Luchetti were courting?"

"Yes, but we fell out. We were always falling out, and then Victor came chasing and caught me when I should have known better." She sighed shook her head. "Will they let him be buried properly?"

"I'm afraid I don't know," Giles said. "Can you tell me anything about Captain Carrington and Victor? Do you know why he was dismissed?"

"It was because of Rosa. Rosa told me that the Captain had been bothering her, and I told Victor. So he had it out with him."

"Mr Luchetti said that he had been pilfering as well as stirring up trouble with the staff."

"He would say that – he hated him and wanted him gone. The moment he started looking at me, to be honest. No, Victor wasn't a thief, but he had a temper on him, and he liked a fight. And there was not enough room in the kitchen for Giancarlo and Victor. So push came to shove. It would have done sooner or later. But I was glad to hear he got a job at The White Hart."

"Did you see him much after he left here?"

"No, never. I decided I'd had enough. That was before I realised I might be, well, you know. It was only the once, you see. Not like with Giancarlo," she added.

"Then he ought to marry you."

"And then you'd have another murder to sort out, sir, for I expect we would cut each other's throats," she said. "Oh poor, poor Victor! What did he have to do that for?"

"I was also told he was a gambler." Polly nodded. "Do you know if he owed money to anyone?"

"To me," said Polly. "I gave him some money, like a fool. I suppose he threw it away on the dice. That was the game he liked."

"Do you know where he went to play?"

"The Fox and Grapes?" she said. "Maybe."

"Thank you," said Giles making a note of the name. "Now, about Rosa, is she one of the girls working with you in the scullery?"

"No, she's a chambermaid – well, she was working here as one. But she's left."

"Was that because the Captain forced himself on her?"

"Aye. He tried to. She wasn't having it, though."

"And was the Captain known to have loose hands generally?"

"Yes. So the other girls said. He never bothered me."

~

"So do you still think Morgueillon had something to do with Carrington's death?" said Felix.

"I don't know," said Major Vernon. "That he was a volatile individual is clear enough, and he had motive to do it. But these things may only be coincidences. I need a better picture of his movements over the last few days."

"I can ask Madame Jacquot about that when I go back to The White Hart. It may be that he never left her kitchen," Felix said. "I need to look in on Miss King." Major Vernon nodded.

They had now entered the entrance hall dominated by the vast statue of Hygeia, but Felix scarcely noticed it because on the far side, by the reception desk, Sukey was talking to Mr Fisher. A little distance away a nursemaid was standing holding a baby, with two small children at her skirts.

"If you could ask him about it, I'd be grateful, ma'am," Fisher was saying.

"Yes, of course I will, Mr Fisher," said Sukey, glancing back at the nurse.

"I have enough till the end of the week, ma'am, because of guests settling their accounts, but I have to pay the tradesmen on Monday. Captain Carrington told me he'd have the money today. I have kept them all on goodwill and promises. I'm not sure I can do it much longer."

"I will do what I can," said Sukey. At this point, one of the children, a boy of about four, came running over to her and tugged at her skirts. Turning to attend to him, she caught sight of Felix and Major Vernon. "Jane, will you take them out into the garden now? I'll join you in a minute. Go back to Jane now, Paul, will you?"

"Yes, ma'am," said the nurse. "Come here, Master Paul."

"But we are going to see the leopards today?" said Paul, not obeying either command.

"I don't think so," said Sukey. "I'm sorry."

"But –" he began. Sukey shook her head and the boy went off, looking miserable. The nurse departed with her charges.

"What is going to happen to those animals, then?" said Mr Fisher to Major Vernon as they approached.

"It has not been determined," said Major Vernon. "I'm sorry – I couldn't help overhearing, but you seem to have a cash flow problem, Mr Fisher."

Mr Fisher nodded and said, "But I am sure Dr Kennedy will be able to deal with it, if I can find him."

"We saw him earlier in the baths," said Felix.

"I will make sure he comes to see you, Mr Fisher, the moment I lay eyes on him," said Sukey. "Now, I really must go."

"Perhaps we might have a word in the garden?" Major Vernon said to her. "Just briefly."

"Yes, of course," she said.

They went outside, and Sukey retrieved the baby from the nurse and sent them off to play at a distance.

"I shall have to feed him, if you don't mind," she said,

and so they went and settled in one of the rose-covered bowers that Felix remembered so well from his last visit. She sat down and rearranged her bodice and wrap in order to set the child feeding without any loss of modesty. Felix was in awe of it. That calm competence had been one of the things that had so impressed him when he had first known her.

"I will come directly to the point," Major Vernon said, "and you will understand why." She nodded. "About Dr Kennedy and Captain Carrington – you said there was friction between them sometimes. Can you tell me anything more?"

"It is hard for me to say. My husband does not confide in me about business matters, but I have sensed that Paul – Dr Kennedy, that is – is not entirely happy about how things are here."

"How did they meet?" Major Vernon said.

"It was at a dinner in Belfast," said Sukey. "When we were in Ballycoghlan, he used to go to Belfast every month or so for a couple of nights and see various people – colleagues, old medical school friends, that sort of thing. Oh, and go to the bank, and the shops and the library – he's a member of the Philosophical Society there. Ballycoghlan is a quiet little town."

"He never took you with him?" Felix said.

"No, that would have been inconvenient for everyone," she said, transferring the child to her other breast. "Anyway, he came back having met this Captain Carrington who was looking for a physician to take charge of his hotel, and I have to say he was mighty fired up about it. He said it was the opportunity he had been looking for, and he was seriously considering it. And before I knew it, it had all been organised. There was an exchange of letters, but I never laid eyes on the Captain before we got here in April."

"He didn't give you a veto?" said Felix.

"What do you think?" she said. "I couldn't very well start bleating about not wanting to come here, in case – well, you know perfectly well what I mean!" She flushed and turned her attention to the baby. "Oh Lorenzo, don't you want any more?"

The baby, full of milk and wind, had begun to howl.

"Let me," said Major Vernon, taking the child deftly from her. She handed him a muslin square, which he tossed over his shoulder, and standing up, draped the square over his shoulder and pressed the baby to him in order to rub its back. He walked away, soothing the child.

"No, I suppose you couldn't say anything," Felix said. "Does he know?"

"Does your wife know?" said Sukey.

"No," he said.

"Then there's your answer," she said.

"Does he really not confide in you?"

"Do you confide in her?" she said.

"This is not a game, Sukey!" he exclaimed.

"No, it certainly is not," she said. At this moment the Major had turned on the gravel path and was now carrying a quiet, contented baby in his arms. She got up, smiling. "I should ask you to be a godfather, Major Vernon," she said, taking the child from him. "You are on the side of the angels, and that's the truth."

"This friction between the two of them," Major Vernon said. "Can you be any more specific?"

"Money," she said. "There was a fight about fees, I know that much. Captain Carrington objected to my husband charging patients who were guests at the Hydropathic, but given there was no salary as yet, Paul had little choice."

"No salary?" said Major Vernon. "Then on what terms did you come here?"

"They were to be partners, and share the profits. But I do know they had not signed a formal agreement. That made me uneasy when I heard it, I must admit."

"Did your husband put capital in?" Felix said.

"I imagine so. There must have been money from the sale

of his practice in Ballycoghlan, and perhaps elsewhere, but as I said, he does not confide in me. I wish he would!" she added, with a fierce glance at Felix.

Major Vernon nodded. "There is something else," he said. "I've heard that Carrington was pestering some of the female staff, in particular a girl called Rosa, one of the chambermaids. Mr Luchetti said he had discussed it with you."

"Yes, she's left now. There's plenty of work elsewhere, so I hope she found a better place. I gave her a character, for what it's worth."

"Apparently she complained to another girl, Polly Roberts, who told Victor Morgueillon, and he confronted Carrington about it?"

"And he was dismissed, yes, I heard that – and that he killed himself," she said. "I never knew him. But my husband did say it was better he was sacked, because he was so unstable. Poor soul. Now, if you will excuse me, I really must get back to the children."

When she had walked away and was out of earshot, Felix said, "He lied to us about how he met Carrington."

"He may have misremembered," said Major Vernon.

"Are you giving him the benefit of the doubt?" said Felix.

"Not at all. I'm going to see what Fitznorton has turned up. You can go and talk to Madame Jacquot."

Chapter Twelve

Returning to The White Hart, Felix found that Eleanor and Miss King had gone out. Miss Stevens was sitting in the window, sewing.

"Jacob has gone with them, sir," she said. "Sorry, I beg his pardon, Moore. How am I to remember that, Mr Carswell, I ask you?"

"I don't know how any of us will," said Felix, and he went in search of Madame Jacquot.

She was in her office: a neat old-fashioned room, panelled and painted blue. A vase of larkspur and lavender decorated her writing table, while she wore a blue and white checked pinafore over her dress. The picturesque harmony of this scene even extended to her blue cap ribbons. It was like one of those serene, domestic eighteenth-century paintings that Lord Rothborough collected. She smiled as he was shown in.

"I'm glad to see you. I had wanted to speak to you," she said. "Do please sit down."

"About what?"

"I have been asking questions – for my own peace of mind – about poor Morgueillon. And when I did, I thought it might be useful to you and Major Vernon."

"Yes, certainly it would be. That is what I wanted to ask you – about what you know of his movements over the last few days."

"Then we have thought alike," she said.

"And your peace of mind?" he said. "That was a horrible thing you experienced. Have you been sleeping?"

"Not entirely as usual," she said. "So, I'm tired. And I feel – oh, how does one put it – nerveuse. As if something is going to jump out of the shadows. That is why I went asking about him. If I knew why he did it, then I thought I would be more calm."

"A good plan," said Felix. "And what did you discover?"

"Gambling," she said. "He owed a lot of money, to a man called – now, what was he called..." She reached for a notebook that was lying with her paperwork. "I wrote it down. Like Major Vernon?" she added with a smile as she consulted it. "Ah, Jack Rivington."

"Who told you that?" Felix said.

"One of my other chefs, Guillaume Roncière. It was as well I asked, for he has been gambling too, and he has a wife and two babies and should know better. He will be more careful now. I told him to tell his wife, who is a good girl, and he looked at me as if I had given him a death sentence. Le con absolu! She will tell him what is what, at least! And this Rivington, he sounds diabolique!"

"Nobody mentioned The Fox and Grapes?"

"Yes, yes, that is the place!" she exclaimed. "It is a dirty hole."

"We will look into it," said Felix. "And no one mentioned Captain Carrington in relation to Morgueillon?"

"Morgueillon did not like him, that was true enough. One or two people said that to me."

"Was Morgueillon at work here all Saturday and Sunday?"

"Yes, we were busy, and he was here on Monday night. But he went out after that, at least that was what Roncière told me. Rivington sent a boy to the kitchen late that night. Several people saw him talking to Morgueillon, and then he went off."

Felix considered again the condition of Carrington's cadaver and his estimate of the time of death. His instinct was that the body had been placed in the cage on Sunday evening.

"Do you think he was definitely here on Sunday night?"

"Yes, and he was quite content. I spoke to him myself after dinner on Sunday night, in fact," said Madame Jacquot.

"I told him I was impressed with his work, that I was pleased with him –" She made a gesture of despair. "Mon Dieu – what happened? Le pauvre."

"At least you were there with him. You tried. He was not alone at the end." She closed her eyes and nodded. "Sometimes that is all that can be said." He said the last phrase in French.

"You speak my language very well, Monsieur," she said, continuing in that tongue.

"I heard little else when I was a small child. I was born in Paris, after all."

"That makes you my honorary countryman," she said, "en effet."

"An honour indeed," he said.

She got up from the table and went to the press. "We should drink to that. It's not too early." She took out a bottle and two tiny glasses. "Ratafia de Mures. Home-made, of course, from last year's blackberries. It will be time to go and get some more. There is a great hedge of them at the back of the field where we keep our milking cows."

"You have your own cows here?" he said, taking the glass from her.

"Of course! I would not trust the milk sold about here for my guests. Lord Rothborough himself told me to get Alderneys, as the best milkers. But perhaps you know that he has a passion for them?"

"Yes, we have them at Ardenthwaite," he said. He sipped the liqueur – it was extremely sweet but had an intense taste of brambles that reminded him of finding a perfect ripe berry on the bush. "That is delicious."

"Lord Rothborough was most appreciative as well," she said.

"I suppose you know that he and I –"

"I guessed, yes – you will forgive me? You are so alike. And he is a most exceptional landlord, I must say."

Felix thought that although Lord Rothborough was attentive to his tenants in general, Madame Jacquot might have been especially favoured. It was not difficult to see why. In physical terms she was alluring, but she was also intelligent and practical, not to say courageous.

"He is lucky with his tenant," he said, raising his glass to her.

"I hope to make this place prosper. It's doing well, though what the effect of Captain Carrington's death will be, who can say? He did a great deal to get people to come here. But perhaps we will do all right without him. I wonder what will happen to the Hydropathic, though. I suppose that charming Irishman will now be in charge. He could certainly make an success of it."

"Dr Kennedy?"

"Yes."

"Charming?" Felix said. "That hasn't been my impression."

"Perhaps it takes a woman to notice it," she said, smiling.

"Perhaps only women get the benefit of it," Felix said. "How well do you know him?"

"Not at all," she said. "I met him once at Mass, with his wife. He was polished, that is all. Perhaps, then, all I saw was charm that is superficial?"

"That may be the case," said Felix. "In fact –"

"Yes?"

"I have a great many doubts about him," said Felix. "I can never be comfortable with a man with medical qualifications who makes sweeping claims. You have read that pamphlet that Captain Carrington put out?" She nodded. "To put your name and your reputation next to such fables – that is first class quackery, no more and no less."

"So does the Hydropathic Institute do no good to anyone?" she said looking alarmed. "The waters? The baths? I recommend them to my guests all the time, Mr Carswell –

should I not?"

"I don't dispute that they can do good, in many cases, but they are not cures. They are comforts. If you had a guest here who was suffering from chronic pain, I would send them to the hot baths, but I would not promise anything but a temporary relief. To claim that hurling buckets of cold water at a man and then wrapping him in wet linen will cure serious conditions is more than irresponsible. It is downright fraud."

"But is there not some effect that if a doctor prescribes sugar water and says it is a marvellous healing drug, people will feel better?"

"Yes, that is true enough, but –"

"And the conviction of a physician in a person's recovery will often help a person to cure themselves? You are priests as much as physicians, Mr Carswell, surely?"

"Some see it that way. I prefer to see my profession more as soldier, and most of the time, I fear, we are fighting unknown enemies. There is no excuse and no time for false claims. I cannot respect a man like Kennedy for going along with Carrington's nonsense. He is a charlatan."

"I see," she said. "And that is all you have against him?"

"Is that not enough?"

"Yes, but you are very passionate, Monsieur! Oh, excuse me – it is of course absolutely right that that should annoy you extremely. It is my fault," she said, laying her hand on her breast. "I'm always too curious. Nosey, is that not the English word?"

"Again, you are impersonating Major Vernon," said Felix, reaching out and tapping her notebook.

"I take that as a compliment."

"And you are right – there is another reason I cannot like Kennedy. I'm annoyed to find that he is not a better man. His wife, you see – she and I were once..."

He had not intended to be so frank with her, but she struck him as someone he could trust with such a confidence, and the burden of his feelings had been growing wearisome.

"Ah, then you don't need to say a thing more!" she said. "I quite understand." She pressed her finger to her lips to indicate her discretion and in that moment, he felt he liked her very much.

"Now, if you want to help your guests, madame, you ought to send them to Mr James Hamilton. He is a dentist, and he took out Miss King's tooth this morning under the influence of ether – a remarkable operation."

"Yes, indeed, Miss King told me herself," said Madame Jacquot. "It sounds extraordinary."

"I hope she is not overtaxing herself," Felix said. "My wife will have insisted on her going out with her, and when she decides a thing –"

"Miss King is tres dévouée," said Madame Jacquot. "She does not like to disappoint her friend. But I don't suppose they have gone far. The bonnet shop I recommended is only a few steps away. A different sort of cure," she added. There was a knock at the door. "Yes?"

A clerk came in and said, "Canon and Mrs Fforde have arrived, ma'am."

"Ah, yes! I will be there at once," she said, getting up. She reached up to unfasten the knot at the back of her pinafore but she was soon struggling with it, so Felix went to help her. The knot had pulled tight and it took him a few moments to loosen it. Standing close to her, as he was obliged to, he was acutely aware of all her womanly charms. It swam into his mind that he would like to help her remove a great deal more than a checked linen apron, an idea which made his fingers unwarrantably clumsy. But he managed to unfasten the knot and she moved away, much to his relief.

They went out to the hall to find the Ffordes, as well as Mrs Vernon and Celia.

"Oh, Mr Carswell, you are here!" exclaimed Celia, rushing over at the sight of him. "Where is Uncle Giles, then?"

"I'm just going to find him," he said.

"Are you both horribly busy?" she said. "You will be able to come to the opera with us?"

"Oh, certainly! I have got the box opposite yours."

"Excellent," said Mrs Fforde. "Now, perhaps we had better see our rooms?"

"Yes, of course, ma'am," said Madame Jacquot. "Please come this way. And I will try and find a better room for you and your husband, Mrs Vernon."

"Oh, I'm sure that won't be necessary," said Mrs Vernon.

"You will dine with us tonight?" Canon Fforde said.

"No, you are dining with us," said Felix. "I insist. It is all arranged."

"I have reserved one of our private dining rooms, just as Mrs Carswell asked," said Madame Jacquot.

"I cannot argue with that! Thank you!" said Canon Fforde. "Tomorrow we will take our turn, yes? Are you making any progress on the case?"

"Hard to say," said Felix. "And I had better go and find the Major. Any messages?"

Mrs Vernon shook her head and Felix left them to settle themselves.

~

"So, by cross referencing those names with the recent arrivals in Stanegate, listed in the Stanegate Intelligencer," Fitznorton said, "I should be able to determine if any of Carrington's victims are in the town."

"Excellent," said Major Vernon. "Any matches yet?"

Fitznorton shook his head.

"I have often thought a form of mandatory identification for the general public would be beneficial. A card of some sort," Fitznorton said. "Do you not think?"

"If you like low-level tyranny, perhaps," said Carswell. "I would find that a great insult to my liberty."

"It would be useful, but since people with criminal intentions are liable to use false names," said Giles, "there would a brisk trade in forgeries. It would create more problems than it solves."

Inspector Harris came in. "There is a Swedish lady in Stanegate," he said. "She goes by the name of Mrs Johnson. Runs a perfume shop in the parade."

"That was near to where Mary Carter saw Carrington talking to the woman he supposed to be his wife," Giles said. "Mr Fitznorton, are you content to continue with this? If so, Mr Carswell and I will go and talk to her."

Chapter Thirteen

"I wonder how much of Carrington's useful knowledge died with him," said Giles to Carswell as they walked to the Parade. "It may be that the aggravating circumstance that drove someone to murder him is not neatly recorded on paper for us to understand. It may have happened years ago, or only recently. Still, one has to be impressed by Mr Fitznorton's efforts. I like the orderliness of his mind."

"He is a machine," said Carswell. "I have been thinking: what was the name of the man who owns the menagerie land?"

"Henderson," said Giles. "I wrote to his solicitor – I am still waiting to hear what he has to say."

"If we assume that Lord Rothborough's offer was an extremely good one," Carswell said, "then Carrington must have promised the earth to make him hesitate."

"Interesting. And your point?"

"What if Carrington was seriously overstretching himself? That would be a serious provocation to those in business with him. Kennedy must have put a great deal of money in – that seems likely, given how vague he was about it to us. It just strikes me that if Carrington loses everything through reckless expansion, then Kennedy would have come down with him. Perhaps Kennedy realised that everything was precarious and decided –"

"To get rid of Carrington? Certainly that financial situation needs to be clarified. But do you really think Kennedy would go to such lengths? Yes, I can imagine he might wish to kill his business partner. Unfortunately, I must share your unease, but think about the method. He was restrained and stabbed."

"We know nothing about Kennedy," said Carswell. "He might well be capable of that."

"Yes, but he's a medical man. He has better tools at his disposal, surely? Why not poison him in his bed and make it look like a natural death? Why stab him and then push him into a leopard cage? That is the whole problem with this case, if you ask me, Carswell. That final action. That is far more than a pragmatic, opportunistic disposal of a body. I cannot help thinking it means something to the murderer. I know that sounds ridiculous but – ah, this must be the place."

They had reached a double-fronted shop with large windows, painted in a fresh green and trimmed with generous amounts of gilding. The window displays were striking, with garlands of flowers and heaps of golden apples, arranged around large flasks of coloured cut glass that glittered in the sun. The interior was equally sumptuous, with heavily carved glazed cabinets full of bottles, and tables laden with piles of soap and pots containing beauty preparations. The air was heavy with the scent of mingling perfumes and there were looking glasses everywhere.

"Why so many apples?" said Carswell. There were artificial gilded apples lying about, as if some mythical tree had caught the breeze and scattered a crop of windfalls.

A smart young woman in a frilled apron came tripping up to them. She was tall, with striking pale hair and blue eyes.

"May I help you, gentlemen?"

"Is it possible to speak to Mrs Johnson?" Giles said.

"She's busy at the moment," she said. "Is there something I could help you with?"

"Forgive me – you are Miss Johnson, perhaps?" Giles ventured.

"I am," she said. "If you wish to speak to my mother, it's best to make an appointment. She is busy, as I said."

"I understand she is Swedish by birth?"

"Yes," she said. "Why do you ask?"

"I should explain," said Giles. "My name is Vernon, and I am a police officer investigating the death of Captain Carrington. Your mother was seen talking to him. We think she might be able to help us."

"Captain Carrington is dead?" she said.

"Unfortunately," he said.

"Oh, dear Lord," she murmured and turned away. "Are you sure?" He nodded. "I don't know him, I mean I scarcely know him, but I do know who he is."

"I'm sorry. Perhaps you had better find your mother, Miss Johnson?"

"Yes, yes," she said. "I'll see if she can come down. Will you wait in there?" she added, indicating a door.

The room they went into was furnished like an extremely precious lady's dressing room – spotted muslin curtains with pink ribbons, pink damask walls and gilded furniture.

"Chances are she is his daughter," said Giles, looking about him at the shelves backed with mirror glass to reflect the careful displays of pots and bottles.

"More fake apples," said Carswell, taking one from the basket on the table, "and fake remedies no doubt. Those pots have that dubious look about them."

"Harmless enough," said Giles examining a pot that was labelled: 'Exquisite extract of gold'.

"Fraudulent though, surely?" said Carswell, reading from a trade card. "'At the sign of the golden apple of youth in Stanegate: a most exclusive selection of perfumes, tonics and beauty preparations of the purest and most efficacious sort. Also home of the celebrated Idunnic Chamber, allowing a perfect restoration of youthful beauty and rigour. Lately of Bath, Tunbridge Wells and Cheltenham. Under the exclusive proprietorship of Mrs Birgitta Johnson.' Idunnic Chamber! Ye Gods, what can that be?"

"Bath, Tunbridge Wells and Cheltenham," said Giles.

"And now here."

The door opened and Miss Johnson returned with a middle-aged woman. Her commanding height was enhanced by the plaits of flaxen hair piled on her head like a crown, with no cap to obscure them. Miss Johnson explained who they were.

"So, how can I help you?" She spoke with a distinct accent.

"Mrs Johnson," Giles said, "are you the Miss Birgitta Halverson who was married in 1819 to George Edwin Carrington, at the Swedish Church in Wapping?" She nodded and went and sat down. "I'm sorry to tell you, then, that your husband is dead."

"Ingrid," she said, turning to her daughter and reaching out for her hand. "Go and find your brother."

She nodded and left.

"How many children do you have, ma'am?" Giles asked, sitting down at the table.

"Two."

"And they both go by the name of Johnson?"

"There is no Johnson," she said. "I took the name when we left him."

"When was that?"

"About eighteen years ago. We were living in Bristol."

"And why did you leave him?"

"We hated each other. He was glad to get rid of me – and the children for that matter. Too much responsibility."

"He did not support you after you left?"

"No! I did not ask him to. I can manage for myself, as you can see," she said, indicating her shop. "Which of course he did not like at all. He did not like my being here one little bit. And now he's dead. Murdered, you think, yes, or you would not be here?"

"Yes," Giles said. "Why did you come to Stanegate, Mrs Johnson, and open your business here?"

"Because it was up and coming. A business like this depends on fashionable people and I go where the fashionable people go."

"But you have been aware that your husband was responsible for the town's recent success?"

"Yes, but I thought I could try my luck here. We have done well in Cheltenham but my son was restless. And as for Carrington – he could not stop me, could he?"

"He did not try to?" Giles said.

"As I said, he did not like it, but that was his problem."

"So you have had some dealings with him since you arrived?"

"Yes. He tried to tell me to leave, but I told him he was being ridiculous. Even his mistress comes here. I charged her double, of course, when I realised who she was."

"And what do your children feel about their father?" said Giles.

"Ingrid is a sensible girl. She knows better than to depend on a man for her fortune. She is too busy with the business to be bothered. Erik – well, twenty is a difficult age."

"You said you came here because he was restless. Could you elaborate?"

"He'd been a bit silly," she said. "Got himself in trouble."

"What sort?"

"He had been running with a rough set. Bare-knuckle fighting, that type of thing. I hope he will grow out of it."

"Do you know if he has seen his father?" he asked, thinking of the old chef's account of Carrington arguing with a strapping young man with golden hair.

She was silent for a moment and then said, "It's possible. I told him that there was no point trying to see him, that the man is a waste of time, but – as I said, he's at a difficult age."

"And it is his father," said Giles. "He may not feel as dispassionate as you, ma'am. What was the precise nature of the trouble in Cheltenham?"

"He was arrested for brawling. He was drunk, and he set on some other boy. They let him off with a fine because – well, because the wife of one of the magistrates was a good customer of mine, and they gave him the benefit of the doubt. So after that, I thought a fresh start would be good for him. He promised me he wouldn't get into any more trouble." Giles could hear the nervousness in her voice.

"Where was your son on Sunday afternoon and evening?" Giles said.

There was a silence, and she said, "I can't tell you. He was at home on Sunday morning, but after that –" She got up from the table and went to the door. "I did not see him until Monday morning. He can tell you yourself where he was, soon enough, I hope." But even as she opened the door, her daughter came in.

"I can't find him," she said.

"Did you see your brother on Sunday afternoon or evening, Miss Johnson?" Giles asked. She looked alarmed at the question and glanced at her mother for guidance.

"Tell them whatever you know," said Mrs Johnson.

"He was back here very late on Sunday, that's all I can say. He came back after you had gone to bed, Mother."

"What time was this?"

"Oh, past midnight, certainly," said Miss Johnson.

"And how did he seem?" said Giles.

"He was drunk," said Miss Johnson. "He went straight to bed. We didn't talk."

"Does he have any favourite haunts? You understand it will be necessary to find him."

"I'm not sure. Mother?"

"Anywhere there are flash young men with money to waste," Mrs Johnson said. She was now fiddling with her rings.

"Do you think your brother may have been to see your father, Miss Johnson?" Giles said.

"He said he wanted to," said Miss Johnson. "But if he did

– I don't know."

"Can you give me a description of him?"

"He's tall, well built," said Mrs Johnson.

"Hair colour?"

"Like mine," she said.

"Thank you, ladies, that will be all for now," Giles said. "Thank you for your time."

They went back into the shop which was now busy with customers. One elaborately dressed woman, catching sight of Mrs Johnson, came over and said, "I hope there won't be too much more delay, Mrs Johnson."

"No, ma'am, there won't be. I'm sorry for any inconvenience. Won't you come upstairs now?" she said. She escorted the lady to the foot of the stairs where one of the shop girls was guarding the entrance – she jumped aside for her mistress and the customer who proceeded upstairs.

"What happens up here?" said Giles.

"Ladies only, I'm afraid, sir," said the shop girl. "That is where the Idunnic Chamber is."

"Which is, precisely?" Carswell said.

"I can't say, sir. It's a secret and for ladies only."

Two women now appeared at the top of the stairs: Mrs Carswell and Miss King.

"Eleanor?" exclaimed Carswell. "What on earth are you doing in here?"

"Buying some soap," she said. "Good day, Major Vernon. Isn't this a lovely place? You should buy something for Mrs Vernon."

"I have your purchases ready now, ma'am," said another of the shop girls, bustling forward with a large beribboned box. "Shall I send it to your hotel or will you take it now?"

"Oh, I will take it now," said Mrs Carswell, taking the parcel. "And since my husband is here, we will pay now."

"Thank you, ma'am," said the girl. "The account desk is over here, sir, if you please."

"That looks like a great deal of soap," said Carswell, frowning.

"Go and settle up, would you?" said Mrs Carswell. He left them, and turning to Miss King, Giles enquired how she was feeling.

"I hear you had an operation under ether," he said.

"Oh yes, it was wonderful," she said. "I felt nothing!"

"So we are celebrating," said Mrs Carswell, hooking her arm into that of her friend. "And the magnetic rays have helped. Does she not look well for it?"

"Very," said Giles. "Magnetic rays?"

"In the Idunnic Chamber," said Mrs Carswell. "We have both tried it. It is so invigorating."

"Is that what's upstairs?" said Giles. Mrs Carswell nodded.

Carswell returned holding a bill.

"Five pounds and seven!" he said, waving it under his wife's nose. "You have nearly cleared me out of cash. What is all this nonsense? Four guineas for the Idunnic Chamber? What does that mean? What have you been doing in here?"

"Perhaps we should go outside?" said Giles.

"Yes, certainly," said Miss King. "Come, Eleanor."

"I'm afraid we must take our leave," said Giles, as they emerged into the street. "We have pressing business. We shall see you later, ladies."

"I do feel tired now, Eleanor," Miss King said. "Let's go back to the hotel."

"A good idea," said Carswell.

The ladies set off, and Carswell stuffed the bill into his pocket.

"It is not the money I care about," he said. "It is her money, after all; it is the –" He broke off, took a deep breath and gestured at the shop front. "Absolute quackery!"

"Undoubtedly, and most aggravating, certainly," said Giles, turning in the opposite direction and beginning to walk.

"But you had best forget about it and concentrate on the business in hand. We need to find Erik Johnson. His mother's manner was interesting, to say the least."

"In what respect?"

"She did not seem surprised. His behaviour has obviously been worrying her for some time. And that was the first thing she did – send her daughter to find him. She is no fool."

"She's a criminal," Carswell said. He glanced back at the shop. "I dread to think what is in that parcel. How can Eleanor be so gullible? She knows perfectly well how foolish this is, and as for Miss King –"

"That is unfair, Mr Carswell."

"I know," he said. "I know! So, how shall we find Erik Johnson?"

"Let us report back to Inspector Harris. We can take a short cut through the gardens."

The Parade Gardens were full of fashionable loungers, enjoying the last sun of the afternoon. As they turned a corner into a more secluded alley, they saw a young man and a woman entwined in a passionate embrace on a bench.

"Isn't that Miss Johnson?" said Giles, recognising her dress. Carswell nodded; she caught sight of them, and swiftly freed herself from her lover's arms. She muttered something to the man and then began to walk briskly away. The man reached after her, but did not make any great effort at it, as if he had drunk his fill. Instead he fixed his gaze on Giles and Carswell, his expression seeming to say, "So what, gentlemen, so what?"

"So Miss Johnson is more susceptible to male charm than her mother imagines," said Giles. "Interesting. I wonder who he is."

~

It was just after six when Giles let himself into his hotel room, and found it in darkness, the curtains drawn and the shutters closed.

"Emma?" he said, seeing a body lying in the bed.

"Hello," she said sleepily.

"Are you all right?"

"Oh! Yes, perfectly," she said, stirring. "I was just having a rest."

He adjusted the curtain and the shutter to allow in a strip of light, and smiled at what it revealed. Her chemise had slipped from her shoulders and she was lying in a languid, voluptuous position on top of the counterpane. He sat down on the bed and kissed her, to which she responded with eagerness.

"What is it about hotels?" he said, feeling stirred.

"It's this hotel," said Emma, reaching to unknot his cravat. "It feels a little French. Although I have never been to France, of course."

"Did you meet Madame Jacquot?" he said, getting up and stripping down to his shirt.

"Yes, I did," she said. "And I'm glad I'm here now. It might have been dangerous to leave you here alone with such a force of nature. You might stray, and I can't risk it."

"There is no danger of that," said Giles, lying down beside her. He began to caress her breasts, making her sigh. They proceeded swiftly to indulge themselves.

"It's being away from the children," said Emma breathlessly, climbing off him. "I'm astonished at myself."

She now had deliciously flushed cheeks, and Giles wondered if there was time for a brief rest and another bout, but the clock chimed to remind them of the world beyond.

"You will have to help me dress," Emma said, "since I have left Patton behind."

"With pleasure," he said, watching as she put on her stockings, which were blue silk and a recent gift from him.

"I should make a confession," she said, picking up her stays. "I spent a fortune on these and I cannot get used to the fit. They are the new style, you see. It was vanity that made me buy them – I wanted to look young and slender."

"You are perfect as you are," he said, getting up to assist.

"You don't want to scold me for extravagance?" she said, turning her back to him. "And I have new drawers as well, and I know that some gentlemen feel that their wives should not wear such things."

"Later, perhaps," he said, seeing perfectly well what she was discreetly displaying to him despite the folds of white linen. He pulled down the tail of her chemise and gave her backside a gentle slap, which made her squeak. "I need a plunge in a cold bath. Now, let us get you laced up and respectable again, Mrs Vernon."

Chapter Fourteen

"So," Felix said, having bitten his tongue for a good half hour on returning to The White Hart, "what on earth is an Idunnic Chamber?"

He had occupied himself in changing for dinner and then looking through his letters, and since Jacob and Stevens had been in the room with them, it had not been so difficult. But now they were alone.

"I shan't tell you," said Eleanor, without glancing up from the libretto for La Sonnambula. "You will not listen properly to a word I say about it."

"At least you see that," he said, returning to his letters. They did not help him much. "I only hope it was not dangerous. Some of these quack remedies –"

"No, of course it wasn't," she said.

"So what was it?" he said. "Seriously, what was it claiming to do?"

"It harnesses the forces."

"The forces?" he said, attempting not to laugh. "The forces of what?"

"This is why I do not want to discuss it with you."

"Because you know you have been gulled for two guineas and don't like to admit it?"

"Because it was restful and stimulating at the same time. There is definitely something in it."

"I very much doubt that. What actually happened?"

"I shall not say a word unless you promise you will not interrupt me? Yes?" He put his finger to his lips and nodded. "Promise?"

"I promise," he said. "So?"

"I know you will think this is nonsense, but you are always saying that there is so much we don't know, and how can we know things unless we try them? Yes?" Felix nodded, squashing his objections as best he could. "And if it works for many people, then surely that means something as well?" He was forced to nod again. "There were so many interesting testimonials." He began to wonder if she had prepared this speech to torture him, and what offence he had committed to deserve it. "There was one from a woman who had terrible migraines – you know, the kind that Major Vernon has so often... perhaps he should try it."

"It was ladies only, surely?" he said, unable to resist. "Sorry, I shall not say another word, I swear."

"It was," she said, as if struck by his remark. "I wonder why. Perhaps it only works on women. Anyway, according to the testimonial, she sat in the chamber three times and was quite cured."

"Oh, really?"

"Yes, really."

"By what mechanism?"

"The crystals, of course, and the silver plates. It is lined with them – and they concentrate the powers of magnetic healing and allow them to pass into the open pores of the skin, which is why you have to sit there quite naked. It wouldn't work otherwise."

"No. Of course not," said Felix, shaking with repressed laughter.

Miss King came in. "Will I do?" she said.

"Oh, Jenny," said Eleanor, jumping up and going to her. "How lovely you look! Does she not, Felix?"

"Very fine," said Felix. This was true enough. She was wearing a dark red satin gown, the colour of a glass of claret.

"The black lace is perfect," she said. "You look like a Spanish noblewoman! Stevens has been so clever!"

"Yes, she has, and she was pleased with me, but I feel so

grand," said Miss King. "I've never been out to a watering place before. Does one really have to be so dressy here?"

"We must make our mark!" said Eleanor, slipping her hand about her waist. "And now we should go down – I want to work out where everyone should sit."

"Your mouth is not giving you any discomfort?" said Felix.

"No, none at all," said Miss King. "It does feel strange, and I will be careful what I eat, just as Mr Hamilton told me."

"And tell me, did you sit in the Idunnic Chamber?" Felix asked, unable to resist.

"Oh, do be quiet!" said Eleanor. "Let us not talk of that again!"

"With pleasure," said Felix, and opened the door. "Shall we go?"

Eleanor swept past him, and Miss King followed in her wake, with something like an apologetic smile. He was sure that she had felt it all to be nonsense, and he wished she might assert herself a little in such circumstances. It would do Eleanor no harm to be checked occasionally, and she would be more likely to listen to Miss King than him.

Madame Jacquot was waiting for them in the dining room. It struck Felix that she had gone to extraordinary trouble over the arrangements, with flowers and ribbons garlanding the table. There would be absolutely no difficulty in giving a good report of it to Lord Rothborough, and this was no doubt her aim. As Eleanor was deliberating where Fitznorton ought to be placed, it struck him as a pity they could not ask Madame Jacquot to join them, as he was sure she would draw him out nicely, though whether it was fair to inflict Fitznorton on her was a different matter entirely.

At this moment the gentleman himself appeared and stared at the handsomely dressed table, as if he had never seen the like before. Madame Jacquot slipped away, and Felix was left to introduce Fitznorton to Miss King.

"The table looks pretty, does it not?" said Miss King.

"Yes, very pretty," said Fitznorton.

"Everything is so sumptuous here," said Miss King. "Not just in the hotel, but the entire town."

"Wait until you see the Roman Baths," said Felix. "I think they allow women to use it at times."

"Then we shall, certainly," said Eleanor, taking her place. "How interesting it is to dine at a round table. No one is at the head nor the foot. Will you go there, Mr Fitznorton?" He went to his place dutifully. "Now, I have been thinking hard about how we may be connected, but I really cannot work it out."

"I'm sure Mr Fitznorton's mother cannot be mistaken," said Miss King.

"Oh, no, I didn't mean to imply that," Eleanor said. "It's just that I don't know all the details of that side of the family. Perhaps I will become more dynastically minded when the baby is born," she said, patting her stomach. "Perhaps that is a consequence of motherhood – a desire to thoroughly master the family tree."

"The connection must be a remote one, and not at all obvious," said Fitznorton.

"It is interesting, really, if you think about it," said Eleanor. "We may meet people all the time who are our relations and never know it. Perhaps people fall in love with long-lost cousins and marry them?"

"They do in novels and in operas, certainly," said Felix. "Speaking of which, what is the plot of La Sonnambula? You were reading the libretto, I noticed."

"But that would spoil it for you," said Eleanor.

"You don't go to the opera for the surprise of the story," said Felix. "It's not like a play. Though that is odd, when one thinks of it. Why sometimes the story has to be absolutely fresh and entirely unknown, and at other times, the same story, repeated again and again, is far more powerful."

"The anticipation of knowing something terrible will

happen, and that nothing can be done to stop it," said Miss King. "There is something moving in that. I have read Romeo and Juliet a hundred times and it always breaks my heart."

"Yes," said Eleanor. "Oh, Felix, do you remember that production we saw on our wedding journey? They changed the ending! It was too much!"

"We didn't know whether to laugh or cry," said Felix. "I should never have gone if I'd known they were going to do that. The rest of the audience liked it, though. So what is the plot?"

"The heroine is a sleepwalker," said Eleanor.

"Obviously," said Felix.

"And she strays into a gentleman's bedroom whilst sleepwalking, and is, of course, completely innocent of anything, but her fiancé is convinced she has been unfaithful and casts her aside. But then –"

The door opened and a waiter showed Canon Fforde, Mrs Fforde and Celia into the room, so Eleanor got no further. A minute or two later, the Vernons joined them and everyone sat down to their dinner. Felix was seated next to Celia who had shot up in height over the summer, and now looked much older than thirteen.

"So are you terrified or excited about school?" he asked.

"Both," she said. "I hope it will be all right."

"I'm sure it will be," he said. "And you will be the only one who knows how to dissect an ox heart."

"Or a bull's eye," she said.

"Your mother was telling me that on some days you will only be allowed to speak French or German," said Mrs Vernon, who was sitting nearby.

"Yes, every third day is English," said Celia.

"That is terrifying," said Felix.

"We had a similar system at my school," said Mrs Vernon. "Girls have to talk, you see – it makes a virtue out of a necessity. I'm sure that's the only reason I have any proficiency at all. That was the only good thing about that school, in fact. I did not learn much else. I am sure you will, though."

"I'm worried I will miss home too much and be laughed at for it," said Celia. "That is the main thing."

"You will not be the only one who is homesick," said Mrs Vernon. "And it does pass, soon enough. I expect you will be far too busy to miss it. It will be Christmas before you know it."

"I hope so," said Celia, and laid down her knife and fork. "Oh dear, this is delicious, but I don't feel very hungry. I haven't felt hungry for days."

"I was the same when I first went to Edinburgh," said Felix. "It's like the homesickness, though – it does pass. In my case, the problem was that the food in my lodgings was inedible so when I did get my appetite back, I couldn't satisfy it."

"Which will not happen with you, Celia," said Mrs Vernon.

"When I got my courage up to complain to Lord Rothborough," Felix went on, "he told me I was lucky he had not sent me to Harrow or some such, where I would surely have been turned on a spit."

"Oh dear," said Mrs Vernon, smiling. "Well, if you cannot eat this, Celia, there are sure to be ices at the opera. At least I hope so!"

~

"This makes the Northminster Playhouse look decidedly shabby," said Giles, as they settled into their seats in the box the Ffordes had taken.

"Stanegate in general makes Northminster look shabby,"

said Emma. "I wonder if there is not some fearful competition brewing between them. Mr Carswell was already talking about building a bath house."

"How lovely Celia looks!" Sally said. Celia had gone to sit with the Carswells in their box, which was opposite theirs.

"She's already taller than Mrs Carswell," said Emma. "Think how tall she will be by Christmas."

"It really is frightening how grown-up she looks. It makes me realise I don't have children any more," said Sally, "but young people. It makes one feel ancient. I shall have to borrow Sandro from you."

"With pleasure!" said Emma. "But he will make you feel even more ancient. He is the world's most exhausting child."

"Now, are you sure you can see there, Mr Fitznorton?" Sally said. "I may be blocking you."

"No, not at all, ma'am," said Fitznorton.

"It looks as if it will be a full house," said Lambert. "Which is excellent. How many of them will be true music lovers is another matter. That is always the problem with the opera – people do not come for the music, but to be seen."

"If the musicians are doing their work properly," said Emma, "there will be a state of enchantment and everyone will be as still as a mouse."

"One can but hope!" said Lambert. "It's not every day that one gets a chance to hear a talent like that of La Fiorella. Have you heard her before, Mr Fitznorton? She was singing at Drury Lane recently. We were lucky to catch her there."

"No," said Fitznorton. "I rarely go to the theatre."

"Who are those gentlemen bowing to us?" said Emma. "Down there in the stalls?"

"That is Signor Luchetti and his son," said Giles, responding with a wave. "The chefs at the Hydropathic."

"The one with the coffee machine?" Emma said. "They look so distinguished!"

"That is because they are princes among chefs," said

Giles. "The food there was superior."

"Could there be any better kitchen here that Madame Jacquot's?" said Lambert.

"It would be hard to say which establishment is better, certainly," said Giles, "and I really am no expert. But the coffee put the edge on it for me."

"And that, and all this –" Emma made a gesture at the elegantly dressed crowd, as the orchestra finished tuning up. Her voice dropped to a whisper: "It is all because of your poor murdered fellow! What a strange case."

The overture began; it was a brief one, and the curtains soon opened on an elaborate set showing a Swiss village, but Giles studied the audience instead, ruminating on what they knew of Carrington's life and unfortunate end. A career blackmailer, whose wife had left him in Bristol nearly twenty years ago, had then become a successful promoter of a watering place, taking over its largest hotel and expanding it, installing vast marble statues and glittering mosaics. How had he funded it?

He scanned the audience again, wondering what secrets they held, and if any of them had any connections to the bizarre events that had unfolded on Sunday night. It had been an execution followed by an attempt to get rid of the body, which spoke either madness or desperation. Had someone been paid to kill him, and having underestimated the difficulty of getting rid of the body, had therefore dumped it at the menagerie in the hope that the leopards would mutilate him out of all recognition? Or was that part significant, and part of the execution? It had struck him previously that murderers did not just kill to remove obstacles. There was often something more than pragmatism at work in what they did. Ordinary people often enough harboured wicked intentions towards a person who had offended them, but they did not act on such fantasies; yet murderers, that special category of human, did. The fear of the gallows meant nothing to them. They acted in spite of it.

His attention was now caught by the beauty of the famous soprano's voice as she reached shimmering heights. Perfect stillness reigned in the audience. As Emma had predicted, they were all apparently enchanted. But he turned a little and saw in a box near the one occupied by the Carswells that the man sitting at the front of it had begun to slide out of view, as if he were fainting. Giles recognised him, even as he vanished. It was the young man who had been kissing Ingrid Johnson in the Parade Gardens.

The aria finished and the house erupted into applause. The young man did not appear again, and Giles wondered if he had been taken ill.

"I need to talk to Mr Carswell," he said to Emma, and took the opportunity of the applause to leave the box.

He dashed round the long passageway to the entrance of their box, which was helpfully signalled as 'The Royal Box', and opened the door. The applause was continuing. Fortunately Carswell was sitting at the back and could come out without the ladies being disturbed.

"I think someone has been taken ill," Giles said. "The man we saw with Miss Johnson, in fact."

They went to the box and opened the door. The man was lying on the floor, and on her knees cradling him in her arms was a woman they at once recognised. It was Mrs Stuart. She must have been sitting in the shadows.

"May I help?" said Carswell, throwing himself onto his knees beside him.

"I think he's dead," she said. "I can't feel his heart."

Carswell began to check for signs of life, but the longer he did so, the clearer the situation became. The man was indeed dead.

Chapter Fifteen

"I can't in all conscience sign a death certificate," said Felix to Major Vernon after they had carried him out to the passageway behind the boxes and he had made a superficial examination. Giles turned to Mrs Stuart.

"You said your husband came here for treatment at the Hydropathic, ma'am?"

"Yes, he did."

"So was he under the care of any particular physician?"

"Dr Kennedy," she said.

"We will have to speak to him, then," he said. "In the meantime we shall have to remove him to the town infirmary."

She nodded.

"You must do what must be done," she said.

Major Vernon went off to make arrangements, and she stood and watched as Felix made further examinations.

"Ma'am, I hope you don't mind me asking this: you knew he was ill, but there was no suggestion his condition might be dangerous?"

"No. But he has not been well for some time."

She sank down onto the floor beside him and took the dead man's hand.

"Headaches," she said. "He suffered dreadfully from them." She bent over his hand and kissed it. "Oh, but he feels so cold already." She began to shake and her composure gave way. She began to sob, still clutching his hand in both hers. "I thought they were just headaches, and..." She straightened and gazed at Felix with wide, glistening eyes. "I was not kind. I have not been kind enough. I have been –"

She broke off and wiped her face with her still gloved

hands.

"Oh! Mrs Carswell asked me to –"

Felix looked up. Celia had come out of the box and was standing in the passageway, her white skirts glowing in the gaslight. Felix got to his feet, pulled off his coat and covered the dead man with it.

"Go and find your father and Mr Fitznorton," he said to Celia. "Send them here, and stay with your mother. Tell them there's been an accident. Oh, and may I borrow your shawl? Mrs Stuart needs something warm about her."

She handed him the shawl and having walked respectfully and slowly past the dead man, ran off. He wrapped her shawl about the now shivering Mrs Stuart. Through the open door of the box the opera continued in an unending stream of glorious melody. He moved Mrs Stuart away from her dead husband and sat with her on a bench, where she clung to him, almost choking on her grief.

Major Vernon returned with assistance, and soon both Canon Fforde and Fitznorton joined them and it was possible to move her to a more secluded spot. A small quantity of brandy and hot water revived her, but she seemed to Felix to be in a dangerous state.

"I will take you home," said Felix. She nodded in agreement.

"I'll get a carriage organised," said the Major. "To the Rustic Cottages, yes?" She nodded again.

It seemed to take a long time to get to her house, and the hackney driver stopped to ask them exactly which house it was.

"Over there," Mrs Stuart gestured. "I can walk from here."

She insisted on climbing out of the carriage, even as she spoke, clambering over Felix to do it. He hurried out after her, telling the cab man to wait for him.

"I want to see you safely inside," he said, gently catching

her arm.

"That won't be necessary," she said. "Truly, I feel a great deal better –" but then she stumbled and was obliged to accept his assistance.

The front door lay at the end of a path, densely planted with shrubbery, and there was little to light their way. She reached under a stone and took out a key to unlock the door.

"Is there no one at home?" he said. He had imagined that a woman servant at least would be there to assist her. She did not answer but went into the house. She lit a candle, and then turning back to him, she took off Celia's shawl. "You must give this back to that young woman," she said. "Good night."

"Are you sure you will be all right?" he said.

"I would prefer to be alone. Thank you for everything you have done."

Felix nodded and was about to say he would call the following day, but the door was shut in his face.

By the time he got back to the theatre, the performance had finished and the audience was flooding out. This pleased his driver who was at once able to catch another fare. Felix paid him and plunged into the crowd in search of Eleanor and Miss King. He soon encountered Mrs Vernon, who led him to the rest of the party, still in the lobby of the theatre. He handed the shawl back to Celia.

"What did he die of?" she asked, wrapping it about her.

"I can't say yet. He wasn't well, though."

"Poor woman," said Mrs Fforde, "to lose your husband like that. And he was so young!"

"Yes. It will be a puzzle, I suspect," Felix said.

"But you will solve it," said Celia with great confidence.

"How was the rest of the opera?"

"Oh, very exciting," Celia said. "When the heroine sleepwalks on the roof of the mill it was really convincing."

"The singing was perfect," said Mrs Fforde. "Poor Lambert will be sorry to have missed it. Let us hope there are no unhappy accidents tomorrow night."

"We should go back to the hotel," said Felix, glancing at Eleanor. She was having an animated conversation with Miss King, and looked flushed, while Miss King looked drained.

"Oh, what horrible news," Eleanor said, "and after such a performance! Oh, Felix it was sublime – when she walked on the rooftop – oh, what an actress La Fiorella is! Her voice is exquisite, of course, but I had not expected her to be so utterly convincing!"

"Thank goodness you were at hand," said Miss King.

"And that Major Vernon noticed it," said Felix. "Shall we go home?"

"Yes, indeed," said Miss King. "I am exhausted."

They walked back to The White Hart where a waiter told him that Major Vernon was waiting for him in the coffee room. The ladies dispersed upstairs to their rooms, and Felix found the Major drinking tea with Canon Fforde and Mr Fitznorton.

"Will no one join me in a brandy?" said Felix, having ordered one for himself. "Not even you, sir?" he added, to Canon Fforde.

"Not this late, Mr Carswell," said Canon Fforde. "And I must go and see to my womenfolk."

"I will retire as well, Major," said Fitznorton. "If I'm not needed?"

"No," said Major Vernon. "We will meet again tomorrow at eight at the police office."

"Certainly, sir. Good night."

"How was Mrs Stuart?" said Major Vernon.

"She will be all right, I hope. She was not receptive to my assistance. She said she preferred to be alone. The house seemed deserted. No sign of any servants. I shall call first thing."

"That's odd," said Major Vernon. "Perhaps they had let them go out because they had gone to the opera."

"I imagine that's the case," said Felix. The waiter delivered his brandy and hot water, and he sipped it. "Of all the doctors he had to be under the care of, it would have to be Kennedy, wouldn't it?"

"It is unfortunate," said the Major. "I hope he will be able to give you a clear explanation. Will you ask him to come and examine him?"

"I suppose I shall have to," said Felix. "What did the attending physician say at the Infirmary?"

"There was only a dresser there," said Major Vernon. "And he was half asleep. What might have caused it? I know it can only be speculative, without knowing his history, but we can rule out foul play, I take it?"

"Why do you ask that?" Felix said. "Is there something that is bothering you?"

"No, just that we ought to rule it out as soon as we can. Such a sudden collapse – well, as a layman, I can't help ascribing an unnatural cause."

"It did cross my mind," said Felix. "Or rather, it did when she shut the door in my face. She was decidedly odd."

"Death can do strange things to a person," Major Vernon said.

"But we saw him this afternoon being unfaithful. What if she knew about that and couldn't bear it? I will request permission to do a post-mortem, whatever Kennedy tells me. If he had some underlying condition which she has somehow hastened for her advantage –"

"Perhaps a little gentle questioning would not go amiss in the first instance," said Major Vernon. "Just to settle the matter."

He finished his tea and said good night, leaving Felix to contemplate his brandy and hot water. He took the opportunity to smoke a cheroot, and made a few notes on the condition of the dead man so that he should not forget his observations. As he did, the coffee room filled up with men who had the look of having endured rather than enjoyed their evening at the opera and were seeking relief. Some ordered champagne and brandy while others settled to a hand of cards, and the air filled with expensive cigar smoke. At the doorway he noticed Madame Jacquot discreetly surveying the scene. She was on the lookout, he was certain, for unruly elements. There was a group of young men who were on the verge of rowdiness, but the head waiter went to speak to them, and they soon dispersed. Felix was only half aware of this happening, being deep in his notes, and looked up to see one of them putting on his hat: a tall, blond-haired, ruddy-faced young man with broad shoulders. The name of Erik Johnson swam into his head, but in a moment more he had gone with his friends and the room was suddenly quiet.

He sat back in his chair, contemplating another drink and another cheroot, and decided he was better off going to bed. The thought of pressing himself against Eleanor's plump, pregnant body spurred him and he made his way upstairs.

He went into their bedroom, but she was not there. He supposed she was saying good night to Miss King – this was not an unusual occurrence; he had a notion they said their prayers together. He readied himself for bed, then sat in the armchair reading a few pages of the French novel he had been dipping into over the last few weeks. It depicted the affair between a grisette and a nobleman, and it was curiously piquant in a sordid way so that he wished his wife would hurry and come to bed. At last, he decided to fetch her, and crossing the sitting room which linked the two bedrooms, he tapped on Miss King's door.

There was no answer, so he opened it a chink and saw the lamp was still burning. He looked in, and saw there were two bodies lying closely together in the bed.

At the sound of the door creaking open, Eleanor stirred and sat up. Her hair was cascading down her back, her cheeks were crimson and her shoulders were bare.

"She was tired, and so was I," she said, in a whisper. "Would you put out the lamp?"

He did so and left without another word. This had happened before, but for some reason he felt profoundly disturbed. Eleanor had looked and sounded exactly as she did after...

He put out the rest of the lights and climbed quickly into bed. As he lay there on his back in the dark, in the cool sheets, it began to torment him. Had Eleanor and Miss King's ardent friendship become something quite different?

He lay there, reviewing all the signs of affection he had seen between them: the kisses, the embraces, the constant smiles between the one and the other. Eleanor had told him a hundred times of their mutual devotion, and he had considered it touching, and had been happy that she was happy. He had seen Eleanor lavish gifts on Miss King, much to the latter's embarrassment. He had seen Eleanor defer to her opinion on occasions when he was certain she would not have deferred to him. It had amused him to see it, and made him grateful for the peace that Miss King instilled in her. Had he read it all wrong?

No, it was impossible. She was flushed and dishevelled because the bedroom was warm and she had been excited by the opera. There was nothing more to it. That Miss King could be involved in such an imbroglio was utterly impossible. She was devout, careful, cool-blooded, self-controlled – everything that Eleanor was not. She would probably be shocked to learn that such relationships might exist. Eleanor loved her as a friend in her generous passionate way, and that was the limit of it. He should not allow himself to stray into febrile territory.

Yet he could not sleep. He tossed about in the great bed, feeling wretched. How he could even allow himself to have such vile suspicions he did not know, yet a profound uneasiness had gripped him. He felt as if he were standing on a crumbling ledge, struggling to remain in place. As the hours passed, he fell deeper and deeper into the idea that it was all exactly as he suspected: that they were lovers.

Chapter Sixteen

"I have laid hands on Erik Johnson for you, sir," said Inspector Harris to Giles when he arrived at the Stanegate station house the next morning.

"Excellent work, Inspector."

"I can't take credit for it, sir," Harris said. "There was a bit of a fight in the small hours in the yard of The Marquis of Granby. They brought in three of them. He had a knife on him."

"Mr Carswell will need to see that," said Giles.

"I have it in my office, sir," said Harris. "Do you want to talk to him now?"

"Yes. I presume the justices are sitting today?"

"They are, but not until the afternoon."

"Bring him up, then, if he's in a fit state. I take it there was strong drink involved in this incident last night?"

"Aye, sir, that's about the sum of it."

Giles turned to Fitznorton who had already settled at his desk.

"Have you found anything relating to his estranged family? They go by the name of Johnson."

Fitznorton consulted his index.

"Nothing as yet," he said.

"And no sign of a will?"

"None."

At this moment Carswell came in, looking for all the world as if he had been involved in a brawl at The Marquis of Granby. He had apparently not shaved, nor even dragged a comb through his hair, and he was not wearing a cravat.

"We have Erik Johnson," said Giles. "And interestingly

he had a knife on him. Will you have a look at it? Inspector Harris has it in his office." Carswell nodded and left without another word. Giles followed him.

The knife was lying on Harris' desk. It was a steel-blade hunting knife, with a carved ivory handle. Carswell picked it up and carried it to the window.

"What do you think?" said Giles.

"Certainly could have done the job," said Carswell, peering at it, and then measuring its width with his fingers. "I estimated two inches, from the appearance of the wounds."

He laid it down on the desk.

"Not a nice piece of work for anyone to have in their possession," said Giles, examining the knife for himself. "So, are we looking at patricide? This will make a good start to the conversation. Will you join me?"

"I have to go and see Mrs Stuart," Carswell said.

"Perhaps you should go back and shave first," Giles said.

Carswell rubbed his chin and grimaced.

"I've been up since five," he said. "I couldn't sleep. I've written to Kennedy about his patient and asked him to come to the Infirmary. It will be interesting to see what he says."

"Any more thoughts on that subject?"

"I had a good look at him this morning," said Carswell. "And really, I cannot draw any firm conclusions. Perhaps the widow will tell me something useful, if she lets me over her threshold, that is."

Giles laid the knife down on the table.

"I had better go and talk to Mr Johnson," he said.

"I hope you get a confession out of him!" said Carswell. "The sooner this is over, the better for all of us!"

"Is something wrong?" Giles said.

Carswell gazed at him and said, "On occasion you have told me, rightly, there is a time and a place for indulging in feelings and, tempting though it might be, I'm painfully aware that this is neither the time nor the place. Besides," he went on, "what good does it do? It changes nothing. There are some things that cannot be remedied, unfortunately."

"That does not mean they should not be spoken of," said Giles.

Carswell went to the door. "I shall ask the coroner for permission to do a post-mortem on Stuart, whatever Kennedy says. I need to settle the matter for myself and I do not think we can consider him an impartial witness."

He left, and Giles wondered if Carswell's feelings for Mrs Kennedy were causing him difficulty. It was not easy for any man to be confronted with an old love. The fire might have been extinguished but the ashes, white and apparently dead, could still conceal a burning ember.

Erik Johnson perfectly fitted the old chef's description of him: flaxen hair, a florid complexion and broad shoulders. He was also extremely hung over, and sat slumped at the table, looking even more dishevelled than Carswell.

"Tell me a little about yourself, Mr Johnson," Giles said when he had introduced himself. The young man stared at him. "Your occupation, for example?"

"Gentleman," he said, sitting up.

"I see," said Giles. "That includes getting into fights, does it? Are you not supposed to be at work in your mother's business in some capacity?"

"Would you care to be involved with that, sir?" said Johnson.

"It strikes me she has worked hard to make sure you never went hungry. Your behaviour is unkind to her, to say the least. I understand you moved to Stanegate because she felt you had fallen into bad company in Cheltenham."

"Is that what she said?" Giles nodded. "Not true. We came here because the game was up."

"Would you care to elaborate on that?"

"People began to realize they were being dunned," he said. "It happens every time. First in Bath, then in Tunbridge, then in Cheltenham. It all goes well, and then – it doesn't. So we pack up the circus and find some more fools." He rubbed his face. "If you want to put someone in a police cell and charge them, then I suggest you look to my dear Mama. She is a fraud, nothing more, nothing less. Why I am here, I don't know."

"You were drunk and disorderly," said Giles, "and apparently threatening someone with a hunting knife," he added, glancing through the notes Harris had given him. "John Perryman states you pressed the tip of the knife to his throat and told him you would not hesitate to kill him if he did not retract his words. Did he insult you?"

"I can't remember what he said, and I didn't do that," said Johnson. "That I do remember."

"But you were carrying a knife."

"Yes."

"Where did you get it?"

"Does that matter?"

"All right, why did you get it?" This question puzzled him. "You see, Mr Johnson, it's not only last night's escapade that has brought you to our attention. I am here to investigate the death of Captain Carrington. Perhaps your mother mentioned that to you?" The young man shuffled in his seat and nodded. "So can you explain to me why you have such a knife in your possession?"

"It's not against the law," he said.

"No, but holding it to a man's throat and saying you will use it, is," said Giles. "Now, if I had found you in a forest in Scotland, having just shot a deer, in possession of such a knife, then perhaps there would be no question to answer. But here?"

"It's just a knife. All the fellows carry them. You'd be a fool not to round here."

"So you bought the knife to be like the others?"

"Pretty much," said Johnson.

"And how did you feel when you learnt that your father was living here?" said Giles.

"What sort of question is that?" he said.

"Were you interested or annoyed? I don't suppose it could have been easy. Did you see him at all?"

"I may have done," Johnson said.

"And how were things between you?"

"How do you think?" Johnson said. Then he added, "And I'm not surprised he's dead. I can't say I liked him. Was I supposed to? Was I supposed to see him and feel like a lovesick girl or something?"

"Do you know why your mother decided to leave him?"

"You've met my mother, you can see what she's like," he said. "She likes to rule the roost, and I suppose that wasn't to his liking. A man has his pride. So he went his way and she went hers."

"There was no question of his taking responsibility for you and your sister?"

"My mother said she wouldn't take a penny from him, but I don't know if that was just to make it seem he'd offered and she'd refused. I don't think he did offer, though. Why should he? She left him. What did he owe her?"

"What did you talk about?"

"I don't know."

"Come now, Mr Johnson, you must have some idea."

"The weather and the Roman Baths."

"Money?"

"No," said Johnson.

"I doubt that," said Giles. "How much money does your mother give you?" The young man looked away. "Not enough for your tastes, I'm sure. This is an expensive town. I find it hard to believe there was no mention of the subject, given how prominent the Captain was here. Did you ask him for money?" Johnson did not answer. "You were seen quarrelling with him, Mr Johnson, on Sunday afternoon. I suggest you are straight with me. Did you ask him for money on that occasion?"

"Yes," he said, at last.

"And he refused you?"

"I didn't kill him," said Johnson, leaning forward. "If that is what you are thinking, you are wrong – I did not!"

Giles left the conversation at that, not giving his opinion one way or the other. He was not entirely convinced by Johnson's protestation of innocence, and wondered if a longer period in the cells would make him more forthcoming. He went back to Fitznorton.

"Anything of interest?" he said.

"Possibly," said Fitznorton. "Cuttings from an Irish newspaper – they report a case where the family have taken issue with the disposition of a will. The deceased, Henry Farrell, left all his fortune to his medical man – a Dr Kennedy of Ballycoghlan."

"And the family didn't like it?"

"No, they alleged that the will was changed under duress."

"From Kennedy?" Fitznorton nodded. "Did they win the case?"

"Seemingly not."

"Perhaps that explains why he left Ireland," said Giles, "with money to invest. And Carrington knew all about it. Very good work, Mr Fitznorton," he added. "That could well be significant." Even as he said it, he was thinking of Sukey, and what an unpleasant piece of information this was.

~

Catching sight of his reflection in the plate glass window of one of the shops in the Parade, Felix understood what had provoked the Major's mild suggestion that he shave. He took himself to the nearest barber's shop, having no wish at that moment to go back to The White Hart.

He was also in need of a haircut, something that he did not trust Jacob to do, so he charged the barber to shave him and trim his hair.

As he lay back in the chair and submitted to be soaped and scraped by the barber, he remembered how Sukey used to cut his hair. She was still the only person he had ever found who cut it to his liking. He recalled the particular pair of scissors she used, and how she had acted with a delicious mixture of timidity and boldness.

"That is a very fine head of hair you have there, sir," said the barber, now taking up his comb and scissors. "And perfect for the latest styles. Yes, I should be able to do something very à la mode with this, sir," he said.

"Just a trim, if you please," Felix said.

"Yes, yes, of course, sir," the barber said, and began. "A little here and there, certainly."

He began by laboriously snipping away tiny amounts and then, taking up a pot of pomade, proceeded with excruciating slowness to smother, smooth down and tweak every last lock into some pattern of his own devising.

"There," said the barber, finally standing back from his creation. He was obviously pleased. "Just as worn in Paris by all the gentlemen of distinction."

Felix gazed at the looking glass in disbelief. A foppish stranger sat before him, his hair slicked down and then pulled forward like the ears of a spaniel. It was beyond ridiculous. He was on the verge of asking the barber to begin again and amend his work, if it were possible, but decided he could not bear to idle in that chair a moment longer. He fumbled in his pocket for some coins and left the shop as fast as he could.

At the next shop window he came to, he tried to rearrange it with his fingers, but only succeeded in making it worse and covering his hands with the vile scented grease with which his hair was now coated. He was then obliged to go and buy a cravat. Here, he was certain that the supercilious shopman, eagerly pushing the most expensive Italian foulard (diamond weave and most exclusive) was laughing up his sleeve.

It was something of a relief to climb up the hill by the menagerie to the Rustic Cottages.

Mrs Stuart answered the door herself.

"I hope I'm not intruding," he said. "I wanted to see if there was anything I could do for you."

"It's kind of you to call," she said.

"I have a few more questions for you, as well, I'm afraid," he said.

"Of course. Please come in," she said.

He followed her into the house and she took him into a sitting room, fitted out like a plate from a house furnisher's catalogue, with strange-shaped chairs and sofas, upholstered in garish pink. Curiously, there was no carpet on the floor, just plain scrubbed boards. The blinds had been drawn and the diffused sunlight softened the gaudy wallpaper and made the curlicues and gilding less offensive. However, the room could never be called charming, and he felt for her having to endure her first widowhood in a place that was so definitely not a home.

She did not offer him a seat and remained standing herself, in the bay window, with the breeze flapping her skirts. He was about to speak when a curious braying began in the distance.

"The camels," she said. "Poor creatures. They do not have enough room in their stable and they often complain of it. There are half a dozen of them. Young males, all of them. It is cruel beyond measure."

"The place will have to be closed down after what happened to Captain Carrington."

"Good," she said. "One can see it in all their eyes, the

utter misery of the life they are forced to lead, for our so-called entertainment. The sooner it is shut, the better."

"The problem will be finding somewhere else for the animals, and I am afraid the leopards will probably have to be destroyed."

"Oh no, surely not?" she said. "How cruel!"

At this she went and sat down, as if exhausted.

"Are you alone here?" he felt he must ask.

"Yes," she said.

"You do not have a servant of some sort?"

"I manage very well on my own," she said. "I'm used to it. What did you want to ask me?"

He was glad she had prompted him, for his surprise at this admission had distracted him. What type of man had her husband been that could allow this? She was obviously not bred to such simplicity, neither did her appearance suggest it. It could not have been lack of money, for this cottage would not have come cheap, nor the opera box nor their elegant clothes. Had it been a fear of strangers? It was curious.

"I wanted to know more about the symptoms your husband described; his headaches, for example. Dr Kennedy will have some history of it, of course, but anything you have observed may be of help."

"In what way?"

"To establish the cause of death. May I ask, for example, when he first became ill?"

She looked down at her hands and considered.

"It was about sixteen months ago. We were living abroad. He began to have these prolonged headaches and some of his natural vitality seemed to leave him. He was always very active, but then he was sluggish. He hated to get up in the morning, complaining of tiredness, and when he did go about his usual pursuits, that exhausted him."

"Did he seek medical advice?"

She shook her head. "He did not like your profession; in

fact, I should say he disliked doctors intensely, and I regret to say I did not dare to suggest it, although I wanted him to see someone. I thought it was his eyes. He complained of blurry sight, but he would do nothing about it, in case he was prescribed eyeglasses. He was vain in that respect..." Her voice faltered at that, and she reached for her handkerchief. "Excuse me."

"I'm sorry, it must be hard to talk about this. Did he complain of nausea, or dizziness?"

"Yes, sometimes." She got up and went to the window, standing with her back to him. "There is something else. He seemed at times quite different in character. That was the hardest thing for me. He was not the man I thought he was. I feel I have lost a stranger."

At this point she was overcome, and began to sob. He helped her back to her chair, and left her, intending to find her something to drink. He went into the kitchen which lay at the back of the cottage. The fire in the hearth had gone out, lacking some diligent soul to tend to it. A pump in the adjoining scullery gave up some water after some vigorous cranking, and failing to find a glass, he filled a pink lustreware souvenir mug from the menagerie that was sitting on the kitchen table.

He went back to her and found her a little more composed. She sipped the water and said, "Might I see him?"

"Yes, of course."

"And will there have to be – you did say, last night, that there would have to be a –"

"A post-mortem? It's possible. It depends on what Dr Kennedy says. I should prefer there to be one, although I know that is hard for you."

"Why would you prefer it?"

"When a death comes on so suddenly, there are questions that must be answered," he said. "If you would like to come with me now, if you feel strong enough?"

"Yes, I will, thank you," she said, handing him back the mug and getting up.

She left the room, and he stared down at the faces of Moonshine and Mercury, in engraving form, pasted on the mug.

They walked down past the menagerie and he was able to find a cab to drive them the rest of the way to the Stanegate Infirmary, which lay on the other side of the town. He took her to the side room where the body had been placed, leaving her to say her farewells, and at once came face to face with Kennedy.

"Good morning," he said. Kennedy gave a curt nod. "The widow is with him," Felix added, indicating the room. "Perhaps we might have a word?"

There was an empty consulting room across the passageway and they went into it.

"What is your difficulty, then?" said Kennedy, laying his silk hat down on the table.

"What was your diagnosis?" said Carswell.

"Malignant inflammation of the heart," said Kennedy. "That it should have become terminal so abruptly was a surprise to me, I admit, but there again, there are precedents."

"In a man of thirty?" said Felix. "What did you make of the headaches?"

"Common enough in such cases," said Kennedy.

"Blurred vision?"

"Again, common enough. I had a patient, a woman, who died suddenly. She had a weak heart – there was a distinct murmur, and she suffered similar symptoms to those of Mr Stuart."

"Was there a post-mortem?"

"No, of course not," said Kennedy. "Your police work has made you suspicious."

"With good reason, I'm afraid."

"Are you looking for another murder?"

"I'm not looking for anything – that is always the worst approach in such cases, as I am sure you know. I am open to whatever the evidence suggests. With the greatest respect," Felix went on, feeling very little respect at this point, "there are questions here that need to be answered. Your diagnosis only adds to the puzzle, I'm afraid. It would be advisable to do a post-mortem."

"To what end? If the widow is satisfied with my explanation, and I am sure she will be, then why pursue the matter?"

"Are you not curious," said Felix, "that a man should just drop dead in such circumstances?"

"My observations of him satisfy my curiosity perfectly, sir," said Kennedy. "He was extremely frail. I may not have predicted such a demise, but it not so unusual. Perhaps you do not have enough practical experience to realise that."

"Perhaps we should both put our case to the coroner," said Felix.

"I have a great deal of pressing business," said Dr Kennedy. "It would be better to settle the matter now. Let us put it to the widow instead. In my experience a post-mortem is a great cruelty to those suffering a bereavement."

"Of course, I would hesitate to inflict it on anyone," said Felix, "but how can anything in medicine be advanced without easy recourse to such procedures?"

"Your Edinburgh training is all too evident," said Kennedy. "That was the city that spawned the body-snatchers, after all. All in the sacred name of science."

"And you don't hold science sacred?" said Felix. "You speak like a layman. Perhaps those who operate an elaborate establishment puffing that fraud Priessnitz's system are better called that!"

Felix was aware that even as he had spoken, he had crossed a line, but everything about Kennedy infuriated him. That his blow had struck hard was all too evident from the way that the man stiffened, and he looked as if he was about to deliver a withering riposte when the door was pushed open and a nurse came in, enquiring bluntly which of them was Mr Carswell.

"I am," he replied.

"There's a boy just come in with his head smashed half open," she said. "Mr Taylor is not here. Can you look at it, sir? It's more than the dresser can deal with it."

Felix followed her at once, glad to have escaped any further words with Kennedy, and grateful to be able to channel his anger into something useful, for it soon emerged that all his skill and knowledge would be necessary.

The boy was in a horrendous state, having collided with a hook hanging on a hoist in his father's workshop. The parents had come with him, and were in despair, as was the dresser, who seemed to have forgotten everything he had ever learnt. Felix was forced to take complete control of the situation, thankfully aided by one of the nurses who had some wit about her. It was a long and complex process to repair what he could of the boy's fragile skull, but he felt Mr Harper himself would have been pleased with the result. He only wished he had recourse to Hamilton and his magical ether.

When at last the boy was in a satisfactory condition and Taylor, the Infirmary surgeon, had appeared, Felix could stand down. It was two in the afternoon, and he was tired and extremely hungry. An orderly managed to find some tea and a bit of bread and cheese for him and he sat in a side room to consume them. Alone with his thoughts, he found himself longing for Sukey, as he had not done since those agonising days when they had first parted. He wanted her to come into the room and smile at him, and then perhaps sit and drink tea, and make idle, pointless conversation, as they had often done. He leant back in his chair, staring up at the badly distempered ceiling, and wondered again how on earth she had come to marry Kennedy. That, of all the puzzles that confronted him, was still the most mysterious.

Chapter Seventeen

They were just passing by the railway station when Giles noticed an open landau in a familiar livery, and a few moments later, in the bustle of the crowd emerging from the newly arrived train, he saw the unmistakable figure of Lord Rothborough, accompanied by his eldest daughter, Lady Charlotte.

Giles hurried forward to make himself known to them. Lord Rothborough saw him at the same moment and they greeted each other with all the pleasure of old friends.

"This is good luck," said Lord Rothborough. "I take it you're here on business?"

Giles saw him glance at Fitznorton with interest.

"Yes," Giles said. "Lady Charlotte, my lord, may I present Mr Edward Fitznorton of the Home Office. Mr Fitznorton, Lady Charlotte Haraald and Lord Rothborough."

"Mr Fitznorton, good to know you," said Lord Rothborough, shaking his hand. "I had heard you were interested in Major Vernon's line of work, from Sir James Ainsworth." It was no surprise to Giles that Lord Rothborough was aware of Mr Fitznorton.

"Yes, my lord, he has been encouraging me," said Fitznorton.

"He knows talent when he sees it," said Lord Rothborough. "And you could not be in better hands, though I suspect whatever it is that brings you here will not be edifying."

"No," said Giles. "It is not. We are looking into the death of Captain Carrington."

"Heavens! Have you any idea who is behind it, yet?"

"No, it's a bit of a tangle, to say the least."

"That doesn't surprise me," said Lord Rothborough, "given the dealings I have had with him."

"Then we should discuss that further," Giles said. "As a matter of fact, we were just going to The White Hart. We have a family party at hand – Mrs Vernon and the Ffordes are here for the opera, as well as Mrs Carswell and Miss King. I take it you are on your way to Holbroke?"

"Yes, but there is no urgency. Let's go. Carrington – well, yes, that deserves a conversation, certainly!"

So they climbed into Lord Rothborough's carriage and set off for The White Hart, while their luggage, James Bodley and Lady Charlotte's maid departed in a second carriage for Holbroke.

"The opera – it is Bartelozzi and his company?" said Lord Rothborough. "Maria has told me all about them."

"We went last night," said Giles. "They were good, at least from what we managed to see of it. There was an incident. I hope we shall see the whole of Mary Stuart tonight. Or is it Mary Queen of Scots?"

"Maria Stuarda," said Lady Charlotte. "Do you like the opera, Mr Fitznorton?"

"I don't think I have enough experience of it to judge whether I care for it or not. But I have to say, from what I saw last night –" He hesitated. "I expected something different, and it was – well, enjoyable, certainly."

"If you have no experience of opera," said Lady Charlotte, "you are lucky to have such an introduction to it. You will have to be careful, though; it might make you into a fervent devotee."

"You are indeed lucky, Mr Fitznorton," said Lord Rothborough. "There is a great deal of caterwauling and boredom that passes for opera. So, what was the incident?"

"A man in the audience died, unfortunately," said Giles.

"Oh, poor man," said Lady Charlotte. "Oh dear, how

horrid. What was the cause of it? Do you know?"

"Mr Carswell was not sure. We are waiting to hear from his doctor before speaking to the coroner."

"George Boothroyd, that is?" said Lord Rothborough.

"Yes."

"He is an excellent man," said Lord Rothborough. "And I dare say he could not resist asking you to play cricket, Mr Fitznorton?"

Giles smiled at Lord Rothborough's apparent omniscience in matters local and national. It was something to wonder at.

"Oh, so you are a cricketer, Mr Fitznorton?" said Lady Charlotte.

"Mr Fitznorton is a Cambridge Blue," said Lord Rothborough.

"Do you like cricket, Lady Charlotte?" said Fitznorton.

"I must parrot your reply to my enquiry about opera," said Charlotte. "I don't have enough experience of it to judge. But I do think it looks splendid from a distance. Do you play, Major Vernon?"

"Not for many years," said Giles. "And even then I was liable to drop catches, and never could manage to hit more than a four."

"You will have to explain to me what that means," said Lady Charlotte.

"You must ask my niece," said Giles. "She is at The White Hart with her parents. She knows the rules better than I do."

They had reached the hotel now, and went up to the Ffordes' rooms where Celia and her parents were drinking tea.

"Emma has gone to gaze at the shops with Mrs Carswell," said Sally.

"I wonder if Mrs Carswell will persuade her to try the Idunnic Chamber," said Giles.

"Yes, what on earth was that?" said Canon Fforde.

"Apparently a piece of expensive nonsense," said Sally. "Mr Carswell was warm on the subject."

"Oh, yes," said Celia. "Mrs Carswell said that ladies take their clothes off and –"

"Celia!" said her mother.

"Absorb the magnetic forces," she went on, unconcernedly, "which the chamber concentrates. Apparently the walls are lined with silver and crystals! It sounds so pretty. I wish I could try it."

"I think, Celia, we should go for our walk," said Sally. "Would you care to come with us, Lady Charlotte?"

"Yes, very much," said Lady Charlotte. "I am longing for a walk after the train. And you can explain the rules of cricket, Miss Fforde."

"I shall take a turn myself," said Canon Fforde. "I expect you gentlemen have business to discuss. I imagine you must have known the late Captain, Lord Rothborough?"

"Indeed. What a strange development," said Lord Rothborough.

Lady Charlotte was examining the playbill lying on the table.

"I see they are giving Norma," she said.

"Would you like join us?" said Canon Fforde.

"Yes, do, Lady Charlotte," said Sally. "You would be doing me a kindness. We are taking Celia to school tomorrow morning, and after that I shall be bereft."

"Oh no, Mama, you won't be," said Celia.

"I should love to!" said Lady Charlotte. "Papa, may I?"

"Of course," said Lord Rothborough.

"And you will join us?" said Canon Fforde.

"Not on this occasion. I can manage without Druidical tragedies at the moment," said Lord Rothborough. "But perhaps you might bring her back to me at Holbroke on Sunday, and I can prevail on you to stay a few nights? It has been too long since you were there."

"I can see no reason why not," said Canon Fforde. "Thank you, my lord."

"Excellent!"

The ladies and Canon Fforde went on their walk, and Giles, Lord Rothborough and Fitznorton repaired to the coffee room, which was fortunately empty. Giles briefly explained the circumstances of Carrington's death.

"You've spoken to Tait, I take it?" said Lord Rothborough.

"Yes, he told me you were anxious to buy the menagerie land."

"I tried and failed," said Lord Rothborough. "As with Carr's Crag. That has been a great mystery to us, how he got hold of the land and then developed it. Carrington cannot have done that alone, if he is the prime mover behind it."

"Who owned it before this?"

"An old gentleman farmer called Robinson. Very respectable, but the estate was not entailed, and his daughter's husband has no interests in the county and disposed of it. I was extremely annoyed when I heard of it. I should have given him a fair price for it, and now the place has been defaced with those terrible houses."

"You can't think who might have wanted that land, other than Carrington? Or someone who was prepared to lease it to Carrington for development?" said Giles.

"There is one name that comes to my mind," said Lord Rothborough, "although I have not mentioned this to Tait, for it has just been a suspicion of mine: the widow Amberleigh."

"The widow of the Earl of Amberleigh?"

"Her son is still in his minority and she has a great deal too much influence over his guardian and trustee. More than influence, if you guess my meaning." He glanced at Fitznorton, and Giles – recalling this lady's name from an incident a few years past – guessed that Lord Rothborough would like the conversation to take a more confidential turn.

He turned to Fitznorton and said, "I have just remembered something, Mr Fitznorton. Might I ask a favour of you? Would you go back to the station house and see if any of those papers relate to the tenancy of Laburnum Cottage? I know it is a great deal to ask, on top of what you have already done."

"No, sir, it will be no trouble at all," said Fitznorton, getting up. "Do you want me to bring them here?"

"No, I shall be coming back there myself presently," said Giles. "Thank you."

"Good day to you, Mr Fitznorton," said Lord Rothborough.

"And to you, my lord," Fitznorton said, and departed.

"You have him trained already," said Lord Rothborough when he had gone.

"Mr Carswell thinks he is a machine, and there is something in that. He is happy to do the most trivial tasks, which in the circumstances is extremely useful, and I am exploiting him without any shame."

"You know his family comes from the circle around Dr Waterbury, the Rector of Fulham?"

"No, and that signifies?"

"Ultra-evangelical. Practically dissenters."

"I see. That explains why he doesn't drink."

"Very likely. They are all idealistic, principled, energetic for reform and entirely admirable in many respects, but they are difficult to deal with, I always find. They cannot seem to understand that the rest of us are deeply flawed and cannot change."

"Or will not, perhaps?" said Giles.

"There is something in that," said Lord Rothborough. "I'm glad you sent him away. What I am about to tell you – well, it's not for such innocent ears. It's mortifying. Lady Amberleigh and I were at one time – you catch my meaning?" Giles nodded. "We did not part as friends. She is not a forgiving woman, and she is a lover of intrigue."

"A dangerous combination," said Giles.

"Exactly. And I have heard that she is overly involved with her son's guardian, Sir Henry Boynton. He is ten years younger than she is, and I suspect she has him thoroughly in her power. I know what she is capable of, and I know Boynton a little. I cannot imagine him resisting her, in any respect."

Giles sat back, drained his coffee cup and considered what Lord Rothborough had said.

"Are you sure she would go to such lengths?"

"I can't be sure," said Rothborough. "But it may have influenced her to invest in Carr's Crag. Perhaps I'm not thinking straight, for I'm still angry about what has been done up there. I would like nothing better than to raze those wretched cottages to the ground, a fact of which she must be perfectly aware."

"How?"

"Because – my vanity does not like to remember this – but we had a conversation once about the duties and responsibilities of landowners. I was telling her how she ought to guide her son, and that there is often a larger good to be considered than mere profit, and she laughed at me, and told me, rightly enough, that I was lucky to be in the position to preach because my ancestors had done all the unpleasant grasping for me. She said she could not afford such niceties on behalf of her boy, that it was her duty as a mother to increase his rent roll as much as she could. Developing Carr's Crag in partnership with the likes of Carrington strikes me as just the kind of scheme she would thoroughly enjoy, especially as she will have heard that we attempted to buy the Crag from the late Mr Robinson. But of course, this is all speculation, and what use to you it may be, I can't say."

"Carrington was a blackmailer," said Giles. "We are trying to ascertain how it is related to his business affairs. I have a theory that he persuaded his victims to invest in his schemes here. But if that has anything to do with the actual commission of his murder, it is impossible to fathom at this stage. However, I like to open my ears to all possibilities. What sort of man is Sir Henry Boynton?"

"Decorative," said Lord Rothborough. "You know the type, I'm sure. Utterly unsuited to the work. His elder brother Thomas was supposed to be trustee – he was an able fellow, but he died not long before Amberleigh did, so the brother inherited the post. Possibly at my lady's request, for she knew she could control him."

"And where are the Amberleigh estates in relation to Stanegate?"

"To the north-east of here. The principal house, Amberleigh Castle, is about five miles away, but the estate runs close to the edges of Stanegate, in places. It's a very impressive piece of property."

The door opened and Madame Jacquot came in, but on seeing them she hesitated at the door.

"Excuse me, my lord," she said, dropping a curtsey. "I did not know you were here."

"Ah, madame!" Rothborough said, getting up. "How good to see you. Business flourishing, I trust?"

"Very much so," said Madame Jacquot. "The opera has seen to that. One can hope it all lasts," she added with a glance at Giles. "Is there any news?"

"Not yet, madame," said Giles. "I'm afraid I shall need my room for a few more days."

"It is a shame Madame Vernon cannot stay with you. She was saying to me this morning that she must go back to Northminster today."

"Unfortunately, yes," said Giles.

"What do you make of Carrington's death, madame?" said Rothborough.

"I hardly know, my lord. It is horrific, certainly. Do you have a theory? You told me of your meeting him and not liking him, that I do remember."

"So I did, madame," said Lord Rothborough. "Yes, it was disagreeable. I was just coming to that, Vernon – you will think I was trying to conceal it from you."

"That I doubt, my lord," said Giles smiling. "I wonder, madame, if we might order some more coffee?"

"Of course," she said, and left them.

"Disagreeable?" said Giles. "Do you think he might have had something against you?"

"I don't know. The whole meeting was curious. I felt at a distinct disadvantage, although there was nothing at stake, ostensibly. But now you have said that, I wonder if she said something to him."

"We don't know whether they knew each other," Giles said.

"No, and I hope there is nothing in my suspicions, but I certainly think she could be meddling in property acquisition here against my interests."

"In the light of Carrington's death, it would be interesting to see if she knew him. Do you think there are things he may have used against her?"

"That," said Lord Rothborough, "is a question in itself. He may know about her and Boynton, for example."

"They are definitely involved?"

"I find it hard to think they are not. But that young man may be more of a saint than I was."

Chapter Eighteen

Giles returned to the station house and was surprised to find that Fitznorton was not there. Such a diversion from his usual diligence was curious, but Giles was not prepared to be annoyed by it, given that it gave him a chance to look over Carrington's papers for himself. He felt that Fitznorton had been protecting them, like a hen defending her eggs.

His conversation with Lord Rothborough had given him some new possibilities. If Lady Amberleigh and her son's guardian were entangled, and Carrington knew about it, they were as likely candidates for blackmail as any. Had the gaining of the development lease on Carr's Crag anything to do with that? On what terms had it been let?

Fitznorton came in after five minutes, carrying some bulky parcels.

"Excuse me, sir," he said. "I took the liberty of doing some shopping." He put the parcels down, and looked at his watch. "I was an hour and ten minutes, so I will, of course, make that up in due course."

"That won't be necessary," said Giles. "What did you buy?"

"Cricket kit," said Fitznorton. "Finding a pair of suitable boots was no easy task and these are a slight risk, being ready-made. I like them well broken in, generally, but necessity demands an experiment."

"Ah yes, the match," Giles said. "Now who is playing, again?" he added, trying to recall the conversation with the coroner.

"The Earl of Amberleigh's men," said Fitznorton, taking a paper from his pocket. "Mr Boothroyd kindly answered my enquiries about them. Know one's enemy."

"Quite," said Giles.

"It should be an interesting encounter. The Earl of Amberleigh himself has just finished at Eton, and opened the batting for them against Harrow this year. He is an impressive player. He made forty-two with very little difficulty – he has a nice, stylish action, but Rumford's bowling got the better of him. He is the man to watch, certainly."

"You know him?"

"Rumford?"

"No, young Amberleigh."

"No. Only of him, and I saw him play, of course. And his guardian –"

"Sir Henry Boynton?" Giles said.

"Yes, he is the Boynton who made ninety-seven not out against Cambridge in '34. I shall be interested to see him play."

"So shall I. You haven't come across any mention of the Amberleigh estates here, have you?"

"No, I don't think so. I presume it is what Lord Rothborough alluded to?"

"Very much so, and this cricket match is fortuitous. Perhaps the dowager herself will come to watch."

"So you believe there may be some connection with the Captain's death?"

"Reputation is everything to such families," said Giles. "If he was pressing them, then there may be something in it. But we will go gently. Now, Laburnum Cottage?"

"Of course, sir, I will get to it at once."

Giles left him and went downstairs, where Erik Johnson was still languishing in his cell. Sitting on the bench, he gazed up miserably at Giles as he came in.

"Inspector Harris is putting you up before the magistrate this afternoon," said Giles. He sat down beside him and said gently, "Have you anything more you wish to say to me? About your father?"

Johnson stared down at his clasped hands.

"What is it you want?" he said. "A confession?"

"Have you something you want to say to me?" Giles said. "Tell me what happened that day when you met him by the menagerie."

"We argued," said Johnson. "I can't deny that. He said – you, see I didn't ask for money. Not like I said earlier."

"So what did you ask for?"

"I asked him for a job," said Johnson. "That's all. I thought I could make something of myself. When we came here, and I realised it was him, that he was behind it all: those Roman Baths and the crowds, and all the money coming into the place, I felt I wanted to be part of it. I wanted to be Carrington, not Johnson, that's all. I wished I could use his name and not feel ashamed of who I was."

"So what was his answer?"

"He said no. I might have been a beggar asking for a penny. He made me feel –"

"Angry?"

"Yes, yes, of course! And yes, I shouted at him, and he told me to go away and not make a nuisance of myself. He said I wasn't to have expectations of any sort. So I told him it was my right, that I could call myself Carrington and tell the whole town who I was, and how would he like that? He said I could do what I liked, that making such threats would make no difference to anything. He said that when my mother left, she sealed my fate, and I could take it up with her. I could scarcely believe it. I know I'm not a son a father could be proud of, but he obviously felt nothing."

"You must have been wretched," said Giles. "That was no way to be treated."

"No, it was not!" said Johnson, springing up. "And I told him so, but he just walked away."

"Which way was he going?"

"He went up the hill," said Johnson. "And before you

ask, I thought of running after him, and pulling him down and giving him a good kicking, yes, I did! But I didn't, and I didn't kill him either! I know where you are trying to lead me, but I won't be led! I did not kill him. What would be the point of going to the gallows for a man who didn't give a damn about me? Yes, I'm glad he's dead, that I can't deny, but I went away that day and decided I wouldn't have anything to do with him again, that he was a lost cause. So no, I am not going to confess to anything."

"Why did you threaten John Perryman last night?" Giles said.

Johnson, who was now leaning against the cell wall as if it were the only means he could stand upright, said, "He called me a bastard." He closed his eyes. "I was angry, yes, but not with him, not really. I was still angry about – that man. I can't even call him my father, can I?"

"Where did you get the knife?"

"I bought it yesterday morning. From Brown's in Franklin Street."

"Yesterday?"

"He will tell you I did."

"We shall check that, certainly."

"Do you not believe me? I did not kill him. I didn't have the knife until yesterday. Isn't that proof enough for you?"

"There are other knives, Mr Johnson," said Giles, getting up. "Perhaps you went to replace one that you had lost."

He left the interview at that and went upstairs, where he found Carswell.

He had shaved and put on a cravat, but his hair now looked like a newly made stook of hay.

"I need you to speak to the coroner," he said. "He does not consider the circumstances of Stuart's death justify a post-mortem. Kennedy has spoken to him, of course, and he was against it as well – which I cannot like! You can talk him round, I am sure of it."

"Did you speak to the coroner yourself?" said Giles, wondering if this burst of passion from Carswell had influenced the matter.

"No, I have had no opportunity," said Carswell. "I was with Kennedy at the Infirmary and then they asked me to assist in a case, so I was only able to scribble a note, and so Kennedy carries off the widow to see him in my absence, and now it is to be recorded as a natural death, and –" He broke off and was about to push his hand through his hair in his characteristic fashion, but then stopped, made an angry gesture with his hand and muttered, "That damned barber and his grease!" He then went and sat down on one of the benches in the passageway. "I have to go back to the Infirmary. I am not happy with my patient. Will you speak to Boothroyd?"

"Yes, of course, but if Kennedy has given him a sensible argument, what can I add?" said Giles. "There is nothing overtly suspicious about the man's death, is there?"

"No," said Carswell.

"And you saw nothing when you visited Mrs Stuart to arouse any suspicion?"

"No," Carswell said again.

"Then what am I to say?"

"I don't know," he said. "The worst of it is that I cannot know unless I'm permitted to do a post-mortem. She spoke to me of headaches and a change of character, of blurry vision. That is what is nagging at me. I want to see if there is any structural cause to it."

"A medical question, then, rather than criminal?" Giles said.

Fitznorton came out into the hallway before Carswell could respond.

"I have found that lease, sir," he said. "And yes, the landlord is the Amberleigh estates."

"Amberleigh?" said Carswell, getting up. "Where do I know that name from – oh."

"Yes, indeed," said Giles.

"Is she mixed up in this?" he said.

"It's possible," Giles said.

"Lord Rothborough will not like that."

"I have spoken to him about it," said Giles.

"He's here?"

Giles nodded. "En route for Holbroke. But he was on his way to Tait's office when I last saw him, and will be back at The White Hart later."

Carswell reached for his hat and bag.

"I'd better get back to the Infirmary," he said.

"Do you still want me to speak to Mr Boothroyd?" said Giles.

"No, I should go myself," said Carswell. "I need to martial my arguments better, I suspect."

"Will you be going to The White Hart?"

"It depends. This boy – it's not a simple matter. Would you explain to my Lord –"

"Of course."

"Thank you," said Carswell, and departed.

"So what should I do now, Major Vernon?" said Fitznorton.

"Let's go to The Fox and Grapes and find Jack Rivington," said Giles. "And before that, I want to try and buy a knife."

~

Brown the ironmonger confirmed that Erik Johnson had bought his expensive knife the previous morning.

"He'd been eyeing it up for a few days, but he didn't have the cash until yesterday," he said.

"Did he say where he got the cash?"

"I know he runs with a bad crowd," said Mr Brown. "His mother told me."

"Gambling?" Giles said.

"Aye, that sort of thing. The dice, she said," Brown added with a shake of his head.

"And this is the only occasion he has bought anything like this from you?"

"Yes."

They left and went to find The Fox and Grapes. This was situated up a remote lane in a yard, and had a quiet appearance about it that made Giles instantly suspicious. It consisted of a room, with a counter in the corner, and a few tables and stools, as well as a settle by a meagre fire. Here an old man sat sucking on a pipe, and seeing them come in, he called out, "Missus!"

The missus now appeared at the counter from the back room. She was a diminutive, sharp-eyed woman, who at once asked them their business.

"And you are, ma'am?" Giles asked, having stated his credentials.

"Magilligan," she said, and then with emphasis, "Miss Magilligan."

"We are looking for Jack Rivington," Giles said.

"And what makes you think you will find him here?" she said.

"But you know him?" She nodded. "We are investigating the death of Victor Morgueillon."

"I heard he killed himself," she said. "What's there to investigate?"

"Who he was mixed up with – which seems to be Jack Rivington. I understand there were debts to be settled. Debts run up in dice games in this establishment, perhaps."

She considered the point.

"Happen you should talk to them, missus," said the old man by the fire. "He don't owe you anything."

"Be quiet, you daft old fool!" she exclaimed. "What do you know?"

"More than you think," he said, tapping his nose, "and that Jack, he's got the mark of the gallows on him, that much I can say."

"And why would you say that?" said Giles, turning to the old man.

"Don't listen to him," said Miss Magilligan. "He knows nothing."

"But you clearly know something." She sighed, flipped up the counter and signalled that they were to follow her into the other room. This was a kitchen, as cheerful as the other room had been bare. Two small, rough-coated dogs lay asleep on a rag-rug in front of the hearth. She gathered one up and sat down with it in her lap.

"I know Rivington," she said, "but what he does is nothing to do with me."

"But he organises gambling here?"

"Aye," she said, and then added, "but it isn't anything to do with me. I couldn't stop it if I tried, could I? I'd lose half my trade. And it's small stuff, nothing worth shedding blood over."

This struck him as a strange thing to say. So he went and sat down opposite her, and reached down and scratched the exposed belly of the dog that remained on the hearth rug.

"How much would be worth shedding blood for?" he said.

"A figure of speech," she said. "Watch yourself, or she'll nip you."

"Does Erik Johnson come here?" Giles asked.

"Maybe."

"That means yes, I take it?" he said. She nodded. "Did Johnson know Morgueillon?"

"I think so," she said.

"And you have seen them together?"

She looked down in annoyance as the bitch on the rug rolled ecstatically and demanded more fussing.

"They have been here from time to time," she said. "That young Johnson is a cocky one, and the Frenchman was trouble, surely enough. No, I don't like it," she said. "I can't stop it, can I? Men will have their fun."

"And what form does this fun take?"

"Dice," she said. "And whether Jack has them straight or not I couldn't tell you. Perhaps sometimes he plays fair, perhaps other times he doesn't."

"But you don't ask him to leave?"

"He brings me trade."

"And when he isn't here, where will I find Jack?"

"I've no idea where he lodges here, but I can tell you where he is now," she said.

"Yes?"

"Ireland," she said. "Somewhere near Cork. He has family there. Left on Tuesday morning. Gone to a wedding, he said."

~

"So," Emma said, as they sat drinking tea at The White Hart, "there will be no hope of you coming home soon?"

"No, unless I have some startling new information," Giles said. The truth was, he was feeling frustrated. Erik Johnson had been bound over to keep the peace and released. "There is so much going on here, I feel at sea with it. Perhaps you could steal away again next week?"

"Too tempting," said Emma. "I could grow accustomed to this sybaritic life. The shops are full of lovely things!"

"Even Mr Fitznorton has succumbed," said Giles.

"Yes, we met him on our walk, laden with parcels."

"Cricket kit," said Giles.

"So he said, but I suspect gloves, cravats and eau de cologne for his handkerchiefs."

"No?"

"What else does a man buy when he is wooing?" said Emma.

"Wooing?" said Giles. "Fitznorton?"

"Charlotte," said Emma.

"No," he said, "surely not."

He glanced across the room. Fitznorton was talking earnestly at Lord Rothborough, while Charlotte was nearby, deep in conversation with Celia.

"You said he was ambitious," Emma said.

"Yes, but –"

"I'm not saying he will succeed," she said, laying her hand on his arm. "Simply that he may attempt it."

He found he was a little tender on the point, and wondered if Emma was teasing or testing him, for she knew that Charlotte had admired him. But that was too fantastical. She would not say such a thing unless she had glimpsed at some possibility.

"Perhaps, but I can't imagine anything coming of it," said Giles. "His opinion of women in general leaves something to be desired."

"Harsh words," said Emma, smiling. The clock on the mantel struck the hour. "Oh," she said, "is that the time already?"

"Unfortunately," he said, getting up and putting his hand out to her. "You don't want to miss the train."

"No, but it will be at the expense of missing everything else!" she said.

Chapter Nineteen

Returning to the Infirmary, Felix determined that his patient was stable but in need of a watchful eye. His intention to remain there the rest of the afternoon was soon noticed by the matron, and he was asked to look at a great many more small cases that had arisen in the absence of the usual attending physician.

"He will be out with his guns and his dogs over the moor after the hares on a day like this," she said, shaking her head. "He cares more for breeding his dogs than this place. But truth be told, we are better off without him, mostly, and Mr Evans" – this was the dresser – "is learning fast. But today, it has been one thing after another, sir, and it's as well you are here to help us."

"How was he appointed?" said Felix.

"I don't know, sir – how are any of these things managed?" she said. "It's a mystery to me." They had reached the door to the women's ward and the conversation turned necessarily to other matters.

By the end of the afternoon, when he judged it safe to leave, he was tired and not much in the mood for a dinner party and the opera, but the thought of some intelligent conversation with Hamilton spurred him.

He got back to The White Hart and scrambled into his evening clothes with the assistance of Jacob, who could not resist telling him that he was late. It cost Felix a great deal not to shout at him, and he went down to the private dining room in a state of some agitation.

He found them all at the table, with the soup served. Eleanor rose at the sight of him and exclaimed, "Oh, Felix, whatever happened to your hair?" before bursting out laughing.

"The barbers here are not be trusted," he said. "It's probably just as well, for the Infirmary was crawling with lice and this stuff must have repelled them!"

"Surely not?" said Mrs Fforde.

"It's in an appalling state of disorganisation and the physician in charge is more interested in hare coursing."

"Yes, I have been wondering about that myself," said Hamilton.

"Have you met the man?" said Felix, sitting down. Hamilton shook his head. "He should be thoroughly ashamed of himself," Felix went on, filling his glass. "I expect it's a good stipend as well."

"Major Vernon told us about the poor little boy. He will be all right?" said Miss Hamilton, who was sitting next to him.

"I hope so," said Felix. "I shall go back after the theatre."

"His poor parents," she said. "I often think, when James is treating children, it is the parents who suffer more. It makes one wonder how anyone manages to be a mother or a father."

"It is certainly a terrifying prospect," said Felix, filling his glass.

"Oh, I'm sorry, I should not have said that," she said, flushing, "given that Mrs Carswell is – I have guessed right?" Felix nodded. "Oh, dear, I am too blunt!"

"No, you are a proper Scotswoman," said Felix, raising his glass to her. "And we are not being particularly coy about it. I don't have much time for that, to be honest."

"I wish you both luck and happiness, then," she said, raising her own glass to him.

She spoke with a warm, civil sincerity, but for a moment he could not respond. Across the table, Eleanor was now chattering to Canon Fforde in her usual animated fashion. She looked, it could not be denied, utterly beautiful: her glowing red hair full of leaves and flowers, her neck and shoulders bare, her neckline more than hinting at her fuller breasts. She had begun to adapt her dress to accommodate her now visibly swelling stomach, and it gave her a timeless look, as if she were a representation of eternal maternity on a monument. He glanced at Miss King, who was looking equally elegant in her own quiet way, and his mind travelled back to the sight of the pair of them the previous evening. Had it all been fancy on his part? He could not settle the question.

"Thank you," he said, and turned his attention to his soup.

Dinner proceeded and Felix was gratified to see Hamilton properly appreciated by his friends. Miss King was particularly lively in recounting the miracle of her tooth extraction, and eager to proclaim him the hero of the hour. Perhaps she was feeling something more than gratitude. He had never observed her inclined to flirt, but there was something about the way she was looking and smiling when Hamilton talked of his ideas, that gave Felix pause. That Hamilton was responding to this was also noticeable. He was, after all, a man looking for a wife, and Miss King, sensible and clever, could be the sort of woman he liked.

After dinner, they walked to the Opera House, and, when they got to their box, Hamilton pointedly asked if Miss King would sit between his sister and himself. Finding his own place at the back of the box, Felix gave this comedy more attention than the overture, and would have taken some pleasure in it, had he not noticed Eleanor glancing uneasily at them, as the chorus of Elizabethan courtiers burst out with enthusiasm and the opera began. She looked for all the world as if she had been deserted.

Their eyes met, and she indicated she wanted her wrap, so he pulled his chair closer to hers and put the shawl about her shoulders. She grabbed his hand and pressed it fervently, evidently in need of comfort, and he could hardly refuse her, although it troubled him that such a tiny act of desertion by

Miss King could prove so significant.

The opera rolled on, splendidly but foolishly, with the Earl of Leicester declaring his undying love for Mary, Queen of Scots, and the facts of history being the real victim of the piece. Eleanor seemed to lose herself in the action, while Felix leant back and wondered what it would mean to them if Miss King and Hamilton were to marry. Eleanor would be bereft and he was not sure he could deal with that. She was necessary to them both, that was clear enough, but the form that necessity took, the aspect he had glimpsed last night in Eleanor's flushed complexion, was extremely disturbing to contemplate.

The interval came at last, and the champagne and the ices with it. Aware that he was of a mind to drink himself stupid out of sheer agitation, he declined a glass and said, "I will go down to the Infirmary now. I really shouldn't be here."

"Oh, Felix, must you?" said Eleanor, gazing up at him.

"Jenny will be here," he said, using her Christian name for the first time.

"Yes, of course," said Miss King, slipping into his place. "That little boy – you must see to him."

He was not sure if this was obedience or preference on her part – perhaps a mixture of the two – and he was glad to close the door of the box behind him. He stood in the passageway staring down at the carpet, which was virulent in colour and pattern. He had not noticed the pattern the night before when Richard Stuart had lain there, with his widow weeping over him.

He glanced up and saw Major Vernon, the Ffordes and Fitznorton coming along the passageway, to take their share of champagne and ices as had been arranged previously. As a result he was obliged to play footman and hold the door open.

"You're not coming in?" said the Major.

"I'm going to the Infirmary," Felix said.

"That boy will owe you a great debt," he said, closing the

door to the box and remaining outside.

"It's not just that," said Felix. "I need – I don't need to be here, that's all. Dear God, this carpet – it would give anyone a migraine. By the way, there was no carpet at the Stuarts' cottage, since we are on the subject of carpets. And no servants. I meant to mention it earlier. A strange couple, certainly."

"That is odd," said Major Vernon.

"I'd better go," said Felix, and hurried away.

~

The opera ended with a heart-rending aria from Mary, reproaching the Earl of Leicester for leading her to the scaffold. La Fiorella surpassed herself, bringing the audience to their feet, and Giles wished Emma could have stayed to see it. Not only had the music and the drama been delightful, but there was even more pleasure in seeing Celia's face as she hung on every note and gesture of the great soprano, with a still-childish intensity but also with the understanding of a young woman.

"Oh, my hands are sore with clapping!" she exclaimed. "Why cannot I stay and hear Norma?" she said, turning to her father. "It is so unfair!"

"It's a great pity," said Lamb. "But we have seen Fiorella at her peak tonight. That role was made for her. She will be tired tomorrow. You will have had the best of her."

"I suppose so," said Celia. "Oh, poor Queen Mary!"

"Poor Queen Elizabeth, I should say," said Sally, "to have to make such an impossible decision, to have that burden on her shoulders, knowing that something so momentous must be done, and that she would be hated for it."

"And all for the good of the nation," said Mr Fitznorton.

"Yes, Mrs Fforde, I agree with you. She is the real heroine of history. A remarkable woman."

Celia yawned. "Oh, please excuse me, Mr Fitznorton, I was not yawning at you."

"I think we should get you back to bed," said Sally. "Perhaps you will sleep better tonight."

"I hope so," said Lamb. "Tomorrow will be exhausting for all of us. Come!"

They made their way downstairs through the crowds, Fitznorton at Giles' side.

"I'm surprised," Fitznorton was saying, "that something that departed so much from historical truth could be so diverting."

"That is the power of music for you, Mr Fitznorton," Lamb said. "And if you enjoyed that, you will be confounded by Norma, I can assure you. It is a much better piece."

"Oh, why can I not see it!" Celia said. "And I am going to miss the cricket at well!"

"Perhaps there will be cricket at school," Giles said.

"I hope so," she said.

"If they do not, you should suggest it," said Giles.

"I don't know if I could be so brave," said Celia.

"Ladies have always played cricket," said Giles. "I can't see how they could object."

"What do you think of young ladies playing cricket, Mr Fitznorton?" said Celia.

"I think it is excellent exercise, Miss Fforde, if done properly."

"I always bowl overarm, you know," she said, and then darted off to speak to Mrs Carswell, as if she knew he might remonstrate with her on the point.

"I wonder why Mr Carswell did not come back," said Sally. "That poor child –"

"I think I will go and find him," said Giles, and having said good night to everyone, turned towards the Infirmary.

The injured boy was sleeping soundly and in no immediate danger, though his head was swathed in monstrous layers of bandages. His mother was sleeping on the floor. The nurse guarding the door told him that Mr Carswell had been in for some time and had gone to look at the other cases, but Giles could not find him on the wards.

He discovered him at last in the room in the basement that served as a morgue. Carswell was standing in his shirtsleeves, surrounded by a blaze of lamps and candles with a knife in his hand, bending over the deceased Richard Stuart and on the verge of making a first incision.

"What are you doing?" Giles said.

"Being delivered from temptation," said Carswell, turning away. He went to lean on the table by the side, breathing hard. The air in the room had been starved by the lamps and the smell of the cadaver was also becoming apparent. Giles took the sheet that Carswell had tossed on the floor and covered the body, before going to open the tiny window.

"I think you had better get out of here," he said, and steered Carswell to the door. He then set about putting out the lamps before joining Carswell in the passageway.

He was sitting on the floor, his head in his hands, his back pressed to the wall, under the light of a guttering candle stub on a bracket. The candle went out and they were in darkness.

"My curiosity got the better of me," said Carswell. "And my stupidity." Giles sat down on the floor beside him. "But I need to know," Carswell went on. "What Kennedy said does not satisfy me."

"I'll speak to Boothroyd tomorrow at the cricket match," said Giles. "Something may be done in light of –" He hesitated, wondering if this was the moment to speak, given Carswell's present mood, but then decided it was best dealt with. "Fitznorton turned up some information about Kennedy that is not to his credit." Carswell said nothing but gave a heavy sigh. "Of course, it may mean nothing to our enquiry, but –"

"How could she marry him?" Carswell said. "I cannot fathom it. And if she is not –" He gave another great sigh. "What did he turn up?"

"That a patient left him a great deal of money, and the deceased's family disputed the will. But the will stood, and he got the money."

"And this lovely tale was in Carrington's papers?"

"Yes."

Carswell clambered to his feet.

"Let's go back to the hotel," he said. "Maybe tomorrow some of this will make sense."

~

"I should not have laughed at your hair," Eleanor said.

He had expected to find her asleep, but she was awake and apparently waiting for him. She was propped up on the pillows, book in hand.

"Has worrying about that kept you awake?" he said. "Or is it that novel?"

"It's not a novel," she said. "I don't only read novels, you know."

"I know," he said, sitting down on the bed.

"I sensed you were offended," she said.

"Only very slightly," he said. "And it is risible."

"I think it becomes you. It makes you look distinguished."

"Distinguished?"

"Like a brilliant young surgeon who goes to a great deal of trouble," she said, moving up behind him. "Everyone was very impressed with you," she added, wrapping her arms about him and kissing his neck.

It was hard to resist this, and so he undressed quickly and climbed into bed. She wriggled into his arms, so that she was sitting between his legs, her nightgown falling from her shoulders.

"When will the milk come, do you suppose?" she said, touching her breasts. "I'm looking forward to that."

"It can be painful," he said.

"I hope I have enough milk," she said.

"That's unlikely to be a difficulty."

"But what if I am ill and can't feed him?" she said.

"We could find a nurse, I dare say," said Felix.

"I do not want him to have any common wet nurse," she said. "Perhaps Jenny might manage to feed him."

"What makes you say that?" he said, alarmed. "It is not likely. Not at all likely, in fact."

"I have heard that it happens."

"She would have to be married with a child of her own. Otherwise, it would be extremely unnatural."

"I can think of nothing more natural," said Eleanor, "than offering one's baby to a friend to suckle. It would be delightful, and I think she would like to share the work."

"Then you had better find her a husband," said Felix.

"No, no, she will never marry," said Eleanor.

"That is for her to say, not you," said Felix.

"She has told me so," she said, leaning back against his chest, and then, guiding his hand to beneath her swollen belly, indicated that she wished to be petted. He obliged, stirred greatly now. He imagined Miss King sitting as he did, with Eleanor pressed against her, pulling her hand down to her waist; and then, hearing Eleanor murmur and gasp, and grow warm and restless, he began to wonder what Eleanor did in return for her dear friend.

Chapter Twenty

Giles breakfasted with Sally, Lamb and Celia, prior to their departure. Celia had now reached such a pitch of excitement and terror that she could not eat or drink anything, no matter how her parents urged her. The long-anticipated day had finally arrived, and to see her standing on the brink of her new life was affecting. He had seen so much of her growing up, it was impossible not to feel what Sally and Lambert were valiantly trying to conceal. Fortunately, there was a distraction in the form of a gift to be delivered, a parcel of books from Mr Carswell: an anatomy textbook, a primer of chemistry and the poetry of Walter Scott.

On being unwrapped and examined by Celia, they provoked a gush of tears.

"Perhaps you had better leave the anatomy with us," said Sally. "The other girls may not be ready for that."

She sniffed and nodded in agreement.

It was just as well that Carswell was not there to see it. His mood the previous evening was of the volatile sort that would not have been helped by the sight of Celia's wet cheeks and red eyes.

As it was, she sat down at once to write a tear-stained note of thanks to him. She sealed it and told Giles that he should deliver it at once.

"So he is to go rushing into their bedroom?" said Lamb.

"I will give it to Jacob," said Giles. "I beg his pardon, to Moore."

"No!" exclaimed Celia. "You must give it to him yourself. Please?"

"Of course," said Giles.

The time of departure soon came, and Giles saw them into their carriage. Celia had got over her tears now, and was thoroughly excited and in high spirits. The moment was crowned by the arrival of a charming posy of flowers, sent by Madame Jacquot from her own garden. Celia pulled out various choice specimens and insisted on decorating her father's buttonhole and her mother's bonnet with them.

"Oh, and one for you, Uncle Giles," she said, leaning out of the carriage and handing him a lavender flower.

He kissed her and they left, with Celia standing in the open carriage and waving enthusiastically in a style Giles was sure her future teachers would not approve of. He stood and watched them go, pressing the memory into his mind, as Sally might press the flowers in blotting paper, to mark the moment when Celia left childhood behind.

At the station house he was met by Inspector Harris.

"There's a young woman here wanting to talk to you, sir. Her name is Rosa Kemp."

He pointed to a pretty young woman sitting in the public waiting room.

"How can I help you, Miss Kemp?"

"I've come because of Erik," she said, getting up as he came in. "You are Major Vernon?"

"Yes, I am."

"I don't have much time. My mistress won't like it when she finds I've gone out, and I can't afford to lose another place."

"You were working at the Hydropathic?" Giles said.

"Yes, I was. How do you know that?"

"Polly told me about you. Now, this may take a little time, so I shall send you home with a note when we are done. Will that help?"

"I suppose," she said. "What did Polly say about me?"

"Let's go and talk somewhere else, shall we?"

He took her into Harris' office.

"Polly told me that you had some trouble with Captain Carrington," he said, when they had sat down.

She avoided his gaze for a minute and then said, "A bit. But it wasn't anything really. He was just that sort. But I know how to look after myself."

"Of course. You have heard, perhaps, that he's been murdered?"

"Eaten by the leopards, yes."

"He was not killed by the leopards," Giles said. "Now, perhaps you could tell me what happened with Captain Carrington. I can't believe it was just nothing. After all, you had to leave a good place."

"It was all right," she said.

"And you are lucky to have got another job."

"There's plenty of work here," she said.

"Were you the only girl that Carrington bothered? Polly and Mr Luchetti thought it was a problem."

"Maybe," she said. "There won't be many tears shed at his funeral, that's sure enough."

"Now, you wanted to talk to me about Erik Johnson," Giles said. "Did you tell him about what Carrington did to you? I take it you know him well?"

"He's sweet on me."

"And you like him?"

"Yes."

"And did he tell you to come here?"

"Yes, but – look, you've got the wrong idea about him. He wouldn't do that."

"So he told you why I had been questioning him?" She nodded. "And he told you why the magistrates have bound him over to keep the peace?"

"He said he was in a fight and it was a lot of fuss about nothing."

"He had a knife and he threatened another man with it. It was a large hunting knife. Does he like knives?"

"A man has to keep himself safe," she said.

"So, he likes knives," Giles said.

"I didn't say that."

"But he usually carries something that you could do real harm with?" She nodded. "And I suppose you told him about the problem with Carrington."

"Yes."

"And how did he take it?"

"I tell you, he didn't do it!" she said.

"But he was angry?"

"Yes, but –" She stared at him. "I just know he didn't do it. I wouldn't be here if I thought so. Anyway, why do you think it was? Everyone says it was the Frenchman who did it, and that's why he killed himself."

"You knew him, I suppose?" said Giles.

"A bit. He was crazy. It was just the sort of thing he would do. I saw him once going at Carrington, yelling his head off, he was. And why else would he kill himself? That's who did it, not Erik."

"Where was he on Sunday night?"

"With me."

"All night?"

"No, not like that. We had a walk about six and then I had to go back. He took me back about eight."

"And you don't know where he went after that?"

"No."

"He didn't tell you his plans?"

"No, why would he?"

"You tell me," he said. "Did he talk about his father at all?"

"His father?" she said. "What has that to do with anything?"

"Captain Carrington was his father."

"No!" she said, frowning. "No. He would have told me that."

"Perhaps he didn't think you worth such a confidence. I'm sorry."

"Maybe he forgot to tell me," she said, but she did not sound as if she believed it. "Was he his bastard, then?" she added. "Is that it?"

"No, not all," said Giles. "In fact, he's his heir. There might be a lot of money coming his way."

"Oh, my Lord," she said softly. "I see."

"Is there anything else you want to tell me?" he said. "About Sunday night, perhaps?"

He was hoping for some crumb now.

"He did say..."

"Yes?"

"I'd been talking about a bonnet I wanted. It's in the window of one of the shops in the Parade. I can't afford such things, but he said that in time, he'd get me everything I wanted, that he was going to be rich. Of course, I laughed at him. He has a bit of money, I know, but it never stays in his pocket long."

"Are you sure you don't know where he went after he had taken you home? Where is it you work now?"

"At Mrs Gilbert's. It's a big lodging house opposite the Incurables."

"Near the menagerie," said Giles.

~

"Who was that?" said Fitznorton, after walking past her as he came along the passageway.

"Erik Johnson's sweetheart, Rosa Kemp," said Giles. "But not for much longer, I suspect. She had some interesting things to say."

They went into the room that he had commandeered for

the investigation. Here, he had begun his usual system of pinning papers to the wall, in order to get some clear view of the situation. He had placed a paper with Carrington's name at the centre, and another near it with 'Erik Johnson' written on it. This sheet also bore the legend: ESTRANGED SON. He unpinned it, took up a pencil and added the word: KNIVES.

"It's crude," said Giles, sensing Fitznorton observing him, "but it helps me keep things straight."

"Might I suggest different coloured papers? In Prussia, that's the way it's done."

"It's done in Prussia?" said Giles.

"Yes, I assumed that was where you had adopted the idea from. Von Gravenhof references it in his book. In a footnote, I think."

"I dare say you are right," said Giles, who had not read the book in question. "What a wretched blow to my vanity – I had thought it was an expression of my own native genius, and had been inclined to congratulate myself on it. Ah well, the Prussians, of course, and coloured paper – that is a good notion. Blue with white chalk springs to mind."

Giles suppressed the urge to send Fitznorton off to the nearest stationers to fetch some.

"Is Erik Johnson still our most likely suspect?" said Fitznorton.

"He asked that young woman to come and plead his innocence," Giles said. "At the same time he has not confided to her his connection to Carrington. He seems more and more interesting to me."

"But he absolutely denied having anything to do with it, in two interviews," Fitznorton said.

"Perhaps I went too gently on him," said Giles. "He's clearly capable of lying when he chooses to. He also likes to carry a knife, which may mean something, or nothing at all. Perhaps he's too obvious. Patricide is such a satisfactory crime."

"Excuse me?"

"I'm thinking aloud," said Giles, turning away. "So, when does the cricket begin?"

"We are to meet at noon at The Red Lion Hotel. The match begins at two. Of course, if you feel that you cannot spare me –"

"No, you must go. After all, Sir Henry Boynton may be of interest."

~

"Felix, where are you going?" Eleanor said, stretching out her arms from the bed. She had woken up to find him dressing. "Don't go. Come back to bed."

"I would, but I have things to do. I'm late already. I'll see you at the cricket."

"You haven't asked the Hamiltons, have you?"

"No. Why? Should I?"

"No," she said. "I'd rather you didn't. I mean, they are nice, but he's too –" She leant back on the pillows. "Oh, I don't know."

Felix went and sat on the edge of the bed as he fastened his cravat. He wondered if he should say, "Attentive to Jenny?" but decided not to. Eleanor had now pushed the covers back and lay in a tempting pose, and it was not the moment for such a conversation. Instead he leant over and kissed her, unable to resist slipping his hand under the neck of her nightgown.

"I don't think either of them cares for cricket," Felix said and kissed her again, and was at that moment extremely tempted to get back into bed. But he pulled himself away and crossed the room.

"Since you must go, I might go back to the Idunnic

Chamber," she said.

"No, no, no!" said Felix, turning back from the looking glass. "Are you saying that to make me stay?"

"We had such a pleasant night," she said. This was undeniable, and to hear her say it, her voice still so sweet and husky with sleep, sorely tempted him.

"Yes, but I have things I must do. Young Jack, for a start –"

Eleanor sighed, and reached down and rubbed her stomach.

"His poor mother," she said. "I suppose his looks will be ruined."

"Not if I can help it," said Felix. "And now I think of it, Hamilton may be able to help me with that. The tip of the hook went in at –"

"Please, no!" exclaimed Eleanor, drawing the covers over her. "It's too horrible. I can't bear to think of it. What if something like that were to happen to our boy, Felix?"

"Rather, what you will do when our boy is a girl?" said Felix. "You really shouldn't –"

"I know it is a boy," she said. "And that is that. And Mrs Johnson was sure. I was surprised, but she took one look at me and said: a boy."

"Do you mean Mrs Johnson of the Idunnic Chamber?" said Felix.

"Yes, and her daughter said she was never wrong. So there you are."

"Good grief," said Felix. "You may believe what you like, of course, but you are setting yourself up for disappointment. And besides, what would be wrong if it was a girl? People say they are easier."

"It is not a question of what I want," said Eleanor sitting up. "It is a boy, not because I want it, it simply is. I know it, and you, as a man who can never experience this, cannot possibly understand. Blanchfort Carswell it is," she added, patting her stomach.

"No, it is not!" said Felix. "And you worry about him walking into a hook on a pulley! That name is ridiculous."

"It is my family name and it must be preserved," said Eleanor.

"Not in that manner," said Felix. "Can you imagine what will be done to him at school with such a name? It would be extremely wicked and selfish to do that to him. No, we will call him something sensible like John, or William, or Giles! There – that is a name I can like, and if that doesn't make a decent man of him, then –"

He broke off, and went to put on his boots. It never ceased to astonish him how the simplest conversations with Eleanor could lead them into the foothills of a quarrel. It was just as well that Jacob came in with his coat, as well as a chambermaid with Eleanor's breakfast tray, and he was able to hurry away.

At the Infirmary his patient was comfortable enough, but he would still require close attention, and Felix promised the exhausted mother he would come back later in the morning. As he left, he met the boy's father in the passageway – he had come from his work, and, much to Felix's embarrassment, insisted on pressing some money into his hand. It was by no means a large amount, but such was the man's pride that he would not accept Felix's services gratis. Charity was for others, he explained, and Felix must take his money. Felix took it, impressed and a little ashamed. He put the money not in his purse with his other loose change, but in his coattail pocket, wanting to feel the weight of it to remind himself it was there.

Having made a round of those other patients he had been called on to see the day before and discovered nothing alarming, he made a considerable effort not to visit Mr Richard Stuart's remains, which still lay in the morgue in the basement. Instead, he decided that he would gather his information on that subject in order to be better prepared to speak to the coroner that afternoon. There was some danger that Mr Boothroyd would not want to talk shop, so he would have to be both brief and effective. He intended to go to the coffee divan on the Parade to put his case together, but passing Mrs Johnson's glittering establishment, he determined to speak to Miss Johnson about her lover's symptoms.

He went into the shop, hoping he would not meet Eleanor carrying out her threat of visiting the absurd Idunnic Chamber again. He was met by Miss Ingrid Johnson herself.

"May I help you?"

"I wanted to speak to you about a personal matter," he said. "About Mr Richard Stuart."

"What about him?" she said. He realised that she might not have heard what had happened to him.

"Could we go somewhere private?"

"Yes, of course."

She led him to the back room where they had spoken to Mrs Johnson previously, only to find that lady sitting there, tying up boxes with silk ribbons. Miss Johnson promptly retreated, but Mrs Johnson asked, "What do you want?"

"Nothing, Mother."

"Why are you here, Mr Carswell?" said Mrs Johnson.

"I want to speak to your daughter."

"Then do," she said.

"I'd rather not," said Miss Johnson, turning to Felix.

"What is this about?" said Mrs Johnson. "Is this something about Erik?"

"No, it's nothing to do with that," said Felix. "I was hoping your daughter might help me with something. I have a case in hand, and –"

"Has he been taken ill?" said Miss Johnson.

"Who?" said Mrs Johnson. "Who? What is this, Ingrid?"

"I'm afraid I have some bad news for you, Miss Johnson," Felix said.

"Bad news..." repeated Miss Johnson, and went and sat

down. "About Dick?"

"Dick!" exclaimed Mrs Johnson. "Who is this? What have you been doing, Ingrid? I thought –"

"You thought wrong, Mother!" exclaimed Miss Johnson. "So what is it?"

Felix sat down opposite her and said, "I'm sorry to have to tell you this, but he's dead. It was on Thursday night, and very sudden. He collapsed, and nothing could be done. I was with him."

"Oh, dear God," said Miss Johnson, leaning back in her seat, her hand covering her mouth. "He said he wasn't well, but he thought he was getting better. What was wrong with him?"

"That's what I'm trying to work out. It's a bit of a mystery, and I'm hoping you might help me. You said he told you he was ill –?"

"Excuse me!" said Mrs Johnson. "Before we go any further, you will tell me exactly what has been going on. Who was this man?"

Miss Johnson now burst into tears. "Someone I loved, that's who! We were going to get married. He gave me a ring."

She reached into her pocket and laid a ring on the table: a fair-sized diamond surrounded by pearls. Mrs Johnson snatched it up and examined it with interest.

Felix doubted this was the time to mention that Dick Stuart had a wife. Mrs Johnson put the ring down again.

"A ring means nothing," she said.

"As you have always said," said Miss Johnson, with a great sniff and wiping her eyes. "I know, I know! Never trust them. But he was different."

"In what way? In that he didn't have the decency to come and speak to me? An honourable man would have done that. Isn't that so, sir?" Mrs Johnson added, gesturing at Felix.

"Oh, you can talk, Mother," said Miss Johnson, picking up the ring. "Talk all you like, but I loved him and I would have married him. And now this is all I have."

"If it was his to give you," said Mrs Johnson, turning away and going to the window. "You stupid girl!"

This provoked another burst of tears and Mrs Johnson, seeming to take some pity on the girl, said, "I shall make us coffee. Will you take some, sir?"

Felix nodded and she left, leaving her daughter to vent her grief with considerable force. At length she managed to compose herself, and slipping the ring on her finger, sat herself up.

"Did he say anything about me?" she said.

"I'm sorry, he did not. It was very sudden: apoplexy, I think. It was while he was at the opera. There was no chance for anyone to say farewell," he added, remembering Mrs Stuart holding him in her arms.

"Oh yes, the opera, he said he was going to that," she said. "He said we would go when we were married – we were going to go to Paris."

"What did he tell you about his illness?"

"That he had headaches and sometimes he felt sick. And I think sometimes he could not see straight, although he would not admit it. He didn't like to talk about it. He wanted to think about the future – always. About the children we'd have, and the house we were going to live in. He wanted to build a house for me. I told him I was tired of living above a shop." This thought made her break down again, and only after a long burst of tears did Felix dare enquire, "What do you mean by not seeing straight? Can you give me an example?"

"It was this eye," she said, pointing to her right eye. "There was something wrong with it. He was blind in it. We were in the gardens and I saw this little dog, and he had to turn his head so, until he could see it. I thought it was odd, because he was sitting just by me, so close." She sighed. "And he got dizzy. Did I say that? He used to joke about it, how sometimes he'd find himself flat on his face for no reason."

"How long had you known him?" Felix asked.

"Third of July," she said. "He came in to buy a present for his sister. He wanted me to help him choose something, and we got talking."

"His sister?" said Felix. "Do you know where she is?"

"Georgiana? She lives in London, I think. She will have to be told. She's his only relative."

"Well, not quite," Felix said.

"What do you mean?"

"There's someone else, and I'm sorry to have to tell you this: another woman – his wife, to be exact. Here, in Stanegate."

Miss Johnson sat in silence, her lower lip trembling. Her mother came in with the tray of coffee, and seeing her, said to Felix, "What have you told her now?"

"That he was married!" Miss Johnson said, and flung the ring across the room at her mother.

Chapter Twenty-one

The cricket match was to take place at the far end of the Stray, on a broad, beautiful stretch of open ground bounded by woodland, and with a long view over the country beyond. Here Stanegate and all its sophisticated pleasures were left behind, as the players gathered by a rustic looking hut, and what spectators there were settled on the grass to watch. It was a perfect day for the game, warm and breezy, the trees rustling with the leaves they would soon shed, a melancholy song of summer's end that made Giles remember the long, idle games of his own youth in Northumberland.

The approach of a barouche landau drawn by a superb pair of bays brought him back to the present. It was Lady Charlotte's carriage. She was sitting, in queen-like solitary state, her parasol open, her bonnet ribbons and muslin flounces fluttering in the breeze.

"You will have an excellent view from there," he said, looking up at her.

"You won't join me?" she said.

"I'll be happier on the grass."

"Do not go far," she said. "I'm in need of an interpreter. Mr Graham" – the Holbroke coachman – "has been attempting to explain the rules, but I am still quite confused."

"I'm sure it will make sense when you actually see the game," said Giles.

"That is what I said, my lady," said Mr Graham. "It will all come clear." He went off to attend to the horses.

"I hope so. I don't want to seem foolish to Mr Fitznorton," said Charlotte. "I suspect he believes women are inherently foolish creatures. It would be pleasant to prove him wrong, don't you think?"

"He does have a slight tendency to put everyone in their place," he said. "Perhaps it comes of having such an organised mind. But the right person could confound him."

"Quite," she said. "So, what else do you think of your protégé ?"

"That he's not my protégé," Giles said.

"Then what is he? Your apprentice?"

"No, God forbid," Giles said. "He is just here to observe what we do, and if he wants to learn anything from it, then that is entirely his business. I expect he might write a politely scathing report at the end."

"Would he dare?" she said.

"He may do as he likes, I suspect," said Giles, "since he is tipped for great things."

"So Papa said. An interesting man, altogether."

"He may become one," said Giles.

"That is also what Papa said," said Charlotte, smiling.

"I'm surprised he didn't come with you today," Giles said.

"He was tired," said Charlotte. "It worried me. I do wonder if Carswell should not come down and look at him. Without making a fuss of it, of course."

"Certainly," said Giles. "Ah, here we are – they are coming out for the first over."

The game began in a leisurely fashion. Lord Amberleigh's team were batting first, and Giles was amused to see Fitznorton being sent out into deep field, as if he were of no consequence, whilst Mr Boothroyd, as captain, was to bowl first. Fitznorton made an incongruous figure in the coroner's team, being young, slender and full of energy. He glanced at Lady Charlotte who was rather obviously not looking at the wicket but at the distant figure of Fitznorton, resplendent with a striped sash about his waist.

The first batsman out was, Giles guessed, Sir Henry Boynton, who had a careless but forceful grace in his batting style that guardsmen often displayed on the cricket pitch. He made a nice collection of runs, apparently effortlessly, before hitting what would surely be a magnificent six, had not Fitznorton, leaping and twisting with spectacular elegance, caught him out. This caused the small crowd to erupt in delight.

"Goodness!" said Lady Charlotte.

"Like a cat after a bluebottle!" said Giles.

"No, no, that is too commonplace," said Charlotte.

"I don't think cats are remotely commonplace," said Giles. "And it was a magnificent catch. He must have asked Mr Boothroyd to put him out there, knowing that Sir Henry was a hard hitter. Sir Henry will not be pleased to be out so soon."

As the players rearranged themselves, Giles noticed Mrs Carswell and Miss King coming towards the pitch. He went to meet them, and they were soon installed alongside Lady Charlotte in her carriage.

"What was the applause for?" Mrs Carswell asked.

"Mr Fitznorton caught Sir Henry Boynton out," said Lady Charlotte.

"Oh, how exciting," said Miss King. "First man out to bat, as well! Rather a humiliation for him, poor fellow."

"Yes, this could get interesting," said Giles. "And I see you are an expert. Lady Charlotte is in want of one, and I am going to commiserate with Sir Henry."

He walked over to the rustic hut where Sir Henry was sitting on a bench, his bat at his feet.

"That was wretched luck," said Giles.

"Certainly was," said Sir Henry. "Who is that fellow? Do you know him, sir?"

"Mr Edward Fitznorton of the Home Office. Late of Cambridge."

"What's he doing here?"

"He's working for me, at present. Allow me to introduce

myself: I am Major Giles Vernon, Superintendent with the Northminster and County Constabulary."

"Oh, that's who you are. I was wondering, seeing you talking there to Lady Charlotte Haraald. I'm surprised her Papa isn't here. So you are Major Vernon."

He got to his feet and they shook hands.

"I take it that is Lord Amberleigh who has just gone out to bat?" said Giles, watching as a pale-haired young man went to the wicket.

"Yes," said Sir Henry. "He will have to watch his step. We expected an easy victory today. Perhaps that won't be the case." He rubbed his face. "What brings you to town, Major?"

"Captain Carrington."

"Oh yes, I heard about that. What a thing."

"Did you know him?"

"We did a bit of business. You may have heard that."

"In relation to Carr's Crag?"

"Yes. Lady Amberleigh wanted a house in Stanegate, so we built half a dozen up there."

"But you had to acquire the land first?"

"You've talked to Lord Rothborough about that, I suppose?" said Sir Henry.

"He did mention it," said Giles.

Young Lord Amberleigh now whacked out what would surely be a six, but it looked for a moment as if he would be caught out, as Fitznorton again leapt for the ball. However, this time he did not succeed, and he looked distinctly peevish as a result.

"Oh, by God, that was close," said Sir Henry. "This man of yours intends to give us trouble, doesn't he?"

"Blame Mr Boothroyd, not me," Giles said. "What did you make of Carrington?"

"He was your typical pusher," said Sir Henry. "Always a little de trop, if you catch my meaning. Made himself popular with the ladies, though."

"Anyone in particular?"

Sir Henry studied the game before answering.

"He amused Lady Amberleigh," he said, "for some reason. He was a good backgammon player, I will give him that."

"So the financing of the Rustic Cottages was partly from the Amberleigh estates?"

"Yes, and it ought to pay out eventually. My lady is pleased with her cottage as well."

"Which one is that?"

"You don't see it at once. It's set a long way back and has the best outlook. Adelaide Lodge. Devil of a business building it but Carrington, to give him his due, got it done. He had a talent for that. The baths as well –"

"Yes, most impressive. So – I have to ask this – he didn't confide about any enemies or difficulties he was having?"

"No," he said, and then threw his hands up as the Earl stumbled back and demolished the wicket. "Oh, the devil! I hope you haven't laid money on us winning, Major. Or maybe you have, on us losing?"

"I'm not a gambler," said Giles.

"Excuse me," said Sir Henry. "I must go and speak to my team."

He began to walk to the pavilion and Giles considered if there was anything more to be got from him at that point. He was certainly interested to hear of Lady Amberleigh being amused by Carrington. At the same time, he became aware of a young woman standing nearby. She was dressed in a fashionable cloud of printed muslin and looked familiar. It was Mary Carter, Mrs Thorne's maid. She did not seem to notice that he had recognised her, for she soon went trotting off, apparently after Sir Henry. This gentleman had not gone to speak to his team at all, for he walked past them with a wave of his hand, and continued on his way. Miss Carter came behind, keeping her distance judiciously, and even stopping for a moment or two, apparently to watch the game. Then she started off again, and Giles followed her, as discreetly as he could. She turned behind the cricket hut where Sir Henry now stood smoking a cigar. He bent to embrace her, with one arm extended to preserve his tobacco, but the kiss was no less passionate for that.

Conscious that he might be observed at any moment, Giles moved quickly away out of sight. He was tempted to intrude into their tête-à-tête and find out more. It was certainly an interesting liaison. Sir Henry must have met Mary Carter at Mrs Thorne's. Perhaps that was where they had played backgammon together.

He was still deliberating the point when he caught sight of Sukey Kennedy pushing a baby carriage, her step-children running ahead of her.

He went to meet them. She looked, he thought, extremely pale and tired.

"That looks laborious," he said. "Allow me?"

"Thank you. It's still better than carrying him," she said, yielding the baby carriage to him. "The children were being impossible. I'm trying to exhaust them, and have only exhausted myself."

"Perhaps we should sit down?" he said as they approached the shelter of a large oak. He pulled off his coat and spread it on the ground for her to sit on. She sat down with a grateful sigh, and then called to the children.

"Why don't you make some houses with twigs and leaves?" she suggested to them. "Like we did at Ballycoghlan." This suggestion was well received and they ran off to play. "They miss the country. I wish we could go back."

"Where is their nurse?" he said, sitting down beside her.

"Off seeing her young man," said Sukey. "She begged me, and really, I didn't have the heart to say no. She works so hard. Those two are little savages sometimes. What are you up to? I never expected to find you idling about like this."

"I'm not strictly idling," said Giles. "I wanted to speak to you about why you really left Ireland."

"Oh," she said. "You know, don't you? About the case against him?"

"About the money your husband inherited? Yes, I'm sorry, I do."

"I should have said something, and I'm sorry for being so vague about it, but he does not like it talked about. If it got back to him – how did you find out?"

"There was a reference to it amongst Captain Carrington's papers."

"What?"

"Some newspaper articles. It seems the Captain was one for gathering useful information and using it for profit."

"Blackmail, you mean? So you think that he might have been blackmailing my husband?"

"I have to explore all the possibilities," he said. "You know that." She nodded.

"Which makes him a suspect," she said.

"Is there anything that has made you uncomfortable?" he said.

She leant back against the trunk of the tree and looked up into the leafy canopy. Her silence was painful, and he disliked having to press her further. He was searching for the words, when she said, "I know they were quarrelling and I understated it. How could I not? He is my husband. Loyalty is important."

"Of course," he said. "I know. What were the quarrels about? Money?"

"Yes, though I don't understand why, because we haven't gone short at all. He gives me more money than I need for the housekeeping, and that is nothing because we are practically living in the hotel, and all our meals and so forth come from the kitchens. I gave him some of it back and said that he ought to put in the bank for another time, when we did need it, but he insisted on my taking it. He told me to go get some new dresses. He wanted me to look the part, he said."

"Perhaps they were quarrelling about how the hotel was run?" Giles said. "About whether it was a hotel or a medical establishment, for example? There must have been some tension there."

"It's possible," she said. "Paul's a proud man, certainly. He had to fight hard to become a doctor and he likes to take command, that's true enough. I haven't heard him say so much, mind, but I sensed sometimes that he was not happy to bend his neck to the Captain. I know he thought him immoral."

"Ah, yes, well, he had a mistress."

"There was a mistress?" said Sukey. "I did wonder."

"Oh yes. She lives in one of the Rustic Cottages. Mrs Thorne is her name, and that young woman over there," he said, pointing out Miss Carter, who was now strolling arm in arm with Sir Henry, "is her maid."

"That dress must be borrowed from her mistress," Sukey said. "And who's that she's with?"

"Sir Henry Boynton. Captain of the visiting cricket team."

"Goodness," said Sukey. "You know, I've seen them together before, now I think of it. It was last Saturday afternoon, at the menagerie. I'd know him anywhere, with that moustache. He clearly thinks himself a fine fellow. The children were staring at him, like he was one of the animals."

"Were you with your husband?"

"He did come with us, yes," said Sukey. "He didn't want to. He thinks the place vulgar and that I shouldn't be indulging the children by taking them there, but he came in the end, and he was fascinated, as we all were, by the leopards. Such lovely creatures. It's hard to imagine that –" She took a sharp breath. "I've just remembered something, and I don't want to tell you it..."

"Yes?"

"It was something he said. He wondered how secure the cage was. How the keepers got in and out without being mauled."

"May I ask you something else?" he said. "Where was your husband on Sunday night?"

"We went to Evensong, and afterwards we had high tea with the children, and then I put them to bed, and he went to see his patients. I didn't see him until the next day, because I slept in the nursery with Lorenzo."

"That will be easy to verify," Giles said.

"Or disprove," she said and got to her feet, shaking out her skirts. "Is that Mr Carswell I see coming towards us? And the lady with him, is that –?"

"Yes, that's his wife."

~

"Oh, Felix, Felix, we must have one of those!" exclaimed Eleanor, catching sight of the baby carriage and the woman bending over it to lift out the child. "What a wonderful thing!"

He could not venture an opinion. Rather, he was watching Sukey holding the baby against her. The Major was putting on his coat.

"Mrs Carswell, Mrs Kennedy," Major Vernon said, with an admirable lack of fuss. "Mrs Kennedy, Mrs Carswell."

"Oh, what a beautiful child!" exclaimed Eleanor, seeing the sleepy child in Sukey's arms. "How old?"

"He's three months."

"Oh, look at him, Felix, look!" Eleanor said. The child's bonnet had fallen off to reveal a soft, dark crop of hair. "His hair – oh, is that his father's hair, Mrs Kennedy?"

"Something like it," said Sukey.

"May I touch it?" said Eleanor, drawing off her glove and

reaching out. "It looks so soft."

"Of course. Would you like to hold him?" Sukey said.

"Yes, please!" said Eleanor, and handing her gloves to Felix, now took the child into her arms with a squeak of pleasure. "Oh, you are so sleepy. What a darling! What's his name?"

"Laurence," said Sukey. "Well, I call him Lorenzo."

Eleanor smiled at this.

"Yes, that is perfect, for such a handsome gentleman," she said. "Lorenzo! Now, you really should put your bonnet on straight. It's not good for you to go without it, but I suppose it is because you want us to see your beautiful hair." He knew that this was said in all innocence, but he felt she had guessed everything, and was determined to pierce him in every spot, like St Sebastian bombarded by arrows. "Lorenzo," she went on. "Perhaps we should put that on our list, Felix."

"You have a list?" said Major Vernon.

"Of course!" said Eleanor. "And it is growing long. But we still have plenty of time to decide."

At this point the baby began to grow restive.

"I think someone is hungry," said Sukey. "Excuse me, won't you?"

She took the child back from Eleanor and walked away behind the shelter of the tree.

"How is the match going?" Major Vernon said.

"I have no idea," said Eleanor, who was examining the baby carriage. "We must have ours painted to match the carriages, don't you think?"

"Yes, whatever you like," said Felix, trying hard not to think of Sukey feeding her child, hidden by the great trunk of the tree.

How did this hurt so much, still, after so much time and change, after so much careful rationalising? What was it about her that still held him in such thrall? They had lived together and for the most part, it had been disastrous, and yet for all that, he still longed for the intimacy they had experienced, and the simplicity of their life together.

Chapter Twenty-two

Eleanor had just sent Stevens away and was regarding her reflection in the looking glass.

"Is this too frivolous for Norma?" she said, touching the rosettes of ribbons with which she had ornamented her ringlets.

"It's the opera," said Felix. "You're not going to church."

"Perhaps I should have worn my silver moiré, even if it is a touch dowagerly."

"Is that a word?" said Felix.

"It should be," she said. "It's too late to change it now. I wonder what Jenny is wearing." She got up from her seat and went to pick up her fan and gloves. "Tell me about Mrs Kennedy."

Sitting on a low stool and pulling on his evening boots, Felix thought he had misheard her.

"What?"

"Mrs Kennedy. Who is she?"

"In what sense?"

"It's obvious, isn't it?" said Eleanor. "Or, did you think I wouldn't guess? So tell me all about it. I never thought Major Vernon, of all people, would be so... but then again, he was a widower, and she is handsome."

"You think that the Major and Mrs Kennedy –?" Felix began.

"I am right, aren't I?" said Eleanor. "There was something about them, sitting there under the tree. It was so... interesting. And it's a good thing Mrs Vernon has gone home! I wonder if she knows about it. Do men tell their wives such things, Felix?"

"It depends, I suppose," said Felix. "You shouldn't make such speculations about the Major, Eleanor. He'd be offended."

"Speculation, I think not!" said Eleanor. "After all, he lived in her house."

"So did I," said Felix. "Who told you that?"

"Jacob."

"How did he know?" said Felix.

"Bodley told him."

"Then he certainly should not have told you!"

"Oh, is it a secret?" Eleanor said. "It is! Then it must be as I suspected. Oh, my goodness. But she is handsome. I can see she is his style."

"He has a style, does he?" said Felix, who could not decide if he ought to be offended or pleased that she could not associate him with Sukey in any way.

"Yes, of course," she said.

"I don't know where you have got the idea of there being anything irregular between them. What did Jacob say to you?"

"Only that you both lodged in her house. He didn't accuse Major Vernon of anything. I am only inferring –"

"Wrongly," said Felix, "I assure you."

"I think not," she said, going to the door. "He is a man who likes women, that is clear enough."

"Is it?" said Felix.

"You wouldn't know. He doesn't look at men the way he looks at women. I suspect he was rather wicked at one time. It's just as well he is married now."

She left the room, to Felix's relief. He wondered if he should fetch her back and tell her why she was wrong. He did not at all like her having such a misguided notion, and perhaps the only way to correct it was to tell her the truth. Yet he was not ready for that conversation, and even as he sat there, he did not know when he would be ready. He had no idea how she would take such information – would she be angry or amused? It was impossible to say.

The worst of telling the truth was that it could do nothing for Sukey except damn her thoroughly. He had a suspicion that his sins might be forgiven after some tears and pouting on Eleanor's part, and a great deal of humility on his, but Sukey would remain a tainted creature, who had misled him.

~

"We were so cruel," Sally said. "We left after half an hour. Lamb would not even let me help her unpack."

"It is the only way to do it," Lamb said. "And Celia knows that."

"It was unfeeling," said Sally.

"So unfeeling," murmured Lamb to Giles, "that I was practically in tears in the carriage."

"Tears after the event mean nothing!" said Sally.

"Which is why you shed so many?" said Lamb.

"We have been wretched," said Sally, throwing herself into Giles' arms, anxious for an embrace. "It was far, far worse than I thought."

"But Celia was dry-eyed, which is how it should be," said Lamb. "And still annoyed about missing the cricket and Norma. How was the match, by the way?"

"The Amberleigh team was decimated as a result of Mr Fitznorton's efforts – no, one should not say effort, because he made it all look effortless."

"I assume the Stanegate team have carried him off for a victory dinner," said Lambert.

"No, he is joining us tonight," said Giles.

"Because of Lady Charlotte?" said Sally.

"I have no idea," said Giles.

"Sally has several," said Lamb.

"As did Emma," Giles said.

"Then that is settled," said Sally.

"In what respect?" said Lamb. "That the wedding will take place or that he admires her?"

"I think it may be mutual," said Sally, "so who knows? And who could object to such a match? His family certainly could not."

"I think his family might be the sticking point," said Lambert. "Those Waterbury-ites are not worldly – or rather they have a worldliness all of their own."

"False humility, you mean?" said Sally. "Then it will be a good test of the young man, to find his heart going against all that!"

The conversation got no further as Lady Charlotte herself joined them, and they went down to meet the others for dinner.

"The hero of the hour, I hear, Mr Fitznorton!" said Lamb, catching sight of him in the passageway ahead of them.

"He ought to have a victor's wreath," said Sally.

"I may have a wayward sprig or two of butchers-broom," said Lady Charlotte, stopping by a looking glass that was hanging in the passageway. She was wearing a fetching confection of leaves and flowers in her hair. "Mr McGillray can be a little enthusiastic when set to making headdresses, although he is marvellously adept. I like to think he makes his wife and daughters wear such things at breakfast." She pulled out two sprigs and offered them to Fitznorton. "Ruscus hypoglossum, as it is properly called. He asked me what the opera was about, and I told him it was about Druids and Romans, so he put some of this in."

"Ah, the marvellous Mr McGillray!" said Sally. "How apt!"

"He is head gardener at Holbroke," said Lamb to Fitznorton, who was looking thoroughly confused.

"Do you remember how he taught Celia how to make

flower crowns and we all went into dinner highly bedecked?" Sally said.

"He must have a great many men under him to have the time for such things," said Fitznorton.

"Fifteen, at present," said Lady Charlotte. "We took on a few more, as my father has been developing the parterre – I say my father; it was all Mr McGillray's notion. It grows more intricate by the year."

"And more spectacular!" said Sally. "I'm looking forward to seeing it again, and I hope he will suffer me to question him on a few trivial topics."

"Of course he will," said Lady Charlotte. "He will be delighted. He knows so much and he loves to share it. We are lucky to have him. I hope he stays with us for the rest of his life, but there is a danger with these men of talent that they will be lured away."

"That will not happen with Mr McGillray, surely?" said Lambert. "His family have been at Holbroke for several generations – I remember Lord Rothborough saying so, and I think you are godmother to one of his children?"

"His youngest girl, yes. Amelia Charlotte – an honour."

"For her, yes," said Mr Fitznorton.

"No, for me!" said Lady Charlotte, laughing. "Oh, it will not stay just like that, Mr Fitznorton," she went on, noticing him struggling to fix the sprigs into his buttonhole. "Let me find you a pin."

"I have one!" said Sally, producing from her pocket a silver fish-shaped needle case, and relieving Lady Charlotte of the honour of fastening the laurel sprigs. In truth, she was better placed to do this, being closer in height to Fitznorton. It was probably a relief for Fitznorton. Lady Charlotte in high spirits, with the beam of her brilliant attention fixed upon one, was a delightful experience for anyone, but Giles wondered if Fitznorton could even allow himself to enjoy it.

Presently the Carswells and Miss King joined them and

they went into dinner. Sally and Lambert, as the hosts of that evening's feast, arranged where they should all sit at that agreeable round table. Sally put Giles between Mrs Carswell and Miss King, with Lady Charlotte across the table next to Mr Fitznorton, where she continued to dazzle.

As the evening passed, he wished that Emma were still with them. The party felt incomplete without her, and he felt the lack of the warm, protective mantle of her affection and the way the mere sound of her voice made him feel rational and calm. He had not expected that the spectacle of Charlotte succumbing to infatuation would unsettle him, but unsettled he was. He had no claim on her, yet he could not prevent his irritation rising at the sight of her unguarded behaviour. Having had the privilege of her admiration, he was forced to see it turned on someone else, on Fitznorton, of all men, who – try as he might – he could not like. He was not even sure he could respect him.

He told himself it was surely only a transient reaction on her part. Fitznorton was a handsome novelty and she was indulging herself after a long period of social seclusion. He knew he should not think less of her for responding to Fitznorton's purely animal charms, but as he watched her turn towards him and smile, her eyes wide with admiration, it irked him, even though he knew it was hardly fair. He could only hope that Fitznorton was even vaguely aware of the compliment he was being paid.

Because they were going to the opera, they abandoned the customary separation of the sexes after the meal, but in practice, the ladies left just as they always did, to go and fetch their wraps and tweak their ribbons.

"If I had known, I would have ordered port," Lamb said. "Madame has such a good cellar. I was tempted."

"We have time to finish the claret," said Carswell, eyeing the decanter. "Which was excellent, by the bye."

"I thought you might appreciate that, Mr Carswell," said

Lamb. "A real Edinburgh claret."

"I never got such good claret in Edinburgh," said Carswell. "Who's with me?"

Lamb took a glass, Fitznorton refused, naturally, and Giles hesitated before saying, "Half a glass, if that does not deprive you?"

"No, not at all," said Carswell. "But that is not like you, Major."

"It must be the prospect of all that female self-sacrifice lying ahead of me," said Giles. "Does not Norma get burnt alive at the end?"

"Yes, and her faithless love repents of his infamy and comes to join her on the pyre," Lambert said.

"Edifying, I suppose," said Giles. "But is it only me who wants an evening where there are lovers in disguise, an unexpected inheritance and no death? Oh, and perhaps a comic miser and a matchmaker."

"And a ballet in the middle?" said Lamb, smiling.

"Yes, with a dozen really pretty young women, wearing not a great deal," said Giles, who had no special interest in ballet girls, but a vague wish to annoy Fitznorton.

"Tragedy has a monopoly on the good tunes," said Carswell.

"It is certainly true that to write affecting music in the opera, an element of misfortune does help," said Lamb. "But you are right, Giles, a little comedy would not go amiss. We have had a heavy program this week."

"Yes, the only one with a happy ending turned into a tragedy," said Carswell, draining his glass. "Regarding the late Mr Stuart, I attempted to talk to Mr Boothroyd about that, but he was too cock-a-hoop to take any notice, for which I blame you entirely, Mr Fitznorton."

"I beg your pardon?" said Fitznorton.

"Your victory made him forget he was a coroner," Carswell went on. "Perhaps I should have got you to speak to him. He clearly has a special regard for those of us who can hit balls into the next county."

"Ah yes, I did try, but it was perhaps not the moment," said Giles. "He said he thought it unlikely he could permit it. As we discussed, I am not sure your grounds are sufficient, Mr Carswell."

"What are we talking about?" said Lamb.

"I want to do a post-mortem on Richard Stuart," said Carswell. "He was exhibiting some interesting symptoms before his death. I spoke to Miss Johnson this morning and she confirmed what his wife said, by the way."

"Did she know there was a wife?" Giles said.

Carswell shook his head.

"I was the bearer of bad news," he said. "He had asked her to marry him, apparently. She flung his ring across the room."

"That's interesting," said Giles. "A potential bigamist."

Carswell went on: "I dare say that wretch Kennedy will have signed the certificate and the man will be in the grave before we can be any wiser about the matter!"

"So you consider Dr Kennedy may be responsible, in some way, for Stuart's death?" said Fitznorton.

"I don't know. I just didn't like his diagnosis, and when a man drops dead like that, there are going to be questions. I'm not saying he killed him, but there are plenty of sins of omission that a medical man can commit that can lead to death."

"We are not here to persecute Kennedy," Giles said, "but to find who killed Carrington."

"And if they are one and the same?" said Carswell. "When you were talking to Su– Mrs Kennedy, did you tell her what Carrington knew about him?"

"Yes," said Giles.

"And what did she say?"

"That they went to the menagerie with the children on

Saturday and he wondered how secure the leopard cage was."

"The devil he did!" said Carswell. "And does he have an alibi for Sunday night?"

"She said he was seeing his patients. That she did not know when he got back."

Carswell fell silent then and it was left for Fitznorton to say, "Should he not warrant formal questioning, then?"

"It may come to that," said Giles.

"If I find –" Carswell began, and then got up from the table and left the room. Giles followed him into the passageway. "What else did she say to you? She looked so tired and I am sure she is not happy. God, I do not think I can bear to think of her – if he has done anything, if he is – why do these things not die?" Carswell went on, fumbling for his cheroot case. "Why does it feel like a red hot poker in my stomach?"

"I don't know," said Giles. "I'm concerned for her as well." Carswell nodded. "But we have to be careful. If he is dangerous –"

"We cannot leave her with him until we are sure! Until he takes a knife to her!"

"I was going to say, we must not provoke him."

"And what if we have provoked him already?" said Carswell. "What then?"

"I don't think she's at any particular risk just now," Giles said.

"On what grounds?" said Carswell. "We have no idea what we are dealing with here."

"Yes, but she does and she has a great deal of sense. If there is any difficulty she will try and get away."

"Try and get away? Men kill their wives all the time!" exclaimed Carswell. "You know that! He is twice the size of her. He could strangle her one-handed."

"You must calm down," said Giles. "You are giving in to fancy."

Carswell took some time to consider the point, and nodding, walked away down the passageway. At the same time, Madame Jacquot came into view at the other end, accompanied by the familiar figure of Tom O'Brien.

"Ah, here you are, sir!" said Madame Jacquot. "This gentleman is asking for you."

"O'Brien, how good to see you," said Giles, shaking his hand. "What brings you here?"

"My nephew's christening," said O'Brien. "I'm not supposed to be here, of course. Bridie has given me a tongue-lashing for it, and she will give me another in due course, but I wanted to come. Ah, Mr Carswell, good evening to you!" he added, nodding to Carswell.

Carswell muttered a greeting in return, just as Lamb and Fitznorton emerged from the dining room.

"You will come to the opera with us, Mr O'Brien?" said Lamb, after the introductions had been got through. "I know you like good music – I've seen you at the Philharmonic."

"That's very kind of you, Canon Fforde," said O'Brien. "I would like that. It's Norma, tonight, isn't it, with La Fiorella?"

"It is," said Lamb. "I'm hoping that La Fiorella will rise to the occasion – she was superb last night in Maria Stuarda, but I worry she may have exhausted herself."

They went off to find the ladies. Coming into the entrance hall they were met by the striking sight of Lady Charlotte standing under the brilliant lamp that hung from the ceiling. She had put on a gauzy, spangled stole which made her look as if she were wrapped in a cloud. Fitznorton plucked a rose from a large vase on a side table, strode over to her and presented it. She accepted it, colouring as she did so.

"I feel I should make up for stealing your laurels," he said.

"Very theatrical," Giles murmured to Sally.

"Oh, don't be sour," said Sally. "It's charming. They might be good for each other. He must be persuaded to come to Holbroke with us tomorrow."

Chapter Twenty-three

"Your brother-in-law," Felix said to O'Brien. "What do you think of him?"

"Why do you ask?" said O'Brien, glancing at Major Vernon. "What's up?"

Two long acts of Italian opera had passed and they were now sitting in the coffee room at The White Hart. Felix had kept his peace but he had no intention of waiting further. He felt overwrought and exhausted. He had been thinking of Sukey and then of Eleanor and Miss King the entire evening. The three of them seemed to perform a diabolical dance in his mind, accompanied by the throbbing beauty of Signor Donizetti's music. Then, at one of the most intense moments of the drama, he had been privy to the sight of Eleanor reaching for Miss King's hand. He could scarcely find an innocent explanation for it, especially when he saw they had both been crying. It was a communion to which he was obviously not admitted and, whatever it meant in terms of their conduct, he had felt wretched for it, and it had cost him a great deal to contain his anger.

Before the Major could speak, the waiter came and asked for their order.

"Tea," said Felix. "As Madame makes it?"

"Oh yes, sir," said the waiter.

"That sounds excellent," said Major Vernon. "O'Brien, will that do for you? Anything stronger?" O'Brien shook his head. "It seems Mr Fitznorton is having an effect on you, Carswell," added the Major with a smile when the waiter had gone.

"He's having an effect on all of us," Felix said. He might

have added, "especially on Charlotte", but that was not a conversation to be had in front of a relative stranger. "So, about Kennedy – what do you know about him?"

"Truth be told, not a great deal. You would have to ask my wife, except she wouldn't speak of him now except to call him the Devil incarnate. But she does know all the ins and outs of him, his family that is. Her father thought a great deal of him, and they were all happy with the match until –"

"He decided to leave the Church?" said Major Vernon.

O'Brien nodded and then leant back in his chair, and rubbed his face.

"What a business! I've had my thoughts over the years about the Church and its undue influence. It's a hard thing when you've been brought up with it, and you love it, and it defines you, and then you feel the yoke on your back and you think: where is my freedom of thought? I respect Kennedy for what he's doing. He is a free man and welcome to his beliefs, and the same goes for Sukey. She wouldn't be coerced. You know what she's like," he added, looking at Felix.

Felix nodded.

"Apart from the religious question," Major Vernon said, "is there anything you can remember hearing about him? How they came to leave Ireland, for example?"

"I didn't pay much attention to it," said O'Brien. "I've been busy – well, you know that, and sometimes family talk doesn't make much impression. You really would need to talk to Bridie, but then again, she's so angry she won't say anything reasonable about him. What is all this about? Is it to do with Carrington's death?"

"It's a possibility we're obliged to look at," said the Major. "They were closely connected, after all, and there are one or two things that are not entirely –"

"That's understating it," said Felix. "The fact is, Mr O'Brien, that Kennedy has been supremely unhelpful to us. Now Carrington is dead he has got control of a considerable business, and there is strong evidence that Carrington was blackmailing him."

"About what?" said O'Brien.

"The money he got from a dead patient," said Felix. "There was a case about it. The family contested the will. Did Mrs O'Brien not mention that?"

"I would imagine that Mrs Kennedy would not have told her about it," said Major Vernon, "given that he did not like the matter to be talked about."

"I should like to know the circumstances of that death," said Felix, getting up. "In fact, we should write to the coroner in Bally – wherever it is – and get the details."

"Ballycoghlan," said O'Brien. "I hope to Heaven you are wrong about this, Mr Carswell."

"So do I!" exclaimed Felix.

The waiter came in with the tea with Madame Jacquot in his wake, which surprised Felix.

"I didn't mean to be taken literally," he said, as she stood and mixed the tea for them.

"It's nothing, and I take it as a compliment. Also, it allows me to give you your key, Monsieur O'Brien, and welcome the distinguished proprietor of The Bugle!"

"Thank you, ma'am," said O'Brien.

She did not stay any longer than it took to make the tea.

"What a woman that is," said O'Brien, glancing behind him as she left. "I should like to know her story."

Sitting down again to drink his tea, Felix shared this curiosity. Her presence lingered with them, like a strong, sweet scent in the air. He had never heard the solidly uxorious O'Brien make any sort of remark about a woman before – it might be ascribed to his having quarrelled with his wife, or perhaps it was that Madame Jacquot's charm was impossible for any red-blooded male to ignore.

"So you are halfway to arresting my brother-in-law," said O'Brien, heaping sugar into his tea.

"By no means," said Major Vernon.

"Bridie would be pleased if you did," said O'Brien. "That's a tale I could go home with. But for Sukey's sake –" He put down his teacup. "At least I can give her a roof over her head these days, if there is any trouble. She can go to my house in Swalecliffe if there's any bother."

"You have a house in Swalecliffe?" Felix said.

"And what else am I supposed to do with my money?" said O'Brien. "Do you think I keep it in a sock under the mattress, Mr Carswell?"

"I thought it was two houses," said Major Vernon.

"It is," said O'Brien, "but one of them is let already. The left hand one."

"With the plaster barely dry, I should think," said Major Vernon.

"Yes. But you were right – that was the part of town to go for – Eastcliffe, they are calling it now."

Felix remembered the walks he and Sukey had taken on those broad sands together, on the glittering tide margin, walking towards the cliffs. There had only been a few cottages scattered along the foreshore then, and on more than one occasion they had talked of taking one, and living there. It had seemed that nothing could ever part them.

"I do know one thing about Kennedy," O'Brien went on, getting up. "He worships the ground Sukey walks on. He wouldn't do anything to hurt her." He picked up his key from the table. "I'd better get to my bed."

When he had gone, Major Vernon said, "Although you may consider this too delicate an approach, I will talk to Kennedy tomorrow at the christening."

"Thank you," said Felix.

"And if I do not like what I hear, then we will consider what to do next."

They said good night and made their way to their respective quarters. But Felix got as far as his door and decided he was not ready for Eleanor, and so turned back towards the coffee room, in need of a smoke. As he did, he discovered Madame Jacquot sitting on an upholstered bench on a half-landing, rubbing one of her stockinged feet. She leapt up at the sight of him, and then darted forward to retrieve her abandoned shoe. This was all done with too much haste, with the result that she almost fell. Felix rushed forward to catch her and she stumbled into his arms.

"Oh, excuse me," she said, falling back onto the bench.

"Are you all right?" he said.

"Yes, yes," she said.

"Are you sure?" he said.

"I'm just tired."

"Then you should go to bed."

"I should but –" She gestured about her.

"What needs to be done that you must do now?" he said.

She considered his question and then yawned.

"You have a point, monsieur," she said, putting on her shoe. She winced as she did so.

"You've been on your feet all day, I imagine," he said, crouching down. "But perhaps I had better check if there is anything wrong?"

She reached out and stayed his hand. He felt a frisson of desire pass over him and when she said, "Not here," he wondered if she had felt the same thing.

"No, not here," he agreed.

He offered her his arm, which she accepted, and they made their way upstairs to the chintz-papered sitting room where she had given them tea that first night. She fell into an armchair and said: "Perhaps you should chop off my feet, Monsieur Surgeon! I am in agony. I have to confess it!"

"I don't think it will have to come to that," he said, going to adjust the lamps.

While his back was turned, he heard her laugh but it was that nervous, desperate laughter that collapsed soon enough into sobbing.

"These stupid, stupid shoes," she said. "You see, monsieur, I have the feet of une paysanne, made for sabots – what is the English?"

"Clogs," said Felix.

"Clogs, yes," she said, choking back her tears and pulling off a white stocking. "Not the pretty little feet of a lady. They are hideous," she added in French, thrusting out her foot from under her frilled petticoats.

"Let me be the judge of that," he said, kneeling down on the floor beside her. "No, not hideous. Just a little swollen. If I may?" She gave a gasp and a nod as he gently manipulated it. "You still have movement, there, so that's all well."

"You have cold fingers," she said.

"I'm sorry."

"No, I like it," she said, and burst into tears again. "Excuse me," she sobbed. "You are being so kind."

He was not sure this was at all kindness on his part. It was too pleasurable. Her straightforward, frank dissatisfaction with her foot, which was battered, red and with the suggestion of a bunion forming, spoke volumes about her: of her determination to make a success of her hotel, and at the same time, of her human vulnerability about her appearance. She was, he concluded, utterly adorable.

"It's a privilege, ma'am," he said, and reached for her hand. He meant only to give it a reassuring squeeze, but ended up kissing it.

"Oh dear," she said, but she did not withdraw her hand. She managed to smile, but with tears rolling down her face.

"You have had a cruel week," he said. "I should have sent you to bed after what happened with Morgueillon."

"And I would have disobeyed you," she said, with a great sniff. "How could I not? I had to carry on. It was all I could do. Especially as..." She paused, and now removed her hand from his. "I think I should be straight with you. I omitted to tell you something important the other night. It was not just that I was there at the moment. I was there for a reason. He and I – we had une petite histoire, if you understand."

"Oh," he said.

"Très petite," she said, holding up her hand and making a tiny space between her finger and thumb. "I soon realised that I could not be seriously involved with a man like that. He was ill in his mind, that was clear enough. So I backed away, and of course that did not help him."

"You must not think you are responsible," he said, and she nodded.

"I have not slept all week."

"Of course not," he said. "It must have broken you in two. I don't know how you have managed. You have been magnificent, you know, to carry on as you have done."

"I'm sorry I didn't tell you this that night. I felt ashamed. I did not want to say it in front of Monsieur le Major."

"You did well to keep it quiet. Usually he prises secrets out of people," said Felix.

"So I understand," she said.

"Perhaps it is because you are good at that as well. You got a secret out of me. About Mrs Kennedy."

"That must be hard," she said. "Even after it is all long over, it still hurts to see someone one once loved married to another."

"It might not hurt so much if I were more sure of myself," he said, getting up from his knees. "We fairly tore each other to pieces. There is nothing to regret, but I do regret it."

"That is how it was with my husband," she said, getting up.

"You probably should not –" he began.

"I am going to fetch my slippers," she said, going to the bedroom door. "Do you wish to smoke? That is why you were coming downstairs, I think."

"Yes. How did you –"

"I saw you in the garden the other day. Cheroots, non?"

"Yes."

"Just like my husband," she said. "I recognised the smell. I like it. There is some Marc de Bourgogne there as well, if you care for that."

She went into her bedroom, and Felix felt that the temperature of the room had become uncomfortably warm, so he took off his coat and then his waistcoat before he lit up his cheroot. He felt certain she would not mind this liberty – even, that it was what she expected of him.

He poured two small glasses of the brandy, took a sip of his own and discovered it was of the quality that would have unleashed a torrent of appreciation from Canon Fforde. He was just loosening his cravat when she returned, dressed now in the loose white wrapper she had worn the other night. But unlike the other evening when she had worn a demure cap, she had uncovered her hair and it was falling down in a dark tangle down her back. She smiled at the sight of him, and he wondered if she had taken off her stays.

He offered her the glass.

"I should not," she said. "But I see you have been moderate."

"It's good," he said.

"From my country," she said, and raised her glass to him before going to sit down again.

"Tell me about your husband," he said, sitting down near to her, "if you can bear to."

"He was a medical man, like you," she said. "You remind me of him. Though he was tall and fair, so I don't know how. Perhaps it was the cheroots."

"Were you happy?"

"That's a question!" she said.

"Forgive me."

"No, it's a good question," she said. "Just hard to answer.

I thought we would be, and then –"

"Yes, I know that," said Felix, leaning back and inhaling his cheroot.

"He died of the cholera," she went on. "It happened so quickly. We had a bad, bad quarrel, he went to work and we never had a minute alone again. And then he was dead. He did not even have the last rites – not that he would have cared, for he did not believe in God, and certainly not in that! But his poor mother..." She sighed. "I think it was worse for her."

"That I can't believe."

"You can only feel so much," she said. "But it is odd, is it not, that sometimes you feel so much and sometimes you feel nothing? I can never understand myself."

"That is the human condition," said Felix. "And the world is divided amongst those who make the attempt to understand it and those who do not, don't you think?"

"Perhaps," she said. "And so, are you happy?"

"Oh, I deserved that!" he said, but he was not much pained. There was great enjoyment in this trading of secrets.

"It strikes me you are not," she said.

"It's just as you said. Sometimes I feel nothing and sometimes I feel everything. My wife is more of a puzzle to me as each day passes."

"There is perhaps a particular puzzle that you wish to solve," she said. "Yes?" He glanced at her. She had pressed her glass to her glowing cheek. "Your wife and her friend."

"Yes?" he said.

"I saw something I was not supposed to see," she said.

"Go on," he said.

"Are you sure you want to know?"

"What did you see?"

"A kiss," she said. "I know women kiss each other but this was..."

"I see," said Felix. "What kind of kiss?"

"It's hard to describe – the lips... very wide, and the

tongue... Oh, I'm sorry," she said, glancing away. "That must hurt you."

"Perhaps it doesn't hurt so much," he said, "given that is what I have begun to guess at. Although I hardly understand it. I can see that Eleanor is impulsive and wayward, but Miss King?"

"Perhaps it is her natural state to love women," she said.

"But not Eleanor," said Felix. "She is..." Madame Jacquot now made an equivocal gesture which eloquently expressed the matter. "Yes. That does happen."

"Pierre told me about a man who loved men as much as women," she said. "It was a patient of his. He was in despair about it – the patient, not my husband."

"What did you husband advise?"

"He did not say. A sea voyage?" she said, and then burst out laughing. "Excuse me!" she said, but Felix was also laughing. "I didn't mean to make such a blague – all those handsome sailors..."

"No, no, it was perfect. And all the better for being unintended." Then when they had recovered from laughing, he said, "What is happening here?"

"We are becoming friends?" she said.

"Yes," he said, although looking at her he felt there would be more to it than the exchange of confidences and lewd jokes. He was feeling increasingly stirred now, and was wondering how much licence she would permit. A languid carelessness had stolen over him, as if nothing beyond the four walls of that room mattered. He was, in short, thoroughly beguiled.

She put down her glass and moved in her armchair so that her wrapper slipped away to reveal her bare legs. Her feet were in red satin slippers.

"How are your feet now?"

"Better," she said.

He got up from his chair and pulled a stool close to her

seat.

"I should look at the other one," he said.

"Should you?" she said, smiling.

"For completeness," he said, taking it into his lap and removing the slipper.

"It is equally hideous," she said.

"Not at all," he said, and stroked the sole of her foot, which caused her to gasp. "It is a handsome foot. I would like it done in marble. It could sit on my desk and remind me of your purposefulness."

"What nonsense," she said, laughing.

"I mean it," he said. "I see no reason we shouldn't we amuse ourselves, madame."

"Elisabeth," she said. "If you like, monsieur?"

"Elisabeth," he said. "That suits you. And Felix, if you please."

"Yes, of course," she said, and then straightening in her chair, said, "I wonder who you were named for."

"That I don't know," he said, and began to caress her leg. She leant back again, her head against the cushion, her eyes closed. Unable to resist any longer, he got up and kissed her. He kissed her as he understood she had seen Eleanor kissing Miss King. She opened her eyes and her lips, permitting the liberty, with evident pleasure.

"Shall we?" she said, gesturing towards the bedroom door, after they had indulged themselves in this way for some minutes. He did not need to be persuaded.

Chapter Twenty-four

"I have something to ask you, Major Vernon," Sukey said, catching sight of him.

"Susanna –" began Kennedy, but she darted forward, and laid her hand on Giles' arm.

"Will you be Lorenzo's godfather?" she said. "I really couldn't think of anyone better. Will you?"

They were standing in the courtyard garden of the Incurables Hospital, and the morning was warm and softly bright, making the old stone buildings and the well-stocked flower beds look especially picturesque. So too was Sukey: perfectly dressed for the christening of her child, in grey silk trimmed with cherry-red ribbons, and a flat straw hat that became her.

"That's a great honour," he said.

"Which you will accept?" she said.

"I –" he began. In any other circumstances he would have accepted at once, for the idea that she should trust him with this flooded him with pleasure. Yet he was acutely aware that Kennedy was looking stone-faced. It was clearly not his wish. "Are you sure?" he said.

"Would I have asked you if I were not?" she said, laying her hand on his arm again, and this time he felt a measure of pressure in it. "Please?"

"Of course, of course," he said, wishing he might take her hand and reassure her, for he sensed she was acting with bravado.

"I knew you would say yes," she said. "I shall go and tell Dr Greville."

There was an awkward pause as she left, and then

Kennedy said: "She is a little over-excited. Please do not feel obliged in any way."

"I'm happy to accept," said Giles.

Kennedy was silent and then said: "Don't you think it would be better for everyone that the connection between my wife and yourself was not prolonged in this way?"

"I think it is an excellent idea," said Giles, not at all liking Kennedy's tone. What did he mean by connection? Had Kennedy come to some erroneous conclusion about his relationship with Sukey? Had he mistaken him for her protector?

"Do you really think it is appropriate?" said Kennedy.

"I can't think why it would be inappropriate," said Giles, as lightly as he could. "Mrs Kennedy did a great service to my late wife. I'm in her debt and this is an opportunity to repay her. I assure you I will take my duties towards your son seriously."

Kennedy looked as if he were about to remonstrate further when Sally and Lady Charlotte came strolling up, arm in arm. They had been admiring the baby, who had been lying in state in his basket.

"Such a perfect child, Dr Kennedy!" said Lady Charlotte. "I am astounded at the beauty of his tiny hands. What do you think he will become? Another medical man? A great surgeon with deft fingers, perhaps?"

"I hear you are to be a sponsor," Sally said to Giles, and then turned to Dr Kennedy. "A good choice, sir. My brother is my son's godfather and it has done him a great deal of good. But I'm biased, of course."

"As you should be, Mrs Fforde," said Lady Charlotte.

The bell for Matins began to ring and they all went into the chapel. Here the old women of the hospital emerged from their quarters by means of a special door, and, all dressed in neat blue cloaks with frilled bonnets and snowy white aprons, went to sit in their allotted stalls adjacent to the altar. Above them carved angels blew on trumpets, as fine as anything in the Minster, and the old stained glass caught the sunlight and distilled it into coloured shadows.

Dr Greville had a plain yet eloquent way of reading the collect and Giles attempted to find some comfort in the message laid out for him. But he could not. Carswell's suspicions about Kennedy had begun to plague him. On the one hand, if Kennedy believed that he, Giles Vernon, was the source of his wife's previous dishonour, then his hostility to the investigation might be explained by that alone. But the man had plenty to hide on his own account. The court case in Ireland over the disputed will was shady, to say the least, and might imply a great deal more. Had Kennedy dispatched a patient before their time for pecuniary gain, and had Carrington come to realise that?

They had come to the general confession, and Giles, repeating the familiar words with the usual rueful sense that they had been written expressly for him, glanced up and saw Kennedy's bare head bent over his prayer book. Had he decided to leave the faith of his birth to avoid the trial of the confessional? If he had gone to confession and admitted to murder, then the priest would have surely demanded that he turn himself in to the appropriate authorities. Absolution would be conditional on accepting civil as well as divine judgement. The Church of England made no such demand. He could confess without any specificity and feel the warm embrace of forgiveness. Did Kennedy care about such things? If so, it was a crack in his defences that might be of use to them.

He could not forget Sukey's hand on his arm and the look in her eyes. Was she telling him to be wary? She was certainly asking for protection. She knew he would not take such a duty lightly. As a custom it was a fine thing, to give a child such protectors.

The baptism took place at the end of the service, through

which Lorenzo had stayed blissfully sleepy in his rush basket. But when Sukey lifted him out to present him to the priest, he bawled, as was traditional, and continued to do so as the Kennedys (who were acting as godparents as well as birth parents) and Giles formally renounced the Devil and all his works, not to mention carnal desires and the vain pomp and glory of the world. It was an impressive show, all in all, especially when Dr Greville's soothing tones quieted him. Perhaps he was destined to be a great actor, for his timing was impeccable. Giles noticed Mrs Greville was crying copiously. At the same time he saw that behind her, a woman wearing a heavy black veil had joined the congregation. It was Mrs Stuart.

~

"It still feels wrong that there was no Mass said," said O'Brien, taking his nephew into his arms. "Oh, but you are a strong one, aren't you!" he exclaimed. "But it was nicely done. I can see why you like that Dr Greville, Sue."

"What will you tell Bridie?" said Sukey.

"I have no idea," he said, kissing Lorenzo. "If I took him back with me, it might help. She never can resist a baby."

"She has resisted mine," said Sukey, and then burst into tears.

"Oh Lord –" said O'Brien, thrusting the baby into Giles' care and going to embrace her. "We will get all this put right, I know it. It will just take time."

He led her away and Giles was left managing his new godchild. He soon became distinctly fractious, from hunger no doubt, but it was clear that O'Brien and Sukey should have some time together undisturbed.

"You will just have to wait," said Giles, and carried him

over to Lady Charlotte and Sally.

"Poor Mrs Kennedy," said Sally. "I cried all through Tom's christening, and I had most of my family about me. I am glad Mr O'Brien came. It is a terrible time to have a rift in the family. Why he could not be allowed to be a godfather I don't know. These silly rules."

"Do you think Mrs Kennedy would mind if I held him?" said Lady Charlotte.

"I can't imagine she would," said Giles, happy now to pass Lorenzo to her. She soon had the measure of him, letting him suck on her finger.

"I shall take him to see the old women," said Lady Charlotte.

The hospital inhabitants were sitting on the benches in the garden enjoying after-church conversation, and Lady Charlotte's arrival with the baby seemed to delight them.

"It's a pity Mr Fitznorton is not here to see that," said Sally.

"It's just as well," said Giles.

"Where did he go this morning? The old parish church, I suppose."

"No, he made a point of telling me that he was going to St Luke's. It's that barn of a place just by the railway station."

"Oh yes, of course, St Luke's!" she said. "There was a fuss about it, as it is extremely low. But the young man who has the charge is supposed to be very good, in his way."

"I'm glad I had the excuse to come here," said Giles.

"It was a beautiful service," said Sally. "Those charming old women and a baby!"

"Not to mention a handsome young widow," said Giles, indicating Mrs Stuart who was speaking to some of the hospital inmates.

"That is the lady from the opera, is it not?" said Sally.

"Yes."

"Poor creature. Still, she has friends here, it seems. I

wonder how Celia is getting on this morning."

"Ruling her new roost, I'm sure," said Giles. Now he noticed that Kennedy was talking to Mrs Stuart. They had moved away from the old women, and seemed to be having an intense conversation.

"What do you make of Dr Kennedy?" he asked Sally.

"I am sure he is most worthy," said Sally, "but he seems cold to me. Perhaps he is too aware of himself. It cannot be easy to be a convert. Imagine if it were the other way. It is such an unusual situation."

"Yes, it is."

"Lamb said that it was almost unprecedented. It happens often enough that dissenters will become members of the established Church, and of course it is not uncommon amongst Jewish families. But since the Catholic emancipation, he cannot be acting thus because he is suffering discrimination. It must be a matter of conviction."

"He didn't want me to be a godfather," Giles said.

"Then he's a fool," said Sally. "Oh, dear me!" she added, for Lorenzo was now screaming in Lady Charlotte's charge. Kennedy looked round from his conversation with a frown, and seeing this, Charlotte carried the howling infant over to his father.

"You want your papa, surely!" she said and presented him to Dr Kennedy, in such a fashion that he had to take the boy from her. He looked discomforted, but was obliged to mutter his thanks while Lady Charlotte dropped a most inappropriate curtsey, with such a sly smile on her face that Giles could not prevent himself laughing. "I am done nursemaiding!" said Charlotte, coming over to them.

"I think Dr Kennedy feels likewise," said Sally, for he had at once taken the child to Sukey. They went inside together – Sukey, presumably to feed Lorenzo, and Dr Kennedy – Giles had a dreadful suspicion – to berate his wife.

"What a great gloomy fellow he is," said Charlotte. "It

ought to be a happy day for him. Does he ever smile?"

This struck him as an interesting observation.

O'Brien joined them and said, "I have to get back to Northminster. There's a train at one. Can I take any messages for you, Mrs Fforde?"

"That's so kind, Mr O'Brien, thank you, but I have none," said Sally. "But please give my best wishes to Mrs O'Brien."

Giles went to the gates of the Incurables Hospital with O'Brien.

"Keep an eye on Sukey, will you?" O'Brien said.

"You know I will," said Giles.

"I told her the house was there if she wants it."

"Do you think it might come to that?"

"Put it this way: I think Carswell may be onto something. You should take him in and do your work on him, Major."

"Tempting. I certainly don't like him, and I don't like what sort of a husband he seems to be, but there is still some distance between that and making an actual accusation of murder. He's no fool and he has a calm head. There is still something about the way that Carrington was disposed of that seems too impulsive to be quite his style. Tell me, did Mrs Kennedy say anything particularly troubling?"

"No. But I think she's afraid." Giles nodded. "That asking you to be godfather against his wishes – well, I don't know what you thought, Major, but..." O'Brien put his hat on, consulted his watch and said, "I'd better get on my way."

Giles watched him walk away before turning back into the hospital garden. Mrs Stuart was coming towards him, putting down her bonnet veil.

"Allow me," he said, holding the gate open for her.

"Thank you," she said, and was about to leave, when one of the old women came shuffling up behind them with more speed than might have been expected given the woman's age.

"Mark you have it tomorrow, my lady!" said the old woman. "I shall not wait any longer."

"I'm sorry, I don't know what you are talking about," said Mrs Stuart.

"You know very well!" exclaimed the old woman.

"Mrs Barnaby, what is wrong?" said Mrs Greville, who had followed the women to gates.

"She owes me money!" said Mrs Barnaby. "She said I should have it today. I gave her ten shillings and she was to give me twenty back for it."

"I really have no idea what you are talking about," said Mrs Stuart. "Now, will you please excuse me, I must go home." She began walking away quickly.

"I will have it tomorrow, my lady!" shouted Mrs Barnaby after her. She was out of the gateway now. "A promise is a promise!"

"Hush, hush, now Mrs Barnaby," said Mrs Greville, taking her arm and leading her back in. "I think you are confused. She gets confused at times," she added to Giles. "Shall we go back to your room and find you a cup of tea?"

"I'm not confused!" said Mrs Barnaby, refusing to move. "She has my money."

Mrs Greville looked as if she were summoning reserves of patience as she said, "Whatever you say, Mrs Barnaby. Perhaps she has gone to fetch it?" This seemed to mollify Mrs Barnaby and she agreed to be steered back into the garden. "I'm sure she will be back later."

Giles closed the gate and followed them across the courtyard, thinking how he would tackle Kennedy. He was not in the best position for such a conversation given the man was already annoyed with him.

Unfortunately, it soon became clear he was not going to able to do anything. The Kennedys had come outside again and were now taking their leave of Dr Greville.

"You won't stay for lunch?" said Dr Greville.

"I'm sorry, but I have a headache," Sukey was saying. "You've been so kind, but I think I must go home." She looked utterly wretched.

~

Felix was struggling to feel like a sinner, though the clergyman was determined on the attempt. Instead, he felt strangely serene, as if he had discovered a truth that few people understood. That this was the high road to libertinism and a most unfashionable stance for the day only increased his pleasure. The cant on display about him in this shiny new preaching box was considerable and he felt that it should be opposed robustly. His night with Elisabeth had been a dazzling excursion, and he had no intention of repenting. Even now, as the clergyman spoke a great deal about the fiery pits of Hell, Felix found himself thinking of the sweetness of her warm lips on his bare skin, her gentle touch and later, her sleepy pleasure in his embrace.

"Why on earth did we bother with that?" he muttered to Eleanor as they came out of the church.

"I don't know. I don't think I care to be shouted at so much, I must say," she said, taking his arm. It was curious how close he felt to her in that moment. If she had been seeking her own amusement elsewhere, he no longer felt annoyed by it. They were more alike than he imagined, and curiously well-suited. "He must be hoarse."

"We shall have to be careful that Mr Fitznorton does not insist on examining us on the principal points," said Felix, glancing back to where Fitznorton was talking to the clergyman.

"I can't remember a thing he said," said Eleanor. "But I can tell you there were some extraordinary bonnets. Did you see that one with the yellow feathers?"

"Yes, from a large canary, apparently," said Felix.

"I think not. They dye feathers, you know," she said.

"Unfortunately yes, I do know that," said Felix. "But I like the idea of monstrously large canaries much better. Bigger than parrots, perhaps."

"It is a nice conceit," said Eleanor. "They would be popular."

"If one was to breed for size," he said, "one might get halfway there. But it would take some time, and a great many generations. How often does husbandry manage that transformation, I wonder?"

"You will have to try it," said Eleanor, and darted off to retrieve Miss King from the crowd. They returned to him, arm and arm, and once again he was filled with a delicious sense of laissez-faire. There was something appealing about the sight of them together and the idea of their intimacy no longer troubled or offended him. On the contrary, it was convenient. He had returned to his room that morning and found the bed had not been slept in. He had not been missed, certainly.

Chapter Twenty-five

"Are you sure you will not drive with us to Holbroke?" said Charlotte to Felix, as they were having lunch.

"I would, but Major Vernon wants me at work," said Felix. "He wants to review all the evidence."

Fitznorton frowned and said, "Does Major Vernon often work on a Sunday?"

"No," said Felix, "but the circumstances demand it. We are on campaign, so to speak."

"I'm afraid I shall not be able to oblige him," said Fitznorton. "I make a point of not working on the Sabbath. Surely, it can wait until tomorrow?"

"You must ask him that yourself," said Felix. "But time is rarely on our side in these matters. Given that our murderer had no respect for a day of rest and went about his work last Sunday, then it behoves us to shift ourselves a little. The ratepayers of Stanegate deserve no less. They pay our wages, after all."

"Wages, Felix?" said Charlotte. "It is hardly that in your case."

"Stipend, then?" he said. "But that sounds pompous."

"You should not worry about that," she said, "since you were behoving just then, which is almost the definition of pomposity. Oh, it's such a shame you cannot come back with us," she went on. "But duty is duty, and you must catch this man as soon as possible. I had hoped you would come as well, Mr Fitznorton, but it seems you will not be at liberty either."

"I shall be at liberty, as I shall not be obliging Major Vernon," said Fitznorton, "but I'm afraid I should not have been able to oblige you in your wishes either, my lady. I shall keep the Sabbath as I always do: no work, no idle leisure and no unnecessary travel."

"Very admirable," said Charlotte, "but I think Carswell has a point. The business in hand would seem to override such personal scruples."

"I cannot agree," said Mr Fitznorton. "The Sabbath must be kept as God ordained it, as a day of rest."

"As far as is possible, yes," said Charlotte. "And it is a fine principle. Of course we all must have our rest, and make sure that those we are responsible for take their ease at least once a week, but it is impossible, surely to adhere to it in all circumstances?"

"All the more reason to attempt it. God has commanded it. That is the point."

"So you think Mr Carswell should not attend upon sick child on the Sabbath?" said Charlotte. "A child who might die otherwise?"

"That is for his conscience," said Fitznorton. "But I should not break the Sabbath for such a reason."

"Then thank goodness you are not a medical man!" said Charlotte, with a brittle laugh. "You were well advised in your choice of profession, Mr Fitznorton."

"You are missing my point, my lady," said Fitznorton. "You must remember God's will in all this. A sick child, however dreadful it is to see, is in the hands of God. His fate depends on God's mercy and grace, not the action of medical men. The more we trust God and honour His commandments, then the better we may accept such events for what they are."

"Which is? A test of the parent's piety?" said Charlotte. "Or even that of the child? Oh no, Mr Fitznorton, I will not have that. For if that is the case, why do we have doctors at all?"

"That is a question I have sometimes considered myself," said Fitznorton. Felix could not prevent letting out a snort.

"Does this amuse you, sir?"

"The last time I had this conversation," Felix said, "I was eighteen, and the fellow taking your line had the most appalling case of erysipelas."

"Which is?" said Charlotte.

"A most unpleasant skin disorder. It was one of the worst cases of it I have ever seen."

"I am glad we have finished eating," said Charlotte.

"That was the difficulty," said Felix. "He was one of the lodgers at Professor Hill's. We were all sick at the sight of him at the dinner table, but he refused to have it treated, although it would not have been a difficult matter. I suggested something to him and he said he would not take any treatment as he considered it a sign of Providence, and he was supposed to suffer it. A candidate for the ministry, of course. I wonder if he ever managed to get himself a charge, let alone a wife."

"Oh dear," said Charlotte. "I'm sure he came to his senses eventually."

"He called medical men the progeny of the Devil!" said Felix.

"I'm sure you did not let that pass," said Charlotte. "I remember how Papa used to sigh over your letters from Edinburgh."

"You should have seen the ones I got back!" said Felix.

"Ah yes, I have had one or two of those myself," said Charlotte, smiling. "Thinking back to your poor fellow lodger, I'm sure a pretty young woman telling him to apply some witch-hazel to his face would have cured him nicely."

"Another reason to admit women to the medical profession," said Felix.

"Are you serious in that?" said Fitznorton.

"Yes, on reflection, it would be a great advance in civilisation," said Felix. "Take a young woman – someone like Miss Fforde, for example, who has a mixture of intelligence, compassion and duty – and train her, and then put her in the service of her own sex in their hour of need –"

"On whatever day of the week it may be required," said Charlotte, pointedly. "Yes, that would be a wonder and such a comfort to women."

"It would unsex them," said Fitznorton. "Those who practise medicine, I mean."

"How?" said Charlotte. "I cannot see it. Now, what is the time?" Felix showed her his watch. "Then the carriage will be here shortly. I must go and get ready," she said, getting up from the table.

Naturally all the men got to their feet as well and she was obliged to pass Fitznorton on her way to the door. He stepped into her path to delay her.

"I hope you will consider what I have said, my lady," he said. "This is a serious matter."

"I'm sure it is," she said. "But really, Mr Fitznorton, is it not rather vain to choose not to work when there is work to be done? Now, if you will please excuse me."

~

"He will be happier with his book of sermons," said Major Vernon as they walked down to the Stanegate Constabulary office, having seen off the carriages to Holbroke. Fitznorton had retired to read until Evensong.

"Greek New Testament," said Felix. "He made a point of telling me so. And you knew he would not come, didn't you?"

"It was a lucky guess."

"Lucky?" said Felix, smiling. "I smell strategy."

"It is most unprofessional of me, of course, to exclude him deliberately, but the truth is he unsettles me. I cannot think when he is in the room. Heavens, what does that sound like?" he went on with a laugh. "A finicky dowager, perhaps –

no, a swooning poet."

"Perhaps there is a touch of the artist in what you do," said Carswell.

"In that my pride enjoys being swollen by approbation?"

"No, not that, and I don't think it's true. No, I was thinking that there is something mysterious about how you sometimes hit on the solution that does seem akin to poetry."

"I'm surprised to hear you say that, as a man of science."

"Think of Newton and his apple. He was in a state of idle contemplation in his apple orchard and voilà, the idea of gravity came to him."

"I don't suppose Newton would have come to his idea unless he was in full possession of all the other necessary facts. Enough of them to give him the confidence to make such a leap into the dark," said Major Vernon.

"Certainly, but it is that leap that I find the mysterious element in this. Not everyone will be inclined to do it. It requires courage and imagination, and a lack of fear of failure. You do not fear being wrong, do you?"

"No, not particularly. One can achieve nothing worthwhile without making a great many mistakes."

"An attitude which is akin to that of a poet or a painter," said Felix. "And by it, you are reaching for something more than the sum of the parts."

"I would not exclude yourself from that method," said Major Vernon. "Is that not the general nature of experiments? Looking for something that might be there, but might as easily not be." They had now reached the station house. "Perhaps we would be better sitting in an orchard," he said, his hand on the door.

Inside, the duty Sergeant was dozing over a copy of the previous day's Bugle, apparently impervious to their arrival.

"Mr O'Brien would be disappointed to see that," said Major Vernon, leaning over the desk and extracting the paper, waking the man as he did so. The Sergeant started up and leapt to his feet, full of apologies.

"I ate too much dinner, sir," he said. "My wife made a plum duff, you see, and brought me a great slice of it." He pointed to an empty plate sitting near to the arrest log.

"Clear that up, please, Sergeant. Perhaps you should make yourself some coffee – and some for us while you are at it? No, we will have tea."

"Of course, sir – at once, sir."

Felix followed Major Vernon into the room he had commandeered for the investigation. It was warm, the sun amplified by the closed Holland blinds. Major Vernon opened the windows but there was barely a breeze to stir the papers pinned to the wall.

"I wonder what Sergeant Browne thinks of working on the Sabbath," said Felix taking off his coat.

"He gets double pay for doing so," said Major Vernon. "So it cannot be too objectionable."

"Especially if that work is making tea for us and reading The Bugle," said Felix, yawning. "Excuse me. Are you sure we should not have coffee?"

"At the risk of sounding again like a finicky dowager," said Major Vernon, also taking off his coat, "I do not trust Sergeant Browne to make coffee that is drinkable."

"Signor Luchetti has spoiled you."

"Apparently," said Major Vernon, taking up his customary place in front of the papers, his hands behind his back. "That is the tendency of Stanegate, perhaps."

He stood in silence for a few minutes and then turned and sat down. Between them on a large baize-covered table lay the neat piles of Carrington's documents made by the assiduous Fitznorton, each tied with tape and bearing a pinned description of their contents.

"One cannot fault it," said Major Vernon. "And yet do we really have any idea of what manner of man Carrington was?"

"Someone who liked everyone else's secrets," said Felix. "That is the fault line, surely?"

Major Vernon nodded and said: "But we need to narrow our field. Let us take the stance that not everyone is disposed to or capable of murder. That leaves us to identify those individuals who are more likely to be able to execute a considerable act of violence and then dispose of the body in such an interesting fashion. That is key. So if we turn to Dr Kennedy, for example..." He began to look through the papers. "Where is Kennedy?"

Felix straightened in his chair, realising that he had been as neglectful of his duty as the hapless sergeant. The intensity of the previous night with Elisabeth had left him suspended in a giddy state of rapture from which he now fell, fast and hard, back into reality.

"Here," said Felix, finding it close at hand. He picked it up. "Not the thickest pile, by any means."

"That's a point in his favour, perhaps," said Major Vernon, taking it from him. "Or it indicates that he may have covered his tracks well."

"What happened this morning?" Felix asked.

"I did not speak to him, not as I would have liked, at least," said Major Vernon, "for which I apologise. The right moment did not arise. Mrs Kennedy was..."

"Yes?" Felix said. The Major's tone was grave and unsettling.

"Seeing O'Brien upset her," he said. "She left with a headache. But that's not all of it. She quarrelled with her husband. Certainly he was angry with her. That was undeniable."

"Angry?"

"She went against his wishes. She asked me to be a godfather, and he clearly did not like it. But I accepted anyway. I think she was asking for protection in some form or other. I am certainly finding it hard not to be concerned about her welfare."

"Dear God," Felix murmured.

"But, as to Kennedy being our man –" Major Vernon said. "Is it really plausible? Yes, he may be an arrogant, domineering husband, but that does not make him a brutal killer. The former is unfortunately as commonplace as the latter is rare."

If this was meant to spare Felix's feelings, it did not.

"A headache?" he said. "I wish I might go and –"

"But that would do no good. If he dislikes me, who knows what he thinks of you!"

"She hasn't told him," said Felix.

"But he has an idea that there was something untoward," said the Major. "However, he may think that I was the guilty party."

"My apologies," said Felix. "Eleanor had that idea too."

"Those who weren't there can't understand, so they perceive the matter wrongly. I can't deny that I have a high regard for her," said Major Vernon. Felix nodded. "Which makes this situation all the more awkward, of course," he concluded, getting up and staring again at the papers pinned to the wall. "There is a part of me which would like to arrest Kennedy and see what he has to say for himself. The business of the leopard cage gives me pause. It is an unlikely way to get rid of a body."

"It may just have been an idle observation on Kennedy's part," said Felix, gathering his thoughts and getting up to stand beside him. "We should not let our feelings get the better of us – as you have pointed out before. If he was responsible, would he have cut Carrington's throat when he has a bag of poisons to hand?"

"And then there is the murder scene itself," said Major Vernon. "We have no idea about that yet." He went to his coat and took out his plan of the town, spreading it on the table. "Where seems likely? It depends how the body was moved.

Where is that blanket?"

"Here," said Felix. It had been folded neatly on a side table along with the remains of Carrington's clothing. He shook it out and held it up.

"So we have bloodstains on that side, I remember you concluded," said Major Vernon. "From the stab wounds?"

"Yes," said Felix. "This side was lying against the body, from the pattern of the stains."

"So what is on the back?"

Felix now flung it over Fitznorton's paperwork.

"Dirt marks," he said.

"Drag marks?" said Major Vernon.

Felix took out his hand lens, drew up the blinds to improve the light and studied the brown-black streaks.

"Possibly," said Felix. "It's dry dirt. It hasn't soaked in, like the blood."

"It's hard work to move a dead man," said Major Vernon, "even if you have transport."

"But no one saw or heard anything of that nature that night, or so they say. Perhaps the menagerie owner – what is his name again?"

"Askham," said Major Vernon.

"Perhaps he is being less than forthcoming. What if Carrington came to see him, there was a fracas, Carrington died and Askham fed him to his leopards?"

"Askham has a perfectly good alibi," said Major Vernon. "As does the keeper Bobby Farr, who lives in the gatehouse. No, they are nothing to do with this, I'm sure of that, at least."

He picked up the map again. "It is easier, of course, to move something when gravity is with you. Downhill. From the Rustic Cottages, perhaps?" He removed the blanket. "Is there anything here about Sir Henry Boynton or Lady Amberleigh?"

"Seemingly not," said Felix, scanning them.

"Remember, these papers were in Mrs Thorne's sideboard. Her maid, Mary Carter, willingly surrendered them to me. Now it appears she is involved with Sir Henry. I presume he met her while he was at Mrs Thorne's cottage with Carrington. Perhaps she removed anything incriminating at his request."

"It's possible."

"Lady Amberleigh has a house up there as well," said Major Vernon, tapping the blank area on the map which the Rustic Cottages now occupied. "Adelaide Lodge, to which I assume Sir Henry has access. How far is that from the leopard cage, I wonder? We should talk to Sir Henry and Lady Amberleigh. Do you fancy a jaunt to the country tomorrow, Mr Carswell?"

"Yes, certainly," said Felix. "Though I don't imagine my presence will make Lady Amberleigh very forthcoming, given her previous relationship with Lord Rothborough."

"It will serve to disconcert her. That can be helpful."

"True enough," said Felix, remembering the occasion two years ago when he had found the Countess, veiled in black lace, waiting in his consulting room to see him. Then she had been determined to cause trouble for Lord Rothborough. "She disconcerted me when she took it into her head to come and see me."

"And while we are paying our call, I shall send Mr Fitznorton out for a day on the beat with one of the constables here," Major Vernon said. "Captain Lazenby should have arranged for him to do that."

"Perhaps he did not dare to," said Felix, amused. "Fitznorton will enjoy that! Although as he is the sort to relish a hair shirt, perhaps he truly will."

"If he has any real interest in the day-to-day business of policing, he will find it instructive," said Major Vernon.

"And perhaps it will take his mind off Charlotte," said Felix. "Though I do not think we shall have to worry on that front after the set-to they had at lunch. He will not care for her after that, thank goodness."

"I don't know," said Major Vernon. "He may see that as a challenge. He has the mentality of a missionary. He may be thinking he might save her."

"As if we are all a pack of heathens?" said Felix. "That is disgusting, but entirely plausible. However, I do not think Charlotte would fall for that."

"I think she is as vulnerable as any of us," said Major Vernon.

Chapter Twenty-six

Elisabeth was an early riser, even after an energetic night.

"You must go and disarrange your bedsheets," she said. "Otherwise you will alarm your faithful Jacob."

"Moore," said Felix. "I suppose so. I cannot have him carrying tales."

"And I do not want my maid seeing you here," she said, handing him his shirt.

"Of course," he said.

"And I think Major Vernon has ordered your horses for nine," she said.

"Is there any detail that does not escape you?"

"Plenty. Sometimes I lie awake wondering if there are enough chamberpots, or if the glaze on the napkins could be done better."

"You were not lying awake last night, I hope?"

"No, I have slept beautifully," she said. "Better than I have for a long time. And believe me, I would like nothing better than to stay in bed and play with you, but we have our work to do."

"Unfortunately," Felix said, kissing her. She allowed it, and then disentangled herself. "Non, enough. This will be all the sweeter for being as rare – as rare as a white truffle. You must go."

"And I was just thinking," Felix said, pulling his shirt over his head, "I should give up everything, and we should run a hotel together. I could count the chamberpots for you."

"That would be a waste of your genius," she said. "And I do not like scandal."

"But you risk it," he said.

"Because I have lost my head over you," she said. "So you had better vanish before I find it again."

"It is squarely on your beautiful shoulders," he said, going and kissing them. She had just put on her chemise and was putting on her stays. He wrapped his arms about her and she allowed the embrace for a brief space, before gently pushing him away.

"Don't tempt me, Felix," she said, "it's not fair. Remember, it is better, far better, that we leave ourselves hungry."

"This is going to be impossible," he said, retrieving his trousers and watching her adjusting her stays, her elegant, deft fingers plucking at the strings at the back to tighten them.

"A test of character," she said, at which he had to laugh.

Deferring to her good sense, he gathered the rest of his clothes, and said a final goodbye. He left her, still dizzy with astonishment at all that had occurred between them over the past two nights. It was not just the physical pleasure of it – although that had been intense – but the frankness of their conversation. They had talked through the wrongs and the rights of it all. She had told him, with charming matter of factness, that she was lonely, but at the same time, she had no wish or desire to be married again.

"I want friendship, not love," she had said. "That is what I want." What was most remarkable to him was that her definition of friendship included all the delights of the bedroom.

"Good morning!"

It was, inevitably, Fitznorton. Ruddy-faced and perspiring, dressed in a striped fisherman's shirt and white trousers, he must have been out pursuing some wholesome exercise. Felix, with his evening coat slung over his shoulder, knew that his appearance betrayed him as coming from a different arena of activity, and Fitznorton's grave expression told him that he perfectly understood this. Determined not to feel any shame, Felix gave a nonchalant wave and responded, "Good morning!"

"The carriage from Holbroke has arrived," Fitznorton said.

"What carriage?" Felix said.

"I don't think I mistook the livery," said Fitznorton. "I recognised it from yesterday."

"I wasn't expecting it," said Felix.

An explanation soon presented itself. Lord Rothborough's loyal Mr Bodley was coming along the passageway with his gleaming silk hat in his hand.

"Oh, there you are Master Felix," said Bodley, laying his hand on his chest. "Thank Heavens!"

"What has happened?"

"It's his Lordship," said Bodley. "He's been ill all night, and I don't like the look of it at all, so I thought I would come and get you."

"Of course," said Felix, knowing that Bodley would not do this unless the situation was serious. "You can tell me what happened while I get changed. Mr Fitznorton, will you please tell Major Vernon I have gone to Holbroke?"

"Yes, certainly. I pray that it is nothing serious."

"Thank you. Let us hope not."

"Young Jacob is packing for you, sir," said Bodley as they went along to his rooms.

"What is wrong with Lord Rothborough?" said Felix.

"He was taken ill yesterday afternoon, just after everyone arrived, and he took to his bed. He did not go down for dinner, and he could not eat a mouthful, and he has been in pain, with a fever. I kept him as cool as I could – I know that is what you advise, and he was calm enough, but he's in much more pain than he says, sir, and I spoke to Lady Charlotte and we agreed you must come."

"Ah, you found him, Mr Bodley," said Jacob, as they went into the bedroom.

"Who pray is 'him', Jacob Moore?" said Bodley. "Watch your tone, my lad. Excuse him, Master Felix, won't you?"

"Sorry, Mr Bodley," said Jacob. "And sorry, sir," he added to Felix. "It was only that your bed not being slept in and all, I was worried, sir, truth be told."

"Whether your master's bed is slept in or not is none of your concern, my lad," said Bodley. "And what are you doing with that waistcoat? That is not the way to fold it. Go and fetch some hot water!" Jacob left looking thoroughly chastened. "You are too easy on him, Master Felix," Bodley continued, shaking out the waistcoat. "He needs a firm hand."

"He's not a dog," said Felix.

"Nothing wrong with a well-trained dog, sir," said Bodley, taking Felix's coat from him. "Now, will you be wanting to shave?"

This was not a request but a command, and Felix – like Jacob, knowing his place in Bodley's orderly world – knew he had no choice but to submit.

~

As he rode up the long drive and caught his first glimpse of Amberleigh Castle, Giles concluded that the Earl of Amberleigh was a lucky young man. The house, ancient and castellated, had been gently modernised in the most picturesque way and was set against a hillside covered with lush plantings. That the parkland of the estate had been landscaped by some ingenious hand was without doubt, probably some fifty years ago, with everything now coming to perfection.

He rode towards the house following a long, twisting drive under a canopy of huge Spanish chestnuts.

As he approached, he saw a young woman and a girl

playing with a dog on the sweeping front lawn. Judging by their elaborate dresses, they were daughters of the house. The dog, a tiny scrap of a thing, was clearly under the impression he was a vast mastiff and came tearing towards him, yapping furiously. Riding a livery horse of uncertain temper, Giles thought it best to dismount.

The younger girl came rushing after the dog and scooped him into her arms, which did nothing to stop the dog's agitation.

"Oh, you are so silly!" she exclaimed to the dog, and then to Giles, "Who are you?"

Giles was briefly lost for words. She was about Celia's age and her features exhibited a curious blend of those of Lady Charlotte and Carswell.

"Major Vernon, of the Northminster Constabulary," he said.

The other young woman now joined them. She was as flaxen-haired as the other was dark.

"The police? What do you want with us, sir?" she said.

"I would like to speak to your mother, if she is at home? Lady Amberleigh."

"Yes, she's at home," said the younger girl. "But she won't see anyone."

"I should like to try my luck, my lady," said Giles. "I've come all the way from Stanegate."

"Perhaps she will see you," said the older girl.

"Thank you," he said.

"Take care of the gentleman's horse," said the older girl to the servant who had come out of the house. "If you would care to come inside, Major Vernon, I can see what can be done."

"That's most kind of you, Lady –?"

"I am Margaret, and this is Clara."

"There's been a murder in Stanegate," said Lady Clara. "My brother said that was all they talked about at the cricket.

Is that why you are here, Major Vernon?"

"Yes. I saw your brother playing yesterday."

"Sir Henry mentioned you," said Lady Margaret.

"Yes, I spoke to him."

"Was it about the murder?" said Lady Clara.

"Clara!" exclaimed her sister.

"Well, he would have to," went on Lady Clara, "since Sir Henry knew Captain Carrington, as did Mama. That's why you are here, isn't it? Yes?" Her manner was as disconcerting as her appearance. "I have read about you in The Bugle, Major Vernon."

"Clara, really, you should not read that! Mama would be very cross."

"She reads it. Everyone does."

"I do not," said Lady Margaret. "Now, I think you had better go, Clara – this business is nothing to do with you."

"Oh, very well," said Lady Clara. "But do stay for lunch, Major Vernon. I have a hundred questions for you. I never thought I should meet you in person!"

"Go away!" said Lady Margaret.

Giles followed Lady Margaret into the house. She took him into a sitting room and said, "I hope you don't mind waiting. It may take me a while to persuade Mama."

"No, of course not. Is Sir Henry here today?"

"Yes, somewhere about. He and my brother went out earlier, fishing or some such. They will be back for lunch. Perhaps you had better stay."

She left him. It was an agreeable room in which to be made to wait. All the signs of a pleasant domestic life adorned it, from the vases of flowers from the garden, to the friendly round table containing all the latest magazines and newspapers. Amongst them was The Bugle. Such was the genius of O'Brien's weekly that it had gained very different readers from the ordinary working families that he had first intended it for. It was beguiling and yet wholesome;

entertaining and yet soundly factual. Hamish, who had scarcely been able to read, now made such a careful weekly study of it that whenever the household copy was wanted, it was usually to be found in his favourite corner.

Giles was just glancing through the much less interesting County Gazette, when the door opened and Lady Clara slipped into the room.

"I knew she'd put you in here," she said, closing the door behind her and leaning on it. "I should be doing my piano practice."

"Is there something you want to tell me, Lady Clara?"

"Yes. I don't know if it's important. But ever since we heard about Captain Carrington's death, it's been very curious here."

"Did you ever meet the Captain?" said Giles, taking out his notebook.

"Oh, yes. He came here lots of times."

"What did you make of him?"

"I didn't like him," she said. "I know one isn't supposed to judge a person, but you know how it is when someone makes you feel uncomfortable?"

"Yes, indeed."

"That was Captain Carrington. He was much too nice. He was as shiny as his boots, and always greasing up to Mama and Sir Henry and Margaret as if they were gods on earth." She paused to catch breath. "I wasn't surprised that someone murdered him. Oh, I know I shouldn't say that, but – well, you know about these things, sir, don't you? Is it true about the leopards?" she added inconsequentially.

"In what respect?"

"That they ate him?"

"Yes, but they did not kill him. He was already dead."

"Oh good!" she said. "Oh, I don't mean that, but they are such beautiful creatures I did not think they would kill anyone."

"I think they could," said Giles. "But in this case, no."

"What will happen to them?"

"I don't know."

"Sir Henry said they would have to be shot," she said.

"You discussed all this with him?"

"I was talking about it with Johnny – my brother, that is – and Sir Henry said that there was no choice but to shoot them. But surely something else could be done?"

"It's a difficult question."

"Moonshine and Mercury are the only things in that menagerie I like," she said. "The rest of it is horrible, especially those camels, and really, it is awful that the leopards should be there as well, although I suppose that cage is large enough. But if you look into their eyes they look so sad. Sir Henry said that he was not surprised that someone got in there by chance, as it was so ramshackle."

"When did he say this?"

"The other day when Johnny and I were talking about it," she said.

"Would you say Sir Henry and Captain Carrington were friends?" said Giles.

"Oh, no, not really. But Mama liked him. That's why she is hiding upstairs, I think. I heard her say she was heartbroken about it."

"Who did she say that to?" said Giles.

"Sir Henry," said Lady Clara. "That's what I want to tell you. They had the most terrible quarrel about it. I know I shouldn't have listened, but I couldn't help it. I was in her dressing room – Mama's, that is – and the door was open to her bedroom, and Sir Henry was there. I was just playing with her dog. I didn't mean to hear it."

"I see," said Giles, wondering how often Sir Henry was in Lady Amberleigh's bedroom and for what reason. "So what was the gist of this argument?"

"It was about Captain Carrington: Sir Henry was saying

that it was a good thing he was dead, and Mama was crying and saying, 'I'm heartbroken.'"

"Are you certain about that?"

"Oh yes. And then there was something about getting something back and then Sir Henry stormed out and banged the door behind him."

"Do they often quarrel?" Giles said.

"I think so," she said. "It's all rather complicated, because it seemed that Mama and Sir Henry were getting married but my sister says she is going to marry him now, but I'm not to tell Mama. I saw them kissing – my sister and Sir Henry, that is. I shouldn't have told you that, probably." She looked embarrassed and awkward now. "Probably I shouldn't have said anything."

"Perhaps you'd better go and do your piano practice," said Giles. "I shan't tell a soul you were here."

"Oh, thank you!" she exclaimed.

"Do you like music?" he said, thinking of Lord Rothborough.

"Yes. Miss Wilson says I'm the only person in the family with an ear, and that she can't teach me anything else. I'm hoping Mama will let Herr Baumer come from Stanegate to give me lessons."

He showed her to the door and she went running off, leaving Giles to make what sense he could of all she had told him. He was now most interested to talk to Lady Amberleigh, and a few moments later a manservant came in to take him to her.

They went upstairs and he was shown into what could only be described as the Countess' boudoir. It was dimly lit, with the windows draped in several layers of muslin, and a powerful scent of musk roses filled the room. The Countess herself was sitting elegantly on a chaise longue, wearing an elaborate silk and lace wrapper that seemed to reveal as much as it concealed. She looked as if she had been arranged 'just so' by a famous portrait painter about to take her image. Her large, liquid blue eyes were both dreamy but fixed on him with sly interest. He could imagine that a skilled artist would wish to capture that, and perhaps create one of those disconcerting likenesses whose gaze followed one about.

"I'm sorry to have to disturb you, ma'am."

She put out a languid hand for him.

"It's no trouble at all. It's useful to put a face to a name, Major Vernon. Won't you sit down?" He took the chair that had been placed by the chaise.

"So you are here to talk to me about poor Captain Carrington?"

"I understand you were friends?"

"Yes, we were. It's a most distressing business. Have you any notion who is responsible?"

"Did he tell you of any enemies he may have had?"

"Oh yes," she said. "He confided in me, you see. But then again, people often do. I suppose it is a gift, but sometimes it feels like a curse." She sighed and glanced at him from under her long lashes.

"I can imagine," he said. "It must be hard." She responded with a crooked smile. "Perhaps he told you he felt threatened?"

"Yes, yes, and not just threatened! He was sure someone was going to kill him!"

"Did he say that to you?" said Giles, feeling that the drama with which she had said this smacked too much of hindsight.

"Perhaps not in so many words," she said. "But he implied it. I could sense it."

"How was it that you became friends?"

"It was Sir Henry Boynton, my son's guardian, who introduced me. They met after the estate acquired the land at Carr's Crag, and naturally, since he wanted to lease it from us, he thought it might be interesting for me to know him."

"Was it your idea to acquire that land?" said Giles.

"It was," she said.

"What has been done is charming," he said.

"Oh, do you think so?" she said, smiling. "I did have a hand in many of the details."

"I understand one of the houses is for your particular use."

"I shall need somewhere to live when my son marries, and the dower house here is really the most miserable hovel. That was why we acquired the land in the first place. Such a romantic spot, don't you think?"

"Very," said Giles.

"Of course, it was wretchedly expensive," she went on, "due to having to bid against a certain person who has more money than sense. I think he wanted it just to spite me. Oh dear." She gave another great sigh. "I suppose he has told you all sorts of outrageous things about me, Major Vernon? Oh, don't worry, I don't expect you to answer that – it would be disloyal and you are loyal to him, of that I am sure. But how pleased I am to have this opportunity to put my side of things! I would hate to have you think ill of me. I have heard only good things of you, you see," she added.

"That's flattering, but I'm sure little of it is deserved," he said. "Tell me about your house at Carr's Crag. You have the eye of an artist to embark on such a project."

"Do you know, my drawing master used to tell me that! He was used to teaching wishy-washy young ladies to paint their mills and their cows and so forth, while I wanted to paint a ravine from nature, all gloom and shadows! When I heard that Carr's Crag was for sale, I knew I had to do something there, something lasting. It has been such a great adventure, but the way it has ended – it is too wretched. Poor, poor, dear Carrington. He was a man of such vision! You have seen the baths, I take it?"

"Yes. Most impressive."

"They are glorious. That will serve as his monument. But it is too awful that he is gone..." She gave a small sob. "Please excuse me. It is just so upsetting to think he may only be remembered for being eaten by those beasts." She reached for her handkerchief.

"It is certainly a tragedy," Giles said, "and anything you can tell me about his business dealings, his acquaintances and so forth, would be of the greatest possible service. We will find who did this, I can assure you of that."

"The thing is, I have a strong suspicion about exactly who is responsible."

"Yes?"

"You will think I am mad for saying it."

"No, I never make any such judgements. Please, ma'am, tell me."

"Very well. Sir Henry Boynton."

"And why?"

"Jealously. He had hoped to marry me, you see, and I may have given him some idea I might accept, that is true enough. I was very low after my husband's death, and Sir Henry was a great solace, but there really was nothing more to it than that, at least not on my side. But he loves me and will not be resigned to it. Why, if he knew you were here, he would be furious! He behaves as if I were his wife, and when he saw that dear Carrington and I had such an affinity, he could not bear it. I fear he has done something terrible!"

How much of this was fancy, Giles could not begin to guess. There was a febrile atmosphere hanging about her, in that airless, overheated, perfumed room. He had a strong desire to throw up the sashes and stick his head out of the window in order to breathe and think clearly.

"Did you see or hear something that made you conclude this?" It struck him that she was entirely capable of attempting to push him in a certain direction for her own ends. "Something specific, perhaps?"

She thought – a trifle too long, it seemed to Giles – before she answered.

"I asked him to go and see Captain Carrington on a business matter, at my request. It was on Sunday night – a week ago yesterday. He went into Stanegate after luncheon. I wish I had not asked him to go. I must have provoked him. At the time I did not guess how upset he was with me. How easy it is to underestimate a man's feelings! 'Why would he care about an old widow like me?' I thought, but it seems the heart is never rational, is it?"

"What was the business?"

"It was nothing at all. Just a few sketches and notes about some villas the Captain and I had been designing together – for the menagerie grounds. But I think Sir Henry misinterpreted my motive. I should not have sent him on such an errand. He took it badly, I fear."

"So he left after lunch on Sunday. When did you next see him?"

"Monday afternoon," she said. "He stayed at my house, I think. He came back and shut himself in his rooms here. He was in a most curious state."

"And when did you learn of the Captain's death?"

"That is the strangest thing," she said, leaning forward now. "This is what alarms me so. It was Sir Henry himself who told me."

"When?"

"On Friday morning. I had been expecting a note from Carrington; he was always a very prompt correspondent and I had begun to think he might be ill. So I mentioned to Sir Henry that I was going to drive into Stanegate and see him, to which Sir Henry said – oh Lord, it was terrible how he said it – he said: no, I should not go because the poor fellow would be in no condition to be called on. Imagine! So I asked him what he meant by that and he said he had been eaten by leopards. I thought he was joking."

"I see," said Giles.

"And spoken in such a hard cold way, as if he meant to hurt me. Which he did."

"Did you ask what he meant?"

"Of course! He said Mr Boothroyd had told him of it on Thursday. He had gone to see him about the cricket, and learnt the news from him. But the way he told me – does that not seem strange to you? It struck me as most alarming. That was when I began to wonder and worry."

"Did you consider approaching the authorities with your suspicions?"

"Perhaps I knew you would seek me out, sooner or later!" she concluded with a dazzling smile.

Chapter Twenty-seven

"Are you not staying for lunch?" said Lady Clara, who, seeing his horse brought round, had come running out of the house. Giles had just got into the saddle and she caught the bridle from the groom, and gazed up at him.

"No, I'm sorry, I can't," he said.

He wanted to tell her he might well be back later, but Sir Henry came lounging out of the house. He struck Giles as civil but wary, and Giles had no wish to show his hand at that point. However strangely Lady Amberleigh had framed her accusations, there was enough substance in them to warrant further investigation. It was better that Sir Henry knew nothing. Giles wanted to corroborate Lady Amberleigh's account – if that were possible. Certainly it would be necessary to talk to Mary Carter and Mrs Thorne again.

As he rode away, he contemplated Lady Amberleigh's unsettling manner. She had been so arch, her demeanour entirely at odds with the subject of a man's death, a man she claimed to care for. She struck him like a spell of unseasonal weather: a heatwave before Easter, or hailstorms in high summer. Did she really care that Carrington was dead? It was difficult to know if she had been sincere. Was she pleased that he had been disposed of, and in that case, was she involved in some way? Or perhaps she was taking her revenge on Sir Henry for throwing her over for her daughter, assuming Lady Clara was correct about that.

The way the girl had looked at him with such disappointment now flashed through his mind as he continued on his way. At that age there was little notion of concealing emotion. She had that frank, open disposition that he had observed in Carswell and Lord Rothborough's daughters. That she was a sister to them was wretchedly obvious, and he wondered why Lord Rothborough had not mentioned this complication. It could be that he was not even aware of it. If he had had nothing to do with Lady Amberleigh for some years and the girl had passed as the daughter of the Earl, her birth unheralded in any newspaper, then he might be ignorant of her existence. This information would grieve him, Giles knew, and it was doubtful whether he should even be told. After all, it was only speculation, and something best kept to himself. It was unkind to both the girl and Lord Rothborough, because there was no way that the matter could be proved definitively.

He had taken directions from the Amberleigh groom and made his way to Stanegate via a field road that turned into a track across the moors. This saved a great deal of time and brought him up to Carr's Crag. Soon enough he had reached the gates of Adelaide Lodge, which were made of fanciful wrought iron, while the gate posts were topped with the hospitable pineapple.

He turned in and found himself in a miniature estate, where the bleakness of the moor gave way to lush planting. There were varieties of trees and shrubs he had never seen before; a winding driveway, similar to that at the Castle but on a smaller scale, led to the front of the house. A large, elaborate conservatory adjoined the house, and it was easy to imagine Lady Amberleigh having designed it. Her hand seemed all about him, and he wondered why she had not yet moved there. He thought she might have enjoyed the pleasures of Stanegate at the height of its season: the opera and the fashionable crowds. She had obviously been interested by Carrington's developments, so why did she not feel inclined to participate in the life of his town?

It could be that the house was not completely finished, and although perfectly habitable by a bachelor like Sir Henry, it might not yet do for a Countess and her household. However, it all looked ready for its mistress and creator – there was even a gardener and two lads hard at work to preserve perfect order. Seeing him ride up, the gardener came to speak to him.

"There's no one at home today, sir," he said.

"Not even any of the indoor servants?"

"No, sir. Sir Henry's man was here yesterday, I think."

"Are you employed by Sir Henry?"

"No, sir, by the Captain. Well, I was, but now –" He shrugged.

"I see," said Giles. "I'm a police officer investigating his death. What did you make of him as a master?"

"I don't know really, sir," said the gardener. "He paid the wages but I didn't have anything to do with him. It's Mr Cuthbert, the groundsman at the Hydropathic, who gives me my orders."

"Do you look after all the gardens up here on the Crag, Mr –?"

"Hayes. Yes, I do, sir."

"Quite a task," said Giles. "So you must be here most days?"

"Pretty much," Hayes said.

"So you see all the comings and goings?" Hayes nodded. "When was Sir Henry last here, do you know?"

Hayes said, "Saturday before last – I remember because he asked for flowers for the house, but I saw Mary Carter carrying them off."

"That would be Mrs Thorne's maid?" said Giles. Hayes nodded. "Have you seen her here often with Sir Henry?"

"Aye, swanning about as if she were the mistress," he said.

"And she was there on that Saturday?" Hayes nodded. "I suppose the house is all locked up?"

"Aye, sir, it is, but if you wanted to let yourself in, I know where the scullery key is."

The key was concealed under a flowerpot in the back court. Giles let himself into the house and Hayes returned to staking the clumps of dark red, velvet-petalled dahlias.

He passed through a series of well-appointed and up-to-date service rooms before entering the main part of the house, which was spacious and generously furnished. Everything in the house seemed to be in perfect order.

The principal living room was on the first floor, and opening the shutters revealed a spectacular view over the gardens and the town beyond. The roofs of the other cottages could just be glimpsed, but on the whole it felt perfectly private.

He crossed the landing to a luxuriously fitted-out bedroom. The ceiling had been tented with crimson silk, and the bed itself dressed in crimson and gold. It struck him as the perfect place to entertain a mistress, and perhaps this was a temptation to which Sir Henry had succumbed.

He went downstairs and discovered another sitting room, this time with doors onto the terrace. It was papered with a panorama of grand Italian views and furnished with delicate chairs and tables, in ebony with mother of pearl decoration, all carefully placed for social drinking and cards. It was then that he noticed that there was an odd number of chairs – one short of half a dozen. This struck him as curious, given how meticulously the room had been arranged, as if waiting for guests to come in at any moment. He realised where he had seen a chair in such a style before. It had been sitting in the back passageway between the kitchen and a serving room. He had only noticed it from the corner of his eye, but he had wondered at its being there. His curiosity piqued, he went back to find it.

The reason for it having been exiled was clear enough. One of the delicate sabre legs had come away at the joint with the seat. It had been moved there by a conscientious servant, presumably to await collection by a joiner for repair.

Giles carried it into the kitchen to examine it in better light. There was a drop-in seat covered with blue satin, like the others, but there was a large dark stain on it – wine, perhaps, or something else entirely? Blood? He used his hand lens, but he could not conclude anything. He wished Carswell were there.

He went back to the sitting room and made a more careful study of the room. There were a few similar dark stains on an area of the carpet, not at all obvious at first because of the gaudy pattern it bore.

He unfastened the French windows and went out onto the terrace. The lawn stretched out in front of him. It was a long way to drag a body across the lawn to the deep border and then the shrubberies beyond, and he speculated about what damage might be caused in the process. He went upstairs again, to see if there was any evidence of this from the superior vantage point of the drawing room, but as he crossed the landing he noticed that the door to the bedroom – which he had carefully closed – was now slightly ajar. Furthermore, he could hear a woman singing in the room. He went to the chink and looked in to see Mary Carter in the act of unhooking her bodice.

He stood back and tapped on the door.

"Harry, is that you?" she said.

"No. May I come in, Miss Carter? It's Major Vernon."

There was silence and then she opened the door, now hastily hooking up her bodice again. Behind her spread on the bed was the muslin dress she had worn at the cricket match.

"What are you doing here?" she said.

"I might ask you the same thing, Miss Carter. Perhaps we might talk in there?" He indicated the drawing room door.

She joined him a minute or two later.

"So?" she said. "What do you want?"

"Are you expecting Sir Henry?" he said.

"Yes."

"Do you often meet here?"

"Often enough."

"What does Mrs Thorne say about that?"

"She doesn't know about it. I don't have to tell her everything."

"Does she know you are here now?"

"She's gone away. To her sister in Liverpool. She's not my mistress any more."

"I take it Sir Henry is supporting you?"

"That's none of your business."

"I think it is," he said, sitting down. "So when did Mrs Thorne depart?"

"Friday," she said.

"And you decided to take your chances here, with Sir Henry? I saw you at the cricket. How long has this been going on?"

"A few months."

"How did you meet?"

"At Mrs Thorne's – where else? Captain Carrington brought him."

"And things went from there?"

"Yes," she said, sitting down opposite him. "What is it you want?"

"Those papers you so helpfully pointed me towards," Giles said. "Was that all of them?"

"As far as I know."

"Did you know what was in them?"

"Just papers," she said.

"Sir Henry didn't ask you to remove anything from them?"

"No," she said.

"Are you sure? He has had some difficult passages with Captain Carrington. You told me yourself that the Captain was a fast one. Are you sure there wasn't anything in those papers that would embarrass him, or Lady Amberleigh for that matter?" She frowned at that. "You know this is her house?"

"Of course!" she said. "The old witch."

"She's not so old," said Giles.

"She's too old for him," she said.

"You mean for your Harry?"

"He talked about marrying her," she said. "And I said, what would be the point of that?"

"I suppose you would like to marry him?"

"As if," she said. "I'm not stupid."

"I'm sure of that," said Giles, getting up and going to the window. He reached for his notebook and looked back at his record of the first conversation he had had with her. "So when did you last see Captain Carrington, Miss Carter?" She hesitated, and had the look of considering a lie. "Tell me the truth or this will not go well for you. Be sensible."

"A week ago Sunday."

"Here?"

"Yes."

"Although he had not visited Mrs Thorne for a fortnight before that, you said?"

"You didn't ask me," she said. "You asked her."

"Fair enough. And this woman you suspected was Carrington's wife – you knew who she was, yes?"

"Yes. He told Sir Henry about her. They were drinking together and talking about women and marriage and all that."

"When was this?"

"Oh, I don't know. One of the nights here. There were a few." She sighed. "I don't know why he always had to be here, to tell the truth."

"That is an interesting point, Miss Carter," said Giles, coming and sitting down again. "What else did they talk about?"

"Money. I didn't trust him – Carrington that is, but Harry wasn't going to listen to me about it. He's greedy. Funny, that – he has all that money and he still wants more. That's why he's going to marry that Lady Margaret. She has thirty thousand a year."

"Does she?" said Giles. "So, tell me what happened on the Sunday night, when you last saw Captain Carrington."

"I don't really remember."

"Come now –"

"I was here earlier with Harry and we had lots of wine and – well, you can guess what we did then. And after that I went to sleep. That big bed is so comfortable. But later I woke up and I heard them."

"Heard them? Then they were being noisy, perhaps?"

"Maybe."

"Tell me," he said.

"All right!" she said. "They were shouting at each other. In their cups. I don't know why or what they were saying. I had a headache and I went downstairs and told them to be quiet and then I went upstairs again. Then Harry came up in a temper and told me off for it, like I was some bit of dirt. So we had a row and I decided to go back to Laburnum Cottage, because I wasn't going to be treated like that."

"I see."

"And then he laughed at me."

"Captain Carrington?"

"Yes. They were in that sitting room downstairs, and I went out that way because the door was open to the garden and that's the way I always go, down through the shrubbery. And he laughed at me and said to Harry that if I were his mistress he'd give me a good walloping. So –"

She broke off and studied her hands.

"Yes?"

"I walloped him." She looked across at him. "I didn't kill him. He was alive when I left. I just gave him a bloody nose, and he was so surprised he fell off his chair, and then the chair got broken and I ran away. I know he was alive because he shouted at me. Called me a little bitch. He was lying on the floor and there was blood everywhere."

"And you ran away?"

"Yes."

"And Sir Henry didn't come after you?"

"No. I didn't see either of them again that night."

"When did you next see Sir Henry?"

"It was the next day, about midday. He was sorry for himself and I was hard on him, but I wasn't ready to let him have his way. I was still angry. So he left."

"But you have forgiven him now?"

"I had to think about my future," she said.

"And when was that?"

"Thursday last."

"After Mrs Thorne decided to go to her sister? Did she let you go?"

"We decided it was better that way," she said. "She doesn't have money for wages."

"And the first you heard of Carrington's death was when I told you of it, on Wednesday?"

"Yes."

"You are sure of that?"

"Yes."

At this moment a voice called out from downstairs.

"Mary! Are you there?"

It was Sir Henry.

~

Sir Henry did not look pleased to see him. No doubt he had been expecting an afternoon of sensual distraction.

"What are you doing here?" he said, just as his mistress had said.

"I understand Captain Carrington was here on Sunday

night, a week ago."

"What have you said to him, Mary?" he said.

"Nothing but what happened," she said.

"You shouldn't have told him that," he muttered, and lit a cigar.

"Miss Carter has given me an account of that evening, up to a point," said Giles. "But obviously she left before the Captain. Perhaps you might elaborate on what happened afterwards?" Sir Henry said nothing but sat down and took a long drag on his cigar.

"We can either talk here or down at the station house," Giles went on.

"Are you proposing to arrest me?"

"Not just yet," said Giles. "And if you give me a satisfactory account of what happened that night, then there will be no need."

"I've no idea what you are talking about."

"You were not entirely straight with me on Saturday, Sir Henry. You talked about Carrington being only a slight acquaintance."

"That's no lie."

"So these drinking evenings were merely business?"

"After a fashion," he said.

"So that night, after Miss Carter had left, what happened?"

"We mopped up the blood," said Sir Henry with a severe glance at Mary Carter. "She told you what she did?"

"Yes."

"He needed to be taught a lesson," said Mary.

"So do you!" said Sir Henry, waving his hand at her. Clearly their reconciliation was perilous, at best.

"Very gallant," said Giles.

"She broke a chair," he said.

"A flimsy design by the look of it," said Giles. "Accidents happen."

Sir Henry's expression suggested that he felt it had been anything but an accident. Had Carrington provoked him further after Mary's departure?

"But I don't suppose Carrington saw it that way," Giles went on, "given he already thought you had no control over your woman. I can't imagine he resisted the temptation to say so, given that he must have been in pain, and all that blood – on the carpet, on the chair – goodness, no, I don't suppose he held back. What did he say to you?"

"Why would I care what he said?"

"Quite," said Giles. "Why would you, Sir Henry? Carrington was a nobody, a vulgar counter-jumper with some nasty habits. Not worth your time or consideration. Why it was necessary to sit up drinking with him, who can guess. Was it that you were afraid of him?"

"I beg your pardon?" said Sir Henry, drawing himself up. As he did, Giles considered again his powerful physique. Dragging a body about would not be any great labour for him, perhaps with the assistance of a loyal manservant.

"This is a man who had meticulously collected unpleasant secrets and used that for his advantage. I can't imagine he spared you. Who among us have no indiscretions that we would rather our families did not know? Or those young ladies whom we intend to marry, for that matter? What would your fiancée think of all this?" He gestured towards Mary.

"Do not mention that lady's name –"

"No, of course not," said Giles. "Nor that of her illustrious mother, which is perhaps more to the point." Sir Henry bristled again and Giles wondered if he were about to take a swipe at him. "Ah yes, you find that offensive. Carrington's stock in trade was offence. He knew all your weaknesses, and I think you were attempting to keep him quiet, but perhaps that night, it was all too much. After all, you had been drinking since lunchtime and maybe you were tired, and angry with Mary here, and angry with him and yourself, and there he is lying on the rug. All ready to be silenced forever. Is that what happened?"

"That is a preposterous accusation, sir!" said Sir Henry.

"So, tell me what happened."

"He left and that was that," he said.

"When?"

"I don't know!" exclaimed Sir Henry. "This is insupportable, sir!"

"It would have been tempting," said Giles. "Like dealing with a mad dog."

"I think you should leave now, sir!" said Sir Henry, marching to the door and holding it open. "And I trust you will think twice before bandying about such accusations!"

"As you wish, Sir Henry," Giles said. "But don't think we have finished talking."

Chapter Twenty-eight

Charlotte and Bodley had summoned Dr Markham, a sensible physician who practised in the environs of Holbroke, and Felix was glad to see him. Since he had arrived first, he had thoroughly examined Lord Rothborough, and given he was in considerable pain, had administered a strong opium draft. This allowed the Marquis to sleep, although fitfully. As a result, Felix was happy not to disturb him further, and instead listened to Dr Markham's account of matters. He felt his own judgement might be compromised by his emotions – another, cooler head was exceptionally welcome, for it was soon clear that the situation was grave.

"The problem is rooted in a widespread peritoneal inflammation, and given the slow onset of symptoms, and the acute phase that has now developed, I suspect some mischief in the caecum and its appendix," said Dr Markham. "What is to be done about it – that is another matter. Sometimes nature takes its course, given careful nursing, but –"

"Yes?" said Felix.

"The distension and the texture of the abdomen does suggest some tumour is present."

"Which we might remove?"

"I am not a surgeon, Mr Carswell," said Dr Markham. "I hesitate to recommend operating in such a dangerous region. I have seen too many accidents in this area, though well intentioned."

Felix nodded. It was not a procedure to be undertaken lightly.

"What would you recommend?"

"Close observation for another day, and then a second

opinion. Mr Harper, perhaps?"

"Certainly," said Felix. "If we were to decide on such a course, he is the only man I would trust to do it. I shall write to him at once rather than wait another day."

"Of course, that is entirely at your discretion. Perhaps we should speak to her Ladyship now?"

They had just come into the sculpture gallery, where Charlotte was waiting. She hurried over to them with three spaniels at her heels: her own Otto, and Lord Rothborough's current pair, Prince and Percy.

"Excuse them, Dr Markham," said Charlotte, as Prince and Percy went fussing round the doctor's ankles. "They are anxious for their walk with their master."

"I'll take them out in a minute," said Felix, catching up Percy. He had never had strong feelings about the Rothborough spaniels, generally preferring large, sturdy dogs, but as Percy allowed himself to be petted, he wondered if he should not ask for a pair from the next litter.

"So?" said Charlotte.

"It's –" Felix began, but failed to find words. He indicated that Dr Markham should speak, which he did, effectively, calmly and with a comforting note in his message that was not entirely justified.

"Another day and then – I see," she said, with a great sigh. "Oh, then that is what we must do. Thank you so much, Dr Markham. Now, will you have some tea?"

"No, if you will excuse me now, my lady, I will go home and see to my other patients, and then I shall be back as soon as I can."

When Dr Markham had left, Charlotte took Felix's arm and leaning against him, said softly, "We cannot lose him. Not yet."

"We will not," he said.

"Should I ask the Ffordes to leave?" she said. "It is a great comfort having them here, I must say."

"I think he would prefer them to stay. I must go and talk to Eleanor."

"You will have to take the dogs with you. They have attached themselves to you. I hope that doesn't mean something terrible," she said. "They would not be calm with me, but with you just now – I wonder why."

"They are simply fickle. It's the novelty," said Felix. "Now, do not give in to gloomy thoughts, promise me?"

"No, I shall not. I am just scared, that is all."

"Of course. So am I, but we have weapons at our disposal," he said, kissing her. "Dr Markham is well informed and he has got to the heart of the problem quickly, which is always beneficial to the patient."

"And we have you," she said, returning his kiss. "Now, go and find Eleanor."

Felix went, with the dogs accompanying him, and found Eleanor still in bed.

"Oh, I'm glad you're here!" she exclaimed, opening her arms to him. "It is all so wretched! How is he?"

"I think it's rather serious," he said, sitting on the end of the bed.

"No! But you can cure him, surely?"

"I don't know. I want Mr Harper to look at him."

"Of course," she said. "He will know what to do. He always does."

"I'm glad you have such faith in him, when you don't like him."

"I never said I didn't like him!" she said. "And I certainly realise he is a genius."

"Where's Miss King?" he said.

"She is in the garden with the Ffordes," said Eleanor. "I could not face getting up, let alone dressing. I cannot lace at all. It's unbearable. I shall have to get some new things. This little gentleman has grown rapidly over the last few days." She rubbed her belly.

"He must like the opera," said Felix, reaching out and laying his hand on it. "Very nourishing."

"Maybe it was Madame's food," said Eleanor.

"Maybe," said Felix. "Do you want to listen to his heart? I have my bag here."

"I see you accept it is a boy," she said. "Perhaps you have a preference after all."

"I don't," he said, getting off the bed and fetching his bag. He took out his stethoscope and offered the hearing tube to Eleanor. But she did not take it.

"Where were you on Saturday night?" she said.

"What?"

"You never came back to our room on Saturday night."

"What do you mean?"

"You didn't sleep there. I came looking for you in the night and you weren't there. I wasn't feeling well. Where were you?"

"At the Infirmary, of course," he said, and wondered if he had betrayed himself in his lie in the manner Major Vernon had taught him to observe in others: in a slight hesitation. "The boy," he added.

"Oh, of course," she said.

She sounded almost too artless.

"Why didn't you say anything on Sunday morning?" he said. "I presume you felt better?"

"Oh yes, I did, and then it didn't seem important, but since we got here and Lord Rothborough being taken so, it started to worry me. You might have left a note for me, at least! What if I had been really ill?"

"I'm sorry," he said, feeling he had had a narrow escape. "I really should have left a message."

"Yes, certainly you must in future," she said, gesturing to him to pass the stethoscope to her. "We have to be careful."

They passed a few minutes listening to the baby's heartbeat, an experience which he had previously thought delightful, but which now unnerved him. He seemed to hear his future son or daughter's voice reproaching him: "So you deserted my mother? How could you?"

It was a question he could not answer. Any attempt to justify himself now seemed mere playing with words. She had needed him and he had not been there. Whatever was going on between her and Jenny King was no excuse for his licence.

Yet it had been exhilarating, and Elisabeth was utterly adorable. Did he have to forswear her and regret it all so soon? Could he not even have a brief season of happy recollection? He could not bring himself to scourge himself at once, especially as he suspected that Eleanor's need for him was not so much for a husband but for an accoucheur.

~

Lord Rothborough stirred from his opium-induced sleep an hour or so later. Felix, who had been sitting with him running through a great many unpleasant thoughts, took his hand and was pleased to see his smile return. Then, as Lord Rothborough strained to lay his own hand over his, and he saw the pain he was in, he forgot all his own troubles and wished only that he could relieve him at once from such obvious suffering.

Dr Markham came back, and assisted by Bodley did everything possible to make him comfortable, but it was clear that it was only mitigation. When they were again alone together, Felix said, "I have sent for Mr Harper. You know what faith I have in him."

"Yes, good." Lord Rothborough struggled to speak, his voice a dry whisper. "Good. And now, will you go to Greystanes?"

This was the village where Mrs Martinez was presently

living.

"Yes, of course. Shall I bring her back here?"

Lord Rothborough nodded and closed his eyes. Mercifully, the opiates seemed to be having an effect and Felix could leave him. Bodley and Mrs Fforde were in the dressing room.

"Mr Bodley is badly in need of rest," said Mrs Fforde. "I will sit with his Lordship."

"No, ma'am," said Bodley. "There's no need for that."

"You must look after yourself, Bodley," said Felix. "I insist you rest. I was thinking that we should send for Mrs Vernon as well."

"A good idea," said Mrs Fforde.

"Both ladies are excellent nurses," said Felix to Bodley. "He will be in the best of hands with them, and you will be able to do your part without making yourself ill, which would not please my Lord, would it?"

"As you wish, Mr Felix," he said. "I'll take the dogs out first, if I may?" The spaniels had quickly transferred their loyalty.

~

The hamlet of Greystanes, crouching on the edge of moorland, was reached by way of an extremely rough back road from Holbroke to Stanegate. It was a journey that Felix imagined would have been better managed on a sturdy highland pony than in a carriage. The old manor lay on the edge of the village, with the moor on its doorstep. It was surrounded by high walls, presumably built to keep out the wind, but it gave the place the look of a fortification, an aspect underlined by the blackened stone of the house itself. Yet there was a garden blazing with colour planted in the forecourt. Here was Mrs Martinez, dead-heading her roses.

She smiled seeing him coming up the path, but as he approached she must have read his expression, for she looked alarmed and said, "What has happened? Something has happened, has it not?"

He took her hand and kissed it, and led her into the house. There, in the dark, flagged hall, cool and scented with stocks and lavender, he explained the situation.

"And you are sure he wants me there?"

"Yes, most certainly," he said.

"And the girls?"

"It is only Charlotte there at present. I told her I was going to fetch you, and she was absolutely in agreement."

She nodded and said, "I must pack. I will not be long," she said, moving towards the stairs. Then she stopped and said, "It's very bad, isn't it?"

"It may be," he said. "But I'm hopeful that if we act fast, something may be done."

"An operation?" she said.

"Yes, if Mr Harper thinks it possible."

She nodded and without another word, went upstairs.

They drove back along that jolting road, not talking a great deal, for her Swiss maid was with them. Yet once or twice she reached discreetly for his hand and squeezed it, and he was not sure it was for her reassurance or for his.

"These are not the circumstances in which I thought I would lay eyes on Holbroke for the first time," she said, as the carriage drew up in front of the portico.

"You've never been here?"

"No. We decided that... oh, I don't know why. Is that Charlotte?" It was indeed Charlotte, standing at the top of the steps. "How kind of her to come out to meet me."

Felix handed her out of the carriage, and for a moment the two women stood and looked at each other. Then Charlotte came down the steps, her hand extended, and Mrs

Martinez dropped a deep curtsey.

"Oh, ma'am, really, there is no need for that!" Charlotte exclaimed, yet she smiled at this elegant show of submission. "Please do come in. My father will be so glad to see you."

They went straight to Lord Rothborough's room, and drawing off her gloves, Mrs Martinez went to the bedside and took both his hands.

"We should leave them be," Felix murmured, and Charlotte nodded. They went into the sculpture gallery as before, and while the dogs went running about, Charlotte sat down as if exhausted and started to cry.

"Oh, Lord!" she exclaimed. "This is all too much." Felix sat down beside her and put his arm about her shoulders, not far from tears himself. She rested her head against him. "He looks so frail. What are we to do?"

"We are doing all we can," said Felix.

"This all my fault. I sensed he was unwell, and I should have been more vigilant. I should have made him see someone when we were in London."

"And I dare say, every time you raised it, he dismissed it? Told you that it was nothing?"

"Yes," she said. "But –"

"Then you cannot blame yourself. And these things are hard to identify. He is strong-willed and physically strong as well, which made him resist as long as he could. In that respect it is a good sign. He will fight, you know that. We will come through."

"Yes, I'm sure," she said, getting up. She walked down the gallery a few paces before stopping and turning back to him. "And she – she is not at all as I thought she would be. She looks so young! How old is she?"

"No more than forty-five, I think," said Felix.

"She is so beautiful! And I can see her face in yours, Felix, although you look so like Papa as well. What will your child look like, I wonder? Will it have that golden hair?"

"Who knows?" said Felix.

"And then I can't help thinking what might have happened if he had married her in Paris. Where would we all be then? I would not be here and you would be –"

"But he did not," said Felix.

"I know, and there are a hundred reasons for it, but I still cannot help wondering. They are obviously devoted to each other."

"Perhaps it's because they weren't married," said Felix. He had not meant to be so blunt.

"What do you mean?"

"Marriage is – I don't know. It is the strangest state. It takes a genius to do it well, I suspect."

"But you and Eleanor – you are happy enough?"

"Yes, yes, but you know yourself these things are not easy, even in the best circumstances."

"You are encouraging my spinsterhood again," she said, getting up.

"I did not mean to," said Felix. "But –"

"But?"

"I have to admit I don't like to see you pursued by people I don't think good enough."

"Pursued? That's an interesting way of putting it. Do you mean Mr Fitznorton, perhaps?"

"Yes, to be frank. Presumptuous prig that he is."

"That is unkind!" said Charlotte.

"Oh, come now, that business about Sabbath day observance – it was ridiculous!"

"He has strong convictions – isn't that admirable?"

"Yes, up to a point," he said.

"He may unbend in time," said Charlotte, gathering Otto into her arms. "I'm sure it is merely that his upbringing has been rather limited."

Felix remembered what Major Vernon had said about her vulnerability and wondered how he might tactfully warn her about embarking on a mission to change a man who undoubtedly would want to change her. He was about to say something when the door opened at the far end of the gallery, and Mrs Martinez came in.

Charlotte dropped the dog and went over to her.

"Is everything all right, ma'am?" she said.

"Yes, yes – he would like to speak to you both."

They went back to Lord Rothborough's bedside. Propped up on the pillows, he appeared comfortable and undoubtedly cheered by Mrs Martinez's presence. He smiled and extended his hand to Charlotte as she approached.

"Now," he said. "I am going to tell you something that is going to astonish you both."

"What is it, Papa?" said Charlotte.

"Mrs Martinez and I are to be married," he said. "And as soon as is possible."

Chapter Twenty-nine

Giles returned to the station house, intending to dispatch Inspector Harris and a constable to Adelaide Lodge to take Sir Henry in for a more formal questioning. He had been both aggressive and defensive, suggesting that there was a deal more to his account. But crossing the threshold, he met with Inspector Harris, hat in hand, about to leave on another errand.

"Ah, Major Vernon, that's timely," he said. "I'm just going to the Hydropathic. I've had a message from Constable Morris. An unexpected death."

"Constable Morris – isn't that who Mr Fitznorton went out with?"

"Yes. It sounds – well, here you are, sir."

He handed him the piece of paper.

Giles glanced it over. Fitznorton's clear hand was as sharp as print: "Dr Kennedy has been discovered dead in his consulting room in the Roman Bath."

"Dear Lord," he murmured, thinking of Sukey. "What the devil is going on?"

"Shall we go, sir?"

"Certainly, at once," said Giles.

Kennedy's consulting room was reached by a passageway leading off the great marble hall of the bath house. Constable Morris was guarding the entrance to the passageway, and indicated their way. The passage led to a small waiting area with benches against the wall where Fitznorton was talking to a portly, white-haired man.

"This is Dr Rosey," said Fitznorton. "He is a guest at here. The manager sent for him when Dr Kennedy was first discovered."

"I'm sorry your holiday was disturbed, sir," said Giles.

"You must understand," said Dr Rosey, "I have not practised in some time, and my forensic experience is most limited."

"I'm sure you have forgotten nothing," said Giles. "So you were called here when?"

"About half an hour ago."

"And he was dead when you first saw him?"

"Yes. The cause is asphyxiation by gas, as far as I can ascertain."

"Gas?"

"The gas cock for the lighting had been left open, it seems," Fitznorton said. "Fortunately the desk clerk who first went into the room recognised the smell, and opened the windows."

"He attempted to revive the poor man but with no success," said Dr Rosey. "One must assume it was a desperate act on the part of Dr Kennedy. Was there not a case – I cannot recall the details, it was in the newspaper – of a bank manager who committed suicide in such a fashion?"

"Hopkinson of the Western Bank," said Fitznorton. "The bank had failed."

"Yes, it only confirmed my idea that gas is not something one should have in one's house. I suppose I am old-fashioned," Dr Rosey said. "But this is a sad business. Mr Fitznorton tells me he was a married man."

"Yes, with a child just christened on Sunday," said Giles.

"Dear me, what a tragic circumstance," said Dr Rosey. "Now perhaps, sir, would you excuse me? My wife will be anxious for me. I will, of course, write up my notes for you, but really I have nothing else to tell you except that the poor man is dead."

"Thank you, sir, you have been most helpful," said Giles. When the old doctor had gone, Giles turned to Fitznorton and said, "I hope Carswell will be back with us soon. Now, let's go and have a look at him."

Fitznorton unlocked the door.

"As little as possible has been touched. Fortunately we were not far off when the body was discovered, and I was able to limit any unnecessary access."

"So, who has been in here?" said Giles, looking about him.

The room was a large one, with a pair of sash windows covered with drawn blinds that were flapping gently in the breeze.

"The clerk, Samuel Bell, the manager Mr Fisher, Dr Rosey, Constable Morris and myself."

"And it was Bell who found the body?"

"Dr Kennedy had a patient waiting for him. According to Bell, Dr Kennedy would come and collect his patients when he was ready for them. When he did not come twenty minutes after the appointed time, Bell went in to remind him, and found him slumped in his chair and apparently unconscious."

"And he smelt the gas?"

"Yes. You cannot smell it now," said Fitznorton, "but even when we arrived and the windows had been open some ten minutes, it was still noticeable. But Bell had the wit to turn it off at once."

"Is that how he was found?" said Giles. Kennedy was slumped forward, his head on the desk.

"Yes," said Fitznorton, who now consulted his notebook. "Bell said: 'I thought he had fainted and then I realised the room stank of gas, so I turned the cock, opened the windows and tried to revive him, but I couldn't.'"

"And the gas cock – where is that?"

"Over here, sir," said Fitznorton, indicating the laboratory bench that lined one side of the room. There were two wall-mounted gas lights above it, and the cock to operate them to one side.

"It doesn't really look like an accident, does it?" Giles said. "I remember when we had gas fitted in the Northern Office, the engineer was careful about placing the cocks so that they could not be accidentally knocked open. The same seems to apply here. So what do we think happened? He falls into a fit of despair for some reason as yet to be determined, and determines to end it all by gassing himself. So he closes the windows and turns the cock and sits down to wait for death?"

"It's what this suggests," said Fitznorton.

"At first glance," said Giles, starting to look through the papers on the desk. "So, what have we got here?" he said, pulling out a slim, unbound pamphlet that was lying open under his hand. It was entitled: 'Digestive complaints and the Priessnitz system.' There was a notebook open in which he had been writing. "It looks as if he was working, not waiting for death."

He yawned. The air in the room seemed heavy. "Excuse me. It strikes me that there must still be a fair amount of gas in here. Perhaps we should leave this for a while. I must go and see Mrs Kennedy."

He walked from the bath house back to the main hotel building. It felt curious that he could now be admitted into Sukey's quarters. If Kennedy had been living, he might not have been allowed across the threshold.

"Is Mrs Kennedy with the children?"

"Yes, sir," said the maid.

"Will you find their nurse?"

"Of course, sir."

The maid showed him into a room where Sukey was sitting on the sofa, with her son asleep in her lap and her stepchildren tucked up on either side as she read to them.

"And then, Little Red Riding Hood said, 'Why, Grandmother dear, what great ears you have...'"

Giles could not bear to interrupt her, so he signalled he

would remain silent, and the story went on. Sukey had a delightful way of reading, and the children were caught up in the drama. He sat down, and the tale ran its inexorable course, with the suitably gruesome ending.

"Again, please, again!" said the little girl.

"Later," said Sukey. "I promise. I need to talk to Major Vernon first. Go and play with Jane, won't you?" The nurse had come to the doorway. "She'll take you for a walk." Jane came and gathered up the sleeping Lorenzo.

"My apologies, Miss Kennedy," said Giles.

Looking delighted to be so addressed, the child scrambled off the sofa and went to her nurse. Master Paul looked at him suspiciously and Giles felt the wretched burden of his news. This boy was old enough to understand his loss.

"Run along, Paul," said Sukey, kissing him. "Please?"

"Do I have to?" he said.

"Yes."

He left with his sister, and Giles closed the door behind them.

"What's wrong?" she said. "There's something wrong, isn't there? What is it?"

He sat down beside her on the sofa.

"I'm sorry – it's your husband. He's dead."

Her eyes widened and she covered her mouth with her hands.

"Dead? How?"

"That's the question. He seems to have gassed himself, either deliberately or accidentally, or –"

"Gassed himself? Oh, dear God! No, surely not? But then –" She screwed up her face. "He had something wrong with his nose – sinuses, is that the thing? He had a really bad sense of smell and I always wondered about gas, because he could hardly smell it. You know how it has such a sickly odour? He didn't smell that. He didn't smell roses or vinegar or..." She broke off, and jumped up from the sofa. "And now he's –"

She stood with her back to him for a while, and then turned towards him. "Where is he?"

"In his consulting room."

She nodded. "Those great big burners. I didn't like them when I first saw them. I said that oil would be safer given his inability to smell, but of course he didn't listen. The light was better, he said – it was more hygienic!" At which she threw herself down on the sofa again and with a sob in her voice went on, "And it's killed him! And we had such a quarrel this morning. We've been quarrelling since yesterday. No, not since yesterday but forever. One long quarrel, it feels like, and now –"

"What do you think?"

"I don't know. It feels as if I don't know him at all, like he was a stranger. How can you be married to someone and know nothing about them?"

"Because he wasn't of an open disposition?"

"That's true enough. But I was as bad. There are things about me that you know, Major, that I never told him."

"May I ask what today's quarrel was about?"

"Oh, I suppose you must ask that," she said, leaning back on the sofa and looking up at the ceiling. "You will have to know everything."

"I know this won't be easy for you," he said. "But the sooner we know exactly what happened, the sooner you can begin to –"

"Grieve?" she said. "But what will I be grieving? Shall I really be sorry for him, or just myself, left here with his children and not knowing what I shall ever say to them about him? I don't like lying to children." She looked at him, her eyes full of tears. "There you have it, Major. I didn't like him much any more. There never was much feeling in it for my part, to be really truthful. I love those children, though. That was why I allowed myself to marry him. Their mother was such a great friend to me, and they needed me."

"And the quarrel?" he prompted, although he did not like to.

"It was about something that happened last night," she said. "He – oh dear, this is shameful to say – he tried to apologise to me for it and I wouldn't accept it. I couldn't see it as an apology. I realise it was now, but at the time it made me so angry and I told him so. I wasn't discreet about it either. We were in the garden and I lost my temper, and that made him angry because it was in public, and that just made him turn on his heel and go storming off. I'm sure half a dozen people will you tell you that they saw me raging at him." She shook her head, the tears returning. "I never used to be so angry. But since I had Laurence – oh, it changes you, being a mother. I never thought it would, but it has!" She pressed her hands to her face. "Oh my poor Laurie, what is he going to think of me? What am I going to tell him?"

"If you continue as you are doing as a mother," said Giles, "you will have nothing to fear. He will understand, I'm sure. What was your husband trying to apologise for?"

There was a long silence before she said, "I was sleeping with the children. It's easier that way when you have a little one to feed, and he came in and said he wanted me as his wife again. You know what I mean?" Giles nodded. "Well, he insisted, so I went to our bedroom, but I wasn't really ready, and it hurt... oh God, do you have to know this? Does this really matter?" She began crying in earnest. "I let him because that is what a good wife does, isn't it?"

Giles could not answer. He was possessed by the notion of being heartily glad that Kennedy was dead.

"The worse of it is," Sukey went on, through her tears, "I did it to mollify him. He was angry with me for asking you to be a godfather, and I suppose I wanted to show him that he had nothing to fear from you. You see, he had an idea that you were the person that –"

"I wondered if that was the case," said Giles.

"I'm so sorry," she said, putting her hand out and touching his arm. "I hate to think he thought that of you. I should have told him everything at the start and faced the consequences. But then he would never have married me, would he? Maybe that would have been better for everyone."

"Except that your friend's children have a mother now," said Giles.

She squeezed his arm and got up, mastering her tears and drying her face on her handkerchief. She went and poured some water from the carafe on the table and drank it, and then sat down across the room from him.

"I said terrible things to him," she said. "I don't know if that had anything to do with it. But I know he cared for me, as much as I didn't care for him. Even last night when... I knew that he loved me and I couldn't love him. I could have left it at that, especially when he tried to make it up, but no – I couldn't. I was just beyond reason. Anger is like a weapon, don't you think? I might as well have taken a knife to him."

"What exactly did you say?"

"That I wouldn't be used like a whore or bought off with baubles. He gave me a ring this morning – he sent it to me, with a note. He didn't have the courage to give it to me directly – I suppose he was already feeling ashamed of himself. And goodness knows what it cost – it's a gaudy thing. I would have thought he knew me better than that. I never wear rings. I would leave off my wedding band if I could. He knew that, but it didn't stop him!"

"Do you have it here?"

She got up and went to the chest of drawers and took out a ring box. "I tried to give it back to him. That's why we had our fight."

The ring, a large lozenge diamond surrounded by seed pearls, sat glittering in a velvet bed.

"It certainly looks valuable," he said.

"I suppose I should have just taken it and kept my mouth

shut, but it felt more like an insult than an apology. It was too much after..." She shook her head. "Did I push him into it, Major? Is that what happened here?"

"We can't say anything so definite at this point. I need Carswell to look at him properly."

"He hasn't already?"

"He went to Holbroke first thing. Lord Rothborough is not well."

"No? Nothing serious, I hope?"

"It may be."

"Oh, that's wretched news."

"What will you do with this?" he said, getting up and handing the ring back to her.

"I'll put it aside for Mary. She can wear it or sell it one day," said Sukey. "Her mother would have liked it. She had beautiful fingers and I think Mary has them too."

"I wonder where he bought it?" Giles said.

"Do you think it might not be paid for yet?"

"Forgive me, I'm always suspicious about jewellery."

"And you are usually right," she said. "Perhaps you'd better take it for now." She handed him back the box. "It may explain something."

"When you say, did you push him into it," Giles said, "do you seriously think he was capable of suicide? Did he ever talk of that with you?"

She gave a deep sigh as she considered the point.

"There were times when the Devil came over him and he'd shut himself away. He was not easy in himself, that's true enough. I didn't help him, did I? He just wanted me to adore him, and I couldn't. He wanted from me what he had from Mary, which was devotion, and I couldn't give it to him. So perhaps it was me, saying those awful things. Humiliating him. I shall pay for that now, shan't I?"

Chapter Thirty

The manager, Mr Fisher, had arranged for them to have the use of the private dining room where they had lunched previously, and Fitznorton began diligently writing up his observations. Jackson, the waiter, went in search of coffee, which Fitznorton rejected, but Giles – thoroughly depressed after his conversation with Sukey – was in need of it.

"I hesitate to say this, but on reflection, ought you to have seen Mrs Kennedy alone?" said Fitznorton, laying down his pen.

"I'm sorry?" said Giles. "On what grounds?"

"She must be considered a suspect, surely? Should you have seen her alone in such circumstances?"

"In the first instance she is a woman who has just lost her husband. She deserves to be told compassionately what has happened, at the very least."

"But is there not a strong probability that she may be involved? Spousal murder is –"

"Extremely common, yes," said Giles. "But if you look at the figures, such as they are, you will see that men who kill their wives far outweigh women who kill their husbands."

"But it is hardly unknown."

"No, but I'm not yet convinced there was any malice involved in this. In any case, I have known Mrs Kennedy for some years and I cannot consider her a likely candidate."

"She was your servant, I understand."

"I beg your pardon?" said Giles. "Who told you that?"

"Mr O'Brien mentioned it."

"She was housekeeper and a nurse to my late wife," said Giles. "Mrs Vernon's condition was such that it required a person of extreme intelligence and diligence. Mrs Connolly, as she then was, came to us because she was an exceptional person in unfortunate circumstances. Her first husband was a scoundrel who had left her unprovided for. She would not have gone to work except out of necessity. To describe her as a servant is not appropriate."

"Nevertheless," said Fitznorton. He hesitated. "Forgive me for having to broach this topic, but it's common enough knowledge that domestics –" He stopped, took a deep breath and went on, "I regret to have to be so blunt, Major Vernon, but we both know how common it is for women servants and their masters to indulge in immoral behaviour, and though we may like to think that our hearths are sacred and pure, it is often far from the case. Your wife was ill and –"

Giles held up his hand.

"Enough, enough! I know exactly what you mean, Mr Fitznorton. Yes, men prey on their maids and boast of it to other men. Yes, it is unfortunately a wretched commonplace. It is a terrible thing; but I can assure you I am not that kind of man." It had cost him something to say this in such a mild tone. He thought of a conversation he had had with Hamish about staying calm under provocation, and this was a fine example. He could easily have struck Fitznorton. "Furthermore," he said, "it is a grave insult to a gentlewoman. What made you feel that such a thing should be said aloud rather than speculated on in private is another matter."

"It is because of all I have observed, sir, of you and your circle. It gives me no pleasure to say so, believe me, but I have been disappointed by the laxity of tone, by the indulgence in luxury and –"

"Because we like to eat good dinners and go to the opera, we are prone to seduce our nursemaids?" said Giles, suspecting now that Fitznorton was deriving an odd sort of pleasure from this. "Is that the evidence on which you base your extraordinary assertion?"

"It is more than that," said Fitznorton. "Mrs Carswell made some light remark about you and Mrs Kennedy. What am I to make of that? It was distressing enough to hear a young woman say something so warm, to even have a comprehension of such behaviour, but I cannot imagine she would fabricate –"

"What did she say?" said Giles.

"She said that it would not surprise her if Mrs Kennedy had been your mistress."

"How on earth did that arise in conversation?" Giles said.

"She was speaking of Mrs Kennedy's child and how at ease you were with him, and then she implied..."

The door opened and Jackson came in with the coffee. "And a glass of Vin Santo, with Signor Luchetti's compliments. In light of the circumstances. Very sad."

"Thank you, Jackson," said Giles, glad of the interruption. "What did you make of Dr Kennedy?"

"I can't say I ever had anything much to do with him," said Jackson. "But we are all wondering what is to happen to the hotel, now he's gone as well as the Captain. Do you know anything about that, sir?"

"No, I'm afraid I don't," Giles said. Jackson left, and Giles went on: "That's an interesting question, certainly. Who owns this place now?"

"Mrs Kennedy?" said Fitznorton.

"As I said before," Giles said, having drunk his cup of coffee in one gulp, "I'm not yet sure there is any malice involved here." He dearly wanted to add that he felt it was Fitznorton who was being malicious, but refilled his cup and restrained himself.

"If it was an accident," said Fitznorton, "then it is of the most unlikely kind."

"That is often the nature of accidents," said Giles. "They are not predictable."

"It requires a most deliberate action to turn the gas on

and off," Fitznorton went on. "The lever is stiff – I tried it myself. It could not have been done accidentally." That there was some truth in this, Giles could not deny. "Bell, who discovered him, also found the lever set to open, for he made a point of stating he closed it. That eliminates the possibility of a leak from some other part of the pipework. It leaves us with suicide and murder as possible causes."

"Then let us look at suicide first," said Giles. "This is a known method of self-murder, as we have already touched on. Kennedy may have been in a depressed state. He had had a serious disagreement with his wife."

"Ah yes," said Fitznorton. "One of the hotel servants I spoke to saw them quarrelling in the garden. Quite a scene, it seems."

"Yes, and it is a source of great regret to Mrs Kennedy that they parted on such terms."

"Did she tell you what it was about?"

Giles leant back in his chair and told himself that it was useful to know what it felt like to be interrogated by someone disagreeable. It did not make it any less painful.

"If I tell you that I think it irrelevant what the subject of their quarrel was, you will not accept it, will you?" he said.

"I think, sir, you are in a privileged position regarding Mrs Kennedy. She has for some reason confided in you, and that cannot in all fairness be allowed when there is a murder enquiry under way."

"If it is murder!" said Giles, getting up. "Until Mr Carswell has seen him I am not prepared to say one way or the other."

"The relevant facts must be laid on the table," said Fitznorton. "Your personal feelings are irrelevant, sir, that is as plain as day. We must look at all parties with a discriminating eye. In the case of Mrs Kennedy, what evidence do you have to rule her out completely? As his wife she knew all his habits and routines, not to mention his weaknesses. For example, your theory that he may have had a poor sense of smell: is that not exactly the sort of thing a wife would know?"

"Indeed," said Giles. "And that was one of the first things that occurred to Mrs Kennedy. She thought his lack of sense of smell may have caused an accident. Now, would she have told me that if she had gone into his room and turned the gas on to murder her husband?"

"How old is her child? A woman who has given birth is subject to violent changes of emotion. She was seen shouting at her husband, Major Vernon."

"That does not make her a murderer. She is fully in command of her faculties. Now, Mr Fitznorton, I salute your thoroughness, but I think we may safely say that Mrs Kennedy has nothing to do with this. Let us think about Dr Kennedy and his state of mind. Are we looking at a deeply troubled soul here? He left Ireland, his home country, under a cloud. He was left money, but the dead man's family objected and there was a lawsuit. Nothing was proved against him, but he was left feeling blemished by the experience. Now, he may have hastened this man to his death, or not – we cannot say. Whatever the case, it may have tormented him. Now he comes here with his wife and suggests they leave the Roman Catholic Church and join the Church of England. Is that not an unusual step for a cradle Catholic?"

"It is," conceded Fitznorton.

"'We have erred, and strayed from thy ways like lost sheep,'" Giles went on, reciting the general Confession. "'We have followed too much the devices and desires of our own hearts, we have offended against thy holy laws, we have left undone those things which we ought to have done, and we have done those things which we ought not to have done, and there is no health in us.' Yes?"

"I don't follow you."

"It occurred to me on Sunday morning that he may have been moved to change his religion because it avoided the need for the confessional. Now, I'm no theologian, but I can imagine that to confess to a priest when you have done something serious is a terrifying thing. Men will go to great lengths to avoid a direct confession. I have seen it time and time again. One must push them into a corner to get them to say: 'yes, I did it'. Now, the general confession such as we have in the prayer book – perhaps to someone raised in the shadow of the confessional, it would seem like a loophole. And yet not."

"What do you mean, sir?"

"Again, I am no expert in these matters, but surely Roman Catholics believe that only their priests have any efficacy and that their sacraments are the only cure for sin? That if you do not confess to a priest you are doomed. Am I right?"

"I believe so. It is an egregious error and I wish so many did not labour under it. The Lord knows all our sins without the need for such interventions. Surely Kennedy must have realised that?"

"Maybe he regretted what he had done? It's a difficult thing to leave the faith of one's birth, especially with a weight on one's conscience. Did he sometimes sit in that room, trying to work but preoccupied with other things, the gas jets blaring, the light as harsh as that in the dock and despair of continuing his life? Did he sometimes wonder if those gas lights were not the means for a gentle, painless self-execution? Perhaps that spirit in him, unfortunately, today drove him to a point beyond which no one could help him. Like that poor fellow Morgueillon, slitting his wrists."

Fitznorton said nothing, and Giles hoped his words had had some impression on him. He went on: "However that may be, until we have a more detailed medical examination, we ought not to speculate. We should establish his movements in the last few hours – perhaps you might oblige me in that? I want to talk to Sir Henry Boynton, and I think I shall send for

Mr O'Brien and his wife. I do not want Mrs Kennedy without family about her."

"It strikes me, sir, that you have interesting friends," said Fitznorton.

"Yes, and it has been of great value to me," Giles said. "It really doesn't do to be narrow, Mr Fitznorton, I find. Life is so brief. Now, shall we press on?"

Chapter Thirty-one

Giles conferred with Inspector Harris to make arrangements for the corpse to be removed to the Infirmary. It irked him that Carswell could not see the crime scene intact, but there was no saying when he would be able to return from Holbroke. If Lord Rothborough's condition was serious, that must take priority. Giles wrote out his other communications first, and then decided that he would wait for news from Holbroke before summoning his colleague. Carswell did not need to be troubled just yet.

These tasks completed and the body removed, he took another look at Kennedy's consulting room, which no longer smelt of the sickly gas. It was now possible to examine the papers on his desk. They did appear to be connected to his work, and he could not find anything that might indicate a suicidal state of mind. He began to doubt his own theory, when opening the top drawer of the desk – which was slightly ajar – he saw a copy of the Book of Common Prayer and a set of rosary beads. The prayer book was inscribed to him from Dr Greville, and Giles decided it might be useful to speak to him about Kennedy's state of mind.

It was after four by the time he arrived at the Incurables Hospital, and Dr Greville received him in his study, offering him tea or sherry, both of which he declined. He described the circumstances of Kennedy's death.

"How extremely strange and sad," said Dr Greville, pouring himself a sherry. "The poor fellow – and Mrs Kennedy – have you seen her already?" Giles nodded. "How has she taken it?"

"I can't really say," said Giles. "She is a strong woman, as you may have noticed, but this is a terrible thing for anyone to have to endure. I did not like leaving her alone. I have written to her brother-in-law – this may heal the rift between the sisters. I imagine you heard something about that?"

"Yes, Mrs Kennedy did confide in me about that. She was most unhappy. I will tell Mrs Greville at once, if you do not mind, Major Vernon? We must go to her."

"If I could just ask you a few questions first, sir?" Giles said, for Greville was halfway to the door.

"Of course," said Dr Greville, sitting down again.

"Could you tell me how it was that Dr Kennedy first came to you about joining the Church of England?"

"Yes, I remember it well because it was so unusual. They came to Matins a couple of times, and then of course Mrs Kennedy's baby was born, and he came to see me to ask about having the child baptised and the possibility of their joining us in a more formal fashion."

"What reasons did he give you?"

"He said that since he had moved here he had realised what an intellectual shackle the Church of Rome was, and that he wished to find a way to exercise his faith in a more rational, less superstitious matter. It was clear he had thought a great deal and prayed about the matter, and that he had received divine guidance. It struck me as remarkable."

"He did not seem to have anything on his conscience?"

"No, I don't think so. Why do you ask?"

"We have to determine whether it was an accident or deliberate."

"Self-murder? Oh dear me, I trust not."

"Was there anything you observed about him that might suggest he had that temperament? You must have seen the signs before in your work."

"Regrettably, yes," said Dr Greville. "But in the case of Dr Kennedy, certainly not. He was not, of course, the most sparkling individual – a serious man, yes, most assuredly, but not melancholic. I would not imagine he could contemplate suicide. He had everything to live for, did he not? A beautiful wife and children and a thriving practice. He was especially pleased by the birth of his son, and he was devoted to Mrs Kennedy. He told me how happy it had made him to marry her. He had felt some despair after the death of his first wife, but Mrs Kennedy had transformed him. Why do you frown, Major Vernon?"

Giles had not meant to betray so much, and amended his expression.

"Thank you, Dr Greville, that's extremely helpful," he said. "And I would be grateful if you and Mrs Greville were to call on Mrs Kennedy."

"Mrs Kennedy chose wisely when it came to a godfather," said Dr Greville. "I feel the Lord's hand in that."

"Although Dr Kennedy did not like it," said Giles. "He did not say anything to you about it that morning?"

Dr Greville shook his head. "If he did object then it must only have been temporary, for he might have stopped it. Perhaps he realised he was being foolish in objecting and was embarrassed."

"They quarrelled that morning," Giles said.

"They had a disagreement, I think, not a quarrel. But all men and their wives have these moments, do they not? You are married, Major?"

"Yes, but –"

"And all men and their wives handle these things according to their varying temperaments. We are talking of the Irish, Major Vernon, after all! They are not like us." At that moment there was a tap on the door. "Yes, my dear?" called out Dr Greville.

"Excuse me for interrupting," said Mrs Greville, slipping into the room. She caught sight of Giles as he rose from his seat. "Oh, good day, Major Vernon! Well, that could not be better."

"I'm not so sure. He is here on sad business," said Dr Greville. "Dr Kennedy is dead."

"No!" said Mrs Greville. "How?"

"It's not entirely clear," said Giles.

"Was he murdered?" she said, with wide eyes.

"Matilda –" murmured Dr Greville.

"Oh, forgive me!" she exclaimed. "But – oh, you will think me wicked to say this, but I have thought on several occasions that he was not – and being in partnership with the Captain, who was as flash and fast as they come –"

"Matilda, what are you saying?"

"Indeed, Mrs Greville, this is interesting," said Giles.

"I suspect it is a froth of speculation," said Dr Greville.

"No, no, not at all!" said Mrs Greville. "You felt it yourself, John. My husband is not speaking ill of the dead, I dare say, Major Vernon, which is laudable in normal life, but in your line of work, must be a great inconvenience."

"Quite, ma'am," said Giles. "Won't you sit down? I would very much like to hear your opinion of Dr Kennedy."

"And I would very much like to tell you it, but I must not forget why I looked in. We have a difficulty, and really it is fortuitous that you are here, Major, because it is unpleasant and perhaps a police matter."

"What has happened?" said Dr Greville.

"Do you remember yesterday after the service, Major Vernon, how Mrs Barnaby was so distressed with Mrs Stuart?"

"Yes," said Giles. "She accused her of owing money."

"I thought it was just some of her nonsense," said Mrs Greville, "for she is prone to that. Her memory is unreliable –"

"To say the least," said Dr Greville. "She thinks I am the Archbishop of Canterbury and that we are in Spain."

"So I thought it was all nonsense," Mrs Greville went on. "But I have just been with some of them in the sewing room, and there was a great deal of muttering and fussing, when usually the dears are as calm as anything. Something had happened."

"Mrs Stuart had not been to visit?" said Giles.

"Exactly. That was the complaint. It seems – well, I cannot make head nor tail of it, but the gist of it is, she has been – but I can't see how this is true – she has been taking money from them and promising to double it."

"Are you sure?" said Dr Greville.

"I had better talk to them," said Giles, taking up his hat. "Mr Carswell said that Mrs Watts – I think that was the name – insisted to him that she was coming into a fortune. I suspect some scheme may have been practised on them."

"But would Mrs Stuart do such a thing?" said Dr Greville.

The question lingered with Giles as he talked to the various old women. This was a slightly exhausting experience that required a great deal of tea and digression to tease out the facts. Their accounts were not perhaps the most focused, but the gist of it emerged at last: Mrs Stuart had seemingly promised to 'manage' their meagre savings for them, and having proved the efficacy of her scheme by doubling Mrs Watts' money in a trice, recruited the others. The sting in the tail was that the old women were an easy target. Another conversation with Dr Greville revealed that the endowment of the Incurables Hospital was plump and well-managed, and as a result paid them all a nice stipend as inmates as well as keeping them in board and lodging. What had been a token by the original founder had now become a useful sum. Previously the women had given over the money to their families, but the temptation to make more had obviously been too much and they had handed over depressingly large sums to Mrs Stuart.

"I have enough to arrest her," Giles said.

"How on earth did we misjudge her so?" said Dr Greville.

"I suspect because she is practised at this and will have done it before, many times," said Giles.

"But she was so kind and good," said Mrs Greville. "The women loved her. She would chat with them for hours."

"And gain their trust? Yes, that's usually part of such operations," said Giles. "A charismatic charmer."

"Like Captain Carrington," said Mrs Greville. "Or perhaps I should say he attempted it and did not succeed. When I heard he had died, it struck me that he was just the type to be murdered."

"My dear, your imagination is running away with you, today!" said Dr Greville. "How is one to tell? How?" He turned to Giles. "So what will you do now?"

"I shall find one of my colleagues and go and arrest her," said Giles. "Assuming she is still in Stanegate."

~

He hurried back to the station house and gave a full account of matters to Inspector Harris.

"And what is to be done about Sir Henry Boynton?" said Harris. "Do you still want him brought in?"

"Can you spare a man to watch Adelaide Lodge?" said Giles.

"Certainly, sir."

One of the constables knocked on the door to say that a lady was here for Major Vernon. Giles went out into the waiting room and saw Emma. The sight of her in her travelling dress, looking a trifle dusty, dishevelled and flushed, was so delightful that he could not resist embracing her effusively, even to the extent that she grew more flushed.

"Giles, please," she murmured. "Not here."

"Forgive me," he said. "It has been quite a day and –" He would have said more but he was forced to release her entirely now, as Fitznorton had come out of the incident room.

"Ma'am," he said.

"Mr Fitznorton," she said.

Turning to Giles, he said, "I trust you do not object, but I have had the papers brought from Dr Kennedy's consulting room. It seemed prudent to have them analysed properly."

"Yes," said Giles. "That may yield something of use."

"I'll go and get started on it. Good day, Mrs Vernon."

"Dr Kennedy?" said Emma, when he had gone. "What has happened?"

"What has not happened," said Giles, taking her hands. "And why are you here? Is it because of Lord Rothborough?"

"Yes, Mr Carswell and Lady Charlotte sent for me. I am wanted to nurse Lord Rothborough."

"Dear God – it's serious, then?"

"Yes, and you should come with me," Emma went on, "if you can. Mr Carswell's letter was, well – it would be a great comfort to everyone if you were there. The children are en route with Greene and Patton as we speak."

"Really?"

"Lady Charlotte thought it would be more convenient for me, which it is, and it is such a large establishment they will not disturb him. At least I hope they will not! I have spoken sternly to them about how they must behave themselves. So, can you get away? What was that about Dr Kennedy?"

"He's dead," said Giles.

"Oh! Goodness. What happened? Was it an accident?" she said.

"It's unclear. I want Mr Carswell's opinion on it."

"Then come to Holbroke with me now and you can talk it over with him. He may be able to come over tomorrow."

"Yes, that's true. Nothing more can be done here today."

"You may safety leave your man-machine in charge," said Emma. "It is only for a night to begin with."

"I will leave Inspector Harris in charge," said Giles. "Mr Fitznorton, for all his merits, is not ready for that."

Chapter Thirty-two

"Your mother?" Eleanor said again. "Mrs Martinez is your real mother?"

"Yes," said Felix.

"How long have you known this?"

"It was a couple of summers ago. She was at Stanegate."

"And you never thought to tell me?"

"It was because she did not want it generally known, so –"

"Generally known?" said Eleanor. "I'm your wife, Felix! Why on earth did you not tell me?"

The simple answer was that he had no wish to confide in her on such matters. He sat thinking of all the things he had not told her. He had resolved that marriage would improve him, but it had not. He had not begun to be honest with her.

"Why?" she said again. "You could have told me when we were engaged, when we were on our wedding journey – oh, I don't know, there must have been a hundred moments when you could have told me!"

"This is not easy for me," he said. "I never expected to know her, let alone – I don't really know what I feel about her, that's the truth. What am I supposed to feel? It just seemed easier not to say anything."

"Easier?" she said.

"It's so complicated –"

"Yes, so complicated that you thought I wouldn't understand?" she said.

"I don't know. I didn't want to bother you with it."

"Oh, I'm not so sure about that!" she said. "You really didn't want me to know, did you? I suppose that is because she was a whore –"

"Where on earth did you get that idea?" exclaimed Felix. "Who told you that?"

"I thought she left you in a brothel for Lord Rothborough to rescue!"

"Who told you that?"

"Does it matter? It's the truth, is it not?"

"Yes, but only after a fashion. It's not as straightforward as that. She was not –" He broke off. He could not use that word in relation to his mother.

"A whore?" Eleanor said again. "A fallen woman? A courtesan?"

"You need to consider your own conduct before you accuse other people of things about which you know nothing!" Felix said.

"I beg your pardon?" she said.

"We have all done foolish things," said Felix. "We are all guilty. Think of that before you speak, for once!"

"Oh, are we?" she said, with the emphasis on the 'we'. "Is there something else you want to tell me, Felix? Something it might also be useful for me to know? Or have you whole libraries of such secrets?" He could not answer, and she went on. "I knew it! I knew it! Mama warned me. That first night after the dance at the Ffordes. She warned me. She told me that you were utterly unsuitable. I should have listened to her!"

"And of course there's nothing you feel guilty about?" said Felix. "Nothing I should know about? You are quite spotless, are you?"

"How dare you!" she said. "How dare you! I have no idea what you mean."

"Oh, come now," said Felix. "Do you think I'm such a fool? Do you think I haven't noticed what is going on in my own house?"

"What do you mean? I won't be accused like this, you know. If you have something to say, say it!" He hesitated and she went on, "Ha, I thought so!"

He turned away and went to the window, pushing up the sash, wondering how on earth this situation could be dealt with. He was so close to spitting out his accusations.

The parkland of Holbroke lay spread out before him, green and gentle and apparently perfect in the dusk of the hour before dinner. He thought of all the time and labour required to make that landscape. It had been made from nothing: those clumps of handsome trees had been planted there as fragile saplings, and the great silvery lake had once been a raw ditch. They had been married a scant year and a half. It was nothing. They had no roots to hold them fixed in the earth together. A simple spell of bad weather could destroy them unless some effort was made. It struck him that he was the one who must make that effort.

He sat down on the window seat and faced her again.

"We must try to be kind to one another," he said. "For the sake of the baby. Yes? I don't want this child born to parents who cannot be civil to each other, who do not attempt to understand the other and forgive. Yes, forgive."

"Do you have something that needs forgiveness?" she said.

"What I am saying is that neither of us is perfect. You have to acknowledge that, Eleanor: it is the human condition."

"If you are trying to make me confess to something, I shall not," she said. "Is this some trick you have learnt from Major Vernon?"

"No, no, that is not what I want. I want us to tolerate each other, faults and all. I know I'm not a saint and I know you are not. Can we not leave it at that?"

"You know I am not a saint? What does that mean?"

"None of us are saints. What I'm trying to say is –"

"What you are trying to say is, I must overlook something wicked you have done, yes? Without even knowing what?" He did not answer but she took that as an affirmative and went on: "How utterly shoddy and entirely unacceptable. This is about Saturday night, isn't it?" she said, advancing on him. "What happened on Saturday night? Where were you? Will you tell me the truth now? I don't believe you were at the Infirmary."

He wanted to say it then: '*I was in another woman's bed. As were you.*' It would have been so easy, and there was a part of him that longed for perfect honesty, however destructive. Yet he knew it would not be reciprocated. He knew he would not get the truth from her.

"I was at the Infirmary," he said. "Just as I said."

She shook her head and exhaled.

"You disgust me," she said, and left the room. He could not blame her.

~

Dinner was a subdued meal, as was to be expected. They ate not in the great dining room but the breakfast room, and neither Mrs Martinez nor Mrs Carswell were present. Emma and Sally valiantly kept an inoffensive, general conversation going, in a manner which Giles knew Lord Rothborough would have appreciated. Before the ladies withdrew, Lambert proposed a toast to Lord Rothborough and Mrs Martinez, an action which brought Charlotte near to tears, and she left the room hastily, with Sally shaking her head at her husband.

"Lamb, really –" she said, and followed Charlotte. The other ladies withdrew, and looking mournfully at Giles and Carswell, Lambert said, "Forgive me, was that ill-judged?"

"No," said Carswell. "It was exactly to his taste. Thank you. I understand he has asked you to make the marriage arrangements?"

"Yes, he has," said Lambert.

"Will there be any difficulty?"

"I don't think so. A special licence from the Bishop will suffice and he will hardly refuse in the circumstances. I have married a man and woman in such a situation before, though it was many years ago. The woman was dying of consumption. It was most affecting. I'm honoured to do it, Carswell," he added, going to Carswell and laying his hand on his shoulder. "And God willing, it will be a long and happy marriage! Now, I shall go and make amends to Lady Charlotte."

Lambert left and Carswell said, "I should go back to my father."

"May I keep you a while longer?" said Giles. "There is something I need to tell you. I would have told you earlier, but there was no moment."

"Yes, of course," said Carswell, sitting down again.

"Dr Kennedy is dead," he said.

"Dead? How?" said Carswell.

"He was found dead in his consulting room about noon today. He appears to have been poisoned by gas."

"Deliberately?"

"That is as yet undetermined. It may have been an accident. Mrs Kennedy tells me he had an imperfect sense of smell. Obviously there will have to be a post-mortem, and I would much prefer you to do it, but given the circumstances –"

"I will do it," said Carswell. "Gas poisoning? How did you come to that conclusion?"

"It's all circumstantial at the moment," said Giles, and went on to give a bare account of what they had already established. Yet he hesitated to repeat what Mrs Kennedy had told him about the state of their marriage and gave only the briefest details.

"What was the quarrel about?" said Carswell, making Giles realise his obfuscation had not gone unnoticed. "It must have been something fairly serious."

"It was many things," Giles said. "I got the impression that he was not an easy man."

Carswell, his elbows on the table, covered his face with his hands and groaned.

"Excuse me," he said, getting up from his seat and crossing the room. "At least she is free of him now! But... oh, dear God, what caused it?"

"I am inclined towards suicide," said Giles. "I think if we dig a little further into his past, we may find something discreditable that had become an intolerable burden to him."

"That he murdered Carrington?" said Carswell.

"I still find that unlikely. But we cannot rule it out. It may be that he commissioned the murder – that is an avenue that we can explore further."

"Have you seen the coroner yet?"

"No, but I have written to him. The body is at the Infirmary."

Carswell nodded and said, "And how is she?"

"Somewhat distressed," said Giles.

"I wish I could go to her," said Carswell. "Is she alone?"

"I have sent for Mr and Mrs O'Brien and I know that Dr and Mrs Greville were going to call on her. They know how to be useful. Ah, yes, and here is something else: Mrs Stuart. She has been defrauding those old women, promising them a fortune in return for their savings."

"Good grief," said Carswell. "That explains a great deal – the lack of servants for one thing."

"Yes, it seems Mr and Mrs Stuart were not at all who we thought they were."

"Did you arrest her?"

"It was put in motion, but I fear she may have left Stanegate already. I wonder who she really is?"

Giles pondered this as he went to look for Emma. He assumed she had gone to see how the children were settled, and went to the nurseries in the north wing. She was not there

– instead there was a scene in progress involving Patton, one of the footmen, Hamish in his nightshirt, and Lord Rothborough's two spaniels.

"Ah, here's your uncle, Master Hamish!" said Patton, "He will put an end to this silliness for once and for all!"

"What is going on?" said Giles.

"They may be his Lordship's dogs," Patton said, "but they have no place on a bed. Especially not your bed, Master Hamish." She picked up one of them and handed it to the footman. "Take them back where they belong, Joseph."

"Thing is, ma'am," said Joseph, struggling with the dog, "I'm not sure where they belong at the moment. They usually have their bed in his Lordship's dressing room."

"You see, Patton, they need someone to look after them," said Hamish, picking up the other dog. "Don't you, Percy?"

"And you will not speak to me like that, young man!" Patton exclaimed. "Did you hear that, sir?"

Prince began yapping furiously and escaped from Joseph's arms, and went running about the nursery. "Come here, Prince! Come now, boy!" Hamish went on, clearly determined to show his authority, but with little success.

"I think Mr Bodley has charge of them at the moment," said Giles, picking up Prince, who tried to bite him. "And I think they will be better with him. So give Percy to Joseph, will you?"

"Charlie Milburne was allowed to have Meg on his bed," said Hamish with a scowl directed towards Patton. He did not surrender the dog.

"No, he certainly was not!" exclaimed Patton. "And if I found her there, he'd get a whipping, which is what you deserve, Master Hamish!"

"Please give the dog to Joseph," said Giles. "And back to bed with you, at once!"

This Hamish could not refuse, but he made a great fuss of handing the dog over, muttering goodbye. He then came to say good night to Prince, who was still squirming in Giles' arms. He made a meal of this, looking up at Giles with huge eyes meant to convey his misery at this terrible injustice, but the rest of his demeanour was so cocky that Giles was hard pressed to be sympathetic.

"Bed!" he said, gesturing towards the open door.

Hamish slunk away, though not without one last glance at the dogs.

"That boy!" muttered Patton. "What he needs is a good hid–"

"No, Patton. You know my views on that."

"I do, sir, but I dare say you had plenty of them, and it didn't do you any harm, did it?" said Patton.

Giles ignored this, and turned to Joseph. "Can you manage both of them?"

"I think so, sir," Joseph said, and departed with the two struggling bundles.

"I hope Mrs What's-her-name likes dogs," said Patton, when he had gone. "Is it true, sir, that she is Mr Carswell's –"

He put up his hand to silence her and went to see if Hamish had gone to bed.

He was sitting cross-legged on the bed, arms folded, his expression defiant.

"I was trying to help Lord Rothborough," he said, "and it's not as if they are dirty dogs, but she said 'oh, we mustn't get anything dirty or else'."

"She?"

"Mrs Patton," said Hamish.

"That's better. Get into bed."

"I'm not tired."

"That's beside the point. In, now!"

"It's not fair," Hamish said, as he got under the covers. "I was only trying to help, and they were good as gold. Why couldn't they stay here? At least until morning. I would have taken them out and everything, walked them, groomed them, played with them..."

"Yes, I know – you were well intentioned, but it was badly executed. I shall speak to Bodley about them and we will see if you can be of use. In the meantime, you will be less impertinent to Mrs Patton."

"I wasn't being impertinent," he said.

"You were," said Giles. "And while you are here she has charge of you."

"But Greene –"

"Greene has her hands full with Sandro," said Giles. "So that is that. Do you understand?"

"Yes," said Hamish, "but –"

"No buts, not now," said Giles. "Go to sleep." Hamish rolled over, turning his face from Giles who laid his hand on his back. "Good night."

"Good night," he muttered in return.

~

"It will be strange for Mr Carswell, I should think," Emma said, climbing into bed.

"What will be?" said Giles.

"This marriage," said Emma.

"Ah yes, I suppose so. But given the circumstances –"

"Yes, but it still feels hasty, I have to say. Don't you think?"

"I don't know. It would have been inevitable."

"It is still very bold. And no amount of time will change that."

"Do you truly think so?" he said.

"People do not forget such things. Even when one is a Marchioness."

"I don't know," Giles said. "I should imagine that merely

being Lady Rothborough counts for a great deal, and there is absolutely nothing about her, if you did not know the circumstances, to suggest that she is anything but entirely respectable."

"Except for Mr Carswell, who can hardly be hidden away, can he? Especially as I know Lord Rothborough would like him to go into public life. How will they manage it all? It is so awkward. I wonder if that was why Mrs Felix was not with us at dinner. I suspect she will find it hard to deal with. A mother-in-law who is and is not a mother-in-law."

"I'm sure that Mrs Martinez would not do this lightly," said Giles. "My feeling is that he wishes to protect her should anything happen to him. They are looking into the jaws of death."

"Oh, don't say that!" said Emma, inching closer to him. He wrapped his arms about her. "He will recover – he must! A world sans Lord Rothborough seems unimaginable."

"It would be a terrible loss," said Giles, embracing her more tightly. She laid her head on his chest and he began to stroke her hair.

"Whatever God wills," she said, after a moment. "It is in His hands."

"Everything will be clearer after he has seen Mr Harper, I'm sure of it," he said, kissing the top of her head. "Perhaps it is not as serious as it seems."

"Amen to that," she said. "And assuming all does go well, it will still be strange his being married again, for all of us. I worry I will not like her."

"I'm sure you will."

"She was not at all what I expected. Of course, I only spoke to her for a moment or two and she cannot possibly be at all at her ease, but I felt –"

"Yes?"

"That she was rather cool."

"In what way?"

"I cannot quite place my finger on it."

"Life has not been kind to her," Giles said. "She is wary, that is all. It may read as coldness. Give it time, and I'm sure you will be friends."

"Of course, you do have the advantage on me in acquaintanceship," said Emma.

"Not much of one," said Giles.

"You saw her in London and there was that intrigue when you first met her. I know you have confidences from her that you are sworn never to disclose, even to me. Sometimes I think you are like a priest who takes confessions, Giles – you have been told so many secrets! Perhaps that is why Catholic priests do not marry – it would not be fair to their wives to have husbands always unable to confide in them."

"I'm sure that is not the reason," said Giles.

"No, of course not," said Emma. "I'm being foolish, because it hurts me."

"It hurts you? Surely –"

"I try not to feel it, but –"

"Oh, Lord," he said. "Truly? You know it is not something I take any pleasure in. There are a dozen things I should like to discuss with you but I cannot."

"I know, and I understand and accept all the reasons why, but I still cannot help feeling that door closed in my face. And when it is a woman, a beautiful, enigmatic woman – well, it stings all the more, that she should speak of you so... reverently."

"She did?" he said.

"You are clearly a saint to her, yes. And goodness, she is handsome, and so thin and elegant." She sighed. "Oh dear – and I felt a mere scrub in comparison."

"Not so. You are not a scrub!" said Giles. "However, you are over-tired and worried. This is a strange situation altogether."

"That's true. Forgive me, I'm being foolish."

"Nothing to forgive," he said, kissing her. "Shall I stroke your back?" This was the usual prelude to intimacy between them, and he slipped his hand inside her nightgown.

"But should we?" she said, and then sighed with pleasure as he began to kiss her now bare shoulders.

"Yes," he said. "Life is brief."

Chapter Thirty-three

Felix woke to the murmur of prayer. He had been sleeping on the sofa at the foot of Lord Rothborough's bed. Opening his eyes, he saw Mrs Martinez, with her back to him and on her knees in the corner of the room. She was kneeling on a prie-dieu and there was a small painting of the Virgin and Child on the wall above it, suggestive of an oratory. He was surprised to discover these objects of private devotion in Lord Rothborough's bedroom. He had never noticed them before.

Judging by the light, it was early morning. He had sent her to bed at one and he wondered how much rest she had allowed herself.

He lay for some minutes watching her, wondering at the rapidity with which she repeated the words of the prayer.

"Pray for us sinners, now and at the hour of our death. Holy Mary, Mother of God, Hail Mary full of grace, blessed art thou among women..."

He sat up and the sofa creaked. She finished the prayer, then rose, crossed herself and turned to him.

"I didn't disturb you, did I?" she said.

"No. I needed to wake anyway," said Felix. He rubbed his face, feeling heavy with sleep.

"You need to rest more than any of us," she said, and went to the bedside. Felix joined her. Lord Rothborough was sleeping still, and gathering his thoughts, Felix set to checking his pulse and his temperature. This made Lord Rothborough stir into wakefulness, and seeing them both there, he managed a wan smile.

"What time is it?" he said, his voice painfully hoarse.

"About six," said Mrs Martinez.

He nodded.

"You should drink something," said Felix. "Some water, if you can keep it down."

He left Mrs Martinez feeding him teaspoonfuls of water and went into the dressing room to find Bodley laying out clean linen.

"He's comfortable," Felix said, in answer to his enquiring glance. "No change."

"That's something, I suppose, sir."

"Yes," said Felix. "It's the best that can be said in the circumstances. Mrs Martinez is with him now. I'm going to get changed."

He went to his own dressing room and – suddenly overwhelmed with tiredness again – stripped down to his shirt and lay down on the bed. He had only slept a few hours, and it had been an imperfect rest, full of vivid and troubling dreams. Sukey had been there, sitting in bed beside him, nursing a baby, but then Eleanor had stormed in and taken the child away from her.

He lay there now, painfully awake and exhausted, remembering the dream without wanting to and wondering how Sukey was at that moment. Major Vernon had talked of them quarrelling, and the fact he had not gone into specific details alarmed him. It was clear the situation between her and Kennedy had been most unpleasant and that she had been suffering. Had he abused her in some way? His death would bring her some relief eventually, he supposed, but the strange circumstances of it could not bring her any immediate comfort. If Kennedy had killed himself, then she would feel herself responsible, that much he knew.

He rolled onto his side, staring at the wallpaper, unable to consider sleep. Had it only been two nights ago that he had been disporting himself so carelessly, like an animal on heat, in Elisabeth Jacquot's bed? He winced at the thought of it. He had used her, and now he felt deeply ashamed of himself.

"Mr Carswell, Mr Carswell!"

Jacob had him by the shoulder.

"What?"

"Mr Harper is here, sir."

"What time is it?"

"Past ten, sir."

"The devil it is..." said Felix. He had fallen asleep again in spite of himself.

"Shouldn't you shave, sir?"

Felix ignored this and left the room, still fastening his braces. In this state of undress he met Mr Harper coming out of Lord Rothborough's bedroom.

"Good morning, Mr Carswell," said Mr Harper.

"Sir, I cannot thank you enough for coming so promptly."

"It was the least I could do," said Mr Harper. "I have made a preliminary examination and I would concur with Dr Markham and yourself that there is an acute and widespread peritoneal inflammation."

"So what do you suggest is causing it?"

Mr Harper knotted his large, elegant hands together as he often did when he was considering something deeply.

"I had a sense of an obstruction to the appendix to the upper caecum, a tumorous lesion, perhaps."

"Yes, that was my impression," said Felix. "Perhaps the appendix itself has become inflamed?"

"Quite," said Mr Harper. "It might be possible to excise it – if, of course, that is what the problem is. I must be frank with you, Mr Carswell. I have operated on a similar case, under such an assumption, only to discover that the damage was far more extensive, and required more exploration and consideration than was possible in the brief time available. There is only so much the human frame can bear."

Felix nodded, and said, "We might consider etherizing him."

"Etherizing? Is that a verb now?"

"Admittedly ether has been a plaything," said Felix, "but it is now being put to serious use. Mr Hamilton, the dental surgeon in Stanegate, has been using it almost routinely for extractions. He operated on Miss King last Wednesday with no bad effects. I witnessed the procedure myself and it was impressive."

"A tooth extraction is a different matter," said Mr Harper.

"Perhaps if you were to talk to Hamilton?"

"Certainly, but you must know I have large reservations about such an innovation, especially when the situation is so grave." Felix nodded and was silent, feeling the full force of Mr Harper's words, expressed as they were in his gentle West Country tones. "Let me explain," Mr Harper went on. "I have two objections – one is that we simply do not yet know the effects of ether on the body when inducing a chemical slumber of that kind. Now, Miss King, what is she – thirty years old and in excellent health, as I remember? She was under for how long, would you say?"

"Some fifteen minutes," said Felix. "And she never quite slept."

"So, about the time it would take a skilled man to extract a tooth without the ether."

"Yes, but –"

"The relief of pain in such a situation is commendable – I am in complete agreement with you there, Mr Carswell. Indeed, I would probably submit myself in those circumstances, if I were confident that a strict time limit were in place and that the hands which were to operate were sufficiently skilled. However, to use ether to buy time when the patient is open on the table – that I cannot be easy with. Lord Rothborough is in a weakened condition. There is no saying how the ether will affect him. It might well may be fatal. There was a case in Southampton –"

"I know the one," said Felix.

"Our profession gives the laurels to those who are deft and quick in all they do. That is the bottom line, Mr Carswell: what can be done in the shortest space of time to the best effect. That is an excellent discipline which I cannot throw aside lightly. It may seem miraculous, this ether, but I have strong reservations. I will consider it, and I will talk to Mr Hamilton. He may concur with me, of course."

"I understand," said Felix.

"In the meantime, I suggest another day of observation. I know this is hard for you," said Mr Harper. "You will be in my prayers." He turned back towards the sickroom. "The lady that is with him –?"

"Mrs Martinez. She's an old friend. They are to be married."

"Ah," said Mr Harper, "that is cheerful news!"

Mr Harper went back into Lord Rothborough's room, but Felix hesitated a while by the window, turning over what had been said. The risks were considerable, that was true enough. To open the affected area and see what might be done at this point might well be disastrous, even in the most skilful hands. However, the alternative of inaction struck him as equally dangerous.

"Good morning, Mr Carswell!"

It was Major and Mrs Vernon.

"I've come to go on duty," said Mrs Vernon. "How is he?"

"He had a reasonably comfortable night. No great change. The principle danger at present is fever: that is what you must watch for. Mr Harper is with him just now."

"Oh, so you are waiting to hear –?" said Major Vernon.

"No, we have discussed it."

His tone must have betrayed him, for in an instant, Mrs Vernon's arms were about him.

"Courage," she murmured, kissing his cheek. "Now, I will go." She released him, went and kissed her husband, and departed.

"Do you think you will be able to come in to Stanegate?" said Major Vernon. "I am leaving just now."

"Yes, I shall later, when Dr Markham gets here. I want to take Mr Harper to see Hamilton."

"Dr Kennedy's remains are at the Infirmary, if you do have time today," said Major Vernon. "Good luck."

They parted, and Felix finished dressing. As Jacob shaved him, it passed through his mind that he ought to go to see Eleanor and attempt to sue for peace. But the effort felt too much at that moment, and he went instead to find some breakfast.

Miss King was in the breakfast room sitting at the table, absently stirring her tea and apparently lost in some deep train of thought. She gave a start as he closed the door behind him.

"Oh!"

"Excuse me," he said, sitting down opposite her.

"How is Lord Rothborough?"

"Comfortable enough, but –" She nodded. "Could I trouble you for some of that tea?" he said, taking up a cup.

"Yes, yes, of course!" she said, getting up to take the cup from him. "I'm only sitting here in idleness. I should make myself useful and earn my keep."

"Is Eleanor still in bed?"

"Yes. She is tired this morning, but nothing to worry about, I think. This pot is fresh," she went on, pouring the tea. "It's Indian. Thomas only just brought it in, but I can ring for more if you wish?"

He shook his head, and went to the sideboard to carve himself a slice of ham.

"I'd better go and see how she is," Miss King said.

"You should finish your breakfast," said Felix.

"I'm not hungry," she said.

"Your mouth isn't giving you trouble again?"

"No, no," she said, "not at all. It's simply –" She gave a

forced smile. "Everything is at sixes and sevens, that's all."

"True enough," said Felix, buttering his bread.

She sat down again and said, "I'm glad to have the chance to speak to you alone, Mr Carswell."

"Yes?" he said.

"What I wanted to say is this," she said. "If there is anything about my presence that you find less than satisfactory, if you feel there is anything I have done that... perturbs you at all..."

He placed his cup back in the saucer.

"Perturbs me?" he said. "In what respect."

"Sometimes I feel I have overstepped the mark. Mrs Carswell is so kind to me. It makes me forget myself and my position. Indeed, I should say that you are both so kind to me, and perhaps it is not deserved."

Was this a confession, he wondered, noticing her averted gaze and scarlet cheeks.

"I fear," she went on, in a quiet voice, "I may not be as useful to you both as I should. That I am perhaps not the person you need."

In that moment it was hard to see her as a viper poisoning his domestic bosom. She looked so miserable, as if she had found herself in a place that she did not understand. Her heart had betrayed her and that he could not censure.

"Are you giving me your notice?"

"I'm trying to face facts: you may wish me to leave. You have every right to dismiss me."

"Why do you think that?"

"Mrs Carswell told me that you argued last night." He nodded. "And I think I was partly to blame for it, and that I cannot allow to pass. I cannot be the cause of unhappiness between you. Therefore..."

He shook his head.

"I can't let you go," he said. "It would break Eleanor's heart, and as for being cause of a quarrel, between us, well, that is nonsense."

"It is?"

"If we squabble it is because we are both a pair of fools who cannot keep our tempers. It is not your fault, Miss King, if we cannot be civil."

"I am not sure you understand me properly, sir," she said, getting up. "You told Mrs Carswell that she should put her house in order, so to speak, did you not? I must be plain with you. I am the cause of that disorder. If there is any fault, it is all mine. I am not a good person." She began to cry. "And therefore I think I should go."

She was halfway across the room now, but he got up and blocked her way.

"No," he said, horrified by her distress. "I can't have both of you with broken hearts, for Heaven's sake!" He caught her hands and said, "And it suits me far better to have you with us, believe me. You say you are not a good person, Miss King. Are any of us truly without fault? I think not! My own conduct is –"

"That does not excuse what I have done," she said, pulling away her hands. "It would be better, surely, if –"

"No, please, Jenny," he said, taking her hands again. "I cannot do without you. We cannot do without you. She cannot be happy without you, and therefore you must stay. And where else would you go? What else would you do? Be a governess again?"

"But, but..." she said, and then broke off, swallowing back her tears and managing an awkward smile. "Are you truly sure that is what you want?"

"Perfectly," he said, and kissed her cheek. "Try to be happy, and I'll try to be kinder to Eleanor."

Chapter Thirty-four

"There is someone here I want you to talk to, Major Vernon," said Mr Fitznorton.

"In relation to what?" Giles said.

"Dr Kennedy's death. A useful witness."

"Very well," said Giles. "There's been no sign of Mrs Stuart, I take it, Inspector?" he said, turning to Harris.

"She hasn't turned up yet, sir, but you'll be the first to know when we find her."

Giles drained his teacup, and followed Fitznorton to the interview room.

"This is Joseph Horton," said Fitznorton, indicating the man who was sitting there. "Bath house attendant at the Hydropathic Institute."

"Thank you, Mr Fitznorton. I'll take it from here."

Giles would not normally have dismissed him, but there was something about his manner that made him wary. It was that of counsel calmly presenting the witness who would make the case for the prosecution, and astonish the court. Given the eagerness with which Fitznorton had accused Sukey the day before, he suspected this must be more of the same. He did not, therefore, want Fitznorton putting leading questions.

"Did you come here of your own accord, Mr Horton?" he asked first, sitting down.

"No, sir, it was that gent who brought you in. He were up at the baths this morning asking us all questions."

"What questions were these?"

"About yesterday morning. Whether we had seen Dr Kennedy about."

"I see. What work do you do in the bath house?"

"I work mostly in the cold baths. I clean and make sure everything is straight for the patients. Take away the damp linen and so forth."

"And you saw Dr Kennedy yesterday?"

"No, not yesterday. But I saw Mrs Kennedy. That's why I'm here."

"So you know Mrs Kennedy to speak to her?"

"Oh aye, sir. She's such a nice lady and she's made a point of knowing us all. She always says good day and smiles, but she wasn't smiling yesterday. Well, not really, it was just a quick smile like, and she was in a hurry. She were walking really fast."

"Where was this?"

"Just in that passageway by Dr Kennedy's office. You know the one."

"Yes," said Giles. "What were you doing there?"

"I was taking some towels down to him. Well, not to him, but there is a cupboard there for towels and I have to check that it's full."

"In the office?"

"No, just outside. I didn't go in. No. I was just going along with the towels, when Mrs Kennedy passed me, in that lobby bit, you know?" Giles nodded. "She'd come from his room and she didn't look happy."

"You are sure it was Mrs Kennedy?"

"Aye, sir."

"Can you describe her dress?"

"Blue, with a white shawl, with a stripe on it. She didn't have her bonnet on."

"What time was this?"

"It were just before my dinner, so fair close to noon. That's when we go for dinner. I always check the towels just before I go for my dinner."

"Thank you, Mr Horton, that was helpful," said Giles, showing him to the door. Left alone he sat down, scratched out some notes in his notebook and then fell into a most uncomfortable train of thought. Sukey had not mentioned going to see him in his consulting room. She had been frank on a great many points, but that she had omitted.

Fitznorton was waiting for him in the passageway.

"So?"

"Yes, interesting. Well done, Mr Fitznorton."

"So you will question her formally now?"

"Mr Carswell has yet to examine the body. When we have his report, I will consider what steps we take next."

"Forgive me, Major Vernon, but that sounds like prevarication. Surely it would be better to take the woman in at once and interview her? I dare say she would not resist confessing if you were in charge of it."

"Was that supposed to be a compliment?" Giles said.

"Sir?"

"Have you any conception how callous that sounds? Not to mention inconsistent. Yesterday it was your opinion I should not speak to her, and now I am to work her over like some petty criminal."

"The evidence is highly suggestive –"

"Highly suggestive, yes, but not at all conclusive, and I will not have her disturbed until we have more on this! Let us think about Sir Henry Boynton and Captain Carrington, shall we? Where are those improper letters we discovered? I have an idea who may have written them." He was thinking of Lady Amberleigh.

"I will look them out, sir," said Fitznorton, going back into the room where they had been collating the papers. Giles took this as his opportunity to leave the station house and head to the Infirmary in the hope he might encounter Carswell there.

However, on his way he reached the bookseller and circulating library where he had bought his map and Fitznorton had disapproved of the elegantly dressed women.

He turned in, struck by a curious memory of one of the old women at the Incurables Hospital talking about Mrs Stuart having probably gone back to Canada. He consulted his notes and saw he was not mistaken: "Says she was once in Toronto."

"Can I help you, sir?"

"Do you have Palmer's Index?"

"Certainly, sir. Upstairs in the gentlemen's coffee room. We have bound copies of The Times for the last five years as well."

"Excellent," Giles said, and sprinted upstairs. Here the waiter showed him to the desired volumes and went to fetch coffee. The place was deserted, and he was able to spread the books out on a large table and make a thorough study. For some years, he had been in the habit of collecting interesting criminal cases and intelligence from newspapers. It was a task he now delegated to a constable, but in the early days, he had cut and gummed the stories himself into large scrapbooks, and as he studied Palmer's useful index to The Times, the details of the case he had begun to recall became clearer. He realised he had remembered this case in particular because it had taken place in a province he had visited – Ontario.

A SINGULAR FRAUD IN LOWER CANADA

– May 1840. A woman, respectable in appearance and habits, is sought in the town of Toronto after the collapse of a savings scheme. The woman, known as Miss Eliza Dunn, residing at Mrs Hope's boarding establishment, was known for her charitable work among the old and unfortunate in the neighbourhood. It seems she had induced them to contribute to a savings scheme, promising a considerable reward in a short period. Such were her powers of persuasion that a group of old women pensioners at St Thomas' Church had given over to her sums in excess of fifty guineas for safekeeping. When Miss Dunn failed to repay the money in the time stipulated and subsequently disappeared from Mrs Hope's house having neglected to pay for her lodging, the alarm was raised. However, Miss Dunn was not found and was not brought to justice.

Was this Mrs Stuart? It struck him as a small scheme – deeply unpleasant, of course, but not especially lucrative, and she had expensive tastes if her appearance at the opera was anything to go by.

"Can I interest you in a cigar with your coffee, sir?" said the waiter.

"No, thank you," said Giles, fumbling for a coin to pay him. He did not touch his coffee.

~

Carswell was in the mortuary at the Infirmary, gazing at Kennedy's corpse, almost as if he had never seen a dead man before.

"It's strange," he said, seeing Giles. "How long was he in there before being discovered?"

Giles consulted his notebook.

"Approximately three and a half hours."

"And you are still leaning towards suicide?"

Giles hesitated and then said, "I wish I could say so. There has been some new evidence."

"What sort of evidence?"

"Joseph Horton, bath house attendant, saw Sukey leaving the consulting room just before noon."

"What?"

"Now, she didn't tell me about this visit, but I suspect it was just an oversight on her part. I've yet to speak to her about it."

"And what if she denies it?" said Carswell.

"We shall see what she says," said Giles.

Carswell leant forward over Kennedy's corpse and pulled open his left eyelid.

"The question is," he said, "how many people knew he

had no sense of smell?"

"Indeed," said Giles. "And the fact that she told me this at once is as good an augur of innocence as anything, surely?"

"I don't think she could do it," said Carswell, letting the eyelid drop. "But then who knows what she has had to suffer from him."

"The danger is," Giles said, "that it may appear that she did it."

"What was that quarrel about?" said Carswell.

"I didn't want to trouble you with it," said Giles. "And I'm not sure she would want you to know."

"What did he do to her?"

"He insisted on his marital rights on Sunday evening."

"Dear God," muttered Carswell, and turned away from the cadaver. Giles took the opportunity to draw the sheet back over him. "That damns her!"

"We don't have all the information yet," said Giles. "The post-mortem may throw up something unexpected. I wrote to the coroner yesterday, so I assume your permission will be forthcoming, but I shall go and see him now, as I want to speak to him about Richard Stuart as well."

"Why now?" said Carswell.

"His wife is a fraudster," said Giles. "Perhaps she might have killed him after all, as you suggested. She seems to have vanished into thin air."

"Since she is not here to object, I could make a start on Stuart's post-mortem," said Carswell. "That was curious," he added. "Kennedy and she seemed to know each other quite well."

"Yes," said Giles, thinking of the christening. "As if there were more to it than her husband being his patient."

"And he was against a post-mortem. Perhaps he knew something."

"And Mrs Stuart killed him for it? And then there is the matter of the blanket." The image of the blanket tangled up in the thorn tree now sprang into his mind.

"The blanket?"

"The Hudson Bay blanket that Carrington was wrapped in. Mrs Stuart had been in Canada – one of the old women at the Incurables Hospital told me so. Now that house is extremely well-placed for entry into the menagerie grounds – how on earth did I not see that before? We have to find her!"

Chapter Thirty-five

Major Vernon suggested that in the first instance they make a search of Mrs Stuart's cottage.

"There is a chance she may have left something of use to us. But you will need to get back to Holbroke."

"Not at once," said Felix. "I'm more use here, to be frank. I left Mr Harper with Hamilton this morning and put it in their hands, and Dr Markham as well, of course. I find it hard to be as clear-headed about it as I should be. It is better I step aside. And this will keep me occupied, at least."

"If you are sure?"

"Quite."

They briskly made their way up the hill to the Rustic Cottages. The Major, who never walked slowly, was now exhibiting the energy that Felix had observed in him previously as they drew closer to a quarry. He felt it himself, and it was a great relief to close the door on all those matters about which he could do nothing in that moment, and concentrate on Mrs Stuart.

"She behaved so curiously when I called here," he said, as they reached the front door. He discovered he was slightly breathless. "I think I need to take to Fitznorton's regime," he added.

Major Vernon smiled at that. "You still beat me at swimming."

"I saw her take the key from under that stone," Felix said, stooping to lift it. The key was there, as before. He handed it to Major Vernon. "People are so foolish in this regard."

"It suggests that she must still be in town," Major Vernon said, turning the key in the lock. "Why lock the house if you are abandoning it?"

"The thing that really strikes me now is that there was no carpet," said Felix, as they went into the drawing room and the bare boards stretched out before them.

"I wonder if it was moved," said Major Vernon, "because something was spilt on it."

"Blood, you mean?"

"Let's see what we can find. We have to ask ourselves, why is she still here?"

"Because she feels confident that no one has uncovered her scheme yet," said Felix.

"But she must know that a trick like that cannot be continued indefinitely. That is the whole point, surely – you promise the payout and then default before you are discovered. And if she is involved in these murders, then what is worth the risk of staying here when she knows we may have already stumbled onto the truth?"

"Money," said Felix.

"Yes," said Major Vernon. "Carrington's money, perhaps."

"Why do you say that?"

"Where is it? He didn't have any bank accounts as far as I can gather. Another sign of a criminal, I'd say. He liked to keep his assets in tangible, portable form." He looked about him. "So we know that Carrington was at Adelaide Lodge on Sunday night. There was a fracas and he left. Perhaps he came here afterwards, for some reason."

"Why would he know the Stuarts?"

"Perhaps they had some business arrangement with him. It's likely that stealing from old women was not their only source of illegitimate income. Spa towns are full of bored rich people. Where better to run a private gaming operation than the Hydropathic Institute?"

"Is that possible?"

"We know that Carrington was crooked, so he will

associate with crooks. Let us imagine him here, on Sunday night. Things take a nasty turn and he is stabbed – most likely by Richard Stuart. Did you not say he had undergone a change of character?"

"Yes, she told me that."

"Perhaps he had become violent. Did you not mention once that sometimes these transformations come over men after head injuries? That they lose their sense of restraint?"

"It has been observed on occasion," said Felix. "She did not say anything about a head injury, but she did mention that he had been having headaches and blurred vision. If he had a tumour on his brain, then that might account for it, and perhaps an internal injury such as that might have the same effect as an external one in regard to behaviour. And of course, that may well have killed him."

"You must do that post-mortem now," said Major Vernon. "You were right to suggest it."

"Unless she killed him," Felix went on.

"We shall come to that later," said Major Vernon, now opening drawers and cupboard doors. "All empty. She is careful, we can say that much. Let's look upstairs and see if there is anything to support my wild imaginings."

Here, more personal possessions were in evidence – a wardrobe full of expensive women's clothing, and what looked like the clothes of a young man.

"Where are Richard Stuart's clothes?" said Major Vernon, holding up a short jacket. "These are too small."

"Maybe she wore them," said Felix. He was examining a waistcoat, a rough fustian item.

"Possibly, which suggests she has a manner of life that involves disguise. She may have sold Richard's clothes already. She might, of course, be selling them as we speak."

"So much for the sentimental widow," said Felix.

Major Vernon was now struggling to extract a portmanteau that had been stuffed into the back of a drawer containing folded linen.

"This looks promising."

He carried it over to the bed. It was locked, but his skeleton keys soon dealt with that, and inside they discovered packs of unopened playing cards, some small velvet bags containing dice and various pamphlets dedicated to systematic gambling. There were also a couple of notebooks, full of abstruse-looking calculations.

"Something for Fitznorton," said Major Vernon, "but at a glance I would say this is to do with increasing odds, or indeed rigging an entire system."

"It looks like it," said Felix, looking through the gambling pamphlets. A business card for a livery stable in Stanegate slipped out. "Is this of interest?"

"I know them," said Major Vernon. "We should ask if they have seen her. Did I see a riding habit in the cupboard?"

"You did," said Felix.

Major Vernon was holding up a diamond bracelet that had been hiding in a leather purse. "Now, I wonder where this came from."

"There is something else in here," Felix said, taking up the purse. He pulled out a playing card. "The three of clubs. That's odd."

"Maybe it's a lucky card. Gamblers have such things."

"There's something written on it," said Felix, going over to the window and peering at it. "I think it says: 'C.H.' What on earth does that mean?"

"May I?" said Major Vernon.

Felix handed him the card. "Looks like it was written in a hurry," he said. "'C.H.'"

~

They returned to the station house. As they entered, the desk sergeant said, "Ah, there you are, sir. We have Mrs Kennedy waiting for you, as requested."

"As I requested?" said Major Vernon.

"Mr Fitznorton said that you wanted her brought in for an interview. She is in the little room at the end of the passageway. She brought a baby with her. I suppose she had to bring it, but it's been howling its head off the whole time."

"Yes, I can hear. Where is Mr Fitznorton?"

"I think he's talking to her, sir," said the sergeant.

"You didn't ask her to be brought in, did you?" said Felix, as they went down the passageway.

"No, of course not," said Major Vernon.

He opened the door and they were met by the sight of Sukey standing with the fractious child held tight against her. Her bonnet had slipped off and was hanging down her back, with the ribbons about her neck like a noose. She looked flushed and uncomfortable. In the meantime, Fitznorton was sitting at the table, with a heap of foolscap in front of him, obviously ready to record a confession, while one of the constables stood in the corner.

"He thinks I killed my husband!" said Sukey, above the screaming of the child. She was on the verge of tears. "What have you said to him? You don't think I have, do you?"

"No," said Major Vernon. "There has been a mistake." He turned to the constable. "Get out at once!" The constable obeyed, but Fitznorton remained in his seat. "Both of you!" Fitznorton now complied and Major Vernon followed him, closing the door on Sukey. "Constable!" he added. "Before you go, I have an errand for you."

"Sir?"

"Go down to Farren's livery stables and find out what business they have had with a Mr or Mrs Stuart. That's Stuart with a 'u'. Come straight back – it's a matter of some urgency."

"Yes, sir, right away, sir!"

The constable went scuttling off, like a rabbit with a backside full of buckshot, and Major Vernon turned to Fitznorton, who now drew himself up as if he wanted to remind Major Vernon that he exceeded him by an inch or two.

"Mr Fitznorton, would you care to explain?"

"I reviewed the evidence and decided that a more formal interview was in order," he said.

"And apparently you thought fit to take my name in vain to accomplish it?"

"It seemed expedient, given the circumstances, which are, I admit, exceptional. I felt that objectivity needed to be brought to bear and that the sooner the suspect was interviewed the more likely it was –"

"That you could get a confession out of her?"

"The bath attendant was a compelling witness. It struck me that you felt that what he said was of value, but were not willing, because of your personal connection with the suspect, to pursue matters to their proper conclusion."

"So you thought you would take matters into your own hands?"

"Yes," said Fitznorton, without a shade of contrition.

"Where do I start, Mr Fitznorton, where do I start?" said Major Vernon. "In the first place, Mrs Kennedy is not a suspect. Even if I did not know her from Eve, she would not be a suspect! To drag her here, on the day after she had been made a widow, and subject her to such an interview –"

"Excuse me, but you are demonstrating my point, Major Vernon. You obviously have some history with this woman and that is making you protect her. Her manner during this interview has given me no cause to doubt that she ought to be considered a suspect. She has been most uncooperative."

"I'm hardly surprised, when you have dragged her from her home and treated her like a common criminal!" said Major Vernon.

"It is my understanding that putting on a certain pressure

can bear results."

"It will not bear results when the subject is entirely innocent. It will only cause great distress, which in this case I find unforgivable!"

"I'm sorry to disagree with you, Major Vernon, but I cannot accept this. Mrs Kennedy was seen leaving her husband's office shortly before the time when we suspect the gas had been turned on. A normal flow of gas from two such burners would be approximately twenty-five cubic feet per hour. This would have been sufficient to kill him in the course of the three hours he was alone in room. She also knew that her husband had no appointments in the course of the next two-and-a-half hours. His diary, which was lying on the table, was there for her to observe when she entered the room. Furthermore, and most importantly, she was fully aware that he had no sense of smell. The facts speak for themselves. Yes?" he added, turning to Felix.

"I haven't done a post-mortem. I can't say anything conclusively."

"But you would agree that it is likely?" Fitznorton said.

"Enough!" said Major Vernon. "Yes, yes, congratulate yourself, sir, you have made an excellent case against her! Bravo! But remember this: you are an observer here, not a serving officer. You are only here because I have allowed it. You have no authority at all! You have absolutely no business taking matters into your own hands in this outrageous fashion. Telling constables to carry out orders in my name, sir? What kind of expediency is that? Grabbing power that does not belong to you because you think you know what happened?"

"Given how little progress has been made in the matter of Carrington's death," said Fitznorton, "I thought you might have welcomed the assistance."

Major Vernon looked as if he were about to make some sharp retort, but shook his head and walked away.

"I'm going to apologise to Mrs Kennedy," he said. "If

you felt inclined to do so also, I am sure she would appreciate it. If you do not care to, I should remind you that her brother-in-law publishes a newspaper with a large and influential circulation. He will not take kindly to hearing that an unauthorised official from the Home Office tried to badger a confession out of his sister-in-law." Major Vernon went and knocked on the door to the interview room. "May I come in, Mrs Kennedy?"

"Yes," Felix heard Sukey say, and the Major entered.

"She was his mistress, I understand," said Fitznorton when the door had closed.

"No, damn you, she was not!" exclaimed Felix, his own reserves of calm now deserting him. "You are a complete and utter ass, Fitznorton!"

"I beg your pardon?"

Fortunately the door opened again, and looking out, Major Vernon said, "Mr Carswell, will you come and have a look at the child? Mrs Kennedy thinks he may have a fever."

He went in to find Sukey now sitting down and struggling to get the child to latch onto her breast. Lorenzo continued to shriek as if he were expressing his outrage at the situation in which his mother had been placed.

"He's like a hot coal," she said. "And he needs to feed, but he won't."

"Here, let me," Felix said, and took him into his arms. "You should both go home."

Major Vernon went to arrange for a carriage, and they were alone.

"What is going on?" she exclaimed, and gave way to tears. "Oh, Lorenzo, hush!" she sobbed, as Felix examined the screaming child.

"He's defending your honour," Felix said. "You should be proud of him."

"Here, give him back to me," said Sukey, taking the child back from him, and attempted again to feed him. This time she had more success. She sat back in her chair and sighed.

"I think you should both go to bed when you get home. You look exhausted," said Felix, touching her forehead. She too, was warm. "If you are rested, it will help him."

"I'm exhausted!" she said. "I didn't sleep at all last night, and then this! I can't believe that fellow had the cheek to say Major Vernon had ordered me here. I wouldn't have come if I'd known that. I hope the Major tore a strip off him."

"More than one, I should say," said Felix.

"He really wanted me to confess to it," she went on. "The worst of it was that he made me feel as if I had done it! He kept going on and on about my quarrelling with him, and how he had three witnesses who will swear that they saw me screaming at him! Which is true, but it doesn't mean I killed him! Oh, and then he said that he'd found someone who'd seen me going into his consulting room. I remember I saw him now, it was Joe who cleans the baths."

"So you did go to his consulting room?"

"Yes! I went to apologise to Paul for screaming my head off, but he wasn't there. So yes, Jo saw me, and I forgot to tell the Major that I'd gone to see him and found he wasn't there, because he'd just told me Paul was dead... but your man there seemed to think I hadn't told him on purpose! As if I was concealing it because I'd killed Paul."

"He had absolutely no business doing it," said Felix. "Any joy?" he added, indicating the child on her breast.

"Yes, he's remembered that he's thirsty, the silly wee thing."

"You should take him to the seaside," he said. "I understand Mr O'Brien has a house at Swalecliffe."

"I have to bury my husband," she said. "I remember when James died, his family had all sorts of ideas about what needed to be done. What am I supposed to do? Do I get a priest to say mass for him? I'm not sure a priest would, if he killed himself. I suppose Dr Greville might have reservations as well. He kept saying, when he called last night, that he was sure it was an accident. But it can't have been. It must have been deliberate."

"Do you really think he killed himself?" said Felix.

"He must have," she said, reaching for her son's small hand. "Who else would have killed him? They'd have to know about his sense of smell – that's what your man was banging on about to me – who else could have known that but me? He had a point."

"Maybe he told it to one of his patients," said Felix, "to put them at their ease?"

"I think you have a different idea of bedside manner, Felix," she said. "Paul wasn't a man to put anyone at their ease. How is Lord Rothborough? I forgot to ask, I'm sorry."

"We don't know yet," he said, touched by her concern. "With luck, Mr Harper can operate and relieve the tumour."

"It's a tumour? Oh, no," she said, and her hand darted out to touch his arm. "Will you give him my best regards? He was always so kind to me. I ought to write."

"I will tell him," he said. "Oh, and he's going to be married."

"No?" she said. "Who to?"

"Can't you guess?"

She stared at him. "My, that will set the world talking," she said.

"Yes, won't it?"

"And what do you think about it?" she said.

"I don't know. It will be strange. My wife –" He broke off. On the one hand he would have enjoyed pouring out his troubles to her, but on the other hand it was hardly fair to burden her with his mistakes. "What will be, will be!" he said. "That's all that can be said, sometimes, don't you think?"

"Yes, indeed," she said, and bent and kissed her child.

Chapter Thirty-six

"That's odd, and no mistake," said Inspector Harris when Giles showed him the playing card. "'C.H.' Is it someone's name, do you think, sir?"

"I cannot say. A name, a place –"

Harris laid the card down on the table and said, "The only place I know with those initials is Crandall's Hole. But that's up on the moor. It's a cave full of tunnels that are easy to get lost in. Nasty dangerous place, all said. I've hauled a few dead bodies out of there in my time – mostly stupid lads going in for a dare."

"Do you have a map of the moor?"

Harris went to fetch it and Giles turned to his wall of notes, the card in his hand. He was alone. Carswell had gone back with Sukey while Fitznorton had at least had the decency to make himself scarce. He was no doubt writing a memorandum somewhere, full of self-justification and liable to cause everyone a great deal of trouble. His manner had struck Giles as entirely impervious to censure.

He concentrated on the puzzle that was Mrs Stuart, carefully testing his own hypothesis against her. The evidence was slim enough – Fitznorton would be the first to point that out. A bloodstained blanket from Canada did not prove she was the Eliza Dunn who had been at work in Toronto, nor that she was involved in Carrington's death. But the facts of the fraud at the Incurables could not be disputed, and that at least gave him a legitimate reason to question her at length.

He stepped back as Harris came in with the map.

"There you are, sir," he said, spreading it on the table. "Crandall's Hole. About three mile as the crow flies."

"You'd be best reaching it on horseback or foot, by the look of it," said Giles, studying the map.

"Oh aye, sir. Carriage wouldn't manage it. We had to carry those poor boys on hurdles across the moor. That were six years ago. Thank the Lord, no one has been so stupid since."

"And anyone who spends any time here would hear of that, I imagine?"

"Yes, sir, they might," said Harris. "Some say it's haunted, of course."

"A useful rumour, if it's so dangerous," Giles said.

Giles studied the map again, tracing the moorland road he had taken from Amberleigh Castle to the Rustic Cottages. At one point it forked, and he realised that if he had taken it he would have reached Crandall's Hole. Whether or not that was significant he did not know.

"We need to keep a constant watch on Mrs Stuart's cottage. She may be nervous of going back in daylight."

"I have already seen to it, sir," said Inspector Harris, and left him alone again.

Giles took the bracelet he had found at the cottage from his pocket. He had hesitated for a while about removing this, but as he had said to Sukey, expensive jewels always made him suspicious. He still had the ring that had caused her so much grief in his pocket, and he took it out now and compared it with the bracelet. They did not match, but they both had a similar feel of quality about them. They made him think of heirloom items belonging to aristocratic families. He felt sure that Mrs Stuart had not come by this bracelet legitimately.

Ten minutes later he was in the Parade, inside a tiny jeweller's shop. The shop might have been small, but it appeared well stocked with glittering novelties. The owner, a dapper young man, was happy to oblige him, impressed by what Giles laid out on the counter.

"Old-fashioned cut, yes," he said, "but superb quality.

Hard to get stones like this, these days, to be honest, sir."

"Are you the only jeweller in Stanegate, Mr Arnott?"

"I am at present! And I hope it will stay that way. But we've been here a while. My late father started the business." He held the ring up to the light. "Oh, that baguette diamond, what a nice thing that is! Are you looking to sell, sir?"

"No," said Giles.

"Very wise," said Mr Arnott. "Pieces like these will only gain value."

"Unfortunately they are not mine to sell or keep. I was hoping you might be able to tell me who they belong to," Giles said, and explained who he was. He went on, "The ring was in the possession of Dr Kennedy, the Irish physician in charge of the Hydropathic. Did you have any dealings with him?"

"No, sir. I would have remembered the name, but I will look at the book."

"Captain Carrington, perhaps?"

"He did buy a few trinkets. Nothing substantial. A pair of earrings. Let me look at the book." He went to fetch his ledger.

"Thank you. Do you do any work for the Countess of Amberleigh or Sir Henry Boynton, by the way?"

"I have reset stones for the Countess once or twice," he said, laying the book on the counter. "Not lately, though. But come to think of it..." He picked up the bracelet again. "That clasp. This looks a little like my father's work. I shall have to get the old ledgers out. It may have been while I was away in Birmingham – I was apprenticed there, you see."

Giles nodded. Mr Arnott was now examining the hallmark through a hand lens. "That's an L – so that will be thirty-five," he said. "The year my father died," he added with a sigh. "It's good to see that, though," he said, rubbing the clasp with an affectionate finger.

It took longer to retrieve this ledger, but the late Mr

Arnott's record-keeping was thorough, and the bracelet repair was soon located.

"Countess of Amberleigh," said Mr Arnott. "Gold, ruby and diamond chip bracelet. New clasp and chain. May 17th, 1835."

"Thank you, Mr Arnott. That's extremely useful. What about the ring? You've never seen it before?"

Mr Arnott shook his head. He looked down at the ledger, and smiled. "Oh, I nearly missed that. My father was a modest man. He has marked that he made the ring in the first place – just his initials here, you see – and the name of the person it was made for: Marquis of R, 1828."

"That would be –?"

"Lord Rothborough," said Mr Arnott. "One of our best customers. Mr Bodley, his man, was in here this morning with an order for him, as it happens."

~

As he walked back towards the station house he passed Mrs Johnson's establishment, and noticed Miss Johnson standing in the window hanging garlands of silk ribbons. He remembered what Carswell had said about her flinging Richard Stuart's ring across the room.

He went into the shop and asked if he might speak to her. She came out of the window, having made him wait a few minutes while she finished her task.

"What do you want?" she said.

"It's about Mr Richard Stuart," he said.

"Oh, what now?" she said.

"Would be possible to see the ring he gave you? My colleague mentioned it."

"Yes, but I don't know where it is. My mother put it away

somewhere. I didn't want to see it. Was he really married?" she said. "Truly?"

"Yes, we are looking for his wife. She has been involved in a fraud."

She screwed up her face. "I feel such a fool," she said.

At this point Mrs Johnson came out from the back of the shop.

"If you are looking for my son," she said, "he's in the back there. I have scarcely let him out of my sight."

"No, it was another matter. The ring that Mr Stuart gave your daughter."

"What has that to do with anything?" she said.

"It may be stolen."

"From whom?" she said.

"That is what I'm trying to determine. Mr Stuart and his wife seem to have been involved in some dubious activities. Some interesting pieces have turned up where they should not be. It would be useful to see the ring."

"I see. To tell you the truth, I don't where I put it. Ingrid was so upset, I just took it away and we've been so busy, and I can't remember what I have done with it. You'll have to excuse me but it may take me some time to find it again. But it was just a trumpery thing, with hardly anything to it. I can't believe it's at all valuable. I mean, I looked at it and thought: that's not the ring an honest man with good intentions would give. Paste, certainly!"

"Oh, Ma!" exclaimed Ingrid. "It was not paste!"

"Of course it was," she said. "A diamond that size? I think not!"

"I really would like to see it, if you can find it, ma'am," said Giles.

"I cannot find it now!" she said. "As you can see, we are busy. If you were to come back later, perhaps?"

"Very well," said Giles. "But if you could just give a description? It was a diamond – how large?"

"A paste diamond," said Mrs Johnson. "Square cut, with chips of glass round it."

"It was real," said Ingrid. "It was!" She ran away, overcome with grief.

"It's a wretched business for her," Giles said.

"If you'll excuse me," said Mrs Johnson. "I had better go to her."

"Yes, of course," said Giles, "but if you could lay hands on that ring, I'd be grateful."

"I'll look for it," she said, "but I can't think what difference it would make. It was nothing, truly."

He left wondering if she had not overstated the point. After all, if the jewel were a valuable one, they might be reluctant to return it. Better, then, to say it was lost and to denigrate its true worth. Mrs Johnson was no stranger to misdirection – her emporium was a stage set for some dubious claims, after all. It was not wise to take what she said at face value.

Chapter Thirty-seven

Sukey opened her front door and Mrs O'Brien appeared in the hallway.

"Oh, Sukey, there you are! Thank goodness!" she exclaimed. "Tom is out looking for you. We just got here, and your girl Jane didn't seem know you had even gone out –" Mrs O'Brien broke off in confusion, seeing Felix with Lorenzo in his arms. "What are you doing here?" she demanded.

"He has a slight fever," said Felix. "I want to have a proper look at him."

"Through here," said Sukey, leading him down the passageway. He followed her into a bedroom, with Mrs O'Brien at his heels.

"Fever?" Mrs O'Brien said. "What sort of fever?"

"Bridey, please, just let him look at him, will you?" said Sukey. "Just for a minute. He knows what he is doing."

Felix laid the howling child down on the bed and did his best to undress him. The child had been sick again in the carriage, this time over Felix, and his soiled napkin soon revealed that he was on the verge of succumbing to a miserably commonplace but potentially dangerous infection amongst infants.

"So?" Sukey said. "What do you think?"

"He has a touch of enteritis," said Felix. "He should get over it soon enough. He's very strong," Felix said, aware that he had said this before and the child had not survived. "He needs to be kept cool, and given plenty of liquid. Your milk is the best thing for him."

Sukey nodded, and reached out to steady herself on the bedpost.

"What a day," she murmured, and then her legs buckled under her, and Felix was obliged to help her into a chair. "He will be all right, won't he?" she said.

"Yes, of course he will," said Mrs O'Brien, who had picked up the baby and was soothing him. "Everything is going to be all right. Poor little man – he is a beauty, though! And yes, you are strong, Laurence, very strong! Let's go and get you all cleaned up," said Mrs O'Brien, carrying him out of the room.

"Thank goodness she's here," said Sukey, sinking back in her chair. "Oh, I never thought I would say that, after all that has happened between us, but –"

"Perhaps she'll take you to Swalecliffe," said Felix, crouching down by her and feeling her forehead, worried that she was also succumbing to a fever. "That would be the best for both of you. I'd take you myself, if I could."

"Oh, Felix," she said, with such plaintiveness that he could scarcely bear it. "Please, no..."

"Of course," he said, jumping up. "Excuse me."

"It's only because... I should like nothing better," she said. There were tears rolling down her face. He longed to take her into his arms and comfort her, but at the same time he was aware it would be to assuage his own pain. He could not be so selfish. He kissed her hand and then left her.

~

Having allowed Mrs O'Brien to scrub down his lapels with a wet cloth and seen that all was as well with the child as could be, Felix made his way to the coffee room of The White Hart. Here, he had arranged to meet Mr Harper and James Hamilton. They were deep in conversation when he arrived and he hesitated to interrupt such a conference, but then

Hamilton caught sight of him, and there was no avoiding it.

"I think at this stage we ought to make another examination of his Lordship," said Mr Harper, "and then discuss frankly with him what might be done. Mr Hamilton, do you agree with me on that?"

"Certainly, I cannot advise anything further until I have seen Lord Rothborough for myself," Hamilton said. "And perhaps this is not the case for attempting an experiment. My work with ether has been of a limited kind. This would be, I have to confess, a step into the dark."

"It may be that his Lordship has thoughts of his own on the subject," said Mr Harper.

"Of course," said Felix. The advice was eminently sensible.

"I will see him again tomorrow," said Mr Harper, "and bring Mr Hamilton with me. In the meantime, I must get back to Northminster."

"Let me take you to the station," Felix said.

"No, I can make my own way," said Harper. "I shall return tomorrow on the early train. How is your other business going? Mr Hamilton told me there had been another curious death."

"Yes, Dr Kennedy. It may be suicide."

"Dear me," said Harper with a frown. "Will you have to do a post-mortem?"

"It's an interesting case. It seemed he died from gas poisoning, but I should probably not do it. I ought to go back to Holbroke. Hamilton, you must know someone here who might be competent to do it? There is that fellow at the Infirmary – I forget his name."

"There will be no one here with your particular skills, Mr Carswell," said Mr Harper. "You owe that dead man the best care. Your duty lies with him."

"Mr Harper is right," said Hamilton. "And it will be a useful occupation for you. We were discussing this – given your connection to Lord Rothborough, it is probably best that you step away from his treatment. It is not always the best thing for a man to treat his own folk, at least not when the matter is so serious."

Mr Harper nodded and said, "I have seen it cause mischief often enough."

There was no arguing with this, but it was hard to accept. Felix saw them to the door and turned back into The White Hart, not at all relishing the prospect of the post-mortem on Kennedy. Any intellectual curiosity was in abeyance. He could think only of Sukey's tear-stained cheeks, and feel the loss of what never could have been.

It was then that he saw Elisabeth standing in front of him, apparently waiting to speak to him.

"Do you have a moment?" she said.

"Yes, of course," he said, and followed her into her office.

"How is Lord Rothborough?" she said.

"It's hard to say," he said. "My instinct is that he's in a dangerous state, and it's not clear what needs to be done. He is in good hands, though – the best, thank God!"

"Yes, thank God," she said, sitting down at the table.

"They have told me to stay away," he went on, sitting down opposite.

"That is good advice," she said. "Difficult for you, though."

"Very," he said.

"And I'm now about to make it all worse," she said with a sigh. "I wanted to talk to you about..." She trailed off, tracing a pattern on the table with her finger. "Oh, this is not easy." She glanced up and met his eyes. "I think," she went on, "I allowed myself to make a mistake. Do you understand?"

"Yes," he said. "That occurred to me. And I should apologise for my part in it. I indulged myself."

She sighed.

"It was not unpleasant," she said. "The trouble was, it was all too pleasant. I thought I could be careless, but now I find myself thinking too much about it. I keep asking myself if I am falling – so I think, all in all, it is better we go no further. I do not wish to break my heart over you, that is the truth. So that must be that."

"You are right," he said, getting up. "Regrettably."

"There are regrets one can bear," she said, "and those one cannot."

Her words lingered with him as he made his way to see Mr Boothroyd to collect his permission for the post-mortem. Major Vernon had been in communication with him, and all was in order. There only remained the dubious pleasure of an afternoon in the company of Sukey's dead husband.

Chapter Thirty-eight

"I knew you would be back, Major Vernon!" said Lady Clara, finding him again in the sitting room at Amberleigh Castle. "And you have come at such an excellent moment. Everyone is at loggerheads! Mama has quarrelled with Sir Henry and my sister, because they have told her they will be married and that is that."

"I see," said Giles.

"And they are to be married as soon as possible and go abroad for at least a year. Margaret wants to see everything before she has a child to bother about."

Fascinating although all this was, her manner was alarming for a child of thirteen, especially given her resemblance to Lord Rothborough's daughters. It was clear that she had caught her mother's taste for drama, and it did not become her.

"My lady –" he began.

"Have I shocked you, sir?" she cut in.

"Perhaps you should consider before you say such things to a stranger."

"I know, but I thought you would need to know. And is it not interesting?"

"Yes," he was forced to concede, and she smiled.

"What has happened to the leopards?"

"It has not yet been decided," said Giles.

At this moment Sir Henry entered the room.

"What the devil do you want?" he said. "Clara, go at once!"

Clara obeyed, but not before throwing a sly smile at Giles.

"What has she said to you?" Sir Henry said, seeing it.

"That congratulations are in order: that you are to marry Lady Margaret."

"Damn her. That child is a... well, I'm sure you of all people know what she is, or rather, who she is. It makes her perverse."

"She is not to be blamed for other people's indiscretions," said Giles.

"I thought you were a friend of his," said Sir Henry, sitting down and taking out his cigar case.

"Some jewellery has turned up in a curious place," said Giles, reaching into his pocket and laying the bracelet and Sukey's ring on the table. "I wonder if you might look at these and see if you recognise them."

"Can't say that's too likely," said Sir Henry, hauling himself up from his chair. Puffing out smoke, he picked up the bracelet up and looked at it. "Nice thing, that."

"Have you ever seen it before?"

"Can't say I have," said Sir Henry.

"Perhaps Lady Amberleigh or Lady Margaret may recognise it," said Giles.

"I doubt it," said Sir Henry. "It might be better not to involve the ladies in this," he added.

"And why might that be?" said Giles.

He had no time to answer, as Lady Margaret herself now entered. She saw the bracelet on the table and exclaimed, "Oh, my goodness! Where did you find that? I thought it had been lost for ever."

She picked it up and kissed it. "Oh, excuse me, but my dear father promised me this – oh, Henry, look – it is the one I told you about! Oh, and this ring as well, I remember that too." She slipped it on her finger, and admired it.

"That is interesting, Lady Margaret," said Giles. "When were they declared lost?"

"The first I knew of it was about two months ago. I wanted to wear the bracelet to a ball, but Mama said it was lost," she said. "Wherever did you find them?"

"The bracelet had come into the possession of a Mrs Stuart," Giles said, turning to Sir Henry. "Did you know Mr and Mrs Stuart, perhaps? They were living across from Adelaide Lodge in one of those cottages, and since your visits there seem to have been fairly frequent, I wonder if you didn't fall into conversation with them. A handsome young couple, the woman especially so."

"No, I don't recall seeing them."

"Captain Carrington didn't mention them?"

"No, never."

"I suppose he wouldn't, Sir Henry," Giles said, taking up the bracelet, "since he gave Mrs Stuart the bracelet that you gave him."

"What!" exclaimed Sir Henry. "That is outrageous, sir! Are you implying that I stole it?"

"Oh no, nothing of that sort," said Giles. "Rather that you were a delivery boy for someone else."

"What do you mean, sir?" said Lady Margaret.

"That Captain Carrington was not the friend to this family that he appeared," said Giles. "Is that not so, Sir Henry?"

"That's true enough," said Sir Henry, going and sitting down.

"What have you done, Henry?" demanded Lady Margaret.

"Just what your mother asked me," he said. "He was getting difficult. He knew all sorts of things he should not have known and he began threatening to expose her, demanding money from her."

"Which it fell to you to deliver," said Giles. "How much in all, do you think?"

"I don't know. She gave over most of the contents of her jewel box over the last month or so. He had apparently promised her some letters in return."

"Letters?" said Lady Margaret.

"Yes, some filth she had written to a lover. I don't know which one!"

"Henry!" said Lady Margaret. "What are you saying?"

"Nothing that you don't already know, I dare say," said Sir Henry. "So yes, Major Vernon, I delivered the jewels to him, but that is the limit of it. I may have wished him dead, and I can't say it isn't a relief that he is dead, but I swear to you that on Sunday night, he was alive when he left the house!"

The door opened and the Countess of Amberleigh entered.

"How good to see you again so soon, Major Vernon," she said, putting out her hand for him to kiss. He did not. "I hope you have good news for us and that you have found the wretch who murdered poor Carrington."

Remembering her accusations against Sir Henry, Giles wondered if she had been listening at the door, so perfect was this timing.

"Poor Carrington?" said Lady Margaret. "Henry says he was blackmailing you, Mama! Is that true?"

"It is no business of yours, Margaret," said Lady Amberleigh.

"It is true, though," said Giles, "that your friendship turned sour."

"And you gave him my bracelet," said Lady Margaret, "so he would not publish your letters."

"It was not your bracelet," said Lady Amberleigh.

"Papa gave it to me!" she said. "He told me it would be mine and you gave it away!"

"It is just a bracelet," said Lady Amberleigh.

"That is not the point!" exclaimed Lady Margaret, growing tearful. "How could you? When you knew what it meant to me. Or was it because of what it meant to him? For you obviously never cared a jot for him if Carrington had letters you had written to other men. Were they to Lord –"

"Be quiet!" said Lady Amberleigh.

"Rothborough, perhaps?" Lady Margaret went on. "Or someone else? Perhaps even to Captain Carrington? I have a fair idea of what went on between you."

"I said, be quiet!" said Lady Amberleigh, and attempted to slap her daughter. Sir Henry naturally could not stand for this and intervened, catching her hand, only to receive a slap of his own from the countess' other hand.

"You –!" muttered Sir Henry, rubbing his cheek.

"You wanted to know about other men, my dear?" said Lady Amberleigh, and indicated Sir Henry. "The letters were ones I wrote to Sir Henry which he was foolish enough to lose in a game of cards to Carrington."

"Henry, is this true?" said Lady Margaret.

"She wrote the letters," he said, after a pause. "I had no choice but to receive them. She had a notion of being in love with me. It was not reciprocated."

"If that was the case, then why did you keep them?" said Giles. "Because you thought they might be useful?"

"Oh Henry, no!" said Lady Margaret. "Please say this is not true?"

"It is, Margaret," said Lady Amberleigh. "Now perhaps you will think twice about marrying him."

"Is this why you do not want me to marry him? You want him for yourself still! When did all this happen between you? Was it while I was at school in Germany?"

"Meg, Meg," said Sir Henry, "it was nothing. Nothing at all. Truly." He attempted to take her hands, but Lady Margaret did not allow it. She retreated across the room to stand by Giles, snatching up the bracelet as she did so. In the meantime, Lady Amberleigh went and sat down, composing herself as she did so.

"You can see why I was suspicious about Sir Henry, Major Vernon," she said. "He has every cause to wish Captain Carrington dead. It is highly likely he is your man."

"No," said Giles. "There is plenty of dirty linen here, but

I doubt it caused his death."

He took his leave and asked a footman to arrange for his horse to be brought round. He went outside to wait, glad for some fresh air.

Here Lady Clara and the young Earl were wrestling on the lawn in the time-honoured fashion of siblings, playfully enough, but not without a hint of real rivalry. At eighteen, the young earl was rather too old and well-developed for such a romp, and although Lady Clara was clearly not suffering, Giles wondered whether if he did not soon desist, she might be injured.

"My lord!" he called out.

This was enough to stop them. They untangled themselves and got to their feet.

"I'm not sure we have been properly introduced, though I had the pleasure of seeing you play on Saturday," said Giles.

"Ah yes," said Lady Clara, shaking down her skirts like a retriever expelling water from its coat. "Major Vernon, this is my brother Johnny."

"My lord," said Giles.

"I'm afraid it wasn't my best performance," said Johnny, shaking his hand. "That fellow Fitznorton caught us all on the back foot."

"You made a respectable number of runs."

"Only by the skin of my teeth," said Johnny. "It made for a much more interesting afternoon, I must say. Cricket is a bit slow here, to be perfectly honest."

"Johnny," said Clara, "you must ask him about the leopards."

"Clara wants to save them," said Johnny.

"So do you!" she said.

"It would be a shame if they had to be shot," Johnny said. "Do you think I might buy them, and bring them here?"

"We could build them the most magnificent cage," said Clara. "Much better than the one at the menagerie. And hire their keeper to look after them."

"I was going to write to Lord Rothborough about it," the young Lord Amberleigh said. "I don't know him, but I think I ought to know him soon enough, given we are neighbours of sorts. He brought forward the Act against dog fighting, and we thought he would care about the leopards. I believe you are a friend of his, sir – at least I heard my mother say something to that effect."

"I have that honour," said Giles, "and I'm sure, in ordinary circumstances, he would be most concerned about the leopards. But he's very ill at the moment –"

"No!" exclaimed Clara, "What's wrong with him?"

"They are not sure."

"Is he going to die?" she said.

"Clara –" said Johnny.

"But he said it so gravely," Clara said.

"Yes, but – excuse my sister, sir, won't you? She always says the first thing that comes into her head."

"I am not sorry for saying it," said Clara. "And I am worried now for poor Lord Rothborough. It would be terrible if he were to die and we were never to meet him. He sounds so interesting. And he is a relation, I think."

"Somehow or other, yes, I believe he is," said Johnny.

"So what should we do about the leopards?" said Clara.

"I can't say," said Giles. "I suspect they would be a costly responsibility, and perhaps, Lord Amberleigh, you are not old enough to take on such a burden. Your trustees might not permit it."

"But they cannot be killed," said Clara.

"It would be a pity," said Johnny. "I ought to be able to do something, surely? What is the point of my being who I am if I cannot do something?"

This was a question to which there was no ready answer, so Giles changed the subject.

"What can you tell me about Crandall's Hole?"

"Oh, it is a thrilling place!" said Clara, now sounding like her mother. "We had a picnic there once and there was a thunderstorm. It was wonderful. We had to shelter in the cave and I felt the ghosts of one those boys brush past me."

"No, you did not," said Johnny.

"So everyone considers it haunted?" said Giles.

"If they believe in such things," said Johnny.

"You weren't there," said Clara.

"Do people often go there for picnics?" said Giles.

"No, I don't think so," said Johnny. "The thought of the ghosts keeps most people away."

"I wonder why those boys went there in the first place," said Clara. "I heard that there was treasure in there."

"What rubbish," said Johnny, and frowned. "Oh, Lupo, what are you doing?" he said, as one of the dogs began to dig up the lawn. "Excuse me, sir." He went off, leaving Giles alone with Clara.

"It's not rubbish. If I had a lot of treasure," she said, "that's exactly where I would hide it."

~

Giles recalled her words as later that day he sat in Lord Rothborough's bedroom. It was not without the bounds of possibility that such a place might be used by criminals. He had come across such cases before. The question remained – why had the name been noted and preserved by Mrs Stuart, in the company of a valuable bracelet?

"Is that you there, Vernon?" said Lord Rothborough.

"It is," said Giles, drawing his chair closer to the bed.

"Good to see you," Lord Rothborough said, managing a smile.

"Would you like something to drink?" Lord Rothborough

nodded, and Giles fed him a few spoonfuls of water from the bowl by the bed, as Emma had instructed him.

This accomplished, Lord Rothborough said, "I hope to be able to get out of bed tomorrow, at least for the ceremony. But I shall need a supporter. Might you do me the honour?"

"Nothing would give me more pleasure."

"Felix is giving away the bride."

"That will be charming," said Giles.

"It will give the world something to talk about," said Lord Rothborough, and laughed, although it was obvious it caused him great pain. "Oh dear," he said. "Especially if I die."

"Oh, we will not allow that," said Giles, reaching for a damp cloth to wipe his Lordship's brow.

"If it is God's will," said Lord Rothborough, closing his eyes. "Then..." He exhaled deeply. "I must face what must be faced, as we all must in time. If this is my end, then –" He reached for Giles' hand. "And I know that those I love will not be without good friends to guide them. You and Mrs Vernon..." He broke off, as the pain again marched over him relentlessly, and caused him to cry out.

Giles watched this loss of composure with some wretchedness, still holding Lord Rothborough's hand.

"Of course," he murmured. When the crisis had passed over, and Lord Rothborough seemed calmer, Giles said, "There is one young woman – well, a child really, who –" He had hesitated to speak of Lady Clara, but now he wondered if it might do Lord Rothborough some good to know of her existence. "I went to call on Lady Amberleigh."

"Yes?" said Lord Rothborough.

"Her youngest child, thirteen or so. She had such a look of –"

"Ah," said Lord Rothborough. "That may well be so." Then he smiled. "Oh dear Lord, forgive me!" The note of repentance was faint, and Giles sensed he had brought him pleasure.

"She is enchanting," Giles said. "She wishes to save the leopards in Stanegate."

"Ah, those poor beasts," said Lord Rothborough. "It would be a pity if they were to be killed, for no fault of their own."

"I'll let you rest now, my lord," said Giles, seeing the door open and Emma come in with Dr Markham.

Chapter Thirty-nine

Lord Rothborough and Mrs Martinez were married the following morning in a brief ceremony in the family chapel at Holbroke, conducted by Canon Fforde. Lord Rothborough had declared he would stand at the altar to make his vows or not at all. Having achieved this through sheer force of will, he was in a state of near collapse by the end of the service. He was obliged to return to the wheeled chair that had brought him to the ceremony, and, accompanied by the new Lady Rothborough and the ever faithful Bodley, departed from the chapel as soon as the blessing had been given.

Felix would have gone after them, but Major Vernon caught his arm, and said, "Perhaps you should give them a moment – rather, you should give yourself a moment. Mrs Vernon said you spent all last night with him." Felix nodded. "And got very little sleep, I dare say?"

"True," said Felix, who had passed another wretched night on the sofa at the foot of the bed.

"Come and have some breakfast," Major Vernon said.

This was sensible advice, and they went with the others up to the state dining room, where Charlotte – presumably in an effort to distract herself – had gone to great trouble arranging large quantities of flowers, covering every available surface, so that the breakfast dishes themselves seemed to be struggling to find a place.

"A wedding breakfast sans bride and groom," she said, smiling at the sight of them. "Unusual, but necessary."

Touched by her manner, Felix put his arms about her, and she clung to him for a few moments. "It was so moving, was it not?" she whispered. He nodded, not trusting his own voice. She broke from him and went back to presiding over the garlanded table.

"May I really have chocolate?" Sophy Gordon was saying.

"Oh yes, Lord Rothborough would expect it," said Major Vernon. The children had been in the gallery with the servants for the ceremony. "Who is that young fellow talking to Hamish?" asked Major Vernon, indicating a young man with soft brown hair.

"Mr Stafford," said Sophy. "He's very nice. He is going to show us how to do simultaneous equations. He says it's just like a conjuring trick." With that she departed, carrying her cup of chocolate carefully.

"Which she will get the knack of in a flash," said Major Vernon, "and Hamish will be struggling behind her again. His battle with arithmetic is painful to watch."

Felix turned back to the sideboard, poured himself a cup of chocolate and laced it with sugar and cream, feeling in need of fortification. He was aware of Eleanor sitting between the Ffordes, looking uncharacteristically tired and subdued. He had not properly spoken to her since their argument of the other day, and he knew he ought to be working on brokering peace between them. But at that moment he had no idea where to begin. He took his cup and plate of meat and went to the other end of the table, where Hamish Gordon and Stafford were sitting. Stafford, he remembered belatedly, was the new curate.

"Mr Carswell," he said, slightly rising from his seat to acknowledge him. "An honour to know you at last. I've heard a great deal about you from Lady Charlotte."

"I hear you have a talent for simultaneous equations," Felix said, shaking his hand. Hamish gave a slight groan.

"I shall endeavour to make it as painless a demonstration as possible," said Stafford. "It is a mere trick, as I said before. And I have a good one with cards as well, which I'm happy to teach you afterwards. You can guess any card a fellow picks out. Lady Charlotte was both mystified and impressed."

This got Hamish's attention.

"Could you show me the trick, sir, and not my sister?" he said. "I mean, I could show her later, but to begin with, might it just be between ourselves?"

"I don't see why not," said Stafford. "Now speaking of magic, we were just talking about ether, Mr Carswell. After what Miss King told us – well, it sounds extraordinary!"

"It was," said Felix. "This is the future of surgery."

"Are you going to operate on Lord Rothborough?" Hamish said.

"Nothing has been decided," Felix said.

"I think you should, sir," said Hamish. "If anyone can help him, it must be you. My uncle has told me you are just as good as Mr Harper."

"Oh, I don't know about that," said Felix.

"He said," Hamish went on, "that surgeons must have more courage than soldiers going into battle to do what they do."

"Perhaps he wants you to become a medical man," said Stafford.

"I have thought of it," said Hamish.

"You're good with your hands," said Felix. "Those dolls you made for Mary Gowans when we were in Scotland – those were clever. He articulated the joints."

"Ah, then, there you have it," said Stafford. "A surgeon in the making, perhaps?"

Hamish went off to find more bread and butter, looking pleased.

"I feel honoured to have been asked here today, since I am still a stranger to you all," Stafford said. "I have had some correspondence with Lord Rothborough, of course – he was most welcoming, even in absentia. You may be sure he will be first in my prayers, Mr Carswell."

"Was it Lady Charlotte who asked you?" Felix said.

"Yes," he said. "I believe she thought I could be of some use to the children."

"Simultaneous equations are useful," said Felix.

"Not as useful as card tricks," said Stafford.

"Ah yes, what was it you said: she was mystified and impressed!"

"Oh, you must excuse me," said Stafford, colouring slightly. "It was just that she was so anxious about her father and I wanted to put her at her ease, and I have found nothing works as well as a card trick. It's an old habit of mine, no doubt a bad one, but I find sleight of hand interesting as a subject – misdirections and so forth. It made her smile at least, and that is probably her characteristic state. It was pleasant to see it, whatever."

Major Vernon now joined them, and Stafford, having been presented, excused himself to go and find Hamish and Sophy, with the intention of taking them for a long walk.

"What a heroic young man," said Major Vernon.

"Charlotte did well to find him," said Felix. "I think he is obliging her, as much as you and Mrs Vernon."

"Maybe so," said Major Vernon. "What young man would not?" He sighed. "Speaking of such young men, what am I to do with Mr Fitznorton? I have not spoken to him since yesterday. I might do it with equanimity now."

"I am not sure I could," said Felix. "Perhaps you should send him back to London."

"Tempting, but I think I need him for the paperwork. The post-mortem reports – I don't imagine you have had a chance to start on them?" said Major Vernon.

"No, but I can tell you what will be in them. Kennedy was poisoned by a large quantity of coal gas. The rate of flow from those pipes in such a short space of time was considerable, because of their unusual width. I suppose he wanted as bright a light as possible in there and specified the diameter accordingly. As a result he will have died quickly."

"Which tends towards an interpretation of suicide," said Major Vernon, "for who else would have known that? The risk element of someone else tampering with the pipes is so great. They would not have known about the rate of flow or how much time was available."

"Are you allowing for desperation?" said Felix.

"Perhaps not enough," said Major Vernon. "And Richard Stuart?"

"A large tumour of the brain."

"Your guess was correct, then."

"Seemingly," said Felix. "It would certainly have had the same effect as an injury to the head, given the size of it."

"That of disinhibition, as we discussed," said Major Vernon. He then fell silent, in a fashion that Felix knew well. At length he said, "I really want to talk to Mrs Stuart, but she has vanished. It's far too convenient. Could you draw her likeness?"

"I think so," said Felix.

Major Vernon handed him his notebook and a pencil, and Felix settled to the task, which was not an easy one.

"It is not the most perfect rendition," he said.

"No, but you have the essence of her. Her eyes are that particular almond shape and pale grey."

"Yes, they were."

"Very fine, some would say. It is a face that will be remembered."

He did not continue. Charlotte was coming towards them.

"Mr Harper and Mr Hamilton are here," she said. "They have gone straight up."

~

"I cannot advise it," said Mr Harper, coming out of Lord Rothborough's bedroom into the dressing room where Felix was waiting with Hamilton. "I have told his Lordship so. He accepts my interpretation of the matter, and is prepared to let nature take its course, as is my Lady Rothborough."

"Do you not think there would be any benefit in a brief exploration?" said Hamilton. "Given my Lord's excellent previous health, I see no great danger in that, and it might give us a better idea of what is going on."

"That is my view," said Felix.

Mr Harper sighed and said, "In the course of my career, I have observed some dozen patients suffering from almost identical symptoms of acute peritoneal inflammation. In three cases, the distress was so great that an operation was embarked upon, as a last resort. I was the surgeon for two of those cases, and although there was some structural relief, any benefit to the patient was only transitory. All three cases were fatal. This is not an area for experiment."

"Until now," said Felix. "We have better tools at our disposal," he added, indicating Hamilton.

"I am sorry, but I will not undertake it," said Mr Harper. "I know this is hard for you to hear, Mr Carswell, but there are times –"

At this moment the new Lady Rothborough, accompanied by Dr Markham, came out of the bedroom. She went straight up to Felix and took both his hands. Looking into her face, he had a sense of her desperation.

"I have told them my opinion, my lady," said Mr Harper.

"Thank you so much for coming," she said.

"I'll make my own way out," he said. "Mr Hamilton, will you come back to Stanegate with me?" he added.

Hamilton glanced at Felix and said, "I won't, thank you. I must check on Miss King."

Harper nodded and went to the door with Dr Markham. But just before he left, he stopped and turned back to Felix.

"Do not be rash, now. You may regret it."

"You do not need to agree with him," said Felix to Lady Rothborough when he had gone.

"I don't know what should be done," she said. "But he was so wary and he has so much experience that –"

"Let me talk to Papa," said Felix.

"No, no, not now," she said. "Let him rest. He is so peaceful just now. So happy." At which she burst into tears.

"I'll leave you two alone," said Hamilton and left them.

Felix sat down beside her, and put his arms around her. She cried for some minutes longer and then, sitting up again, dried her tears. "I'm sorry," she said.

"For what?" Felix said.

"I know you want to do something," she said. "But to be frank I can't bear the thought of it. Not yet, not today. Can we not just have this time? I feel it may be all we have. Do you understand?"

"Yes," he said. "But –"

She pressed her finger to his lips.

"You should go and rest yourself," she went on. "Then you might see it all a bit clearer."

Felix doubted this, but obeyed her and went to his own quarters. From the dressing room he could see Eleanor sitting reading, and he wondered if he ought to disturb her, even if he wanted to. But she had obviously heard him come in, and got up and came to the dressing room door.

"Is it very bad?" she said. "He looked so ill."

"It's not promising," he said.

She came and pressed herself against him. "I'm sorry."

He was surprised at her tenderness. "Thank you. I was going to have a rest. Do you want to join me?"

"Yes, I'm quite tired. This little thing is jumping about today," she added.

He could not resist putting his hand to her belly and, feeling the movement, his emotions got the better of him and he could no longer prevent himself from crying. He sat down and allowed himself the indulgence of it, his mind full of Sukey, and his father and his mother, and then of Eleanor, who came and sat beside him and rubbed his back.

"I have never seen you cry before," she said. There was some distress in her voice. She had been moved by his grief.

"Excuse me," he said, getting up and going back into the dressing room to wash his face. She again followed him.

"You were right," she said, "about trying to be kind. It is important. We should try."

He nodded and dried his face. She went back into the bedroom and climbed onto the bed, and he followed. She lay in his arms, and they slept.

~

Stevens woke them.

"It's Mrs Vernon, sir," she said. "She wants to speak to you urgently. She's just outside."

Felix went out at once. Mrs Vernon, wearing an apron and with a look of the sickroom about her, said, "I am a little concerned. His temperature has gone up and he is on the cusp of fever. He vomited twice, and there was blood in the bowl."

He went with her, still in his shirtsleeves.

What he found was most discouraging. As Mrs Vernon had observed, Lord Rothborough was feverish and in a great deal of pain, thrashing about in the bed almost as if he were having a fit. Lady Rothborough seemed overwhelmed by the situation, although she was trying to soothe him, so Felix was obliged to ask Mrs Vernon to gently draw her aside so he could attempt to examine Lord Rothborough for himself. He sounded him and then as gently as he could, felt the distension of his abdomen, and became certain that the inflammation had increased since the morning.

Hamilton, whom he had sent for, soon arrived, and going into the dressing room with him, Felix said, "I have to see what is causing the problem. But I do not know if he is in a fit state to consent to it."

"Do you have a specific plan?"

"An incision from the spine of the ilium, above Poupart's ligament," Felix said, "taken down to the inner side of the internal abdominal ring above that distinctly hardened spot – you felt it yourself, this morning."

"Yes," said Hamilton. "And?"

"If there is a tangle of the intestine I can free it, or if it is hardened matter, collected in the iliac fossa, that can be removed."

"How long would this take you?"

"I'm not sure. No more than twenty minutes. Could he be safely etherized in his present condition?"

"I would hesitate to say entirely safely, but there is a good chance that there would be no lasting damage. It is a risk I would submit to myself."

"Then we must tell him that," said Felix.

They went back into the bedroom. Lord Rothborough was calmer, leaning against his wife, who had her arms about him, and was telling him to steady his breathing.

"Papa," Felix said, "I think we can help you. There is some risk, but there is more risk in doing nothing. Hamilton will etherize you and I will perform the procedure. The ether will give me time to see what needs to be done."

Lord Rothborough closed his eyes and appeared to be considering the point.

"But Mr Harper said –" began Lady Rothborough.

Speaking with great effort and scarcely audible, Lord Rothborough said, "Do what you will, Felix. I trust you. My life is in your hands."

Chapter Forty

"Where would you hide in Stanegate, Mr Fitznorton?" said Giles, coming into the office.

Fitznorton stumbled to his feet at the sight of him. "I'm not sure, sir."

"Are you dressed for riding?"

"Yes, if required."

"Then, shall we go? We are going to enquire for her at every hotel, every lodging house, every inn in this town and the villages about here."

Fitznorton took up his hat, saying, "How is Lord Rothborough? Is there any improvement?"

"Unfortunately not," said Giles.

"His death would be a loss to the nation," Fitznorton said.

"I should have said that to him," said Giles. "It would have encouraged him. But he knows his worth, and God willing, he will live. He is too vigorous a spirit to be easily defeated."

They set out on foot to make their laborious enquiries. The first dozen establishments yielded no hints, nor the next twelve; it was midafternoon and Giles was beginning to feel weary and dry-throated with frustration. They were in the Parade, and so he decided to turn into the accommodating coffee room above the circulating library which he had visited previously. He had ordered coffee and spread out the map, wondering which quarter should be their next target, when he noticed Eric Johnson sitting in the far corner. He was in earnest conversation with a smartly dressed, white-haired man and they appeared to have important business in hand. It ended with a handshake and the young man looking pleased. He stopped to buy a cigar and Giles went to speak to him.

"Oh, how do you do, sir," Johnson said.

"May I ask the name of the gentleman you were with?" said Giles, who was forming his own ideas about it.

"That is Colonel Brightholme, late of the Ninth."

"Interesting. And your business with him?"

"He is assisting with my purchase."

"Your purchase? By which I take it you mean a commission?"

"Yes."

"Congratulations," said Giles. "Where are you bound?"

"Light Infantry," said Johnson, drawing himself up a little.

"Excellent," said Giles. "But costly, even if you are paying only the regulation fee, which I doubt."

"I wouldn't know," said Johnson.

"Oh, I think you do," said Giles, glancing at Brightholme who was now looking at him with interest. "The usual supply and demand problem apart, you will have paid more to give you a clean record, I imagine. A man who has just had a brush with the magistrates is not the ideal candidate."

"He doesn't know about that," said Johnson.

"Probably just as well," said Giles. "Where does this sudden interest in a commission come from, Mr Johnson? I had no hint of this from you mother. I'm surprised you can afford it."

"It's only what is due to me," said Johnson.

"Would you care to elaborate?" said Giles.

"Not really," said Johnson.

"What a surprise," said Giles. "So, you either tell me now where the money has come from, or you can come down to the station house and tell me there."

"I don't know," said Johnson. "My mother arranged it all. She said she had the money now and I could arrange for my purchase. Why don't you talk to her?"

"I certainly shall," said Giles, remembering how Mary Carter had seen Mrs Johnson talking to Carrington.

Giles signalled to Fitznorton to gather up their map and pay the waiter.

It was only a few steps to Mrs Johnson's luxurious establishment. That afternoon it was thronged with the sort of women who made Fitznorton both nervous and censorious. In this case, he was right to be uneasy, for there was something about them that suggested they were not ordinary, respectable spa visitors: there was too much lace and decoration on their bonnets; their arms were heavy with ribboned parcels, and some of them were definitely painted. That Stanegate, full of luxurious pleasures, should host such women was no surprise, but Giles had not yet seen such a flock of them on open display.

Mrs Johnson, her flaxen hair blazing in the bright shop light, came sailing through this crowd of customers in her dark silk dress, offering only the thinnest-lipped smile to welcome them.

"How may I help you, Major Vernon?" she said.

"I hear your son is to become a military man," said Giles. "An excellent choice of profession, I must say, but an expensive one. Six hundred guineas or so I should say is the going rate for an ensign in a reasonable regiment, and that's before you have got him a decent pair of breeches. Remarkable."

"Business has been good and he needs direction."

"Yes, quite, but that is very good business! From all this – well, my colleague was convinced this was all charlatanry, but he must be wrong. You must be selling something truly wondrous. These ladies all look very well, certainly. Do they go and sit in your magic chamber as well?"

"What is your point, sir?" she said.

"I should like to know where this sudden good fortune came from. It cannot be that one of your golden apples is real."

"I don't know what you are talking about. Hard work and economy, that is all."

"The fact that your husband, one of the richest men in this town, is dead, has nothing to do with it?"

"How could it? I have had nothing to do with him for years."

"And yet you come to the very town where he has had his greatest success?" Giles said. "Shall we go and talk somewhere quieter? Perhaps we should go upstairs. I'm curious to see what's there."

He approached the staircase which had previously been barred to them. One of the shop girls attempted to block him now, but Mrs Johnson shook her head, and she stood back.

"Thank you," said Giles, and began to climb the stairs. "Come, Mr Fitznorton. And you too, if you please, ma'am."

Mr Fitznorton stepped back to allow Mrs Johnson to come up.

"I don't know what you expect to find," she said, behind him.

Giles was not sure either, but he was certain that she was hiding something.

They went into a large room with two tall windows overlooking the street. The light was filtered through pink muslin curtains and the air was heavy with scent; clouds and cherubs had been painted on the ceiling and the walls were hung with soft blue silk. At one end of the room was an extremely large cupboard, painted with bunches of flowers on a silvery background. The two door handles were fastened with a satin ribbon so wide it resembled a sash. Miss Johnson was sitting at a small table bearing a hand-bell and a clock. She rose at the sight of them, putting her finger to her lips to quiet them.

"It's all right," said Mrs Johnson, and rang the bell. She then went to the doors and opened them. "How are you feeling, ma'am?"

"Oh!" replied the woman within. "That was fast."

"Time moves mysteriously when you are in the chamber, ma'am," said Mrs Johnson. "I hope it was satisfactory."

"Yes, I feel quite refreshed," said the woman.

"Allow me to assist you," said Mrs Johnson, taking a fabulous dressing-gown from a hook and stepping into the cupboard. She closed the door behind her and then emerged with the customer clad in the gown. "Ingrid, take madam to the resting room, will you?" she said.

"Yes, of course – this way, ma'am."

Ingrid left with the customer on her arm. "So this is the famous Idunnic Chamber?" said Giles.

"That is it," she said. "What do you want?"

Giles entered the chamber: it was capacious. A window of coloured glass had been placed in the top, the effect of which was to bathe the space in different tints and create an other-worldly effect. The floor was covered by a soft rug and there was an easy chair to sit upon.

The interior walls were covered with little tiles of silver that reminded him of fish scales, and then decorated with crystals in different sizes and tints. Celia would not have been disappointed.

"Very curious," he said, tapping the walls. He then moved the chair, bent down and rolled back the carpet.

"What are you doing?" Mrs Johnson said. "Please stop!"

"Some people put their money in the bank," he said, feeling the bare floor of the Idunnic Chamber and finding a ring handle set in a recess. He lifted it, for it was attached, as he had guessed, to a hinged panel that concealed a cavity in the floor of the cupboard. Inside the cavity was a substantial japanned box, which he lifted out, noting that it was heavy and chinked when it was moved.

"Would you please unlock it, ma'am?" he said, bringing it out and laying it on the table.

"I don't see why I should."

"Because I will force the lock otherwise," he said.

"Oh, very well," she said, and took a key from her pocket.

Just as he had guessed, it contained many purses and packages. The first he took up was full of guineas.

"So what if I keep my money there?" she protested. "What is wrong with that?"

"Nothing at all. It is how you came by all this money that concerns me. There really does seem to be a great deal in here. Ah, jewellery, very interesting. I have already seen some of this. Perhaps the pieces that your husband did not give to you. He kept a few trinkets back."

"What are you saying?" she said.

"That some of this is your savings, of course, and hard won. Even if this is nonsense" – he indicated the chamber – "it is a clever way of gulling people. For that I applaud you. However, my feeling is that a great deal of this money came from elsewhere. You were seen talking to Captain Carrington, and I think sentiment got the better of him. After all, a wife is a wife. Despite everything, he felt he could trust you to take care of it. He saw his children grown up and felt some regret, perhaps. And so you took it into your safekeeping and promised to guard it faithfully for him. Admirable really. Am I right?"

She nodded, and said, "You are right. It was surprising to see him after so much time, but as you say, old sentiment. I felt for him still, and I think he felt for me, because he gave me the money to look after, just as you said, and there were no conditions, no cheating, no nothing. It was just that he trusted me. And when you told me what had happened to him, I thought I would not care, but I do, and it grieves me."

"Do you know how he acquired all this?"

"That's the worst of it," she said with a sigh, sitting down on the chair vacated by her daughter. "The way he came by it. I know you think that my business is dishonest, but I never stole people's secrets and profited by them. I sell happiness to women. But the way he used people – that was why I left him. I hated it. Those baths and the hotel – it is all paid for with his threats. It is all false coin, and I am a fool for feeling anything for him."

~

"So you don't think she or her son had anything to do with Carrington's murder?" said Fitznorton as they walked along the Parade together.

"It seems unlikely," said Giles, scanning the crowds in the gardens, hoping for a glimpse of Mrs Stuart.

They returned to the station house, and Inspector Harris came out to greet them.

"There is news from the livery stable," he said. "She came in and hired a hack. About an hour ago."

"Excellent," said Giles.

"It is?" said Fitznorton.

"She has no notion we are watching her. She will be going about her business."

"Doing what?"

"Trying to find Carrington's money. I think she believes it to be somewhere quite different and that he spun her a tale about its whereabouts. He must have been very convincing."

"You have no proof of any of this."

"No, none at all," said Giles. "Now, are you dressed for riding, Mr Fitznorton? I have a country jaunt in mind. Can I trouble you for a couple of hacks, Inspector?"

"Where are you intending to go, sir?" said Harris.

"Crandall's Hole. In fact, you had better come with us."

"Of course, sir, but –"

"It may be a wild goose chase. I admit that now. But it's a

fine day for it. She may be taking her chance while she can, and so should we."

Chapter Forty-one

Giles was prepared to look a fool – it would not be the first time, and a dead end was a common occurrence in an investigation. However, as they rode up onto the moor, he was pleasantly surprised to see a horse with a side saddle on it, tethered to a thorn bush.

He glanced back at Inspector Harris.

"Piebald skew pony," said Harris. "That's what they said at Farren's."

Giles dismounted.

"I take it the path to the cave goes up that way?" he said, handing his reins to Harris.

"Aye, sir, about half a mile along. It's quite steep."

"I'll go and see if there is any sign of her," he said. "If I don't come back within half an hour, then –"

"Are you sure you want to go alone, sir?"

"I think she will be persuadable. And I have cuffs."

"We'll come for you in twenty minutes," said Harris.

Giles nodded and began to make his way up the path towards Crandall's Hole.

As he climbed higher, he began to be aware of the glorious aspect of the place, giving as it did a view of the magnificent moorland country that lay above Stanegate, and which ran almost to the coast, and Swalecliffe beyond. This afternoon was sunny and clear with a brisk breeze, and it was possible to see the blue distant haze of the sea. He was astonished that there were not any excursion parties picnicking by the cave – the sinister reputation of the place had done its work. It appeared to be deserted.

However, climbing up the side of the cave mouth to

where there was a natural, if rough, staircase of broad stones, he turned and saw Mrs Stuart. She seated on a rocky ledge, gazing out over the open country towards the sea. She was dressed in the smart, dark green riding habit they had noticed in her cupboard. A woman in a riding habit was always appealing, and Mrs Stuart was no exception, the black veiling on her high hat flowing like a pennant in the wind. If she had been sitting for her portrait, she could not have improved on the pose.

The wind changed direction, throwing the veil into her face, and she reached up to push it away. It was then that she saw him.

"Good afternoon," he said, removing his hat. "I'm not the only person in search of a fine view this afternoon. I had no idea you could see so far from here."

"It is beautiful," she said.

"How did you learn about it?"

"I don't know," she said. "Someone may have mentioned it in passing."

"It has a reputation for being haunted."

"That does not worry me," she said.

"May I join you for a while?" he said, moving towards her. Now she gave him a wary glance, and he knew he must stay as mild and inoffensive as possible.

"As you like," she said.

He perched on a rock nearby and looked out, contemplating how he might begin.

"I should tell you, I have been trying to find you," he said at last. "There was some nonsense being talked at the Incurables Hospital. One of those poor old women was saying things about you that seemed most unlikely."

"What did she say?" she said.

"She alleged that you had taken money from her."

"How strange," she said. "What can have given her such an idea?"

"It's a mystery," he said. "She said that you promised to give her double the money back in a matter of weeks: that you had some clever means of investing."

"Goodness," she said. "Why would I do that?"

He let silence fall on this flat denial.

"Indeed, why?" he said. "It's interesting. Of course, I have heard of such a scheme attempted before. In Canada, of all places."

"Canada?" she said.

"By a woman called Eliza Dunn. Does that name mean anything to you, Mrs Stuart?"

"No."

"Think about it, would you?" She stirred a little, and he hoped it was from discomfort. "You've never been to Toronto?"

Now, she gave him a sly glance, as if making a calculation. Had she noticed that her possessions had been disturbed? Did she know that the bracelet and the playing card had gone missing?

"Why would you ask me that?" she said.

That she had answered him with a question struck him as both interesting and annoying. She was clearly well versed in dissimulation and deflection. He was convinced in that moment that his instincts were correct, that she was involved in Carrington's death and perhaps a great deal more, but whether she would ever admit anything he could not know. Self-preservation was a powerful force, and if she was, as he suspected, a woman with a criminal career behind her, then she would have developed it as part of her trade. How could he break her down? What was her weakest spot?

He recalled how she had wept over her husband's body in the passageway at the opera. Her grief had not seemed forced. She had been in a genuine state of shock, although she had known he was unwell. She was in mourning. He could perhaps use that to some advantage.

"Is that where you met your husband?" he said. "It's a lively town, though everyone says it is not. I met my first wife there, as it happens."

"You have been in Canada?"

"Yes. That was what why that story came to my attention. I notice such things because of my time there."

"You were not a policeman?" she said.

"No, I was in the army. So is that where you met him?"

She was silent and then said, "No, I have known him since I was a child," she said.

"And where was that?"

"Somerset."

"Ah, Somerset," he said. "Not so far from Bristol. That was where Captain Carrington came from, you know."

"Captain Carrington?"

"Yes," he said, "Captain Carrington. I believe your late husband knew him."

"He may have done," she said, and Giles was pleased that she had made this tiny admission.

"They had tastes in common, perhaps," said Giles. "He called on you a few times, I imagine. I know he was in the habit of visiting Adelaide Lodge, and his mistress was installed in the cottage across the green from yours. So, why not call on Mr and Mrs Stuart? After all, your husband was a professional card player, was he not?"

"He did from time to time supplement our income by cards," she said. "He was clever and lucky at it, that is all. Life here is expensive."

"Goodness, yes it is," said Giles. "Boxes at the opera do not come cheap by any means. And those old women were meagre pickings. Not enough shillings for all the yards of silk in your veil."

"I told you, I don't know anything about that."

"Because if you admit that, I will know what you are? The thing is, ma'am, I already know what you are."

"How fascinating," she said, taking up her whip and flicking it idly. He caught her hand and took it from her. "Sir!"

He examined the mother of pearl fixings and laid it down out of her reach. "Something tells me that fleecing poor old widows and playing cards will not pay for such things as this. Even if you keep no servants. But it isn't because of the cost that you keep no servants. Servants are too leaky. It is the sign of a thoroughly professional confidence trickster: such utter self-reliance."

"A confidence trickster? What is that?"

"Oh, very good," he said. "You have the perfect manner of a lady, ma'am. Dr and Mrs Greville could not speak an ill word about you, and that is because I suspect you were gently raised, by people of some taste and breeding. But something happened, didn't it? Some wretched circumstance spoiled everything and reduced you to the condition of an emigrant. You went to Canada. Perhaps a kind clergyman paid for your passage. You were to go as a governess, and hoped to find a husband. But something happened. Something changed you. You found you could not prosper decently."

"What are you implying?"

"That you found another way to prosper. You used your wits and your charm and took to stealing from poor old women, promising to make silk purses out of sows' ears. It's an easy game if you set it up right. You find your first mark, and promise to repay them within, say, a week, double what they gave you using funds you already have, and the victim is so impressed that they tell all their friends. She gives you more money to double, as do the friends, and you pay everyone out of what you already have, and cream off some for yourself. It mounts up quickly and then you stop paying out, and run away with the proceeds. I've heard it called the ladies' savings bank. It wasn't just in Toronto. You went to Halifax, Montreal and then Quebec. Each time under a different name, of course. And then you crossed the border into the United States."

"You cannot prove anything."

"No, unfortunately; you have been very clever. But I do have the evidence of the old women at the Incurables Hospital. I have spoken to them all at some length and I can assure you that you will be charged. But that was not really why I wanted to speak to you. There is another more pressing matter we need to discuss. That of Captain Carrington and his murder."

"That is nothing to do with me," she said.

"He was stabbed," he said, "before he was fed to the leopards. Five or six times, with great force. The surgeon's opinion is that he was at his ease when it happened, that he was then restrained in his chair and attacked, without any provocation. He would have suffered greatly. His attacker stood and watched him die. It was, in effect, an execution." He saw she had bent her head and was studying her gloved hands. "There would have been a large quantity of blood shed. The carpet on which the chair was standing would have been soaked through, and perhaps there was blood on his attacker's face and hands, and perhaps on the clothes of someone else in the room. Perhaps on their face or hair. It must have been appalling."

"It was nothing to do with me," she said.

"But you were there. You saw it happen." She bowed her head still lower. "Your husband, who by your own admission had changed in character, took up a knife and stabbed Captain Carrington until he was dead, while he was sitting in your drawing room at the Rustic Cottages."

"Not my husband," she said, quietly. "Richard was not my husband."

"Your lover, then."

"No. My little brother. Dick was my brother."

This he had not expected, but it made a great deal of sense, and he felt a certain satisfaction that she had revealed so much. She appeared to be weakening.

"Did you both go to Canada?"

"Yes. Our parents were dead. We had nothing to lose. We had already lost everything."

"Tell me what happened," he said, gently.

"It was Carrington," she said. "He was the cause of our ruin. He came to my father in the guise of a friend and destroyed everything. He stole from my father, and seduced my mother and myself. I was a girl of sixteen. I did not have it in my power to resist him. I was flattered by his attentions – I was such a foolish girl and he took me, and my innocence with it. I would have become his mistress if he had wanted it. That was how I felt for him, but of course, he did not care. He abandoned us when he had taken what he wanted."

"What happened to your parents?"

"My father killed himself and my mother, who was already an invalid, followed him to the grave soon after. We were left alone and penniless by that wretch. Richard wanted to kill him then, but I told him that Carrington was not worth such a revenge and for a while he was persuaded. But over the last few years, since we came back here and his health began to fail, he began to be consumed with the idea of it. Then he decided we must come here for the cure, and he promised me –" She gave a great sigh and said, "Oh dear God, why am I saying this? Why am I putting the noose around my neck?"

"Because it is better you tell me. It will be easier in every way once you have told me everything," he said. "The burden of your secrets will kill you just as surely as the noose, if you have even a shred of goodness in you. And I believe that you do. I sense it. You need to tell me the truth because it is like a stone pressing on your chest."

"That is true! Ever since we came here, it has been nothing but torture. Richard went mad. Truly mad. To begin with we were going to swindle Carrington. We had a marvellous scheme worked out – infallible and most profitable, and I thought that would satisfy Dick, but seemingly it did not. And then that night... I still don't know where he got that knife. If I had known about it, I might have hidden it, and then he would not have been able to..." She covered her eyes. "It was so... there was so much blood, and he made such a sound when the knife went in him. His face..." She was rocking back and forth. "And I could do nothing. Richard was like an animal. I thought he was going to kill me as well for a minute, then he put the knife down and went out for a smoke, as if nothing had happened. And so then I had to think about what we would do. How it could all be made right."

"It was your idea to put the body in the leopard cage?"

"Yes. They always seemed so hungry to me, so unhappy, and I felt for them. So I thought they might destroy him, or at least some of him. I know it sounds like madness, and perhaps it was. Dick's madness had taken me over."

"You wrapped him in a Hudson Bay blanket and dragged him down the slope."

"Dick helped me. He thought it was a capital notion. Just as he said we must go to the opera. He seemed to feel that he had done nothing wrong. It was just as if he had swatted a fly... I can't understand it. It wasn't like him. He was so changed. That he could do such a thing – that he could kill a man so calmly."

"But perhaps you do understand. After all, you also killed a man calmly," Giles said. "Dr Kennedy."

"How do you know about that?" she said.

"He gave his wife a ring which you gave him. One that Carrington had given to you."

"I had to keep him quiet somehow. He was going to talk. I promised him everything, but he was being impossible. Dick had told him, you see, in his madness, exactly what had happened! He'd boasted about it, and Kennedy told me he would turn me over to you. So he had to go. I didn't mean to, it was just – necessary."

"Necessary," said Giles, feeling a cold chill in the air, despite the sunshine.

"I saw him arguing with his wife – well, that was quite a scene, and I thought it might seem she had done it. She was so angry with him. It would have been amusing in other circumstances, truly. I knew, you see, that he had no sense of smell, and I thought that the gas might do the trick. He had told Dick that, and Dick told me everything. It was just part of the tidying up. Like scrubbing the floor at the cottage. Perhaps I'm as mad as he was. Perhaps we were both ill. I've thought for years that we should not be alive, that my father should have killed us all, and then taken his own life. That would have been better for everyone. That happens, does it not?"

"On occasion, yes."

"If I had died then, I would still be clean in my heart – even though I had let Carrington have me, he didn't take my soul. But now I feel so dirty and so tired." She turned to him and rested her gaze on him. "What is there for me to live for now? The gallows, if I'm lucky, prison if I'm not. I have nothing. Carrington's money isn't here. Why was I such a fool as to think it was!" she finished, and leapt to her feet. "He told me it was here!"

Mrs Stuart began to climb further along the ridge, to where the path grew steep and dangerous, and he realised that she was heading toward the most exposed outcrop, which formed a ledge, with the ground falling away so sharply beneath it. As he dashed after her, it was plain what her intention was: to destroy herself.

She stopped at the furthermost edge and stood, her head thrown back as if at any minute she would jump. He was now within a few feet of her and he grabbed at her long habit skirt, hoping to drag her back with it, but she twisted round and yanked it from him. He stumbled forward again, trying to regain it, only to have her step down and repel him with a startlingly well-aimed kick of her booted foot.

"Don't you try and stop me! Don't you dare!" she said, and stepped back to the ledge. She was within inches of the edge now, and Giles, dry-mouthed and reeling, lunged forward again to tackle her. He managed to get his arms clamped about her and pull her back but she put up a terrible struggle, fighting him with an animal fierceness. Her desperation gave her a strength that he was finding it hard to match.

"I will take you with me!" she screamed at him, "if you do not let go!"

She shoved her knee in his rib cage, which being the site of several old injuries, knocked the breath from him, and he felt his grip on her loosen. He wondered how long he could hold her back when she was so determined.

Just when he felt failure was certain, a great shadow loomed over them and she was plucked off him like a lamb by an eagle, by none other than the athletic Mr Fitznorton.

"Excuse me, ma'am," Fitznorton muttered.

"No!" she screamed. She continued to fight, lunging towards the edge, locked in Fitznorton's arms. Then with one sudden burst of strength, she escaped him and launched herself over the edge. Fitznorton stood teetering there, and might have followed her had not Giles pulled him back at the very last moment.

Mrs Stuart's scream as she fell was quickly terminated by a thud, followed by a chilling silence that was punctuated only by the laboured breathing of the two men.

Chapter Forty-two

After some deliberation, Felix and Hamilton decided that they would perform the operation in the sculpture gallery. This had the advantage of being extremely well lit by the windows in the ceiling, and close to Lord Rothborough's private rooms.

Hamilton drove into Stanegate and fetched his equipment – and his sister, to act as his assistant – while Felix gave directions for the room to be arranged and tables set up. He laid out his own tools on a linen-covered side table, close to the famous Holbroke Recumbent Venus dreaming on her couch in all her naked perfection. The white marble statues and reliefs were to make strange companions.

Mrs Vernon, whom Felix knew to have a cool head and a steady hand, came to assist him, and Hamilton and Miss Hamilton arrived soon after. Miss Hamilton offered him one of the smocks, such as those she and Hamilton had donned.

"It will make you look like an artist," said Mrs Vernon, who was putting on her own. "And is not medicine an art as much as science?"

He thought of the frock coats of elderly Edinburgh professors he had seen in his first days of medical school, their sleeves protected by linen guards, but their lapels sometimes stained with blood. It had been a sign of experience, but Felix was glad it was a custom that was passing away.

He put on the smock and walked up and down to calm his nerves, rehearsing in his mind what he intended to do. He had discussed this at length with Dr Markham and Hamilton and they had agreed it was the most sensible course.

Dr Markham and James Bodley brought in Lord Rothborough, and they made him as comfortable as could be on the table that they had arranged for the purpose. Then Hamilton set about his work of etherizing, aided by his sister, in that calm, methodical manner that had so impressed Felix. In a few minutes, Lord Rothborough was in a state of near sleep, with Miss Hamilton holding his wrist and keeping a constant watch on his pulse, while Hamilton administered the ether.

Mrs Vernon carefully removed the sheets.

"You see the swelling and redness in the skin there?" Felix explained to her. "That is the abnormality. I am going to make an incision from here – to here, and we will see what is causing this."

There was nothing to do now but to take up his scalpel and begin.

It was a curious experience. Making such an incision on a fully conscious patient, even one laced with brandy, would normally have caused an immediate, physical response: a shuddering, jerking motion. For this reason, a patient was always held down upon the table, for otherwise it was impossible for the surgeon to accomplish anything. But Lord Rothborough did not flinch. He lay as still as the white marble statues that surrounded him.

Felix continued, and as he opened up the flesh, a vile acrid stench became apparent, as did a distressing quantity of turbid liquid material inside the abdomen.

"Clearly something has gone awry, but I can't see what," he said. "Let us turn him on his side and drain this away."

Hamilton assisted him with this, while Mrs Vernon, showing no revulsion or loss of nerve, placed and replaced the folded linen and basins until the draining of the offensive matter was partially accomplished.

Felix now had a better view of the problem.

"It looks as it the appendix vermiformis is severely ulcerated and inflamed." He gently touched the offending organ. "Full of stones. Which is what Melis described."

"So?" said Hamilton.

"I think we should take it out," he said. "It is doing no good. Mrs Vernon, if you would cut me a length of silk, about twelve inches?"

"So apply a ligature, and then extirpate it?" said Hamilton.

"That ought to be quickest way," said Felix. "If we might lay him on his back again. Now Mrs Vernon, if you do not mind, the plan is to wrap the silk thread about here and tie it fast, to cut off the blood supply."

"How ingenious," she murmured, handing him the silk. "And deft," she added, when he had accomplished the task.

"His pulse has slowed," said Miss Hamilton. "And his hand is cooler."

"Scalpel and forceps, please Mrs Vernon, and stand by with the basin," said Felix, bending over his patient. He felt a frisson of fear pass over him, and had to take a deep breath to steady himself before he began to cut through the flesh of the diseased appendix. Having removed it to the bowl, he noticed a livid red mass beneath it, an abscess of some sort, which he also excised, before scraping the cavity with a curette.

"Pulse?"

"As before, no change," said Miss Hamilton.

There was a considerable chance that all might still be lost. He hastened to clean out the cavity, as best he could, before turning to the matter of closing his original incisions with suture.

By the time he tied the last suture, having constructed an elaborate piece of needle work that he hoped would still allow the escape of noxious matters, he felt faint with exhaustion.

"Wake him," he said.

This was Miss Hamilton's duty, and she did it very well, raising Lord Rothborough's head and shoulders and resting him against her in order to apply sal volatile. This was most effective and he came to, looking startled, and then gave a roar of pain and fell back against her in a faint. But he was soon again revived, and checking his pulse for himself, Felix was pleased to feel it was regular again.

"Let us get you more comfortable," said Felix. Dr Markham went to fetch Bodley and one of the footmen, who carried his Lordship away on a hurdle. The others departed with them, while Felix and Mrs Vernon remained behind. Felix struggled out of his now stained smock and threw it into the pile of dirty linen on the floor, before going to wash his hands in the basin that had been placed, incongruously, on a side table by a particularly beautiful white bust of Pysche.

Mrs Vernon handed him a towel.

"Thank you, ma'am," he said, "for everything. I could not have managed that without you."

"I did not want to lose a good friend," she said.

"Only in the next day or two will we know if –"

She nodded and patted his forearm.

"Whatever happens," she said, "what you just did was remarkable. Your courage was something to witness."

"No, it was just as you said," he said. "I didn't want to lose him."

"You must put your coat on and go and talk to Lady Rothborough," she said.

"And we must work out a nursing system. I want those dressings changed regularly, and it is not going to be a job for the faint-hearted."

He glanced around him at the gallery where a strange mixture of marble drapery and real linen now prevailed. Outside he could hear dogs barking, and he went to the window to see the Gordon children along with Mr Stafford enjoying the afternoon sunshine, playing what looked like tag in the intricate borders of the famous Holbroke parterre. Mrs Vernon came and joined him at the window.

"Why are they so quiet?" he said. "The children, I mean?"

"I told them they needed to be quiet, and Mr Stafford has kept them to it. But how clever to make a game out of it. How beautiful they look – of course, I would say that because they are my children, but really they are. It looks like a ballet! I'd never have thought Hamish could be so graceful."

"It's a shame Lord Rothborough can't see it," said Felix. "That would be better than any tonic."

~

Lord Rothborough was feverish for the next few hours, and in a degree of pain, but he was increasingly lucid, and by six that evening Felix felt that something might have been accomplished. He and Mrs Vernon surrendered their watch to Lady Rothborough and Bodley and joined the family party in the green drawing room.

Mr Stafford was reading Ivanhoe aloud, with the children sitting at his feet. He read well, it seemed, for Eleanor was utterly rapt. Ivanhoe was one of her favourites, and a bad reading she would never tolerate. Miss King had stopped her sewing to listen, while Charlotte – who had been anxious – seemed calm enough, sitting with Mrs Fforde on the long sofa.

Mr Stafford stopped as they came in, and they were met with many enquiring glances.

"He is comfortable," Felix said.

"Thank God!" murmured Mrs Fforde. Charlotte leapt up and kissed him.

"We are not through the woods yet," he said, taking both her hands.

"But you look encouraged. Does he not look encouraged?" she said.

"Certainly," said Canon Fforde.

The tea was brought in, and getting up from his place, Mr Stafford said, "I think I had better take my leave."

"You will not read us another chapter, sir?" said Sophy.

"Tomorrow, perhaps? If I'm late for dinner my housekeeper will scold me."

"There is no Mrs Stafford to scold you?" said Mrs Vernon.

"Oh no, ma'am. I might wish so, but not as yet." He went up to Lady Charlotte who was dispensing the tea. "Thank you, my lady, for asking me today. It has been a great privilege."

"Will you come tomorrow? You have become indispensable," she said, indicating Sophy and Hamish. "And with luck my father may be able to see you. He would certainly enjoy hearing you read to him when he is more recovered."

"God willing that will be soon," said Stafford, and took his leave.

"Sophy, Hamish," said Mrs Vernon. "You should go back up to the nursery now. Mrs Patton will be wondering what has become of you."

"I will take them," said Sally, and ushered them out of the room. Canon Fforde left with them.

The sound of a carriage outside took Mrs Vernon to the window.

"My husband," she said, smiling, and then added, "and Mr Fitznorton."

Felix felt rather irritated at this intrusion. He assumed that Fitznorton had prevailed on Major Vernon in some fashion.

When the two men came in, Fitznorton went straight up to Charlotte.

"You must excuse me coming here unbidden, my lady," he said to her, "but I am going back to London tomorrow. A colleague is ill and I am needed in the office urgently. But I wanted to see if there were any commissions I could execute for you in town or any messages you would like me to deliver? I am entirely at your service." He bowed to her.

"That is most kind," said Charlotte, flushing. "And of course I can think of nothing and you have had a long drive here as well! But I can offer you some refreshments. Some tea, perhaps?"

"Thank you. How is your father?"

"Carswell has operated and removed – what have you removed again, Felix?" Charlotte said. "Mr Hamilton explained it all to me, but the name escapes me."

"The appendix vermiformis," Felix said.

"Goodness," said Major Vernon.

"Your wife has been the best dresser a surgeon could have," said Felix. "She was heroic."

"I only did as I was told," said Mrs Vernon.

"Are you sure you must go back tomorrow, Mr Fitznorton?" said Charlotte.

"I'm afraid so, my lady. The case that brought me here has been concluded."

"You found her?" said Felix, turning to Major Vernon.

"Yes," said Major Vernon.

"Who?" said Charlotte.

"The wife of the man who died at the opera," said Felix. "And she admitted it?"

"Pretty much."

"So you have arrested her?"

"No," said Major Vernon. "Unfortunately, she died."

"I should not be here if it were not for Major Vernon's prompt actions," said Fitznorton, with the most humility that Felix had yet observed in him.

"What on earth happened?" said Felix.

"So, Mr Fitznorton," said Charlotte. "What did Major Vernon do?"

"Nothing," said Major Vernon.

"He prevented me from falling over a cliff edge," said Fitznorton. "He saved my life."

"Mr Fitznorton was struggling with the suspect. I only gave him a little assistance. Unfortunately neither of us was able to stop her from destroying herself. She was utterly determined."

"It was a remarkable recovery on your part, Major Vernon," said Fitznorton, "given that you were injured by her."

"Oh Lord, where?" said Mrs Vernon, crossing the room. "Not on your ribs, I hope."

"I was winded for a moment or two," said Major Vernon, "but no damage was done."

"You will look at him, Mr Carswell," said Mrs Vernon. "At once!"

She was most insistent, and the three of them went out of the room and into a side room. Here, Mrs Vernon made her husband take off his coat and waistcoat.

"It was a trifle," said Major Vernon, loosening his cravat and leaning back in his chair. Felix made a cursory examination and Major Vernon winced when his fingers discovered some tender spot.

"There is a slight contusion," Felix said, "but arnica will deal with it."

"One day you will be killed!" Mrs Vernon exclaimed. "Do you ever think of that? Forgive me," she said, with a sigh. "But sometimes it is impossible not to worry. I think I should go up to the sickroom again and make myself useful."

"No," said Felix, "not for another hour at least. You have done quite enough. And if there is any change, we will be told. You would be better going to rest, ma'am. Both of you, in fact."

"A good plan," said Major Vernon. Mrs Vernon nodded, and put out her hand to her husband. He took it and kissed it. "I shall be up soon – I must speak to Mr Carswell first," he said. She kissed him in return and left.

"You cannot conceive how magnificent she was," Felix said, when the door had closed behind her. "It would not have been possible without her."

"And you have both saved a life today," said Major Vernon. "I failed to save Mrs Stuart's."

"If she was determined, then –" Felix began.

"It still might have been prevented. If I had said something differently, done something differently, then perhaps I could have brought her to safety. It is a wretched conclusion and I cannot think it will be anything but a black mark against me."

"Nonsense," said Felix. "It was her choice."

"I should not have spoken to her as I did," he said. "I was too eager for a confession. That is my great failing. My wretched vanity demands to be satisfied. I have to hear I am right from the suspect's own mouth! But this was not the time nor the place for that. I was, at the least, wickedly negligent."

"But what else could you have done?"

"I might have brought her down from there on some pretext!" he said. "It would have been easy enough. But, instead, I lost her and damn well nearly lost Fitznorton in the process! It was close. What would I have told his mother? I cannot believe I was so foolish. I could see that Inspector Harris thought me reckless, and I have no doubt he will tell Lazenby exactly what happened. And Emma is right!" he added. "I might have been killed myself, and where would that have left her and the children..." He struggled to master his emotions. "Forgive me," he said. He got up and retrieved his coat and waistcoat. "I will go and make sure Emma is resting. I'm glad she was so magnificent, but it is hardly a surprise to me. It is a shame her husband is a wretch."

"You must forgive yourself for this," Felix said, not liking to see him in such a state. "Time will help you. And at least you have Fitznorton in your debt. Surely that is worth something?"

"Perhaps, but I would rather it was not seen in that way," Major Vernon said, and left.

"He isn't injured, is he?" said Charlotte, when Felix returned to the drawing room.

"No, it's nothing," Felix said.

"Thank goodness!"

Fitznorton had picked up the copy of Ivanhoe and was leafing through it.

"Who do you like best, Mr Fitznorton?" said Eleanor. "Rebecca or Rowena?"

"It strikes me," he said, "that they are both ideal women, but on reflection, Rebecca – she has such great courage and steadfastness. She is not pliant in the face of worldly temptation. She is offered a crown, but chooses the harder path of virtue. Yes, Rebecca, Mrs Carswell."

"A good answer," said Charlotte. "Now, will you please stay for dinner, Mr Fitznorton? We can even find you a bed for the night."

"No, I must go back to Stanegate," said Fitznorton. "But thank you. And my best wishes to your father. Are you sure you have no commissions for me in London?"

Charlotte shook her head, and said, "I will go and order your carriage," and left the room.

Fitznorton made some hasty farewells and went after her.

Felix was now alone with Eleanor and Miss King. Contrary to the usual decorum of Holbroke, he stretched himself out on the sofa. Miss King picked up her needlework again. She was, Felix noted, making a tiny garment. Eleanor strolled across the room and took up the copy of Ivanhoe.

"Mr Stafford read well, don't you think?" she said.

"He was as good as an actor," said Miss King.

"That's always useful in a clergyman," said Eleanor. "To be able to read well."

"And in a husband," said Miss King. "I thought Lady Charlotte was quite captivated by his reading."

"Mr Stafford is charming, yes, and clever and funny," said Eleanor.

"And very good with children," Miss King went on, snipping a thread.

"But," Eleanor said, "he does not excite the imagination.

He is not that type, and Charlotte is..." She broke off.

"Is?" said Felix.

"I think she is like you," said Eleanor. "She is idealistic and warm-blooded. She will wish to fall in love, and violently."

"And you are so cool and rational, madam?" said Felix, getting up from the sofa, much amused by this.

"I am. Or at least I am growing so."

"You may have been, until you paid two guineas to sit in that wretched Idiotic Chamber," said Felix, at which Miss King burst out laughing.

"Oh, excuse me," she said, when Eleanor glared at her. "No, we should not tease you for that, should we?" she added.

"No!" Eleanor exclaimed. "And yes, it was foolish, but it was interesting. It was like going to the opera. You knew it was nonsense and yet it made sense at the same time. Now, I am going to go and dress for dinner, even if we are only eating in the breakfast room again and even if Lord Rothborough cannot see it – we are at Holbroke, after all! Besides, Lady Rothborough may join us tonight, and in that case I have no wish to look anything but perfect!"

Felix made his way back to the sickroom, and found the new Lady Rothborough and Sophy Gordon sitting together on a sofa in the passageway, like old friends.

"Miss Gordon has brought some flowers for our patient," said Lady Rothborough, seeing him. There was a posy in her lap.

"Mr McGillray helped me choose them," said Sophy.

"I'll go and tell him you are here," said Lady Rothborough. "And show him these, Miss Gordon," she added, indicating the little bunch of flowers.

"She's very nice," Sophy said, when she had gone. "Is it true that she is your real mama, Mr Carswell?"

"Yes."

"And Lord Rothborough is your papa," Sophy went on, stating a fact.

"Yes, but Mr and Mrs Carswell looked after me as if I were their own. Just as your uncle and aunt do. Sometimes things do not work out in the ordinary way. I suppose you might say I'm rather fortunate."

"Perhaps my mama and papa will come back one day," she said, after a moment. It was so plaintively said that he sat down and put his arm about her shoulders. She leant against him and yawned.

"You should run along to bed," Felix went on, "or Patten will be after you."

She kissed him and left, and Felix went into the sickroom considering the depressing mystery of Captain Gordon's continued silence. Despite many efforts, Major Vernon had not yet heard anything from him, and the longer the silence, the more he suspected he was dead.

Lady Rothborough was at the bedside. "Felix is here, Will," she said.

Lord Rothborough looked exhausted and pale, and Felix could not like the coolness of his hand, nor his slow pulse, when he took his hand. He went to examine the state of the dressing, and found that one of the sutures had come loose and the wound had begun to bleed copiously.

Angry that his handiwork had not proved durable, Felix threw off his coat, called for Bodley to assist him, and set to doing what he could to improve matters. It was a tense twenty minutes, with Lord Rothborough acutely conscious and in great pain, before Felix felt he had control of the situation and the wound was safely closed again.

"Thank you, Mr Bodley," he said, stepping back. "I think that should be sufficient."

Lord Rothborough gave an exhausted groan and sank back on the pillows.

"I'm sorry, Papa," said Felix. "This is a long road and a hard one."

His eyes closed, Lord Rothborough said, "I'm not alone,"

he said. "I will not complain. Thank you. Blanche –"

"I'm here, my love," she said, taking his hand. "What a clever man our son is!"

~

Unable to sleep and unwilling to disturb Emma, Giles left their bedroom and tried to pace out his unease in the broad passageways of the great house. The hour struck two, as he passed a handsome old clock, and he wished he might turn the hands back to the previous morning, and take his chances again with Mrs Stuart.

He turned a corner and came across the new Lady Rothborough, also in her dressing gown, candle in hand. It was a strange wedding night for her, certainly.

"How is your husband?" he said.

"He is comfortable. Felix is with him," she said. "In fact, we were just talking about what happened today. He is concerned about you," she added, laying her hand on his arm. "And it reminded me – well, you can guess, I think?"

He nodded, the incident clear in his mind. She had been in despair, with a gun in her hand, and he had persuaded her to live.

"I can never forget it," she went on. "You gave me back my life."

"I wish I had such a chance again with Mrs Stuart."

"Of course," she said, "and this will pain you for some time, but you must console yourself with the knowledge that for every failure, there is a success, and that you are a valiant spirit."

"Ma'am," he said. "That is too –"

"I am not overstating matters," she continued. "You must give me the privilege of speaking so frankly. I am the bride, after all! I would not be here, with this ring on my finger, facing this extraordinary new life" – she gestured about her – "if it were not for you, sir. For which I thank you, as does my husband." She made a little curtsey and he was forced to smile. "Now, go up to the nursery and look at your children sleeping," she added. "That will be the best comfort for you."

Epilogue

It was a week before Felix felt that he could at last leave Holbroke and Lord Rothborough's bedside. Major Vernon had told him that Sukey and her family had now moved to Mr O'Brien's new house in Swalecliffe. It seemed that Lorenzo had recovered and was thriving, but Felix felt he must see for himself. So, on a fine, clear September day he ordered a horse, and accompanied by one of the grooms, set off early to ride to Swalecliffe; not as he had once done with Major Vernon across the high moorland, but along the new metalled road that now ran into Stanegate.

Mr O'Brien's two villas were situated in a street running parallel to the new promenade. They had a pattern-book look about them, each a mirror image of the other, with fresh pale render, brightly-painted barge boards cut like lace, and large front gardens, as yet untended. He made his way up the white brick path with some trepidation, and the maid who opened the door to him – a girl of fifteen or so – seemed not to know what to do, and fetched Mrs O'Brien.

"Is Mrs Kennedy at home?" he asked.

"I'm not sure she should be at home to you," said Mrs O'Brien, "but since you are here, you can have a look at Laurence."

"Thank you," he said, following her into a sitting room at the back of the house that was full of boxes in various stages of unpacking. Sukey was sitting in an armchair by the open door to the garden, with the baby sleeping in her lap.

"I hear he is mostly recovered," said Felix, bending over her to take up the child. As he did, he caught the scent of Sukey's hair and a hundred recollections came to him.

"Yes, we had a day or two of anxiety, but he's much better now," said Mrs O'Brien.

"He's feeding all right?"

"Like a Trojan," said Mrs O'Brien.

Felix sat down with the child on his knees and attempted to loosen the layers of flannel in which he was enveloped. Naturally this wakened the child.

"A little less flannel, perhaps," he said. "It keeps him too warm."

"Less flannel?" said Mrs O'Brien. "And what do you know about baby clothes?"

"Infants are liable to overheating if over-swaddled. Just as a precaution?"

He glanced at Sukey, who smiled and said, "I like linen better anyway."

Felix completed his examination and then it was necessary to change the napkin, so Mrs O'Brien carried him out of the room.

"He is doing well," he said to Sukey, "but you know that."

"I was terrified one night," she said. "I wanted to send for you but I knew you had business of your own. Fortunately, Bridie has fallen in love with him."

"Hence the hundred weight of flannel."

"She wants another baby of her own."

"Isn't seven enough?" said Felix. The house, although generous, seemed noisy with children – a tribe of them were banging about in a room upstairs.

"You didn't come all this way just to see how Lorenzo was, I suppose," said Sukey.

"No," said Felix.

"So?"

"I came to ask you to cut my hair." She burst out laughing. "No, I'm serious. It looks ridiculous."

"I never had you as so vain!" she said, still laughing.

"I trust I'm not, at least not excessively," he said, "but you are the only person who could ever deal with it."

"I could, I suppose," she said. She got up and walked around his chair, looking at him from every angle. "I'll go and find some scissors."

He had decided on this idea during the ride over, thinking it would amuse her – but having come to it, he felt a sudden nervousness. Would he be able to bear her touching him?

She came back in carrying a folded towel and her scissors, and he rose from his seat. "I was being a fool. There is no need to trouble yourself."

"No," she said, "I want to. Sit down."

So he sat down and she put the towel about his shoulders, and made him hold it so it would not slip. Then she began to comb his hair with her fingers.

"So," she said, taking up the scissors and beginning to cut. "What is all the news from Holbroke? Major Vernon said you saved Lord Rothborough's life."

"I wouldn't say that," said Felix. "And he isn't entirely well yet."

"But he will be?"

"He is determined," said Felix. "It will be hard to make a good convalescent of him. He is already scheming to acquire the Hydropathic and the Baths. I think the plan is to let Mr Fisher and Chef Luchetti run the place as partners."

"That would be excellent," she said. "Now, I shouldn't go too short here, should I?"

"Do whatever you think fit," he said. "You always did it so well before."

She stood back, regarding him and her handiwork.

"Not much more," she said.

"Are you going to stay here?"

"Why?"

"I shall need my hair cut again." She laughed. "Not just for that reason, of course."

"I've hardly thought about it. Tom says I can stay here as long as I need to."

"Do you have enough –"

"Yes, thank you!" she said. "Paul took out life insurance – a great deal of it, in fact, so we are well provided for, which is awful to say given the circumstances."

"I'm glad to hear it."

"I didn't know he had done it. It's just as well. If I'd known that, and had had to admit it to your Mr Fitznorton, he'd have got me to confess to everything! There, what do you think of that?" she said, concluding the business of the haircut with a few last little snips.

He got up and went to the looking glass above the fireplace, trying hard not to be disappointed that she had finished.

"Quite dashing," she said, coming to brush the stray hairs from his shoulders. "You can't be too dashing, you're a respectable married man."

"Not entirely respectable," he said.

"Oh?"

"I did a foolish thing when we were all at Stanegate. I indulged myself grossly."

He had said this to chasten himself, for at that moment, she was so close to him, he might have taken her into his arms and kissed her.

"With a woman?" she said. He nodded, and felt a flush of shame as he said it.

"You are wicked," she said, with a sigh.

The door opened and Mrs O'Brien came in carrying Lorenzo.

"He's hungry again," she said. "Oh, you're still here."

"I am about to go, ma'am," said Felix, taking up his hat. "I have a long ride back," and feeling provoked by Mrs O'Brien's manner, gave Sukey a fleeting kiss on the cheek.

He rode back to Stanegate where he had arranged to meet

Major Vernon at the station house. However, on arriving there he was told that Major Vernon had gone to the menagerie.

He was supervising the release of Moonshine and Mercury back into their old enclosure. The animals had just left the confines of their painted van and were now warily exploring their old quarters, sniffing and marking every rock and tree root with a rub of the face, just like their domesticated cousins.

"I thought they were to be destroyed?" said Felix.

"I pleaded for them with the magistrates this morning," said Major Vernon.

"You should have been an advocate. That is a marvellous sight," he added, indicating the cats.

"It would have grieved too many people to have them killed," said Major Vernon, "and, Heaven knows, there has been enough misery in the last two weeks. How was Mrs Kennedy?"

"Quite well, and your godson is in perfect health again."

At this moment old Askham, the menagerie keeper, came up.

"I have something for you gentlemen," he said, and produced from behind his back two pink lustre tankards bearing the words: 'Askham's Famous Stanegate Menagerie and Pleasure Ground' and decorated with the engraved image of Moonshine and Mercury, surrounded by a garland of laurels. "A souvenir. The last of these I have. I shall have to order more. I'm sure they will be in high demand now the cats have become so celebrated."

"Notorious, I think, Mr Askham," said Major Vernon.

"It's a good job that other gent has gone back to London, for I only had two," said Askham. He went to the bars of the cage. "Now, you will see, sir, what a good job the blacksmith has made out of that roof. There will be no danger of anything now, and so I should hope, given the money it cost me."

"I'm sure you will be repaid soon enough by an increase

of visitors," said Major Vernon.

"I'm not sure Mr Fitznorton would have appreciated such a magnificent object," said Felix, admiring his tankard. "This will have pride of place in my study, Mr Askham."

They walked back down to The White Hart where the carriage from Holbroke was waiting for them. They passed the Opera House which now was advertising a melodrama called 'The Modern Age' – 'The Company Recently Triumphing in London! Sensational Tale of Depravity in Paris!'

"Have you heard anything from Fitznorton?" said Felix.

"An ominous silence," said Major Vernon. "I have unkind suspicions that he will complain about me to Captain Lazenby rather than coming to me with his grievances. But perhaps he will say nothing."

"I can't believe he will not make trouble," said Felix, "since he disapproves of us all. What was it he accused us all of: oh yes, laxity of tone! Good God!"

"He does not disapprove of Lady Charlotte," said Major Vernon.

They had reached the Parade Gardens now, where the same fashionable crowds were swirling about, just as they had been during their earlier visit.

"This is a strange town," said Felix. "It's as if it's made out of spun silk and spangled paper. There seems to be nothing to it, except chasing pleasure."

"Which Carrington understood perfectly," said Major Vernon. "And exploited so brilliantly."

"Until his sins caught up with him. How long had they been waiting?"

"It was at least twenty years."

"If Richard Stuart had not had that inflammation of the brain, it might not have happened at all. The tumour completely transformed him. I wonder how many similar cases there are."

"It is certainly an interesting question. If he had no

control over the growth of the tumour, how responsible was he?"

"But she was responsible," said Felix. "Of that there is no doubt. She could have gone straight to the police that first night instead of feeding a corpse to two hungry leopards!"

"She was afraid for her own life, perhaps."

"But then to calmly gas Kennedy? It's extraordinary."

"I wish we had managed to save her," said Major Vernon.

"To see her hanged?" said Felix. "Which we both agree is barbaric."

"The judge might have spared her," said Major Vernon. "Public opinion is shifting on this."

"Unlikely," said Felix.

"Dear Lord, as each year passes, I find the practice more and more heinous. It must be stopped."

"Then you must write pamphlets and get yourself elected to Parliament," said Felix. "Lord Rothborough is always telling me that is your proper destiny."

"With the greatest respect to my Lord," said Major Vernon, climbing into the waiting carriage, "I would rather be hanged myself. No, I belong with the honest sinners: the thieves and the murderers."

"And where do I belong, I wonder?" said Felix. "With the living or the dead? When I think what Hamilton is doing, and what we accomplished the other day, and what might be possible in future, then I wonder if that is not my path. What do you think?"

"I can't answer that for you," said Major Vernon, "except to hope you choose to keep me company a while longer."

"It will be my pleasure, Major Vernon," said Felix.

~ THE END ~

Dramatis Personae

The Vernon household

Major Giles Vernon: Chief Superintendent, Northminster Constabulary

Emma Vernon: Major Vernon's wife

Hamish, Sophy and Sandro Gordon: Emma's nephews and niece

Mrs Patton: Emma's maid

The Carswell household

Felix Carswell MD: consultant surgeon to the Northern Investigation Office, natural son of Lord Rothborough

Eleanor Carswell: Felix's wife

Miss Jenny King: companion to Eleanor

Jacob Moore: Felix's manservant

Miss Stevens: Eleanor's maid

The Rothborough household

Lord Rothborough: Felix's natural father

Lady Charlotte Haraald: Lord Rothborough's eldest daughter

James Bodley: manservant to Lord Rothborough

Mrs Blanche Martinez: Felix's natural mother

Dr Markham: physician in the district

At The White Hart Hotel

Elisabeth Jacquot: landlady of The White Hart

Canon Lambert Fforde: Giles' brother-in-law

Mrs Sally Fforde: Giles' sister

Celia Fforde: Giles' niece

Edward Fitznorton: on secondment from the Home Office

Victor Morgueillon: a French chef

In Stanegate

Mr Tait: Lord Rothborough's land agent in Stanegate

Mr Boothroyd: coroner and cricketer

Inspector Harris

Sergeant Gale

Dr Greville: warden of the Incurables Hospital

Mrs Greville: Dr Greville's wife

Mr James Hamilton: dental surgeon

Miss Lucy Hamilton: James Hamilton's sister

Mrs Birgitta Johnson: proprietor of the Idunnic Chamber

Eric Johnson: Mrs Johnson's son

Ingrid Johnson: Mrs Johnson's daughter

Mr Askham: menagerie owner

Bobby Farr: leopard wrangler

Georgiana Stuart: visitor to Stanegate

Richard Stuart: visitor to Stanegate

At the Hydropathic Institute

Signor Luchetti: emeritus Chef at the Hydropathic Institute

Giancarlo Luchetti: Signor Luchetti's son

Dr Paul Kennedy: physician at the Hydropathic Institute

Susanna 'Sukey' Kennedy: Dr Kennedy's wife and Felix's former mistress

Paul, Mary and Laurence: Dr Kennedy's children

Mr Fisher: manager of the Hydropathic Institute

At Amberleigh Castle

Lady Amberleigh: dowager Countess of Amberleigh

Lady Clara: Lady Amberleigh's daughter

Lady Margaret: Lady Amberleigh's daughter

The Earl of Amberleigh: son and heir to the late Earl of Amberleigh

Sir Henry Boynton: trustee and guardian of the present Earl of Amberleigh

Animals

Moonshine and Mercury: celebrated leopards

Prince and Percy: Lord Rothborough's spaniels

About the Author

Harriet Smart was born and brought up in Birmingham. She attended the University of St Andrews, where she read History of Art, and married a fellow student. She now lives with her husband in an eighteenth-century house in Northumberland.

Harriet has an M.A. in screenwriting. She has published twenty novels as well as helping to design the creative writing software Writer's Café and the e-book editor software Jutoh.

She has been writing the Northminster Mysteries since 2010.

You can follow Harriet at www.harrietsmart.com and BookBub.

Manufactured by Amazon.ca
Acheson, AB

12669232R00259